The Dog Made to Think

Martin Lucas

Science brought a dream alive. It also awakened a nightmare…

Contents

Prologue

Part One: Jess and Daisy
Chapter 1 *April 2015*
Chapter 2

Part Two: The Canine Project
Chapter 3 *April 2014*
Chapter 4
Chapter 5
Chapter 6
Chapter 7
Chapter 8 *September 2014*
Chapter 9

Part Three: Machinery of War
Chapter 10 *December 2014*
Chapter 11
Chapter 12 *March 2015*

Part Four: Three Days in April
Chapter 13 *April 2015*
Chapter 14
Chapter 15
Chapter 16
Chapter 17
Chapter 18
Chapter 19
Chapter 20
Chapter 21
Chapter 22
Chapter 23
Chapter 24
Chapter 25

Chapter 26
Chapter 27
Chapter 28
Chapter 29
Chapter 30
Chapter 31
Chapter 32
Chapter 33
Chapter 34
Chapter 35
Chapter 36
Chapter 37
Chapter 38
Chapter 39
Chapter 40
Chapter 41
Chapter 42
Chapter 43
Chapter 44
Chapter 45
Chapter 46
Chapter 47
Chapter 48
Chapter 49
Chapter 50
Chapter 51
Chapter 52
Chapter 53
Chapter 54
Chapter 55
Chapter 56
Chapter 57
Chapter 58
Postscript

Amazon Kindle Edition

Copyright 2017 Martin Lucas

All rights reserved

No part of this book may be reproduced in any form without the prior permission in writing of the author, except for brief quotations used for promotion or reviews.

This is a work of fiction. Names, characters, places and incidents are used fictitiously and any resemblance to any persons, businesses, locales or events is entirely coincidental.

By the same author

The Human Race
(with Terence Dixon)

All in the Mind
(with John Nicholson)

How to Survive the 9-5
(with Kim Wilson & Emma Hart)

To The Real 'Daisy'

The story that follows is imaginative fiction but in the last ten years a vast amount of experimental work has revealed that dogs possess a much wider range of abilities than was previously recognised.

With the exception of the specially bred dogs in the story that are able to develop a sign language, (which even then some researchers argue may be possible) all the behaviour of the dogs described in this story is solidly based on my reading of that research. It is an extraordinary revelation of capability.

Where robotic and military technologies are mentioned I have extended the possibilities of the work that is publicly known about, but it's likely that covert work has already gone far beyond my imaginings.

The character of Daisy is based on a real dog, and although as yet she lacks the ability to communicate quite as clearly as her fictional counterpart, she already does a very good job of letting me know what she wants, and this was what first gave me the idea for this story…

Martin Lucas

Prologue

A man was running through a dark forest. He was very tired, and very frightened, and he was seriously expecting to die very soon. Beneath his feet, layers of pine needles muffled the sound of his steps and, as the late winter afternoon began to slip into night, the dense foliage of the conifers above him cast a gloomy shade, but the creature pursuing him seemed to have no difficulty in tracking him.

He could just make out its dark shape moving between the trees about a hundred metres behind him. It wasn't moving particularly fast, just matching its pace to his, but it was unrelenting. He knew that no matter how far he ran or how fast, it would eventually decide to move in. All he could hope to do was buy time.

He stopped and glanced back. Among the shadows the creature paused too. It stood very still. He tapped the microphone of the headset attached to his helmet and got an answering burp in the earpiece. "What are you doing?" he said. "It's still tracking me."

Behind him the enormous head of the creature turned very slightly.

"Any closer?" The tinny little voice said in his ear

"Never mind that? What's happening?"

"We haven't re-established control yet."

"Christ, I know that. Well give up, for God's sake. Get some people out here and put the sodding thing down. Where are they?"

"They're on their way, but you're nearly a mile out now."

"Well order self-destruct!"

"You know the protocol Jack. We've got to make every effort to bring it back under control first, that thing's worth twenty million dollars. It's not armed. We don't know for sure it'll hurt you."

"Look! I designed the fucking thing. It will seriously hurt me. That's what it does. That's what it for."

"Take it steady Jack, we'll be right there, OK? Jack?"

But there was no reply. All the man's attention was on the spot where the creature had been standing. Except that it wasn't there any more.

His nostrils suddenly filled with the characteristic reek of machine oil. He turned to run, but there standing quietly in front of him loomed the huge mass of the creature. Incongruously it occurred to him, not for the first time that it looked a lot like an enormous dog, but if so it was a dog conceived in the perverse imagination of some depraved robot scientist, which is pretty much what it was.

And just like a dog it could be directed, under the control of its makers, to track, to hunt to the kill, or, even more important, to stop when directed to. Except that this one had discarded that control and was now single-mindedly following the imperatives built into its deepest nature. It was not armed in any formal way but it had its feet and it had its weight. So it leaned down and systematically set about bludgeoning the man to a pulp.

Part One

Jess and Daisy

Chapter 1

Saturday 21ˢᵗ April 2015

The little dog woke up.

The angle of the new daylight squeezing between the bedroom curtains confirmed it was just a little time before the Big One would also wake up. The dog got up from her little bed in the corner and with great satisfaction slowly arched her back, leaning forward to fully stretch her hind legs, then right back to stretch her front legs.

She got a sudden urge to scratch and folded herself neatly so that she could get one paw behind her ear. She scratched enthusiastically, but was careful to avoid the area around the little plastic cap fixed to the top of her skull. That was still very sensitive. As she scratched she moaned gently and rhythmically with pleasure, until suddenly the ear wasn't itchy any more, so she stopped and stood up.

She lifted her head, opened her mouth slightly, and within the space of a second or two inhaled several times. She was immediately assailed by a rich mix of aromas far beyond anything a human being could ever experience; a base note of different ages of dust and old mouse droppings, echoes of various soaps, shampoos and deodorants, the delicious odour of the Big One's breath, the list went on and on. Like all dogs the complex honeycomb of her nasal passages was constructed so that she could differentiate the airflow even as she breathed. One flow of air simply cooled her oesophagus, but part of the inhalation was diverted to a sensitive receptacle at the back of her throat that allowed her to take her time to savour and analyse the odours reaching her. She could also distinguish between the odours she sensed via each nostril to give her a stereoscopic description of the room. It was all reassuringly familiar. The room smelled...fine. Nothing was wrong.

She silently padded over to the bed where the Big One slept until it loomed above her. To one side of the bed was a small table. On it a human would have recognised a clock radio and next to that a small black speaker unit.

A tiny blue light glowed rhythmically on its side and it emanated a low hum, fluctuating slightly in pitch from moment to moment.

On the other side of the bed the clothes of the still sleeping Big One were draped over a chair, radiating her adorable personal smell. The decline in the odour of the clothes told the dog that they hadn't been worn for a little over seven hours. She knew the duration precisely, though she didn't measure time in any kind of units.

Close to, the delicate miasma of the Big One's odour and the gentle pulse of her heartbeat confirmed she was close to waking up, but the dog decided to leave her be for now. She heard faint noises from outside and got her front paws onto the windowsill to look out. About a hundred yards away, in the big field beyond the garden, something was noisily grazing. The few molecules that leaked through the double glazed window reassured her that it was just the old horse that was always in that field.

Beyond the horse was a high wire fence, and beyond that a thick copse masked the road outside. In the woods on the other side of the road a few birds were singing but nothing moved. She lost interest. She felt thirsty but her water bowl smelt empty. At the same moment she detected a tiny movement of air and followed its flow back to the bedroom door. The Big One hadn't quite closed it last night. She successfully hooked a paw around the edge and pulled the gap wider. She felt a little glow of success.

In the corridor outside, the dust in the air was hazed by the sunlight streaming through the window. Apart from the distant drip of a tap the old house was very still. She strolled carefully towards the white room at the end of the corridor. To her perception the passage was hung about with odours, some new some very old, like layers of spiders web, substantial but fragile. There were many tracks of the Big One, many odour prints from her own feet, each with their own history.

She went into the white room. It was painted everywhere with all kinds of interesting astringent smells. She sniffed at the closed toilet seat. It had been used and flushed the night before. The odour said the woman had urinated in it last night, and her period was due very shortly. She made her way to the shower. The door stood open and she used the opportunity to lap up some water left in the corner but otherwise there wasn't much of interest. She decided to go back and wake the Big One.

She made her way back to the bedroom and smoothly hopped up onto the bed via the bedside chair. The Big One moved comfortably in her sleep. The dog lay down with its head between its paws and contemplated her with easy-going devotion. The Word for the Big One was Jess. The Word for the dog was Daisy.

In a very real sense, most of the time, Daisy had no separate identity or consciousness of herself as an individual. She didn't experience the world she was *the world*. Her feelings were the feelings of the world, food loved being eaten, toys loved being chewed, and everything enjoyed being smelled and licked. The nearest she got to experiencing herself as a separate individual was when she was with the wonderful Jess, or to put it more accurately when she experienced herself as one pole of the amazing Daisy/Jess binary team.

Jess was so extraordinarily glamorous. She was not only adorable but endlessly fascinating. Her dexterity was beyond all comprehension, and her power over objects absolute. She could pick up anything, produce food from nowhere, make the car go, oh, so fast, and even throw things a long way. She provided games and toys, walks and ear scratches, and a host of other bits and pieces that made life pleasurable.

Then again life wasn't all fun. There were the endless training routines and tests. A lot of what Jess did was understandable but a lot wasn't. Indeed an average dog might have found much of Daisy's usual day highly stressful, but experimental canine DAC32, was no ordinary dog. She was the survivor of 14 generations of ruthless accelerated breeding and some extremely sophisticated surgery and computer programming.

It was time Jess woke. Daisy nudged the sleeping woman gently and focused her mind a little. For a second or two the steady hum coming from the speaker next to the bed dissolved into a more complex warble. There was a pause then a girl's voice said clearly, "Wake Up!"

Jess Stewart woke up to discover the black and white cocker spaniel lying calmly facing her on the bed cover. A few moments later the radio alarm buzzed quietly and she stretched to turn it off. The covers were warm and cosy, and she felt no urge to stir. "Who woke me up?" she said. The dog waited. "Who woke me up?" she repeated. The dog huffed, bared its teeth, and wagged the tip of its tail.

"Me!" announced the speaker on the bedside table. "Me wake you up. Me! Me!" It was one of their basic but most fundamental exercises and the dog seemed never to tire of it. Huffing seemed to be its version of laughing. The dog rolled over onto its back and waved its legs in the air, wet tongue hanging out. "Me, Me!" said the speaker.

"Oh. It's Daisy!" said Jess. The dog huffed again and covered its eyes with its paws. It may have thought it was hiding, Jess couldn't tell.

'Daisy' was the private call sign between her and the dog. Within the experimental project of which it was a part, its official title was DAC32, the acronym that indicated its unique breeding and training background, but 'DAC' had easily become 'Daisy'.

'Me' was a much more fundamental self reference. It signalled a moment of genuine separate self-awareness, and the signals generated by the little transmitter in the dog's skull to the speaker by Jess's bed indicated it gave her immense pleasure to assert it.

Jess struggled out of the bed. Although it was still April, it was a lovely day, full of promise. She opened the window and allowed the fresh air to bathe her face and her long naked body.

She was a tall, attractive woman in her early twenties with noticeably thick dark hair, though it always looked a bit unruly. In fact, although she subscribed to the general idea of personal care, she wasn't particularly committed to it, providing she was clean and tidy. The sum total of her feminine care kit comprised of one lipstick which she didn't use very often, one small bottle of perfume, and a pair of high heels which she hadn't worn for months.

Faced with the new information from the naked body in front of her, Daisy observed that Jess's period would start tomorrow but said nothing. Jess slipped into a wrap and sat on the edge of the bed. "Sit up," she said to the dog. Obediently the dog sat back on its haunches and waited quietly as Jess checked the transmitter cap wired into its head. The fusion between the skin of its scalp and the edge of the cap was still perfect, no leakage of lymphatic fluid. "Well Daisy," she said, "your little hat looks fine today. Does it feel OK?"

The rising inflection of Jess's voice and the fingers on her head seemed to give Daisy a fair idea of the question. "Me fine," the speaker said. It would have been useful to have the computer interpretation of her brain and hormonal activity identify a separate neural activity spike for 'me' as subject rather than object, but so far the translator system couldn't reliably make such a subtle identification, and indeed all the research indicated that dog's thought was not in that sense grammatical. She seemed to be able to experience, and therefore verbalise, objects and processes, including herself, but usually slapped verbs or adjectives fairly haphazardly alongside objects. The computer translator tidied up the sequences using a mixture of grammatical convention and best fit.

The dog gazed into her eyes. "Me like you," it said, reaching forward to lick the tip of Jess's nose. "Yes, I like you too," she said, stroking the dog's ears. A more accurate verbalisation of the signal might have been "I love you," but Jess, who had final responsibility for the association of verbalised meanings to the dog's neural activity, thought it would be cloying. However the dog had worked out its own way of expressing intensity.

"Me like-like you," the speaker said, the dog still gazing into her eyes.

"Me like-like you too," Jess said. "Do you want a pee?"

"No pee. Dinner!" said the speaker, and the dog jumped off the bed and ran out of the room.

Jess knew that was a combination of a pious hope and a joke, since there was no was way the dog got any breakfast until she herself had showered and got herself organised for the day. She went into the bathroom and sat on the toilet. The ache in her lower stomach told her that her period was near.

From downstairs the proximal speakers in the kitchen bawled "Dinner!" Then there was the sound of the dog clattering up the wooden stairs and padding back into the bathroom. She approached Jess as she sat, and pushed her head between her knees. It was hard to tell if she was checking out her odour or only, as she often did, offering a friendly gesture.

"I'm sure my period's coming," she said to the dog. "Yes," said the speaker on the shelf next to the toilet, but she knew the dog had no idea what she was talking about. It was just being polite. "Dinner soon," the speaker said hopefully.

Jess got into the shower and Daisy, since she knew that nothing very significant was going to happen for a while, lay down with her nose between her paws and appeared to be watching her. In fact she had expertly slipped herself into a nice state of reduced arousal, the Calm. Her eyes were half open but unfocused. The neat little scanner fed back to the extremely powerful computer downstairs the information that deep within her brain, alpha waves had begun to pulse from her thalamus and irradiate the occipital region behind her eyes. This was expressed as a gentle hum from the bathroom speaker. She waited calmly in this amiable doze for the ten-minute ritual to be over, as indeed she would have if the shower took several hours.

In Daisy's time sense there were basically four allocations of events: 'before', 'now', 'coming soon', and 'just wait'. 'Now' was the dominant experience and, since she lived in a world dominated by odours and the memories of odours, her perception of objects and events was far more fluid than that of a human being. The significance of an object, indeed its very existence, depended heavily on her experiences with it. So for example Jess's slippers were nothing like any other pair of slippers. Their meaning was dramatically shaped by all the 'before' information they carried, including the last time they had been worn. Similarly an object that was due to be 'coming soon', carried almost as much impact as an object or experience that was already there. Her anticipation could reach such levels that she had to repeatedly groom herself or run about just to relieve the tension. However if the object didn't turn up she would eventually simply switch herself off, and, as now, 'just wait'.

After Jess's shower they went downstairs together and organised breakfast. Daisy keenly enjoyed not only breakfast, but also the anticipation of it. While Jess brewed up her coffee and laid out her own cereals and berries, the dog wandered about muttering, "Ah dinner, dinner, good dinner."

Jess had tried distinguishing between breakfast and dinner as separate words in the computer lexicon but, measured by her occipital response, the distinction seemed a nicety to Daisy, so all served meals were verbalised as 'dinner'. However she did appear to make fine distinctions between constituents, and enjoyed variety, so Jess had assigned labels as appropriate.

She said, "What would you like for dinner?"
"Chunky Chunks!"
"It's all gone."

"All gone?" The speaker shouted.

When the dog had been implanted with the scanner that sat neatly on its head like a little plastic cap, hundreds of thousands of organic nano-fibre filaments had successfully been diffused deep into its brain. Many were concentrated in the region that seemed to be equivalent to what was called Broca's area in human brains, believed to be a key language making area, though it was much smaller than that of a human. Many more fibres reached as far as the basal ganglia, the old primitive part of the brain that processes the most basic urges and fears. Consequently, the translator could convey useful information not only on the most appropriate verbalisation of Daisy's attempts to communicate, but on the intensity of her feelings, and it had been surprisingly straightforward to link this to volume and pitch variation.

"Yep, anything else?"

"Chunky Chunks!!"

Like many other individuals of her mental age, which in her case was about equivalent to a six year old human, Daisy had difficulty believing that asking for something twice wouldn't make it happen.

"All gone." Jess said.

Daisy considered. The speaker in the kitchen produced a gentle oscillating note to indicate that, although she was thinking hard, the system could not localise among the wash of activity, too many dendrite links were involved, and in any case the dog was not trying to communicate but to decide. Finally, reluctantly, "Rustlers."

"Rustlers what?"

"Rustlers, please."

The dog sat and waited politely while she opened a tin of 'Rustlers', a mixed biscuit and meat product, and set out two bowls on a low table. Its surface was a little higher than the dog's eye line. "Are you ready?" she said. All the dog's attention was on the two bowls. Its tail was twitching gently. Without speaking aloud, Jess counted out four spoonfuls of the food into one bowl, and then five spoonfuls into the other.

"Which one?" she said. The dog considered carefully. Although, like many dogs, she could easily distinguish between, say, two spoonfuls being ladled out and five, this was a much narrower margin, and required real counting. Finally she pointed with her nose to the more substantial portion and said "My Rustlers!"

"My little genius," Jess said, and placed the bowl on the floor in front of her. The little dog set to with enthusiasm. Finished, she sat and waited hopefully as Jess ate her breakfast, occasionally returning to the bowl to give it a lick, just on the off chance. Afterwards, as the dog waited patiently by the back door to go off for its regular morning evacuations, Jess turned off the alarms and then slid back various bolts and locks to open the door. She realised she had left its comms collar back in the office, where she had been re-initialising it the night before, but she didn't plan to work the dog outside that morning so it didn't matter too much.

The collar itself was a masterpiece of micro engineering. Its core chip carried all the accumulated interpretations of signals from the transmitter cap, originally analysed by Jess with the help of the master computer in her office. It also carried a small Bluetooth powered speaker, linked to the cap, which allowed the dog to communicate with someone while it was away from the fixed speaker system. Clipped on to it was a small tracker unit that combined both GPS satellite links and backup LBS technology. Using mobile phone cells this could locate the dog at any time to within about 15 feet, but right now there was no urgency for it to wear it.

As she entered the little room next to the kitchen that she used as an office to fetch the collar, she noticed the light flashing on the telephone that was her direct link to the headquarters of the Canine Division, the readout showed it was Peter Guy. Her mild irritation that a call was interrupting her work was replaced by the pleasure of seeing his name. He ran the security services at the Canine Division of BSDL and they had begun to see each other not long after she joined the organisation. They had soon become lovers.

Of both white and African American origin he was slightly older than her, but seemed to Jess to have the dark good looks of an Elvis Presley in his prime. Although he was no intellectual he had a quick and witty mind and an athlete's body that she found highly attractive. She had never formed a huge passion for him, indeed she sometimes wondered if she would ever really fall in love with anyone, but they had become very good friends. If his feelings for her were stronger than hers were for him, he apparently had enough insight into her nature to keep them to himself.

She decided to let the dog out before she answered the telephone. Released, the dog sprang through the door and disappeared into the garden. Jess put the kitchen dishes into the washer and then went back into the office and pressed the telephone's answer button. The message it produces was terse and to the point: "Hi, I must speak to you. I can't take a call for a few minutes but please stay by the phone and I'll call right back."

Intrigued, she decided to use the time while she waited to start filing her training records.

She usually used this time of the week get her training records organized to present to the organisation that supervised her work. Jointly funded by the US and British governments, it was euphemistically titled the Biological Sciences Defence Laboratories but its main objective was to investigate the military potential of the behaviour and abilities of a range of species. She worked for the Canine Research Division, and officially she was part of the Canine Project; 'to investigate the potential value of dogs with enhanced communication abilities in providing intelligence in battle field situations', but to her, and the elite group of researchers of which she was a part, it was mainly a wonderful opportunity to get a real insight just what kind of world dogs lived in.

This was all every well, but the primary objective of training the dog was to develop a vocabulary which would allow it to report back on tactically important objects and conditions. A key problem was that the dog's responses to a given object were far less stable than those of a human. Factors like changes in odour and the emotional tone of previous encounters were highly important and were reflected in the variations in the neural spikes that were the basis of allocating a vocabulary. A major part of Jess's task, with the help of digital analysis, was to distinguish the common theme among a cluster of responses that would allow them to be connected to a single word. In many ways this was more of an art than a science, but working closely with the dog she had developed an almost intuitive ability to distinguish the patterns.

So far she had accumulated almost six months of data on Daisy's progress. There were still many problems of interpretation, but the dog was beginning to accumulate a vocabulary of current weaponry and hardware that would have impressed the most demanding of ordnance officers. As a secondary effect the dog's comprehension of spoken words was increasing by leaps and bounds, there was clearly some kind of neurological link between its own growing verbal ability and its understanding of what was said to it. All in all it was going pretty well and Jess was in an extremely good mood.

She had decided the previous evening that things had reached a stage where she could start to tease out the trends in the dog's language development over the duration of the Project so far. She was already pretty sure that, compared with most of the other dogs participating, Daisy was far ahead, not just in vocalisation but also in language comprehension. Her progress was extra-ordinary, and despite her determination to maintain a scientific detachment Jess could not help being fond of the dog. The personality that had been revealed as her skills increased was both determined and infectiously cheerful.

As she loaded the files the Bluetooth speaker next to her desk continued to produce the gentle oscillating note that signalled that the transmitter fixed to the dog's skull was operating normally, but after all these months she was so used to it that she didn't really hear it any more.

The telephone rang again. With a smile she picked it up the receiver.

Chapter 2

Daisy stood outside the back door of The Stone House, lifted her head, opened her mouth slightly and took a couple of nice long breaths of the back garden. With an ability to sense odours roughly forty times more sensitive than that of a human being, she was hit by a huge panorama of smells, full of rich detail and fascinating potential, but before she began to investigate them she ran to the little patch of rough ground that Jess preferred her to use for her toilet. This pleasant duty carried out, she ran on past the little lawn with the slide and into the vegetable garden. There was a straight broad path down through the vegetables, but she took the far more interesting route up and down the rows, making occasional short cuts to follow up an interesting new scent. There was no wind but the light breeze that wafted across the vegetable plots was packed with the morning news.

To eyes with only two kinds of photoreceptors the garden didn't look like much. The plants varied in colour from pale lemon to something like custard yellow with the odd dash of dull blue, but their colour and indeed their appearance, was of no real significance to her. In any case, as she grew close to a particular plant it conveniently floated out of focus so she could concentrate on its scent profile.

It was still early spring and there was not yet that much to see but there was a lot to smell. Not only did every variety of plant have its own scent, each growing plant sent out its own scent messages about its state of maturity and health. To Daisy's nose the brassica shoots (recently fertilised by rich chocolate compost, which was almost edible if you were hungry) were virtually shouting their exuberance, but she wasn't particularly interested in plants. She was much more interested in the crisp musky smell of field mice, criss-crossing the rows as they had sought out low lying treats like carrot tops and crisp early lettuce heads. There were many old tracks of various vintages, but also some new ones from last night, one of them from a recently weaned litter still following their mother. Just for fun Daisy tracked them just to follow the convolutions back to the nest, but she was constantly diverted by new scents, some of them of no more than a molecule or two.

It was dead easy to tell where Jess had been. Here she had walked in her Wellington boots, bearing some of the delicious rich smell of the compost she had previously packed around the young cabbages; there she had turned over fresh earth around the tiny lettuce shoots. Here she had stopped to eat a biscuit bar and dropped two tiny crumbs.

Through all of this, Daisy was mentally doing the equivalent of humming to herself. Building the scent landscape always put her in a good mood, but her spirits lifted even more when she suddenly detected a great blast of the sharp gamey smell of what Jess had taught her was called Fox. The scent was so strong and clear that for a moment it was if the fox was right in front of her, but her eyes confirmed that it had gone.

She concentrated her analysis. It was fairly easy to work out the age of the spoor and the amount of drift. The fox had crossed the bottom of the garden in the early hours of the morning. It had scratched about at various points in the newly turned soil. It had then retraced its steps to the door in the fences at the bottom of the garden. The door was open...

Daisy considered carefully, she was busting to track down the source of the odour trail but as a rule she didn't go through the door without Jess. She looked back up to the house. No sign of her.

Without making a conscious decision, she found herself on the other side of the door, out in the meadow. The meadow was big, over two acres. She came here every day with Jess to play games and have conversations via the headset that Jess wore. The meadow had an even richer scent landscape than the garden, but she ignored all the other information calling out to her and, head down, sprinted across the grass until she came to the high wire fence. The scent led her straight to a small pile of fresh dug earth and the weak point between the link fencing and the fence post where the fox had squeezed in, and then out again.

Daisy considered again. This was really exciting; she had never encountered such a situation before, a new chance to search and find, then report back. She shivered gently and her tail thrashed in the air. This was important work and she was carrying it out really well. Jess would be really pleased with her, but then again, if she went outside alone, what would she say? She called to Jess. The signal would have said, "DAC32 operational, make reconnaissance," then, as an afterthought. "Me OK. Me go, me come back," but she was already outside the range of the Bluetooth receivers in the garden. She wriggled her way through the gap and out.

Back in the house, Jess was completely unaware that a chain of events had now been set in motion that would disrupt her life, and that of the dog, in ways she could not possibly imagine.

She picked up the phone call from Peter. "Hi honey," she said. She started to tell him about her intention to review her work with the dog, but he interrupted. "Jess, I'm sorry to sound abrupt but I want to come straight to the point. Are you and Daisy OK?" He sounded a bit breathless.

"Yes, she's outside playing, we're fine. Why?"

"Good. I've got a bit of a security scare up here, and it might just have a bearing on your project. For the time being, just to be on the safe side, I'm imposing a security shutdown on the local centres, including Stone House."

"What do you mean?"

"For the time being neither you nor Daisy should leave the Stone House security area, and no one should come in. I've alerted Joe at the gate. Is that OK?"

"Of course," she said, "but can't you tell me a bit more? It all sounds a bit dramatic."

"Sorry, but the main thing is that I don't want you to let Daisy out of your sight."

"But Peter..."

"And for now, disregard any emails you might get from Division Central until I can speak to you personally. I promise I'll explain more soon. I'll be out of touch for a few hours, but I'll get back to you. Don't worry, I'm sure it'll all sort out."

Before she could speak he disconnected.

She sat looking at the silent phone, a complex of emotions passing through her, mostly anger that he should dismiss her enquiries so peremptorily, but there was also a tinge of anxiety. In her experience he was a confident as well as kind and thoughtful man. If he wouldn't explain what was happening things must be pretty bad.

It was then that she realised she had lost contact with Daisy.

As always, as they had been speaking, the speaker next to her desk had been producing its gentle background note to tell her that the tiny transmitter fixed to the dog's skull was operating properly. She had just registered that the frequency of the tone was going up, which indicated the dog was getting excited about something, when the tone abruptly stopped.

She suddenly remembered that in her rush to pick up Peter's call she had neglected to put the dog's collar on. She got up from her chair. She told herself not to worry. The dog was in the garden and chances were that it was simply in a spot where a Bluetooth monitor had gone down. It had happened before. Strictly speaking she wasn't supposed to let the dog out without accompanying it, but the garden area was well fenced and Daisy could amuse herself for hours on the small lawn.

She switched the computer down to standby, picked up her headset and went out to the little lawn. There was no sign of the dog. She went into the vegetable patch and immediately saw that somehow the door at the bottom of the garden had opened. She ran down and out into the meadow. There was no sign of the dog and she suddenly recalled that it wasn't wearing its tracker collar. Her heart started thumping and she started running across the grass calling, "Daisy, Daisy, good girl, come on, come to Jess."

There was no sign of the dog and no signal in her headphones. She got to the edge of the meadow and ran along the perimeter fence, edged outside by the dense copse of trees and bushes that led to the outer hedge. Then she saw the gap in the fence...

Jess Stewart, rising star of the Canine Research Division of the Biological Science Defence Laboratories, had lost the most valuable dog of the entire Canine Project.

Part Two

The Canine Project

Chapter 3

April 2014

On another crisp April morning a year earlier Jess had, for the first time, made her way along the broad pathways and well tended lawns that separated the administration area of the Biological Sciences Defence Laboratories from the buildings of its Canine Research Division. The view was softened by the remnants of dawn mist, and the more distant buildings hung like grey ghosts in the still air. She drew her coat collar around her. Beneath, in an effort to look professional on her first day, she'd carefully chosen a dark classic business suit and she had drawn her dark hair back into a ponytail, but it appeared that her concerns had been misplaced. The people she passed, also on their way to work, were wearing anything from casual sports gear to military fatigues, but business suits were rare.

  The buildings she passed were a curious mixture too. Some were just refurbished brick buildings, others new curved shapes dominated by vast areas of darkened glass. There was no way to tell what went on in most of them, but long before she got to the group of buildings in which Canine Research Division was based she could hear the distant barking of dogs.

  Her pulse went up. She was both excited and nervous about working with new people. She was not a naturally sociable person. She made friends with difficulty, and at the age of twenty-five she had still never had a permanent relationship. When she was a little girl her parents, both science teachers, had dropped out of their jobs in England to set up a small farm in rural Ireland, and apart from the local school, she had grown up with little contact with other children.

Instead her social life had focused on the various animals around the farm, and her fascination with their behaviour had evolved over the years from her first voluminous notes on the social life of the farm chickens to formal postgraduate research on the communication skills of African baboons.

Now, about to begin her first real job, she mounted the broad steps that fronted the entrance to the main building. A young man was sitting a desk in the reception area within, and he sat up straighter as she gave him the envelope containing her authorisation papers.

"Right Miss Stewart," he said eventually. "Welcome to Canine Division. From now on at any checkpoint just show this ID." He had the warm vowels of East Anglia, a local man. He passed over a prepared plastic identity card featuring the usual almost unrecognisable passport image, and checked the monitor in front of him. "You're expected in the main lecture theatre. Second floor." He checked again and raised his eyebrows very slightly. "You might be a little bit late." He nodded in the direction of the gleaming stainless steel lifts behind him.

She crossed the reception area briskly and pressed the button to the second floor level. On emerging, she presented her ID to the scanner mounted next to a substantial glass door. The lock clicked open reassuringly and she joined various people going about their business in a well-lit central corridor with various sub-corridors off. It was surprisingly wide, and with its discreet signs and moulded skirting, she could have been in any well-managed modern hospital.

A couple of minutes later, slightly breathless, she opened the door into a lecture theatre. It looked as if it could seat a hundred or more, but now held only half a dozen people, two of them women, all quite young, sitting in front of the tall man who stood on the podium. She saw that he was in his early thirties, conventionally good looking, with striking almost blonde hair and the confident smile of perfect dentistry. He looked up as Jess trotted down the steeply angled steps to join the others.

"This must be Miss Stewart. Come in, come in. Take a seat." There was just the slightest note of disapproval. "Now we can start properly. OK, as I was saying, I'm Alex Leicemann, Deputy Head of Canine Division. My particular responsibility is Breeding and

Selection and you'll be working with me for your first few months here." He spoke with a very slight European inflection. She couldn't trace it.

"Now," he went on, "you've got all the background information in your orientation packs and if you haven't read it yet, get on with it. You'll find all the basic data on the canine genome, gene variations, physiology, psychology, and preference for chewing slippers, that you'll ever need, but, before we let you loose on our little buddies, I want to make sure you understand some of the key elements of what we're doing here."

A PowerPoint display came to life on the big screen behind him to mirror his presentation.

"Our work in the Division is part of a much broader project within BSDL which aims to extend the behaviour potential of a whole range of species. The final uses to which much of *our* work is put are related to the military potential of dogs, but frankly I wouldn't worry about that aspect too much. We get a pretty free hand, there's a lot of valuable academic research to be done here, and it's all well funded."

He gave them all a broad confident smile.

"The first step in the process is breeding," he went on. "The key to success is speed. At first we had real problems. There are several legal constraints on what we can do; a bitch can't be inseminated until she's a year old, she can only produce one litter a year and so on. All well and good but it was all going very slowly."

A video appeared on the screen showing a white-coated team gathered around an operating table on which lay an anaesthetised dog.

"The breakthrough came when this team in America finally mastered *in vitro* fertilization in dogs." The screen showed a highly magnified image of moving single cells.

"The natural process is pretty weird. A bitch produces immature eggs that have to hang around in the oviduct for a few days before being fertilised by sperm that's reached just the right stage of development, but the team discovered that if you match that catch up time and then hit the mature eggs with artificially stimulated sperm you can get eighty or ninety per cent successful fertilizations. Check the details out in your packs. So now we can use implantation on overlapping generations of host mothers. That way we've been able to fast breed for anything up to 10 or 20 generations for a given characteristic until it either starts to look interesting or it doesn't."

Behind him the screen showed an animated flow plan of generations, then switched to the removal of puppies from a dog by caesarean section. They scarcely moved, but a few shots later were amiably crawling over one another.

"We get the pups out as early as possible. They're theoretically premature, but it's not that difficult to get them up to speed, and it turns out that extends the period during which the tots are confident and exploratory by an extra couple of weeks, which is useful. Drawing on techniques like these, it's taken a remarkably short time to get a crop of individuals who are reliably showing enhanced levels of a range of characteristics. Some of these are straight forward; physical endurance, resistance to disease and so on, but we're also interested in changes in behaviour that imply enhanced analytic intelligence, emotional stability, empathy, even creativity. We study them by tracking what we call signifying motor patterns. We also chart how these changes are in turn reflected in changes in the physical structure and hormone balances of the dogs. All these variables interact in a complex fashion."

He stopped to take a sip of water from the glass in front of him. Jess decided it was to give his audience time to realise just how complicated it all was, and how clever he was to be on top of it. As he continued to sip in silence his audience sat quietly too, apparently slightly daunted at the realisation of what a complex endeavour they had got themselves into.

"The Division Head, Dr. Blake, organises further research investigating the potential applications of our work. You'll find out which unit you're allocated to in a few months, after you've served your time in this department."

The general mood of the audience lifted, people smiled and winked at one another. They were on their way.

The screen behind him flashed to a new heading.

"Now, selection: the second key to success is efficient selection. As we breed the dogs, we select and reselect ruthlessly until we can see a clear step forward in a motor pattern, or group of behaviour patterns, we're looking to develop, then we breed from that and so on."

"Doesn't that require an awful lot of dogs?" Jess said tentatively. Several people turned to see who had had the temerity to interrupt.

"It certainly does, both puppies and host mothers."

"And what happens to the puppies who don't make it?"

Leicemann frowned. "A few, a very few, are made available for adoption, but most of them, I'm sure you'll have realised, go quietly and painlessly to the big kennel in the sky while they're still quite small." The young woman next to Jess paused in her note taking, looked across and gave a wry lift of one eyebrow. There was now a slight but perceptible uneasiness among the listeners.

Leicemann caught the mood. "I know that that's a reality you can all handle, otherwise you wouldn't have accepted the job. Yes, we get through quite a few dogs, but remember, we're working to Home Office and Federal ethical regulations, and then again it's not exactly a threatened species."

There were one or two attempts at knowing chuckles but one else spoke. Jess could almost feel the people around her reassuring themselves that there were indeed an awful lot of dogs in the world and the ones that survived here would no doubt have lovely lives.

"Now, pressing on. The key to efficient selection is effective observation. That's where you will come in."

There was another stirring of anticipation in his listeners.

"Of course we set standard tests and challenges to the dogs in order to assess their abilities, but we're also on the look out for the emergence of *new* abilities. That takes very careful observation. Dogs constantly display subtle changes in posture and movement, and produce very small sounds, some of them outside the human hearing range. Often the new abilities appear as a new behaviour so briefly that if you blink you'll miss it.
You can't learn to observe out of a book; so all of you will serve at least three months in my department, helping with selections, before you're allowed on to any other stage of the project. I warn you that not all of you will make it."

The mood of his audience dropped slightly. He smiled generously. "But of course you'll have help. You'll have access to our existing logs, and we have the benefit of EVM and other analytic software, but there's one key intervening variable that gives us real problems…" Next to Jess the woman who had been taking notes waited, pen poised. "That's the mind set of the human that's observing the dogs. They've got to be conscious not only of what the dogs are doing but also their own assumptions about what that behaviour means. Now what's the key challenge to doing that?"

He waited but no one in the audience was going to risk a guess. "The key challenge is the simple fact that most human beings think they already know about dogs. Most folks think it's pretty easy; 'dogs wag their tails when they're happy, bark when they're angry and don't know how to lie'. 'They're like very simple-minded little children, with an additional urge to eat anything edible and chew anything that isn't'. 'They're descended from wolves so they still worry about pack status and stuff like that.' Well none of that is true. As you'll find out, a dog is not some kind of analogue of a human child, and it's nothing like its closest relative, the wolf." Some members of his audience looked slightly dubious.

Leicemann looked at them with an expression that conveyed all his frustration with the uninformed masses.

"The point is; domestic dogs have lost almost all contact with their primeval ancestors. Over at least ten thousand years, maybe much more, humans have systematically created a species that's happier among us than among its own, happy to carry out our purposes rather than its own, constantly revealing new uses. Our work here is just a continuation of that process of creation, done more quickly and a lot more efficiently than ever before. I tell you now, if you do your job properly, we can create creatures that will do almost anything we can imagine. Think about that. I'll leave you now to go through your packs, and I'll be meeting you all separately this afternoon."

He swept out of the room and all at once, as if released from muteness, there was a babble of sound as the new recruits started sharing their reactions to his presentation.

The dark girl next to Jess turned to her. "Bit of a hunk eh? And knows his stuff."

Jess frowned. "He can talk the talk," she said, " and he's clever and good looking. But I'm not sure I like him."

Chapter 4

On the very same day that Jess was first introduced to the work of the Canine Division, the puppy DAC32 was twenty-nine days old, and she had begun to realise that in the World were many Things. Some were Good. Some were Not Good.

At first there had been only one Thing in the whole World, the nipple. That was Good. When she found the nipple she would suck it until she was full and then the World would just stop. When the World started again, the big hands would come in and stroke her tummy and she would have a delicious defecation. Then she had to find a nipple again... Round and round it went. Suck, sleep, and defecate, forever. Then she realised there was another Thing; the warm bulk from which the nipples protruded. It was soft and cosy and smelt of milk and love but no matter how much she snuggled up to it, or licked it, it made no response.

Eventually she came to realise that there were Things that did respond, many Things with many smells. She loved the other Things. They were warm and they pushed snugly against her and she licked them and they licked her, which was Good... Then one time she realised she had eyes and soon after that she had legs, then teeth. Life just got better and better.

But then things changed. It began to happen that sometimes the other Things were in the way when she needed to suck. That was Not Good. That was a Problem...

That afternoon of her first day at Canine Research Division, Jess had her first encounter with the mechanics of the breeding process and, unknown to either of them, her first encounter with DAC32, the dog that was to change her life.

In the reception area of one of the smaller Division buildings, a strange figure shrouded in white stood waiting for her. It was Leicemann; wrapped up in an overall suit very much like the kind she had seen police wearing in murder investigation footage on the TV. Close up Jess realised that he was not only tall but had very broad shoulders and a slim waistline. He pretty obviously worked out. He checked the tablet he was holding.

"Doctor Stewart, come in, come in, you're my two fifteen. Good to see you again, nice and early too. Come on through and have a look at the tanks." Away from the podium his voice sounded softer, almost camp, she thought.

"Actually it's not Doctor. I never completed my Ph.D."

"Oh I see," he said, managing to make it sound as if she was admitting to not being able to read. "Still, your references obviously satisfied the interview board. I'm sure you'll manage."

She waited as he made a little adjustment to his tablet, dreading that he would go on to ask her why she had dropped her research. She hurried to fill the gap.

"Do I need to suit up?"

"No, you're fine for a brief visit Miss Stewart, we won't be opening any tanks near you today." Opening a sturdy glass door, he led the way into a long broad corridor.

The first thing that struck her was the abrupt change in temperature and humidity. It was a comfortably warm fug, with an odour that reminded her of nothing so much as talcum powder. Unlike everywhere else she had been so far, the light levels were low, and immediately tranquillising. The next thing that struck her was the rows of glass-covered tanks lining the walls. It was very quiet; the only sound was a distant hum. In the distance a couple of people, white suited like Leicemann, were tending to one of the tanks but they paid her no attention.

Leicemann led her along the main passageway. "We built this whole set up ourselves. Happily my first degrees were in engineering so I was able to make one or two small contributions to the design." He actually smirked. She got a clear impression that he very much enjoyed introducing visitors to the tanks. She looked down into the first one. Below her, lying in a bed of polystyrene granules, was a long bolster shaped padded tube. Nuzzling at a long row of teats on the tube was a couple of dozen tiny puppies. They were too young for her to distinguish breeds. Each one had found a teat and was contentedly suckling. A golden glow suffused the interior of the tank.

"There's everything a pup could need in there, temperature controlled at a comfy thirty two degrees, absolutely reliable Mum, and we use Dap of course to make sure they're all feeling loved."

"Dap?"

"D.A.P. dog appeasing pheromone, it's the essence of motherly doggy love."

Jess noticed the delicate stir of the puppies' fur as a gentle breeze wafted over them from above the feeding bolster.

"So the units are completely self-sufficient?"

"Virtually, of course we have to remove soiled bedding and lick their bums for them."

Jess looked at him.

"Not literally Miss Stewart." He gave a deprecating little chuckle; it was obviously a favourite joke. "We mimic the licking that their Mums would use to stimulate defecation. But we just use a damp cloth."

Jess noticed that both the floor and sides of the tank were marked out with a series of parallel lines blocked in with various shades of grey.

"What are the lines for?"

"Good question. Very young pups have to develop their sense of distance from the cues around them. Since they can't wander about we provide the necessary geometrical cues within the tanks."

"This may sound naive, but wouldn't it be easier to just place them with their own mothers?"

"There has been some discussion about that, but I take a very clear view, the secret of accelerated breeding is precise control and monitoring. We can't afford any random interference from Mum, and it's crucial that the pups are socialised to humans as early as possible." He checked his tablet. "Apparently, in this cohort my colleague Dr. Blake has asked us to select for puppies with 'enhanced social behaviours'."

"What do 'enhanced social behaviours' look like?"

"That's a very good point. You can see that more clearly if you come along here."

He led her further down the passage between the tanks, but as they passed an open door, she stopped and glanced through it. It had white tiled walls, with a wet-room floor. There were sinks and other equipment around the walls but the most striking feature was a large stainless steel table set in the centre. Leicemann had followed her gaze. "Where it's appropriate I sometimes carry out anatomical analysis to see if we can detect physical changes in the brain when an enhanced ability appears."

"Can you actually see anything?"

"Of course. Changes in arousal levels for example, are mirrored by changes in the brain's dopamine levels. These in turn affect the shape and organisation of areas like the amygdala." His face abruptly hardened and he said almost bitterly, "I would do a lot more, but sadly at the moment neuroanatomy is not seen as a focus of the Division's activities. Still," he gave a thin almost sinister smile, "I'm working on that. Shall we move on?"

As she stood reluctant to pull her gaze away from the room, a tall white suited figure carrying a freezer box appeared behind her. It was a woman, and even if the way she moved had not revealed her gender, the heavily made up eyes above the mask would have. "Ah, good," Leicemann murmured. "Let me introduce you to my personal assistant, Dr. Sophie Bezel. She's particularly interested in the neurophysiological implications of our work here. Sophie, this is a new recruit, Jess Stewart."

The kohled eyes regarded her calmly.

Jess glanced down at the box Bezel was holding. It had a clear glass top and although it was frosted with a thin skim of ice she could see clearly that it contained a small neatly excised brain.

"Good to meet you Jess," Bezel said. Despite the muffling effect of the mask it the voice was confident and melodious.

"You too," Jess began, but the woman was already starting to turn away. "Excuse me, but I've got to get this stuff into OACF as quick as I can," she said briskly.

"That's alright Sophie," Leicemann interjected, "just let me have it for a moment."

"Fine Doc." Bezel handed him the box. "You're the boss. When you're ready." Without further comment, she disappeared into the room, closing the heavy door behind her.

"What's OACF?" Jess said.

"It stands for 'oxygenated artificial cerebrospinal fluid'," Leicemann replied. "A cocktail of a half dozen common minerals and a dash of glucose. It keeps neural material alive outside the body, a very effective way of studying brain function. This will survive a few minutes more without active support. It's nice and cool."

He looked down into the box in his hand.

"Look at that little blob of jelly, Miss Stewart," he said. "It weighs about three ounces, and a big chunk if that is devoted to nothing but analysing scents, but this same little package of neurones organises the behaviour of one of the most subtle and responsive species in existence."

"I'm coming to realise they have some extraordinary abilities."

"That's true. Of course the sense of smell is almost unbelievable. The more we find out the more astonishing it is. Dogs have frequently led searchers to objects hidden beneath umpteen feet of water, or buried deep beneath the earth many years ago." She nodded.

"But then again," he went on smoothly, "the same dog may well be blocked in its progress by a simple fence, not thinking to move to a gate a few yards away. We must never forget their limitations, never get carried away by fantasies of consciousness." He paused whilst they both looked at the sample. He sensed her discomfort.

"Our job is to be open to new insights Miss Stewart," he said firmly, "but also to be rigorous in our investigations. Lots of people want to believe there's conscious personality in there somewhere, but I doubt it. It might look like it but there's no real evidence for it. The theoretical construct we depend on here involves the teasing out of interactions of canid motor patterns of behaviour, that's all. Are you familiar with that approach?"

"Yes of course. The idea is that the animal's behaviour consists of a series of little packages, and each package of behaviour is a semi-automatic releaser for the next in prewired sequence."

Leicemann beamed at her. "Precisely, and there's absolutely no need to assume any kind of conscious involvement."

Jess suddenly noticed that a little way behind them one of the tanks had been opened. Two of the assistants were lifting puppies out of a tank. One was put into a neat white carrying cage, the rest into a larger cage with a small red circle on the side. The single puppy began a melancholy yipping as it realised it was alone. The assistants walked away briskly with the cages, the sounds from the puppy fading. She turned back. Leicemann appeared not to have noticed.

"Of course many people hate to let the notion of animal consciousness go. They love stories like the Edinburgh dog that was supposed to have kept guard by the grave of its owner for years," he went on, "but it's much more likely that, as its spurious reputation built up, it simply connected staying there with getting food from visitors. Dogs are adaptive and very opportunistic."

As he was speaking they were strolling past bank upon bank of incubator tanks, each with its pack of puppies, feeding, playing or sleeping. Jess realised the whole set up was much bigger than she had first imagined.

"They're nice enough creatures, most of them. I'm sure they have something like feelings," Leicemann went on, pausing to look down almost fondly at yet another little gang of puppies tumbling over one another in happy ignorance of their bizarre situation, "but I don't believe there's really much depth to those feelings, and there's lots of data to support me. You know, dogs have been observed to just sit and watch for a while as an owner pretends to writhe in agony on the floor, then just wander away."

"Could it be that the dogs could tell the owner was just acting?" Jess said tentatively.

This produced a long hard look.

"As I have said, we attempt to keep our hypotheses on the mental powers of dogs on the conservative side, Dr Stewart," Leicemann said carefully. "I hope you'll be able to work within that framework. Every dog we breed here can give us new insights, but only if we maintain the strictest scientific discipline."

He came down strong on that one, she thought. It was time to calm him down.

"I understand completely Dr Leicemann," she said, equally carefully. "I too am utterly convinced of the absolute need for rigour in science. I hope I can demonstrate that while working with you."

Her answer seemed that lift his mood, "I'm sure you will, Miss Stewart," he said. "I'm sure you will. I have great hopes for our work together." The pale blue eyes regarded her intensely.

My God, she thought suddenly, is he flirting with me? Her habitual distrust of her own ability to read other people kicked in. She didn't know what to say. Abruptly the moment passed. He stepped back a little. "Let's carry on," he said, as if nothing had happened.

He handed the box over to yet another passing white-suited figure and, taking Jess's elbow, led her further along the corridor to a new row of tanks. He stopped at the first one. They both looked down at the puppies within.

"Ah, here we are. This lot is a selection from several previous batches. They all show above average social behaviour skills. This particular group is..." he checked the screens above the tank, "twenty nine days and four hours old. Still at the teat, but they'll be moving on to solids soon. By this stage, if we've set the situation up right, I should be able to show you some of the behaviour we're looking for."

Jess studied the puppies in the new tank; most were suckling away at the mother tube.

"They look pretty happy eh?" Leicemann said.

"Yes, but none of them are wagging their tails."

"I'm surprised at you Miss Stewart. I thought you'd know. They won't start using their tails for another couple of weeks yet." He smiled at her slightly condescendingly.

Damn, I should know that, she thought. Still, no harm, mental superiority means a lot to this man.

"Notice anything else?"

The whole setup looked identical to the first tank until she realised that, although there were twelve puppies, there were only eleven teats on the artificial mother. One puppy was wandering along the line of feeding kin. He went up and down a couple of times and then stopped behind one puppy and nipped his tail. The feeding puppy at first ignored him but after a couple of nips he turned from the nipple to snarl at the nuisance. Quick as a flash the first puppy pushed in and grabbed the vacant nipple.

"That's good," said Leicemann, "but it's not the kind of approach Dr Blake's looking for here, we're after more complex behaviours than that. That little girl who is now without a nipple to suck is…" he leaned over to look at the tattooed barcode, then checked his notes, "DAC32. She's more the type we're looking for in this batch. We keep 'em pretty hungry so she won't hang about."

Now short of a nipple, DAC32 also wandered up and down the line but then she stopped and began working her way between two feeding puppies until her head was between theirs. She began nudging and licking at the puppies until eventually one of them stopped feeding to lick her back. DAC32 calmly took the vacant nipple and began sucking but, after only 30 seconds or so, she yielded it back to its previous owner. Then she started licking the puppy on her other side…

"That's a very sophisticated set of behaviour patterns for any dog, never mind a puppy. She'll probably make it to the next stage," Leicemann said, and indeed, as it turned out she did.

And that was the first time Jess met DAC32, one day to be known as Daisy.

Chapter 5

Jess woke the next morning to the sound of her tablet alarm. Instead of getting up immediately she lay still, gazing abstractedly up at the ceiling of her little bed sitting room. She was trying to absorb and evaluate everything she had seen the day before. She was in some conflict. The job at the Defence Laboratories had come to her after a period in which she had been completely unable to get the kind of work, studying animal behaviour, which she wanted. It had seemed a great opportunity, but now she was beginning to realise that although the dogs involved were well looked after they were really only fodder for the aims and objectives of it's projects. Those that met the aims of its ambitions would survive, the rest eased into oblivion. Did she really want to be a part of that?

A part of her was deeply revolted by the idea, but she couldn't help being fascinated by what the scientists at the Laboratories were trying to do, and the new kinds of dogs that were emerging from the project. If she stayed who knew what she might discover?

She simply couldn't make up her mind whether to go ahead, or to call in to say that she'd decided it wasn't the right kind of job for her. She let her mind go blank and then a few moments later, without conscious decision, found herself getting out of bed and preparing to set off for the Laboratories. For better or worse she would go ahead. There would always be time to change her mind…

During the next few months, like the other probationers, Jess was attached to Leicemanns's section. She spent the first few days being briefed on the use of the preformatted observation logs, which didn't present her with many difficulties, and was then set to work carrying out the various tests and observation protocols with groups of seven to ten week-olds. She was pleased to discover that the survivors of the tanks were kept in more open pens than the tiny pups and even had access to the outdoors.

Her specific brief was not only to socialise the groups she supervised to humans but to select puppies that showed signs of enhanced emotional stability and assertiveness, but whatever their individual abilities, she found the interplay of their behaviour as a group quite beautiful to watch, especially when they were grooming one another. To her it was like a subtle and elegant dance that must have its own rhythms and symmetries, if she could only get in tune with them, and she was happy to spend hours pursuing that hidden choreography.

She quickly realised that they constantly used almost ever part of their bodies to communicate, especially using facial muscles, eyes and ears, but the signals were usually over in a second, often no more than a brief movement of the mouth or widening of the nostrils. She discovered that there was a whole range of barks from a very quiet low pitched 'woof', just to remind another dog that an individual wasn't going to stand for being trifled with, through to the jolly yapping of shared play.

She also realised that they signalled their emotions with their tails to an extent she would never previously have imagined. When a puppy was happy it kept its tail high with a confident gentle wagging rhythm. If it was nervous or angry it might also wag its tail vigorously but angled down to the ground. A puppy just wandering about checking the environment would usually just keep its tail parallel to the ground. A dog that merely wanted to send a little hello might wag just the very tip of its tail briefly, and so on. There were dozens of subtle variations. Most interesting of all, a happy dog would usually wag its tail slightly to the right, an unhappy or frightened one to the left.

When she wasn't observing the dogs she spent a lot of time following up the available literature on communication between dogs and as her skill at recognising the meaning of all the subtle signs and signals grew, the work increasingly absorbed her. As the days lengthened into summer, she spent far more hours with the litters she was assigned to than her schedule required. The other probationers couldn't make up there minds if she was fiercely ambitious or just slightly odd, and, though one or two of the men made a few half-hearted attempts to get to know her, she tended to be left out of any social activities. In any case, since they were aware of Leicemann's promise that not all of them would survive their probation, there was an underlying competitiveness that tended to inhibit the formation of close friendships in the group.

She was used to spending time on her own and it was no great burden for her. She had no great problem organising here sustenance either, the staff canteen was open nearly twenty-four hours a day and the cooking was good. She would usually go down at the end of a long session and devour whatever was left of the dishes of the day.

It was during one of these meals, her mind focused on her recent observations, that she realised that a tall young man carrying a tray was standing next to her table.

"Hi," he said, "I don't want to bother you but do you mind if I join you? It's kinda quiet in here, and I hate eating alone."

As usual at such a late hour, the canteen was indeed almost empty. She considered for a moment, and then more to be polite than anything else, invited him to sit down. He thanked her and sat down across the table. He was a bit older than her, but still young, Afro-American, with the warm voice and easy manner that was typical of so many of the Americans attached to the Division. He smiled at her and reached out his hand.

"I'm Peter Guy," he said. "I work in Security. I've noticed you before. Like you, I guess I usually finish pretty late."

She accepted the extended hand. "Jess Stewart, I work in Selections."

"Oh, Dr Leicemann." He dropped his voice conspiratorially, "The Iceman."

She looked at him.

"I hear he can be pretty tough."

"Sometimes. He has his foibles. I can't say it bothers me. Anyway it's worth it to work with the dogs."

He gave a broad genuine smile. "You enjoy it?"

"Love it." She found herself smiling back.

"I bet. Are you allowed to talk about it?"

"You should know!"

They both laughed and she began to tell him about her work with the dogs.

After that first meeting they somehow managed to bump into each other most evenings, and, though it was not in her nature to enter easily into intimate conversation, she became more and more confident about sharing her enthusiasms with him. He was an attentive listener and often made perceptive and thoughtful comments. He didn't talk so much about what he did, but she understood that was probably part of working in Security. They became tentatively comfortable with one another and she even started checking her hair and putting on a spot of lipstick before she went down to the canteen.

However, at the same time, as the weeks went by, her contacts with Leicemann became more and more strained. Despite her best efforts to retain a sceptical detachment, the more she observed the dogs, and the more she read up on the research literature, the more convinced she became that the creatures she was studying did possess a form of consciousness. It was simpler than that of human beings, and easily diverted by emotion and instinct, but every so often she spotted interactions between the dogs that she could only interpret as reflecting awareness. She noted these moments in her logs, but no matter how carefully she phrased it, Leicemann refused to accept her conclusions.

She'd been particularly impressed by one incident. The group she studied had no particular hierarchy, any more than the average group of human beings might, but one young dog, seemed to have emerged as a natural leader. He wasn't at all aggressive, he just seemed to be more adept at negotiating the various conflicts and issues that came up in the group, equally ready to take a firm stand or dilute a dispute into a game as seemed the best judgement. On this one occasion a real fight began to develop between two of the dogs, one of whom was prone to being bullied, and as it was in danger of being injured.

Jess was about to step in, but before she could do so the leader pushed his way between the two and gave a clear message both with posture and snarls that the stronger dog should back off. As it did so, the lead dog turned to the now quivering loser and set about giving it a good lick before settling down next to it until it recovered. Jess was really excited at observing what was to her a clear demonstration of altruistic behaviour but Leicemann would have none of it.

'You must remember Dr. Stewart,' his written comment on her notes said, 'when trying to understand animal behaviour, a good scientist first looks for instinct or habit rather than some hypothetical conscious activity. Please go back and specify the most likely reflex chain. There's no ghost in these little machines.'

However to her, if she had to make a choice between reporting what she believed she was observing and what she was supposed to observe, the choice was clear, and she continued to include her interpretations in her reports. She wasn't really surprised when, one morning early in July, only a couple of months after she started, he called her into his office.

When she went in he was reading her latest report. "Sit down Miss Stewart," he said, without looking up. She sat down carefully and waited patiently as he made a play of going again through her reports, flipping from page to page, frowning every so often. Her pulse rate had gone up and her breathing was shallow. She had the distinct feeling that he detected her discomfort and was even enjoying it. I'm not the first probationer to sit here quaking, she thought.

Finally he spoke. "I must say that when you first came here I had very high hopes of you, Jess. Can I call you Jess?" She nodded.

"Frankly I'm usually reluctant to give female probationers extra responsibility until I've seen how they perform, but I put you straight on to one of our more demanding projects because I sensed you had a keen eye and a real interest in what we're trying to do here."

"Thank you."

"At first your reports were highly satisfactory but then you began to insert these frankly sentimental ideas about conscious mental activity. I have warned you about this and I've tried to reserve my judgement for as long as possible, but if anything your bias got worse. I can't continue to accept it. I've told you before. Unless you can work within the discipline and guide rules set out in my protocols, there's no place for you here."

Her face dropped.

"Don't get me wrong," he said almost kindly. "I like you, you're intelligent, attractive and a breath of fresh air about this place." He looked at her a little too long. She felt her heart sink. "I'd like you to go on here," he continued, "I think you could have a real future and I'm prepared to work with you on what may only be, who knows, a slightly feminine bias. We can go through these reports in detail together and see if we can't knock them into shape."

He smirked slightly. "I have quite a good track record. Sophie, Sophie Bezel, you remember her? She had some difficulty settling down to the way we work here until she and I had a couple of re-orientation sessions. Now she's completely on board with my approach."

He gave her one of his dazzling smiles.

She took a deep breath. "Dr Leicemann," she said quietly, "I have the greatest respect for the work you do here, and I'm grateful to be part of it, but my approach is solidly based on my past experience and research into the cognitive potential of dogs. I deeply believe in the accuracy of my observations."

She paused but he just watched her in silence. "Look, I'm very willing to closely follow the protocols of the department," she said, "but I just can't withdraw my personal observations. I see what I see." Her voice quavered slightly but it came out fairly confidently since she had rehearsed it to herself several times since she got the call to his office.

They stared at each other some more. His smile had vanished.

"Well you may see what you see, but leaving aside your more florid perceptions, my analysis of the data from your records is that there is nothing remarkable about any member of your study group. I'm having it terminated immediately."

"What!" she burst out, "you can't do that! You know there's real talent in that group. I can't accept that!"

The characteristic thin smile reappeared. "Oh can't you?" he said briskly. "In that case Miss Stewart, it seems I have to remind you who runs this unit. I'm going to recommend to Dr Blake that your contract with us be not renewed, with immediate effect. I should warn you that my decision is final. Meantime, I thank you for your work here, and I wish you the best of luck with your future career." He turned back to his papers.

She was devastated. She had not only lost what was to her the best job in the world but the dogs she had lived with for months and come to know so well were facing obliteration. Fighting back the tears, her face a mask, she stood up and without a word left his office.

Half an hour later she was sitting with Peter at their usual table in the canteen, a little pool of misery in the comings and goings of the daytime staff around them. She had called him as soon as she left Leicemann's office. She was annoyed with herself for her weakness in doing so but she had been in despair. She hadn't known where else to turn. His response had been immediate. Now, managing to keep her voice steady, she finished her account of the meeting in Leicemann's office, then sat back and disconsolately sipped her latte. He waited quietly as she struggled calm herself.

"You did the right thing. There was nothing else you could do. 'Re-orientation sessions?' What the hell was that about?" She wouldn't meet his gaze.

"Look, I know you feel bad now but I'm sure it's going to be OK," he said at last.

"Thank you for your sympathy Peter,' she said. "You know I appreciate it, I really do. But something like this has happened to me before."

"What?"

She paused reluctant to go further, and then took a deep breath. "A couple of years ago I started to do a PH.D in Kenya, studying baboons. I loved it, all of it. It was hot and miles from anywhere but I didn't mind."

He looked at her keenly. "And something went wrong?"

"My field supervisor started coming on to me. I let him know pretty strongly I wasn't interested, maybe too strongly. After that he started dissing my reports. He said my stuff was sloppy and amateur. He went so far as to say he'd make sure I never got a degree."

"That must have hurt."

"It did. This guy is a really big name in ethology. He's got influence. He was so disparaging."

She paused for a moment, as the memory seemed in danger of overwhelming her, and then visibly gathered herself together. "I stuck it out for a while but I got completely confused. I've never been any good at assessing people. Was he just putting me down, or was I really no good? Maybe I didn't have what it takes to be a scientist. Maybe I still don't."

She looked so unhappy that he couldn't help taking her hand. She didn't seem to notice.

"Anyway in the end I just left, chucked it in. I guess you could say I had a bit of a nervous breakdown. I packed shelves in a supermarket for a while, stuff like that. Then I saw the ads for this job. I'd lost so much confidence I was amazed when I got it."

"And you've done great. You're a natural. Look at me, I'm a moron but I've learnt such a lot just listening to you."

She gave a weak smile. "Thanks Peter. I can't tell you how much I appreciate your support." She realised they were looking into each other's eyes. She withdrew her hand.

"Anyway, he's the boss. His word is final. Maybe, I don't know, I should have just agreed to edit my reports."

"You don't really mean that." He was right, she didn't, but what could she do now?

"Even if you have a disagreement about procedure," he went on, "there's no excuse for him giving you such a hard time, you have the right of appeal. As it happens I'm pretty close to Sam Blake and I know quite a bit about his way of working. He's no behaviourist."

"You know Dr Blake?"

"A bit. I know most people around here. I have to. I'm Head of Security for the Division."

She looked up sharply. "Somebody has to do it," he said ruefully.

She was suspicious. "Head of Security? Why didn't you tell me before? Is it a secret?"

"Not really but, you know, I wanted to get to know you, and I didn't want to look like I was grandstanding."

He looked almost embarrassed for a moment. "You know what I mean."

She felt a warm glow. Her previous experiences with men had been often been marred by their apparently relentless need to overstate their accomplishments. She was never entirely confident of her own feelings but now she admitted to herself that she had developed a real sense of attraction to him. He really was very good looking man, perhaps a good man.

"Look," he said, "I wouldn't dream of trying to intervene in your career, but just let me check that Blake is fully up to speed on your work. Leicemann can be tricky. He and Blake don't get on that well. It goes back to when Blake found out Leicemann was using his neurophysiology labs to do some off the record stuff using something called optogenetics. I don't really know the details but it was something about creating dogs that would go into action at the touch of a switch. Is that possible?"

"Apparently," she said, "I've read a bit about it. It's a bit disturbing, to me, anyway. I've only heard of it done with mice. It's horrible but ingenious. They take a light-sensitive alga and extract the gene that gives it that ability. Then you insert the gene into specific neurones in the animal's amygdala."

He looked baffled. "Sorry," she said, with a smile, "I'm coming over all technical."

"No," he said, "really. I'm fascinated. Go on, I'll struggle with it."

"OK," she said, "the amygdala is the bit of the brain that runs motivation and emotion. That in turn controls various behaviours, like running, but more to the point attacking and biting as well. The idea is that when you shine a laser down a fibre into the amygdala, and into neurones that have been sensitised, a protein produced by the gene kicks them off and the mouse, or whatever it is, goes into action. With a flick of a switch you could, theoretically, produce a killer dog that attacks, even kills, the quarry you direct it to, whether it likes it or not. When you've finished, you just switch off."

"Amazing. Yeah, well, when Blake found out Leicemann was doing this stuff behind his back he blew his stack. He tried to get Leicemann chucked out, but he managed to hang onto his job, because of his influence with the Board I guess. They work on a kind of cold war basis now. I'm sure he'd have some sympathy for your situation. Let me speak to him."

"Please," she said, "I can look after myself."

"Of course you can, but big research set ups like this can get very compartmentalised, for all kinds of reasons. The flow of information doesn't always work like it should. I'd just be checking." Eventually, reluctantly, she nodded, and he left soon after.

Later that afternoon she got a call from Dr Blake's secretary to go to and see him first thing the next day.

Chapter 6

The next morning Jess made her way to the unit to which Blake's secretary had directed her. It was there that she would have her second encounter with DAC32, though she didn't realise it at the time and, like so many events in real life, it was purely by coincidence.

After working her way through the usual maze of corridors, she knocked on the door to which she had been directed. She heard a muffled call to come in. She entered a large airy room. There were several large windows, but the white blinds over them diffused the daylight, and there was a very slight odour of disinfectant in the air.

In the centre of the room she saw that a young dog, practically still a puppy, was standing very still at one end of a narrow platform. It was about twelve feet long with closed sides to the floor, set at a height of about four feet. The little dog was looking down at a biscuit placed on the floor in front of it and below the platform. The only access to the floor was a set of steps behind it, on the far end of the platform from the biscuit. The dog showed no interest in her entrance, all of its attention was on the biscuit.

A chubby untidy man in his late forties was sitting to one side of the room behind a simple screen. There was a small table in front of him. On the table was a large monitor. He was studying it and taking notes on a tablet. Without looking up he waved to Jess to come and sit in the chair next to him.

The monitor showed various angles of the puppy standing on the platform. It was a young cocker spaniel.

DAC32 stood on the High Place and looked down at the biscuit on the floor below. She could see it only vaguely but its smell image was clear. It was a delicious biscuit. It wanted to be eaten. She decided she had to get down to get that biscuit, but she was frightened to jump so far. She walked all round the high place smelling for a way down and then she found the steps. They were a bit frightening but she had descended steps before, so she flip-flopped her way down to the floor. When she got there the biscuit had gone, not even leaving an odour. Where was that biscuit?

She ran briskly back up the steps and crossed over the platform to look down again. There it was! She ran back to the steps and descended them again. The biscuit had gone again. How? She was disappointed, and then her spirits rose. This wasn't just a disappearing biscuit, this was a Test. She loved Tests.

*She ran back up to the steps, crossed the platform and looked down again. There it was again! There was a Key here. In the Tests there was always a Key. She stood and studied it carefully and then suddenly, all of a piece, she knew just where that biscuit was. She ran back to the steps, threw herself down and sprinted along the side the platform, **to the other end**. And of course that clever biscuit was there. She felt so good that even before she ate that clever biscuit, now **her** biscuit, she took it to show to the Big Ones to get some Love, because, of course, being loved by Big Ones was the best thing ever, even better than eating a biscuit.*

"One minute, twenty four seconds," said Blake. "I'm doing some trial selections for a new project. It's big for us. What do you think of her?"

Before she could answer the puppy came dancing triumphantly across to them and its head popped round the screen, biscuit still in its mouth. Jess instinctively reached down to give it a stroke then stopped herself.

"It's all right," Blake said, "a little reinforcement won't do any harm. I think she may well be suitable for our needs. There's more tests to do yet but she's certainly bright enough."

"To be honest that looked pretty obvious. Is that a tough task for a dog?"

"It's not so much what she did as the way that she did it. For a start she has to go down and *away* from the biscuit to find it. That's tough for a puppy. Then when she gets to the floor she's completely disoriented, there's no sign of it, and the most obvious way to find it is to snuffle about until she eventually bumps into it, which frankly is what most dogs do. The clever thing to do is go back up on the platform and review the situation. She took the clever option. Easy for us but it requires a moment of real insight on the part of the dog. Anne will take her back now."

A small dark woman in white lab coat came in as he spoke, and with a brief nod to both of them, gathered up the puppy and whisked it away. Jess was sorry to see it go. It was such a bright cheerful creature.

Blake shut his tablet and turned to her. "Miss Stewart isn't it?" he said, holding out his hand. "Good to meet you." They shook hands. His touch was pleasantly warm and dry. For some reason she felt reassured. "Now," he said, indicating a neat pile of files on the table, "the reports of the man some of your colleagues call 'The Iceman' reveal that you've been doing some very valuable work over the last few months."

"Iceman?" She said politely.

"Doctor Leicemann," he said gently. "Don't tell me you don't know his nickname, 'Iceman Leicemann'. We've all got one. They call me Fat Sam behind my back, fair comment."

"To tell you the truth, I think he isn't very impressed with me."

"He isn't, in fact I see from his report that he intends to shut down your study group and he recommends that you be allowed to leave the project."

Jess felt a pit open in her stomach and her pulse rate went up. She started to speak, but he interrupted.

"Hold on. Stay calm. You're not leaving the project and we'll take another look at those dogs before we rush to any decisions. I'll tell you, in confidence, there's sometimes a bit of a divergence between Doctor Leicemann's definitions of science and mine. For a start I'm not quite as impressed as he is with mechanical Mums. It makes it easier to standardise the conditions the litters are raised in and it helps with a fast turnover, but it's a compromise. Pups thrive best with their own mothers." She nodded her agreement.

"I'm not as keen as he is to interpret all behaviour in terms of neurophysiology and conditioning either," he went on. "As scientists we can't afford to leave out any possible interpretations of what we observe. What we're doing here is trying to extend dogs' latent abilities, and to do *that* we have to follow every clue, not ignore the data we don't like." She began to feel more cheerful.

"There's been one or two other issues we've had but you don't need the details. By and large I leave the Doctor on a pretty long leash. He's very able and very ambitious, very good at working the Board. He's managed to expand his department dramatically in just a couple of years. Good luck to him. The powers that be love his breeding tanks, and it helps get me funds, so what the heck."

Jess had the distinct impression that Blake was not made of the same material as Leicemann. There was no ravening ambition here she sensed. Perhaps that was a weakness…

Blake looked down at the folders in front of him.

"The problem is that it looks to me as if in this case Dr. Leicemann might have imposed some of his more radical views on how we should assess dogs for selection. It's something he's done before."

He paused, apparently realising that he might have spoken too openly. "Anyway, I see no lack of scientific rigour in your notes. What may read to the good Doctor as anthropomorphism looks more like sensitive interpretation to me, and that's what I'm looking for."

She breathed a sigh of relief. He looked a bit uncomfortable.

"As usual I've probably spoken too freely. Never mind, all that's between you and me," he went on, "OK?" He looked at her keenly. She nodded. He was apparently satisfied. "Now, before we take another step, let's go and get a coffee. They do a very good latte in the canteen."

A few minutes later she was waiting at a table in the brightly lit canteen. There were only a few other people there but they still managed to fill the large room with a background mumble of casual chatter. He bought over two coffees and a substantial doughnut. "Don't tell me, very bad for me," he said, sitting down, "it's all part of my secret diet plan. Like a slice?" She shook her head.

He took a large bite out of his doughnut and gave a groan of appreciation. She smiled. This man was a far cry from the cool disciplined Leicemann.

"Right," he said, "I'll tell you what we're up to and how you might help. I'm sure I don't need to tell you how good dogs are not only at reading each other but at reading human body language too. We've known for years, for example, that almost any dog can go straight to a hidden object simply by observing where a human is looking. But we need to find out a lot more about this ability to respond to humans. What do you know about that?"

She realised she was getting an impromptu job interview and tried to run over her sources in her mind.

"OK. We know, using MRI scanners, that dogs do respond to a human voice and its emotional tone, and they're using about the same part of the auditory cortex as us. They also recognise the difference between laughing and crying, and scowling and smiling. They use the same side of their brain, the left, as we do to listen to meaningful speech, but not if it's babble."

He nodded and took another bite out of his doughnut.

"How much do they actually understand what we say though?"

She realised that behind his easy-going manner he was listening very carefully.

"They seem to learn the basic meanings of words in much the same way as we do. Some dogs have learned to understand hundreds of different words for different objects, and not just the separate word for each object, but the generic word for groups of objects that share the same property, like 'balls', or 'toys'."

Another giant bite of doughnut.

"Sounds good, but how do you know that they've really learned the names of things, not just commands to fetch them?"

She felt a little flush of pleasure that she was on sure ground with the question.

"Because it's been shown they can understand the difference between words *for* objects and words that are commands *about* objects. They can grasp dozens of different commands. Not just 'fetch' but phrases like 'stand close to the lady', or 'walk around the room'. They can identify the names, and the faces of people too. That means you can tell them to go to another room, fetch a particular object and bring it to a named person. They even scan a face like we do, gazing from the right side to the left."

"Anything else?" She realised that in her enthusiasm she had slid forward to the edge of her chair and surreptitiously pulled herself back.

"Well, one of the things I personally find amazing is that if you give them a new word for an object they haven't yet seen, and tell them to go fetch it from a pile of stuff, they'll search out the only object they *don't* recognise and bring it back. That must mean they can infer things a lot like we do."

"That's right, the 'principle of exclusion.' Pictures?"

Jess was on sure ground here too. "Yes, you can show a bright dog nothing more than a picture of a new object and he'll go and fetch it. That means they must in some sense be able to understand two-dimensional images, just like us. I've even seen references to them being able to obey written commands!"

Reassured by his attentive listening and occasional nods, she ploughed on, surprising herself at the volume of material she had accumulated over the period of her studies. Eventually he put up a restraining hand.

"OK, that'll do for now. Well done. You seem to know your stuff." The doughnut was long finished now and he slowly dusted off his fingers with a napkin. "But the big question is; if dogs *do* have some kind of mind, can we put all those pieces together to begin to understand how it works? If they can understand so much why is their range of responses so limited? Or are we just missing the signals? Could we teach them to generate more signals that we *can* understand? Do they even have that capacity? That's what we're trying to find out. Do you want to get involved in that? You could risk a sip of your latte now by the way, it must be getting cold."

She took a grateful sip and suddenly realised she'd passed a test she hadn't even been prepared for. Her face shone. "Yes indeed. Thank you so much. I'd be so pleased to have the chance to work with you."

"Then you can have your chance. I'm going to give you a little project of your own. I've already got a couple of teams working in this area but think you might bring a fresh approach to it. It'll be a challenge, and we'll need to see some results, but don't worry, I won't be standing over you. I believe in letting good people get on with it." He got up from his chair and shook her hand. "You can start fresh in the morning."

She left his office in a whirl of relief, and that night, despite her resolution never to mix business and pleasure, she went to bed with Peter Guy for the first time.

Chapter 7

The next day Jess met Blake in his office. His enthusiasm was undiminished from their previous meeting, and he briskly led her to a new section of the Canine Unit and into yet another large but anonymous room. The only furniture was a table and two chairs but the room was set up with a full compliment of cameras and microphones. Anne, the technician she had met the day before was waiting there. They exchanged nods.

"You're in the Communications Studies Unit now and this room will be your research lab. You'll remember Anne from yesterday. She'll be your husbandry assistant. You couldn't have better," Blake announced. "Just order any further equipment you need from her. We've already selected a group of dogs that have already shown unusual empathy with human beings, well beyond the average. Your brief is to investigate their potential ability to communicate with humans, and see how far you can build on it."

She felt her pulse rate go up with a mixture of excitement and apprehension. She nodded and tried to look confident.

"I leave your research strategy to you. There's other people working on this too, but it's a wide open brief, and it'll take time. I'll check on how you're doing in a month or two. Let me know if you need anything... Good luck," and without any further briefing, he swept out of the room.

As Jess sat trying to digest the sudden change in her responsibilities, Anne led in the first dog. "I'm in shock," she said ruefully.

"It's the way he works," Anne said. " Don't worry, when he believes in somebody he backs them all the way. You'll be OK. Say hello to Betsy."

It occurred to Jess that perhaps Blake's hands-off approach to administration was the flaw behind the growth of Leicemann's burgeoning empire. However, it had given her a chance to show what she could accomplish, so she swiftly dismissed the thought and turned to the dog in front of her.

Betsy was a beautiful black and white border collie, logged as BC42 G19. The G signified it was the nineteenth generation of its breed. It gave Jess a brief glance and then set about sniffing all around. Eventually, apparently satisfied, it sat down in front of her chair and regarded her steadily. She looked deep into its mild dark eyes. It gazed calmly back. It had a curious kind of charisma and presence. After a while, as if some kind of decision had been made it advanced to delicately smell her hand and give it a little lick. Jess felt as if she'd passed some kind of test.

She checked Betsy's abilities as recorded on her tablet, including the dog's ability to recognise words and gestures, copy human behaviour, and solve problems. It was a pretty impressive list, but most importantly, like the other dogs she would work with, the logs showed that the Betsy was unusually vocal and expressive.

Over the next couple of hours she met more dogs. Physically they didn't look any different from a random selection of normal dogs, but working from their reaction to her and their records she eventually short-listed six of them. Along with Betsy there was a sprightly cocker-poodle, a Yorkshire terrier, a couple of Labradors, and a wiry haired mongrel that could have been sired by a whole range of breeds. They all had different temperaments, but what they all had in common was a kind of intelligent self possession and intense interest in her every word and movement.

Introductions made, Jess went back to her own office to devise her research plan. She sat at her desk computer, typed in a heading, 'Procedures to reveal and develop canine communication skills.' then sat and looked at the blank screen. Where to start?

That afternoon she worked her way through all the relevant sounding research papers in the journals to which the Division subscribed. There were hundreds. Rather prosaic papers pointed out that the average family dog uses dozens of signals to try and communicate its needs to its human owners, even though they might fail to recognise many of them. A lead or a ball picked up and dropped in front of a human being usually gets the message across, but, for example, the slight rolling of the eyes or lip licking often produced by an anxious dog is invisible to most owners. There wasn't much evidence of humans trying to understand the subtle messages dogs often send, since they were usually much more interested in making sure dogs understood what they wanted rather than the other way round.

There were exceptions of course, dogs innately gaze at an object they want someone to pay attention to and had been easily trained to 'freeze and point' at likely prey for generations. More lately they'd been trained to signal their recognition of a whole range of odour traces, from marijuana to the presence in a patient of cancer or diabetes, but she couldn't find any examples of them producing anything remotely equivalent to actual words.

Still, all of her dogs had already demonstrated their recognition of a whole range of words and gestures, so she at least had a starting point of connection with them. But how could she get them to understand that it was important for them to try and communicate back to her in just as much detail? She set to work trawling the Internet for more information.

That evening she made her way to the canteen as usual and Peter was waiting at their usual table. They looked at each other a little shyly. The night before had been energetic. They had seemed to complement each other very easily and both had been reluctant to sleep. "You look happy," he said finally.

"I am. In lots of ways."

He smiled into her eyes. "Me too, but tell me about the new work."

"It's great! I couldn't ask to be in a better project, and I've got so much personal responsibility. It's terrific and scary at the same time."

"Life often is, especially when it's going well."

They exchanged smiles. "Look, I'll tell you all about this new project," she said, "but first but I've got to clear something up with you, it's very important to me."

He interrupted. "Yes, I did make sure that Blake saw your reports, as Leicemann should have done before he started firing you, and no, I made no comments whatsoever. I promise. I know you well enough to know what kind of trouble that would get me in."

She looked into his eyes. He was telling the truth.

"Leicemann is in trouble though. I've made an enemy there."

"I'm sorry," she said.

"No," he said calmly, "what's much more important is that I've made a friend."

The next day Jess started the first stage of building the ability of the dogs to refer to objects. The most common technique used to let a dog know that it had carried out an approved action was by using a 'clicker' which produced a distinct sound the dog had been trained to associate with a reward, but she decided that with such responsive dogs it would be better simply to use a stroke and an approving word. She began by sending each dog in turn into a separate room with instructions to find a specific object of which it already knew the name. This was normally no problem for them but the twist was that the object couldn't be removed, so the dog had to return without it and then somehow let her know if it was back in the room or not.

At first when she repeated, "Is it there?" the dog would either start looking around the room or run back into the other room and wait for her to join it, but, over a day or two, most of the dogs realised surprisingly quickly that they could gain her approval simply by coming back with a slightly different signal if the object was there or not. The most natural response was usually a short yip sound for the presence of the object, usually a toy, and a little whine for its absence, often with a tail position to go with it. She now had a kind of basic 'yes' and 'no'.

Surprisingly none of this took very long either. The dogs had been bred for brainpower and curiosity in the first place. To them these were all new games and they plainly found the exercises fascinating. Anne reported that a couple of the dogs even used their new found ability to signal 'yes' or 'no' back in the kennels.

The real challenge was for the dogs to grasp the idea that they could signal the presence of a particular object by creating a specific sign to go with it, and this seemed to be much more difficult for them. Given that dogs naturally use almost every part of their bodies as signals, she knew they had a vast repertoire of postures and gestures to draw on, but they didn't seem very ready to do so.

However she persisted, rewarding them every time she spotted even the ghost of a signal that appeared linked to a particular object. Two of the dogs just couldn't grasp what she was getting at, and never did, but Betsy and the other three, especially the cocker poodle, gradually seemed to realise what the new game was, and eventually she was spotting and reinforcing a whole range minute gestures of eyes, ears, or even nostrils, that had a high statistical probability of being associated with a specific quality like shape or colour.

It was slow work. The problem was that the signs kept changing, and even the best performing dog, the cocker poodle, now nicknamed Star, didn't seem to be able to refer to more than one quality at a time. At first she'd hoped their abilities would somehow evolve out of her games with them, which they clearly enjoyed, but the weeks went by and they seemed to make no further progress. She got very close to giving up, but deep down she was convinced that the real problem was that she was missing something very subtle, but very obvious. She studied the data tapes again and again, and made renewed searches of the Internet.

A couple of weeks later, at about one o'clock in the morning Anne was woken at home by a phone call. Barely awake she picked the phone up then struggled to make out what she was hearing until she realised it was Jess, apparently crying and laughing at the same time. "I've got it Anne! I've got it," she shouted. "It was staring us in the face the whole time. They've been chatting away to us like maniacs."

In another time and another place, DAC32 woke up to find she was strapped comfortably but firmly to a small table. Although she didn't know it, she was mildly tranquilised, and the various measuring devices taped to her body indicated she was calm and relaxed. This was despite the piece of equipment that surrounded her head and restricted her vision to a cone of visibility straight in front of her. Although the tranquiliser was effective, the main reason that she was showing no signs of stress was that ever since she'd been selected for this particular piece of research, a large part of her young life had been spent learning to lie calmly with her head in an MRI scanner for several minutes at a time. She confidently expected the usual rewards and fussing that went with the procedures.

This time however was different. She seemed to have been asleep for a very long time and she felt…strange. The top of her head felt itchy too, and she was bursting to give it a scratch but she couldn't move, which was frustrating.

Out of her range of vision a voice said, "Oh that's great. She's woken up. And she's annoyed! I'm getting a lovely spike from the basal ganglia. Give her a look at you Mike."

Almost immediately a Big One appeared in her field of vision. She had already smelt that it was The Mike, the one with big shiny eyes that came off sometimes. He smelt happy and she was happy to see him too. She wagged her tail, which was about all she could move.

"Oh boy, look at that lovely inferior temporal spike, virtually no time lag. She still loves you Mike," the voice said.

"And I love you too Baby," The Mike said. He lifted his hand and waved to her. She didn't fully understand what he was saying but she understood the tone of his words and the friendly wave. She wagged her tail faster to show she knew he was being friendly.

"Nice response from the motor cortex there. She's mirroring your wave. Let me try," said the voice. The Mike disappeared. DAC32 waited to see what would happen next. They always played such interesting games in the place called The Lab. Then the Big One who was The Dave appeared. She wagged her tail again.

"Beautiful!" She heard The Mike say. "It's a slightly different locus, but clear as a bell. She knows the difference between you and me all right."

"Course she does," The Pete said. DAC32 wagged her tail again.

"What the hell," said the voice of The Mike, "these signals are so clear. Blake will love it. Walk back out of her field of vision. I'm going to slap a vocal on the neural response to seeing me." The Mike disappeared and there was a pause, Then The Pete stepped back into her field of vision. It was him again!

The little speaker near her head made a little click and then it said, "Hello Pete!"

Chapter 8

September 2014

True to his word for the first weeks of her study Sam Blake did not press Jess for detailed reports on her progress in the dog communications unit, but she knew from Anne that he was under considerable pressure within the broader organisation to demonstrate results. According to Anne, who seemed to know everything about what went on in the Division, he was also in the middle of a bitter dispute with Leicemann. After Blake had over ridden his decision to fire Jess, Leicemann had gone further up the chain to complain that Blake was risking the scientific detachment of the project by encouraging sloppy and sentimental analysis. Blake had riposted that Jess's case was the last straw in a campaign by Leicemann to take control of the entire Division. The word was that Blake had held onto his position but he hadn't been able to oust Leicemann either. She wasn't surprised when, a couple of months after she had first been given the project, she received an official note saying that it was time for an evaluation of her progress.

Two days later Jess was waiting in her room with Anne and the star dog of her team, the cocker poodle who she had nicknamed 'Star'. His official name was LPX 17/9. The women were both nervous and for once Anne, who was a natural chatterbox, sat quietly, abstractedly stroking Star's head.

There was a polite knock at the door and Blake came in. A middle aged black man accompanied him. He was smartly dressed and radiated the calm assurance of someone in some position of power. He advanced towards her, hand outstretched, Star gave him a tentative tail wag.

"Hi, I'm Oliver Donovan. I'm a Project Co-ordinator." He had a pronounced American accent.

"I'm afraid I'm one of the guys who has to finally decide whether we can afford to take on the bright ideas that come out of the divisions, especially this one, but I stay pretty close to Sam. I was really interested to hear about the signing project." Jess nodded her thanks.

"So, is it OK with you if I kind of sit in for a while today?" He gave her another big confident smile. He was used to getting his own way with that smile, she thought.

"Not at all," Jess said brightly, though the reality was that she'd been dreading presenting her results to Blake on his own, never mind about a senior manager. It was typical of Blake's poor grasp of organisational politics, she thought, that he hadn't apparently thought that it would be wiser to get a detailed report on her progress before presenting her work as an example of his approach.

She made herself focus on the task at hand. "Let me introduce you. This is one of the dogs we've been working with, LPX17, but we call him Star. He's a bit excited, he's not used to being with more than a couple of people at a time but I think he's OK."

"Lovely dog," Donovan crooned, confidently patting Star's head. The dog wagged its tail enthusiastically. This man could get on with anyone.

"OK," Blake interrupted briskly, "if everyone's happy, we'll go through into the observation room and you can take us through some exercises." With Anne, he led Donovan back out of the door and a moment later there was a click and his voice came over the speaker next to the one-way glass window of the observation kiosk.

"How do you want to do it?"

"Well, you can see me in here through the screen and you've also got live feeds both from here and the room next to us. There's a catalogue in there of all the toys and objects Star is familiar with. Switch me off and then ask Anne to set out the ones you've chosen next door. Then Star will go in and come back here, hopefully to tell me what they are."

"Terrific, got it," Blake's voice came through the speaker, and then it went dead.

She and the dog waited quietly. After a moment it patted her foot twice as it gave a tiny sniff, while briefly cocking an ear. " I know, I saw you tell Anne," Jess said. "Two visitors, one of them new. Good report. They've gone next door." The dog gave a single tail wag as it lifted its chin and tilted its head slightly. "We have to wait, then there will be a Test," Jess explained.

"Right," said the speaker, "off you go."

Without waiting for a word from Jess, the dog sprinted over to the door to the next room and waited expectantly, occasionally looking back over its shoulder. The door opened and it disappeared. Thirty seconds later it was back. "Talk to me," Jess said.

A minute or so later she called up to the screen. "OK, I have Star's statement."

"We'll come back in." It was Donovan's voice.

The three trooped back in, Anne was smiling.

"Right," Jess said, "I'd say you put out three objects; a big red cube, a yellow tennis ball, and a soft toy duck, called Oscar." Star wagged his tail.

"As it happens he's Star's favourite toy," she went on, "that's why he's a bit chewed, oh, and it wasn't Anne who placed them. I think it was probably you Dr Donovan."

There was a silence and her audience looked at one another. " OK, you got the ball wrong, but that's pretty impressive," Donovan said, "I gotta hand it to you."

"OK, I don't speak perfect dog, my fault. Not a tennis ball, a yellow Frisbee?"

"Correct. You're right on the money. Outstanding."

"Tell it to Star, he's the talent. I'm bragging on his behalf but on a really good day, if I'm on form, he could have told me about anything up to four items, roughly where they were, and if they were moving."

"Great. How does it work?" Donovan said with another big smile. "Give us the headlines."

"OK, we've assembled some clips. If you'd like to get a seat." She hit the remote control and an image appeared on the big monitor on the wall. It showed a dog standing normally. It didn't seem to be moving but a caption appeared at the bottom of the screen 'round object'. That image was replaced by one of another dog, this time with the caption 'yellow object'. This was in turn replaced, and the series of similar clips went on until finally Donovan coughed and interjected. "Excuse me but what are we looking at here?"

"The signals that we spotted in the dogs," Jess replied..

"What signals?" Donovan said.

Jess and Anne looked at each other. Blake smiled.

"OK, I confess we were pretty sure that was what you would say," Jess said at last. "The point is that the signals are usually so brief and often very small, what's been called 'micro-expressions'. Without a lot of experience, most humans can't spot them. Let's look again in slow motion."

"Ah!" Donovan said a few moments later, "I think I see it now. Is 'round object' that flick of the ear?"

"For that dog indeed it is," Jess agreed. Donovan gave a triumphant laugh. "But the real breakthrough came when we realised that the dogs *were* organising their signals, but according to *their* logic and priorities, not ours."

Blake nodded. Jess went on. "We had to keep reminding ourselves that to dogs, odour really is everything. Their world is busting with odour information, and that's what matters. Look at this. This dog's called Winnie. This is her sign for a tennis ball, it looks like a cross between a cough and a tail wag, but when I show her another tennis ball the sign is very slightly modified. Why? The answer is that I had handled the second ball an hour earlier. The sign would be modified differently again if I were to show her a ball I'd handled two hours earlier. That's more important to Winnie than the colour or even shape."

"As you can see here," Jess went on as more sequences were presented, "each dog uses different signs, and some are clearer than others. Star is exceptional. Look at this." The sequence showed Star neatly presenting a variety of ear movements, headshakes and yips in normal motion. "Great stuff! Go Star!" Donovan hooted. Star looked round at them all, tail wagging gently, basking in the approval.

"We were very excited weren't we Anne?" Jess went on. "It all seemed to be going well. We began try and get them to get them to give us signs for verbs or at least action words but, apart from 'lets go play' or 'give me biscuit', they just didn't seem to be able to grasp the concept. We'd hit a brick wall. The system just seemed to break down, with no discernable logic to their signals. I was missing something. In desperation really, we eased back on the training schedules and I spent a lot more time re-examining the records, even extending my research into human sign languages."

"It was that and Star's beautiful clear signs that gave us the clue. We finally realised that dogs just don't communicate in sequences. He was *simultaneously* combining his signs to create sentences. Watch this." The image of Star came up on the screen. "There's no need to yip, then tap a paw, then cock one ear in sequence when you can do all three things at once. But, even more important the way he does them will change the meaning. Watch!" They watched the screen carefully first at normal speed then in slow motion.

"See, 'Anne throws the ball up,' is yip, tap, ear cock all at once, as the dog flings its head up. 'Anne puts the ball *down*,' is also yip, tap, and ear cock, but the dog looks down slightly at the same time. The dogs had been creating different messages by inflecting the basic signs; we just didn't read them right."

"An inflected vocabulary. Fantastic." Donovan breathed.

"This is terrific Jess!" Donovan enthused." Just terrific!"

"Thank you," Jess said. "We've got all the results logged up for you to examine, but I don't know how much of what we've done is transferable to anyone else's work."

"Oh, but it is Jess," Blake said. "Your research gives us a firm bedrock for an even more ambitious project. You've shown that our dogs will deliberately attempt complex communication with us and we can even make some sense of those efforts. It's a huge step. Well done." There were murmurs of agreement from Donovan.

"Well thank you," Jess said, "but please know that I couldn't have done this on my own. Anne has been terrific at every level." Blake nodded at Anne, who quietly nodded back, and Jess suddenly realised that, through Anne, Blake had kept a close eye on her progress over the previous weeks. He'd already known the results would impress Donovan.

"We'll go off now to discuss the next step," Blake said, "but don't worry, you've both done incredibly well." He looked at Donovan then back at her. "If Oliver agrees, I'm pretty sure we can introduce you to another project we're pretty excited about."

"Too right," Donovan said, "somebody up there is really looking after you Sam. This is the kind of results we need." With more handshakes, and a pat on the head for Star, they swept out of the room.

Jess and Anne just looked at each other. "Looks like you survived," Anne said, stroking Star's head.

"Thank you," Jess said quietly, "for everything."

"You did it," Anne said, "and don't you forget it. Let's take this chap out for some play time."

Chapter 9

Three hours later Jess was sitting in Blake's unpretentious little office in a state that was mixture of shock and excitement. "I almost can't believe it," she said at last, "dogs made to talk? Is that really possible?"

"Well, we've known for some time that, in theory, MRI signals can be interpreted as pictures or sounds, but until recently it's been almost impossible to make sense of events occurring very close together. But there's been a breakthrough. Now we can sort out dozens of linked neural events using machine-learning algorithms to measure what they call 'neurally plausible semantic features'".

She looked at him blankly.

"Don't worry," he said with a grin. "It's hard for any of us to get our heads round but you don't really need to, what it means for us is that by linking the analysed signals from the dog's brain to a speaker we can 'hear' the dog's brain activity. As your own research confirmed, it turns out that they have a much wider range of precise responses than we ever realised, especially to people."

"But don't the dogs have to sit in an MRI machine?"

"Good point. In the first trials we had the dogs wearing a kind of helmet version of an MRI, and carrying transmitter packs on their shoulders but the whole set up was too cumbersome and unreliable. The breakthrough came when our people realised they could suffuse a dog's brain with a modified version of a long chain bacterium that uses weak electric signals as part of its metabolism. It responds very sensitively to neuro-electrical activity in the brain. In effect we have an internalised brain scanner. We detect its responses by a harvesting device; it looks like a little cap, attached to the dog's skull. It passes them on to an interpreting computer via Bluetooth or something similar. It's still early days but BioMed are very optimistic. Look, I know it's a lot to take in, but you'll be OK. You can read the detailed papers later."

Jess still looked confused. He smiled again.

"Of course, it may well turn out that it won't really work. We know that dogs can understand an enormous range of words about objects, but can they also generate words? We know they can make signals, but do they have any kind of true syntactical ability? Could they possibly think in a way that really combines nouns and adjectives or even verbs? I believe you're one of the few people who can help us find out. One or two members of the Board are a bit sceptical about it all, but Donovan's right behind the project, and he's got influence and the budgets. He'll stay in touch with all of you on this."

"I wouldn't be the only one doing this?"

"No, there'll be half a dozen parallel trials, all running much the same programme. We've been working on the neurology for a couple of years now. There were more dogs involved originally, but to be frank not all of them made it."

His look became more serious. "This is a high security operation, the military implications are immediate and obvious, and we know that other people are as interested as we are in enhanced animal communications. Peter Guy will co-ordinate security and we'll keep all references low key. We'll simply call it the Canine Project."

She nodded.

"We're splitting the teams up," he went on. "For this to work there has to be a really close relationship between each dog and its trainer. You'll have visits from various specialists, and there'll be times when the dog will have to come in for checks, but I won't lie, it'll cut down on your social life."

"That's no problem," she said.

"Good. Each trainer and dog pair will be in a separate location, all within about twenty miles of here and all linked to us by custom-built high-speed fibre, plus your own local mainframe outfit. As I said, we've been working on this for a long time, but I started thinking about you playing a role as soon as I met you. To tell you the truth, I put you on the signing project as much to assess your abilities as to find out about the dogs. You'll have all the software support Cybernetics can give you, but in the end these dogs will learn to speak, if they ever do, because a trainer like you can correctly interpret their behaviour as well as the neural signals."

'Learn to talk.' The words went round in her head.

"It's like a dream," she said, "but putting that stuff in their skulls. I know I can be frank. It seems so unnatural. Doesn't it hurt, don't they have headaches or something?"

"As you must know, I'm always very sceptical about neurological interventions, but everything I've discovered about this project re-assures me that it keeps well with guidelines on the wellbeing of the dogs. BioMed are doing the actual insertion, they reckon that the only part of the whole package that weighs anything at all is the little transmitter cap in the top of their heads, and that's only a few grams. The internal network weighs next to nothing. It involves several hundred yards of nano-fibre, but it's so fine it's literally invisible to the naked eye. The dog can't have any sense of its presence."

Jess was still dubious. "I don't mean to sound argumentative, but isn't there danger of infection or rejection?"

Blake sat back in his chair. "Biomed say not, but I won't lie to you, we don't really know. On balance I believe, and I hope you agree, that it's worth the risk. For people like us, to be able to really know how a dog thinks, what he really wants, what he's capable of, it's going to feel like Einstein discovering Relativity."

Jess nodded slowly. "Yes, I guess it would feel something like that. Can you tell me anything yet about the dog I'd be working with?"

He smiled. "It's a seven month old cocker spaniel, they've got probably the best sense of smell of any breed, but this one's immensely talented generally, cute as mustard. Your brief will be to develop her talents, not just to search and find but to verbally report on what she's found."

They were both silent for a moment as the implications of what he'd said struck both of them. "Anyway," he went on, "her official designation is DAC32, but no doubt you'll come up with something a bit more user friendly. I'm sure that won't disturb your scientific detachment."

The reference struck a chord.

"What about Dr. Leicemann? What's his role?"

Blake's face hardened. "No role at all. This is nothing to do with his department. As Division Deputy he'll be kept in touch with the broad thrust of the project of course, but that's all. You will work direct to me. Don't worry about him."

Twenty minutes later she was sitting at a table in a quiet corner of the canteen with Peter.

"So, what did you say?" he asked.

She took a long slow sip of her coffee. "I asked for time to think about it."

"Really?"

"Yes, I said I wanted to think about the direction my career was going in. He was kind, said I could have a day or two."

"Is that the truth? You're concerned about your career path?"

"Not really. It's something much more basic than that. If I'm honest I just don't know how I feel about the whole idea of messing about with a dog's brain. I've always wanted to understand animals better you know that. I'm sure there's much more going on in their brains, their minds even, than we've realised yet, but there's something a bit mad scientist about all this. What am I doing involving myself in it?"

"But don't you trust Blake? You always said his heart seems to be in the right place."

"I do, but that's another thing I don't really understand. The whole project sounds like something that Leicemann would run, but apparently he's to be kept right off it."

"Yes, Blake told me. I think the Iceman shot himself in the foot with Blake over the optogenetics long ago. He doesn't like his approach and, even more, I think he's finally beginning to realise just how ambitious he is. He'll do everything he can to slow him down."

"He is a slimy piece of work, but I wish I had that kind of self-confidence. If I'm honest, even if I can get my head around the idea, what's really putting me off is the fear that if I do it, I'll mess up somehow."

She suddenly looked very vulnerable.

"Hey!" he said, "is this the star of the communications unit I'm hearing? The scientist with the magic touch? Blake isn't doing you any favours. He knows that if anybody can teach those mutts to talk it'll be you." She looked at him and knew he meant it.

"Thank you Peter, I never know whether to believe what most people say, but I believe you." A thought struck her. "There's another thing though. I'll be working away from the Labs mostly. It's just the dog and me. We'll see a lot less of each other."

"Is that really putting you off?"

She suddenly burst out laughing. "I know I ought to say it's a big worry, but you know me, disgustingly self-sufficient. But of course I'll miss you, a bit."

He felt the familiar ache of realising that she meant a lot more to him than he did to her. Unconsciously his face fell and her look softened.

"You're a true friend Peter," she said. "Believe me, I know it. You mean such a lot to me." She reached across the table and took his hand, and for a few moments he almost felt as if she were in love with him. They both sat in silence for a moment.

"So, are you going to do it?"

"I'll sleep on it," she said finally, withdrawing her hand.

The next morning she took up the post.

Part Three

Machinery of War

Chapter 10

December 2014

The early afternoon sky over the Northumberland moors was grey and gloomy, and the dark clouds drifting in from the west were heavy with rain. Leicemann got out of his car, lit a cigarette and contemplated the view. Long rolling hills of dull green and brown stretched away into the dim distance below him, relieved only by patches of dark coniferous woodland. Eventually he checked his watch, took out his mobile phone, dialled, and spoke briefly into it. Then he disconnected, threw away the cigarette stub, and got back into the car.

     He drove on for a few minutes as the road descended steeply, and then turned right into a side road. It was well made and recently resurfaced. Next to it a sign said 'No through access'. He drove on, past a small electricity sub station, into dense woodlands, then, for the next half mile or so the road to his left was edged by a substantial link fence topped with barbed wire. It was finally interrupted by a substantial entrance guarded by a gatehouse and pole barrier. There were two signs by the gate. The larger one said 'Another Project of the Sustainable Rural Development Authority'. The other said 'Angelo Control Systems Inc. No Unauthorised Visitors. Camera Surveillance At All Times'.

     At the gate entrance two uniformed guards were questioning the driver of a large lorry, and as Leicemann drove up, one of them came over to him. He took a cursory glance at Leicemann's car and checked Leicemann's ID against a list. He nodded and waved him through.

     Further on, within a hundred yards, the protective screen of trees and bushes fell away, opening up into a large cleared area organised into dun gravel roads and car parks and a selection of buildings. There was a substantial administration building at the centre but a large windowless building behind it, about thirty metres high and easily three hundred metres across, dominated the site.

Various people were moving around the space, some in military fatigues, and the place had the indefinable aura of installations with military links.

Ignoring the various signs directing personnel where to put their vehicles, he parked the car right outside the entrance to the main building and went in.

He was immediately confronted by two stony faced young men. Both were dressed in the neat dark suits apparently favoured by security men the world over. They politely stood in his way but, before they could speak, a tall middle-aged man in faded but scrupulously pressed military fatigues arrived to interrupt them with a nod. The men briskly turned away. The tall man extended his hand.

"Alex, thank you for coming. It's been a long time."

"It has Peter, a long time. But you're still looking pretty good." The tall man gave a dismissive flick of his hand but couldn't resist a self-satisfied little smile. Cadogan's always been vain about his physique, Leicemann thought. He had always worked hard to give an impression of confidence, success, and discipline, especially to himself. Now, although well into middle age, he had the characteristic body mass of someone who works out regularly and with purpose.

"It's a very impressive set up you've got here too," Leicemann went on, "but with respect, I'm surprised by how casual your security seems Peter. It's a lot more difficult to get into the Canine Division of BSDL."

"Might look like that," the other answered confidently, "but my boys saw you have that last cigarette twenty minutes ago. There are eyes everywhere around here, old chap. This is a very confidential operation. I make sure of it."

Still a pompous bastard, Leicemann thought, as he nodded amiably. "Very impressive," he said, "and reassuring. As I stressed I can't afford for BDSL to know anything about my contact with you, even on this preliminary basis."

"Don't worry about that, our security is rock solid. Officially we're here to develop industrial hydraulic systems. We even have a government grant. That section does some quite useful work in fact. Your reputation is safe with us." He raised an eyebrow. "As I trust ours is with you…"

"Of course. I know how important it is that you keep this…setback under wraps. I hope I can help."

"So do I old chum, so do I." For a moment the veneer of total confidence wavered. "I tell you frankly there's no one else I would have trusted with the information I'm going to share with you."

Christ, he must be desperate, Leicemann thought, and I better be careful. He knew from experience that if anything or anyone should ever threaten Cadogan's work, his reaction would be swift and ruthless. "I'm flattered to be approached Peter, truly," he said with a smile.

Cadogan smiled back equally warmly. "We can convene immediately, the others are waiting. Follow me." He turned briskly and strode off.

Leicemann followed him to one of several substantial doors at the rear of the reception area and waited as Cadogan pressed his open hand against an illuminated plate of glass mounted beside it. When the door opened he followed down a long broad corridor with various minor corridors leading off. They had clearly been constructed with an eye more to function than aesthetics, lined with painted but unplastered concrete block. None of the corridors were signposted in any way.

They finally entered a windowless average sized meeting room with a table down the middle and a blank presentation screen at one end. Two young men were waiting for them. One was standing by the screen, the other seated at the table. The standing man was obviously of Asian extraction. He turned away from the screen to welcome Cadogan and Leicemann. His face was impassive. Only a slight cough signaled his nervousness. Beside him the seated man was trying to look busy with his laptop.

"Right, this is Doctor Alex Leicemann," Cadogan said briskly. "Alex, this is Chen, department head," he indicated the standing man, "and Harris is his deputy." The seated man looked up warily.

He was a good deal younger than Chen but, faced with one of his own kind, Leicemann immediately recognised the sharp gaze of the intensely ambitious.

Leicemann nodded to both men.

"Good morning Doctor, thank you for coming." Chen was clearly unhappy, he had a slight Scottish lilt to his voice but that didn't mask his annoyance. "We really appreciate your input."

"Let's cut to the chase, Jim," Cadogan interrupted, sitting down and gesturing to Leicemann to join him. "Lets start by explaining what happened six days ago."

Chen and Harris exchanged glances. "OK," Chen said carefully, "six days ago we started a standard test on a BD5 of the BCI link with the DNS. Dyson was the DT."

"Look son," Cadogan said almost kindly, "don't talk to the Doctor in acronyms."

There was a pause as Chen swallowed the condescension, then he went on.

"Well, as you will know, my department is just one part of the SETDD project." Leicemann looked at him steadily. "As I'm sure you will also know, that stands for 'Semi Autonomous Track and Destroy Device', working code name 'Predator'."

"Indeed," Leicemann said quietly. "I've been given the broad picture."

"The overall brief is to develop a highly flexible and self-organising weapons unit capable of working in problematic environments like dense woodland or highly constricted urban settings," Chen continued.

"Stuff like narrow stairs, tunnels, like that," Harris said helpfully. He got a glance from both Chen and Cadogan and subsided into silence.

"Our part of the project is developing the control system," Chen continued. "There's been various proposals as to how a device can be deployed with maximum speed and flexibility at long range. The preliminary feasibility study determined the best option would be a hybrid AI control system; a deep neural network, supervised from a distance by a human operator via BCI." He paused. "That's 'brain computer interface'. We referred to the model we're working with as BD5, simply because it's our fifth iteration of the control system."

"That's short for Bad Dog Five," Harris said helpfully.

"Why Bad Dog?" Leicemann said to Chen.

"It's just a working name, a nickname really. Working from first principles, the engineering section worked out that the optimum structure was a unit with four legs and a front end control unit."

"A few years ago that would have been impossible," Cadogan said, "but in the last year or two the control dynamics for this kind of movement have pretty well been cracked by various companies working for DARPA; the U.S. military research agency. It's very impressive. They've solved all sorts of problems that wouldn't even occur to most people. The sensors for the legs alone have to be able to co-ordinate and optimise joint position and force, ground contact, a load of stuff, but they've done it. And a lot of it's not even classified."

"Some of the quadrupeds look a bit like a dog," Chen added. "The guys got to calling our model Bad Dog."

"Hell of a dog," Harris muttered.

"Hence BD5," Chen said.

"So what went wrong?"

Chen and Harris again exchanged glances, then Chen continued reluctantly. "OK, this time one of our senior engineers, Jack Dyson, was the designated target. That's the guy who acts as quarry for the hunting tests, the DT."

"There's an indoor test facility behind us here, but we can run long distance tests out in the woodland, back of the labs. It goes back miles. The test area is all fenced off for security obviously," Harris chipped in.

"What the hell was Dyson doing out there anyway?" Cadogan said.

"Well, strictly speaking, as part of the development team he shouldn't have been there at all," Chen said, "but he said he wanted to get out in the woods..."

"It was kind of his baby," Harris chipped in. "He'd had a lot to do with the latest development of the onboard control system and he wanted to observe it first hand."

"And you let him," Leicemann said to Chen.

"Yes, there was no real risk…" Chen's voice faded away. It was clear there was to be a reckoning for that error.

"So, what happened?" Leicemann said. He was getting impatient.

"It all started fine. We gave Dyson a half mile start then fired up Bad Dog."

"Who was driving?" Cadogan said.

"Schulz sir," Harris said.

"Driving?" Leicemann asked.

"That's the control officer based back at the lab," Chen said. "His mental activity is detected through the brain computer interface, a BCI, a kind of helmet with sensors, and beamed out to the device. Again a pretty well established technology, it's used to help paralysed patients regain limb function for example, but nobody's applied it to a remote weapons system like we have." Chen suddenly looked a lot more confident. "It's a terrific system, virtually instantaneous execution of the driver's intention."

"But its not all plain sailing," Cadogan said evenly.

"That's true, there can be random dispersal of the sensor's signals because they're transmitted through the skull bone." Chen conceded.

"And the output signal is vulnerable to being jammed, all kinds of things can happen," Harris chipped in.

"The ideal solution is to have an AI control system on board as well as the remote human controller," Cadogan continued. "There's several huge advantages to that; the control data stream can't be intercepted or compromised, and even more important, the device can go into a stealth mode until it's picked up again."

"So the idea is that the Predator is driven by the BCI operator until it reaches the active combat area?" Leicemann said.

"You've got it," Cadogan said. "After that the remote control system is switched off, it goes to the onboard pre-programmed neural control system and it becomes an autonomous weapon. That's our key objective, our USP. If we can achieve it there's billions of dollars waiting out there to buy in."

"Aren't autonomous weapons illegal under international conventions?"

"At the moment, but in time the fact that you don't need to put boots on the ground will become a crucial issue in persuading voters to back military action. Our customer is thinking ahead. Does that worry you?"

Leicemann paused then shook his head slightly.

Cadogan nodded to Chen. "The outboard controlled walk-through went well so then we cut that and went over to the DNS, the on-board deep neural system," Chen went on. He paused.

"And then?"

"At first everything went fine, Bad Dog still tracked his every move. It was a good session. We were all pretty high. It looked like we'd cracked it. We switched back to remote driver control."

"Only it didn't happen," Harris said, ignoring Chen's gaze. "It refused to accept the outboard driver signal. It went hell for leather after Dyson, despite everything we did to stop it."

"Couldn't it be destroyed?"

"That wasn't an option," Cadogan said firmly.

"So what happened?"

"Eventually it caught him," Chen said quietly, "it didn't have any weapons, but…"

"It beat him to death," Harris said.

"What went wrong? How can a machine get carried away like that?"

"It didn't get carried away, it doesn't have feelings. In our terms its operating system simply lost top level equilibrium," Chen said.

"It's not just a machine, it's a *fighting* machine," Harris chipped in. "It's difficult enough to construct a system that can discriminate between friend and enemy, but we have to go beyond that, the heuristics have got to be mission targeted and flexible. If one strategy fails it has to be able to proceed to others. If it's on-board weapons systems fail or it gets damaged for example, it has to be able to devise other tactics to accomplish the mission. The DNS's got to be able to control an enormous number of things at once, from the most basic levels of balance and movement all the way up to making high level decisions."

"Of course a living creature breaks the job up into different levels of organisation," Leicemann said, "from the frontal lobes for highly focused but relatively 'slow' thinking, right down to the amygdala."

Chen looked nonplussed.

"That's where too much specialisation gets you," Cadogan said to Leicemann.

"The amygdala's the part of the brain that controls motivation and action," Harris said almost smugly. "Any creature with a brain has one in there somewhere."

Chen just looked at him.

"It's the same issue for the Predator," Cadogan said to Leicemann. "It has to be able to respond appropriately to the pace of the action, and ramp itself up when things get hot, but in this case when it reached a high activity level, the discrimination protocols collapsed."

"And it tried to kill everything in sight," Harris said triumphantly

"That's exaggerating, and we will crack it in time," Chen said weakly.

"Except there's absolutely no sign of that," Cadogan said pointedly. Chen couldn't hide his scowl. Harris studied his laptop.

"That's where I come in?" Leicemann said quietly.

"That's where you may well come in. I had Harris do a literature review including a check on work on trans-organic systems, what we used to call cyborgs, and your name came up. Of course I've kept my eye on you since we were post-grads anyway. I never waste a contact. If you're interested, your work in optogenetics might just be relevant, though Harris says it's a while since you published anything new. Did you hit a block?"

"With the optogenetics? Not at all, the research was going really well, it just got stopped by the cretinous director of Canine Division." He looked at Cadogan. "This might be an opportunity for both of us. It's a possibility. Can I have a look at one of these things?"

"The team are waiting for us." Cadogan said.

Chapter 11

Leicemann followed Cadogan, Harris and Chen through a new maze of corridors, on the way passing various side areas and workshops. At first encounter, he wasn't able to grasp how it was all organised. Looking through the large glass screens that separated each room from the corridor, he saw that some sections were dominated by rows of studious young people quietly studying computer screens, others were more like motor repair shops, raucous with the screech of drills and the sizzle of welding equipment.

One room was dominated by a static rolling track above which, suspended by numerous cables and tubes, hung a machine that vaguely resembled a badly constructed mechanical cheetah with no head. The device was running on the track at an extraordinary speed while being gravely observed by a couple of young women with tablets. He stopped a moment to watch.

"They're trying to incorporate the spinal action that gives cheetahs such a turn of speed," Cadogan said over his shoulder, "but that means the whole spine has to be able to move as well as provide a stable base for the legs. It's a challenge but they'll crack it."

"What we would call a synthetic ethogram in my business," Leicemann murmured, "I guess if nature can do it so can you."

Cadogan grunted non-committally and they carried on down the corridor to enter a high ceilinged room that looked like a cross between a control room and a machine shop. To one side was a long desk with several large screens, supervised by a young man incongruously dressed in a combination of camouflage fatigues and a hairnet, but what immediately drew Leicemann's eye was the creature standing quietly in the middle of the room.

His breath shortened. The creature was mechanically constructed, but to compare it to the clumsy cheetah device outside was like comparing a WWI biplane to a stealth fighter.

It was big, the size of a small horse, constructed broadly along the lines of a greyhound, but the heavy shoulders, big chest and huge low hung head made it look more like a stylish hyena. Its dark metallic exoskeleton was smooth and aerodynamic except where it was interrupted by the bumps and knobs that provided leverage points for its pneumatic muscles and the two long thin aerials arching back from the shoulders. A thin rod looking rather like a rifle barrel extended from a swivel on one shoulder

Leicemann decided he needed to try and build at least a rudimentary bridge with Chen. If he was going to work with this man he'd have to get past his resentment.

"My goodness it looks very impressive."

For the first time since he had met him Chen's face almost brightened. "This is Bad Dog Six. Beautiful ain't he? The series specs get better all the time. The DNS and its batteries are packed away into his chest."

"It's got full lidar support now too," Harris added.

"Lidar?"

"Light radar laser senses, we can now use the 3D feedback from his surroundings to keep him balanced, even under intense stress," Chen said triumphantly.

"They use something similar in driverless cars," Cadogan said dismissively. "Never mind that. Let's see some action. Is it safe?"

Chen scowled defensively. "Don't worry, I've doubled up on the emergency links. I can slap a shutdown on him the moment there's any deviation." He turned to Harris. "Let's fire him up." Harris moved across to the control desk, and closed some switches.

An almost imperceptible change took place in the creature. Where before it had stood like a statue, it was now standing in balance, its weight shifting slightly from one broad foot to the other and the head nodding gently. With a little click, shutters flicked up, revealing large dark lenses. The lenses looked extraordinarily like eyes and Leicemann realised it was because they continuously made tiny involuntary movements, just like living eyes.

Chen had put on a simple headphone and mike set. "Climb in Schultz," he said quietly into the microphone.

The young man by the desk took off his hair net, revealing a perfectly smooth shaved head. He sat down in a comfortable chair next to the desk, put what looked like a motorcycle helmet with cables attached over his head, and pulled an opaque visor down over his face.

Within seconds one of the big screens at the desk flickered and after a moment showed the area in front of the creature. As Leicemann watched, the image panned across until he saw himself and Cadogan. He looked back at the creature. It was looking straight at him. In the chair on the other side of the room Schulz had turned his head very slightly.

"OK," Chen said. "Open the doors, Harris." Harris went over to a pair of enormous sliding doors at one side of the room and pressed a switch. With a grumble of gears the doors smoothly slid apart. Chen, Leicemann and Cadogan went through. Behind them, in the smaller room, the creature still stood waiting and Schultz still sat quietly at the desk, his head enclosed in the opaque helmet, his arms and hands occasionally twitching slightly.

The three men were now standing at the edge of a large high space, roughly the size of a small aircraft hanger. It was illuminated by the harsh glare of powerful strip lights. From ground level it was difficult to see very far into it because it was closely packed with a selection of barriers, and screens, interspersed with flights of steps and freestanding doors. Together they formed a daunting series of spaces and corridors.

"Goes back about a quarter mile," Cadogan said. "You could lose a small army in there." Waiting near them were a couple of dozen men dressed in military fatigues and helmets with clear glass goggles.

Although the fabrics of their outfits were marked with a typical military camouflage pattern, about half of them of them were wearing tan coloured desert kit, the others wore the dark green fatigues usually worn in jungle conditions. All the men had what looked like blocks of miniature solar panels sewn into the front and back of their tunics. Leicemann remembered that the creature had a similar panel fixed to its chest.

"OK," Chen explained, "this is a pretty typical testing setup." He waved towards the men in the light coloured fatigues. "Once we switch to DNS, Bad Dog will recognise the sandy guys as enemy, the chaps in greens as allies. They're wearing standard laser sensitive chest packs. We can't afford to risk shooting anyone for real." Leicemann realised it was an attempt at humour. "Both the men and Bad Dog are equipped with laser rifles."

At a wave from Chen the men disappeared among the obstacles.

"Right, walk him in Schultz," Chen said into his mike. Behind them, with a tiny whine of electric motors, the creature lurched forward and then, as if finding its feet, trotted smoothly and confidently into the testing area, the feet making a light scratching sound on the polished concrete. As it passed Leicemann the impenetrable lenses flicked across to look down at him, and at close range he could hear a faint buzzing noise coming from the head.

"Are we OK standing here?" he said. He tried not to sound nervous but the proximity of the huge sentient machine was deeply disturbing

"If we did it would be sensible to keep fairly still and very quiet," Cadogan grunted, "but don't worry, we'll go back to the control desk and observe through monitors. It's not in self-drive yet, and even then it's programmed to respond only to the uniformed combatants."

"Is that what the lights are for? To help it?"

"Not at all, among other things it's got infra red vision and radar, but the lighting helps our cameras." Chen said. Cadogan said nothing. There was a palpable air of tension surrounding both him and Chen. Leicemann realised both men were a lot less confident than they were trying to appear.

They all made their way back to the observation desk where a bank of monitors presented several perspectives of the big room next door, particularly from directly above. From this angle Leicemann could see that the mass of obstructions constituted a gigantic untidy maze. Behind them Harris closed the big doors.

"Right," Chen said as they sat down in front of the monitors, "as I said, the mission is pretty straightforward, Bad Dog has to reach the other side of the combat area, and to do that it has to cooperate with the Greens to wipe out the Sandies, the bad boys. There is no other objective."

He paused and he and Cadogan exchanged glances. "Go to low illumination," he said into the microphone. The lights dimmed perceptibly. "OK. Give me smoke."

"So we can video the laser beams," Harris whispered in Leicemann's ear. On the screen in front of him Leicemann watched the test area dim further as a thin veil of grey smoke spread through it. The gloom gave the whole scene a brooding surreal air.

"Mark time. Go to DNS, initiate mission… now," Chen said quietly. Harris leaned over Schultz's shoulder and pressed some switches.

Schultz sat back, suddenly relaxed, and on the monitor in front of him Leicemann saw the creature abruptly tense then drop slightly, Leicemann was reminded of a cat about to pounce. After a pause the big head slowly rotated to observe the entire test area. Then, still crouched, it slowly paced forward, the head still weaving from side to side. Leicemann suddenly realised that there was a third eye high up at the back of the head.

When it was about thirty feet into the room there was a flash of green uniform to one side as one of the men popped out from behind a screen. Without a pause the creature whirled and the articulated mount on its shoulder aimed the muzzle of the laser rifle straight at him, then after the slightest pause the rifle dropped again. As it did, a figure in desert fatigues appeared at the far side of the room. The creature whirled, dashed forward, there was a loud crack, and a thin beam of bright green light struck the man right in the chest. A stab of light flashed on the screen in front of Chen.

"Kill hit!" he exulted, then collected himself a little. "You're dead fella," he said into his mike. The man obligingly fell down and lay still. The creature abruptly sprinted to a position so that it was masked behind one of the screens. "Evasive action is a damn sight easier than controlling aggressive," Harris said quietly. The creature went very still. After a minute or so Leicemann said carefully, "Has it stopped?"

"It's listening," Chen said reverently. The creature suddenly scuttled across the room to take up a position behind another screen.

"Let's get on with it," Cadogan said. Chen leaned forward to the screens, "OK, bad boys, hit him with everything you've got." Abruptly several of the remaining target troops appeared out of the murk, running towards the creature, lasers cutting through the pall of smoke. With almost contemptuous ease the creature lasered two of them. The others vanished back into the maze and the creature scuttled after them.

The monitor giving a top shot showed the men scattering in various directions but the creature simply picked up speed and confidently followed them, briskly lasering them one by one over the next minute or two.

Seconds later when three men in green stepped from behind their hidden positions, it turned to them, hesitated briefly and then also shot them one by one, firing at the recumbent forms long after they had stopped moving. "Cut the laser!" Cadogan shouted to Harris. As its laser stopped working the creature paused and then advanced to one of the sprawled men in green.

"Keep still!" Cadogan shouted urgently but the man had lost his nerve and scrambled to his feet, about to try and run for it. Before he could move the creature abruptly shot forward and loomed menacingly over him. Cadogan leapt out of his chair. "Oh for fuck's sake, cut, cut DNS!" he shouted. "Take control Schulz, for Christ's sake!"

Harris hit switches as Chen whispered urgently into his mike. Schulz sat up abruptly. As the man scrambled clear, the creature equally abruptly stopped moving, shook itself vigorously, rotated its head through 360 degrees, and became completely immobile. "BD6 has a level seven freeze," Harris said, almost with satisfaction Leicemann thought. Chen had his head in his hands.

"That's the worst performance yet Chen!" Cadogan said. Chen studied his screens. "Twenty million dollars and counting," Cadogan said.

"At least it stopped," Chen said quietly.

Schulz took off his helmet and scratched his bald head. It was covered with dozens of tiny red marks. Spiller shut down a number of switches. The screens went blank.

All three men sat in silence. Finally Cadogan spoke. "Well?" he said. "That's the problem."

He turned to the young man at the desk, "OK Schulz," he said calmly. "Thanks, you can go now, well done. Tell maintenance to give the Predator a complete shake down. I want a full system report before the end of the day."

When Schulz had left, he turned to Leicemann.

Leicemann felt his pulse rising. "It's a big task you've taken on," he said carefully.

"Big rewards if we can solve it, for all of us," Cadogan said. He seemed suddenly to tire of circumspection. "Can you help or not?"

"I think I can." Leicemann said. Chen didn't move. Harris sat up.

"Why attempt the massive task of building an artificial neural control system when perfectly effective ones exist in nature?" Leicemann said. "Your key problem is that you're asking the DNS to do too much at once. You need much more on-board AI resources, way beyond present technology, and a hell of a sophisticated heuristics hierarchy. A mammalian brain's got billions of available neural connections and millions of neural circuits to organise them."

"The point is, can you help?" Cadogan said.

"I'm pretty sure I could put you a fully functioning dog's brain in there. Once it's in and settled it can control the Predator's behaviour by focused neural activity in just the same way that Schulz does by remote. But it's *inside*…"

There was a shocked pause.

"A dog's brain?" Chen was deliberately incredulous. "Look Leicemann," he said, "don't get carried away just because we call it Bad Dog. It just happens to look a lot like a dog. It's pure coincidence. It's just based on the most efficient shape for a predatory four-legged structure. It just comes out that way, the same way you get a fish shape when you ask a computer to show the best design for moving through water."

He turned to Cadogan. "Anyway, I thought this sort of stuff was still at an experimental stage. A very *early* experimental stage." There was the slightest sneer in his tone.

"Not in my labs, no, we've come a long way," Leicemann said. "Despite the fact that most of our research was done behind the back of BSDL, my people can now deliver a stable life support package to a detached brain, and they're still alive after two months."

Chen was expressionless.

"More to the point we were developing control procedures using optogenetics," Leicemann went on. "We were using laser fibre nets to identify specific neural circuits and then fire off a whole range of precisely controlled behaviours." He turned to Cadogan. "I've got a load more data on our progress. I'm genuinely optimistic. Once we get a unit inside the Predator, and link to the sensory-motor system direct…" Chen looked dubious. Cadogan's face was a mask.

"Look," Leicemann continued, "if you know what you're doing, and we do, it's now as straightforward to control a dog's brain as it is to programme a computer. Better than that, a dog's brain is pre-wired for a whole gang of co-ordinated action patterns: stalk, chase, leap, paw slap. Christ, we can even make it bite if you want."

A flicker of interest passed across Chen's face. Cadogan's expression eased. Leicemann grabbed his chance. "What you'll get is an incredibly fast weapon, driven by an organic computer that only weighs about 75 grams and uses about 3 watts of power, leaving loads of spare power to carry heavy armour *and* weaponry."

Chen interrupted him. "How do you give this *thing* senses; eyes, ears?"

"You don't have to," Leicemann said. "We know how to hook up the existing organic sensory system either directly or via intermediaries; miniscreens to feed the eyes, speakers to the remaining inner cochlea, and so on. We can even use the nasal system."

He paused at looked at Cadogan. "Totally loyal, totally obedient. Just give him his orders then go dark. He'll kill who you want, when you want and check back in when it's safe."

"Are you really sure of that?" Cadogan said. "It seems a lot of ask. As Chen says, in the end it's just a dog."

"It *was* a dog, now it's a self-directed tactical weapon."

There was a long pause. "OK," Cadogan said abruptly. "Show us the numbers." Leicemann opened his briefcase and took out his laptop.

For the next hour he worked his way through all the data that Bezel's team, had accumulated before Blake stopped his work. Despite Chen's frequent and sometimes aggressive questions he could feel Cadogan warming to the idea. Finally he abruptly interrupted Leicemann and turned to Chen.

"OK Jim, I've decided. We'll carry on with the existing trials but I want you give Leicemann a Predator and a good team of your people, and see if he can get any of this stuff to work. Give him a Seven."

He looked at Leicemann. "I'm sure you'll understand. If you don't get results quickly, we'll have to drop it."

Chen looked carefully at Cadogan. "So you want us to help him put a lump of goo into a Bad Boy? A Seven even." There was a pause, then, under Cadogan's unremitting gaze, he nodded reluctantly. "OK, OK. We can give it a try I guess," he said finally, "but I stay in charge of the overall project."

"You will, but for this Harris you will act as liaison between Jim and Alex, and me, understood?"

Chen's face went blank. Harris allowed himself a small smile and nodded.

"When can you start, Alex?" Cadogan said.

"We'll need at least a of couple weeks to set up" Leicemann said carefully. "Can you give me lab facilities on site here? I can organise a unit under my number two, Doctor Bezel. She's outstanding. I trained her myself."

"OK," Cadogan said, "but when do you think you can deliver a trial? If we miss the deadline we're all stone dead."

"I won't bullshit you. It's new territory, but I'm pretty sure we can deliver something worthwhile in say, three months max."

"OK, but no longer. If it doesn't work out we'll drop it OK?" Leicemann nodded.

"Harris," Cadogan continued, "go with Doctor Leicemann right now and start organising some facilities."

After Leicemann and Harris had gone, Chen and Cadogan sat in the empty control room. "Are you really going to do this?" Chen said quietly.

"We're in the shit Jim. You know that. I'll give him a shot. I've never liked him but he's good at what he does. He'll put his back into it, I do know. If it doesn't work he's back to being a glorified assistant to Blake at BSDL. He knows that."

Chen looked hard at Cadogan. "I still think it's all bullshit," he said. "What if he leaks our problems? You can't trust him."

"Who says I do?" Cadogan said. "I don't need to. He's got some dark days locked away in his past, and I know all about them. He can't afford to cross me. Don't worry about that."

Chapter 12

March 2015

Three months later

Leicemann, masked and dressed in blue medical coveralls, passed through the airlock that was the only access into the substantial laboratory that Cadogan had provide for him at Anglo Systems three months before.

Inside, shrouded figures tended a series of incubator-like boxes on a long bench. Through the hazy glass of the incubators he could just discern the contents. Some were simply strips of glistening grey brain samples, others were recognisably parts of dogs' heads, in once case a complete skull. Each box was connected to screens monitoring various life functions. Layers of sine waves endlessly flexed and flowed.

Incongruously, 'Music for Lifts' was playing quietly in the background. To one side a solitary figure was bending over an aluminium case. Thin wisps of vapour trailed from the case. The figure straightened up and moved towards him, pulling the lower side of the facemask down to reveal a carefully made up face. "Well, hi there boss," a female voice drawled.

It was Sophie Bezel. "Thank God you sent me some new stuff. The ACF support systems are working pretty well now, but we've been going through samples likes there's no tomorrow."

"Don't worry, there's still plenty more where that came from," Leicemann said. "How about the BCI control systems?"

"They're still cooking," she said.

She led him over to a bench that carried a row of a variety of mechanisms connected by clear fibre cables to the incubators. The fibres glowed with flickering pulses of blue light. The overall effect was nightmarish.

The mechanisms themselves were like creatures from a horror film. Some had single eyes, others jointed limbs. Little heads wobbled and nodded, and claws reached out snapping and clattering. They seemed to be constructed largely of plastic and metal although some components looked almost organic and glistened with fluid. A couple of the bigger units looked a bit like crude copies of a Predator but they lay fixed on their backs legs twitching, as if they had fallen over and couldn't get up again.

"OK. How about the mobile units?" Leicemann said.

"Come and have a look," Bezel replied. She led him down the length of the room past the rows of clicking and clattering creatures, to another chamber.

Inside, two masked figures were watching a creature roughly the size and shape of a dog move about a practise area. It was also much more roughly constructed than a Predator and its movements were jerky, but they were co-ordinated There was no visible connection between it and the operators but the open top of its head flickered with the same eerie blue light as the devices in the other room. A simple maze involving about a dozen choices was laid out in the floor at the back of the room "Send it in," Bezel said. An operator pressed a control. The little mechanical creature surged forward and almost tripped over, then righted itself and confidently trotted forward at considerable speed.

"It's fast," Bezel enthused, "faster than Chen's set up I bet." She'd never been allowed near Chen's non-organic unit but Leicemann passed on every fragment of intelligence he could pick up.

"It's going into the wall," Leicemann said quietly, "slow it down." The operator pressed another control. The creature obligingly slowed. "Walk it through."

Over the next five minutes the little robot dutifully trotted around as directed inside the maze.

"OK," Leicemann finally said grudgingly. "You've mastered the basic moves. Now give it a broad instruction to get through the maze on its own, let's see how it works it out."

Bezel's face fell. "We're not quite there yet," she said. "The basic operations work fine, especially the attack mode, but we're still working on finding neural structures that can operate more strategically. But we'll get there eventually. It's going to work."

Leicemann looked at her. "Tell me straight Sophie. Are you kidding yourself?"

Her eyes shifted slightly to the left. "No Alex," she said. "We know we can build autonomous units. The operating system is just another step."

Leicemann looked at her sceptically.

"'Just another step', Cadogan's pressing for a proper test with a real Bad Dog. So am I."

She looked at him shocked. "But we're not ready. What are you doing? You know we need more time."

"*You're* not ready. *You* haven't got the time," Cadogan said bitterly. "If we don't come first, we come nowhere. Unless we come up with a working model soon, Cadogan will just pull us out of the whole project and put all his budget back into Chen."

Bezel's face fell. "But we're close. We've cracked sensory-motor stability, the optogenic controls work well, and the little buggers are fast! The only real problem is that we can't get right in there to connect with the existing deep neural network. It's just in there waiting for us but I still can't connect with it."

"Right. So?"

She paused as if wondering whether to go on with her next proposal but then abruptly decided to take a chance. "I've been chasing up every little leak from the Canine Project. The dogs are carrying a monitoring system in their brains that detects and transmits multiple levels of neural activity. They've been live testing it for six months now. It works. That's exactly what we need. Using that we could build a fully operational robot in a fraction of the time it would take us otherwise."

Leicemann paused to examine the thought. "I see what you're getting at," he said finally. "OK, that might even work for us I admit. But I don't have any access to that technology. Blake's made sure of that, and it took them years to develop."

"Then let's just take it."

There was another long pause while she looked at him steadily.

"I'm not against the principle," he said eventually, "our work is far more important than their half baked fantasies, but those dogs are Blake's pride and joy. He's got them distributed in a half dozen secure locations. Even if we could managed to get hold of one, what if we're detected?"

"Fuck them!" the words were deeply shocking coming from Bezels elegant lips. "If we get hold of even one of those dogs, and the control system even half works, you can say goodbye to that weakling Fat Sam and his mob for ever. We can do it Alex! Think of the rewards! If we can make this thing work you'd be welcome in any military research centre in the world."

"You think I don't know that? Why do you think I'm willing to work with that moron Chen?" he said bitterly. She didn't reply, but waited. Apparently abstractedly she pulled the open top of her overall a little looser to reveal a neat little dog collar around her neck. She toyed with the little dog tag that hung from it.

"Alex," she said, "I'll do whatever it takes. My loyalty to you is total. You know that. I swear we can do it."

"It's not the financial reward that matters, you understand," he said. "It's about proving that I'm right. That we're right."

Bezel smiled, and waited.

"Sod it," he said eventually. "Let's go for it. It's the only option. But we'll need two at least. One to test the system until it pops, and then one to build the finished demonstrator when we know the limits."

She squeezed his hand. "Where do we start?"

"Keep on with the neural samples. Push them to destruction if need be. Meantime use your contacts to find out which of the Canine Project dogs are doing best. I'll do some snooping too. We might as well give ourselves the best option. Then we'll move in."

"How will you do it?"

"Don't you worry about that," he said. "You'd be surprised at some of my connections...

Part Four

Three Days in April

Chapter 13

April 2015

Just twenty-eight days after Leicemann's conversation with Sophie Bezel, and on the same bright spring morning that Jess was to realise that Daisy had disappeared, a small boy was walking along the narrow road that ran about three hundred yards from The Stone House.

Luke Davies was eleven years old but looked even younger. He was a small and thin, with permanent wrinkles across his forehead that betrayed his underlying anxiety. He was a careful and conservative boy. The world had always seemed to him to be a dangerous and uncertain place, and nothing in his experience had given him reason to change his opinion.

And then there were his personal failings. Almost since he could remember, whatever he tried to do, he'd been chased and chivvied by Chas for failing to be whatever a real boy was supposed to be. Chas was the young man who lived with his mother and who was the bane of his life. He was a tall, heavily built man with unbelievably hairy arms. He cultivated a Mexican style moustache that he called 'My Zapata'. He was prone to sudden bursts of anger.

Everything about Luke seemed to make Chas angry, and he had a cruel and sarcastic wit that could appear from nowhere. He insisted on calling Luke; 'Lulu', and Luke hated it. He'd decided early on in his young life that when Chas was around it was safer to stay quiet and wherever possible melt into the background, and that attitude had gradually seeped into his whole life.

His mother offered some support, but it was arbitrary and confusing and, he suspected, not quite real. Luke couldn't understand why she had even let Chas into their lives in the first place, but he was pretty sure it was because Chas's job on the farm carried a cottage with it.

Although it was tiny it was a lot nicer than the single room they had lived in before she met Chas. She had been in her thirties then, and complaining that she was too old and fat to ever meet another man, and he suspected she was somehow surprised and grateful when Chas turned up. Anyway, in the final analysis, she always deferred to him.

This morning Luke was walking along the back road that connected the tied cottage with the nearby village of Little Oakingham. His mother had sent him to buy sugar, eggs and bacon from the single shop, and now he was on his way back. They did their weekly shopping in the big supermarket in Tamborough, but the little village shop, which called itself a mini-supermarket, was handy and useful to top up on basics. Chas had an enormous appetite for what he called a proper fry up, and supplies almost always ran out by the end of the week.

Today he would usually have used his bicycle but a couple of weeks ago Chas had distorted the back wheel by attempting to show him how to do wheelies on it, and then insisted that he would fix it using a spoke key, when he got hold of one. It hadn't happened yet.

It was a long walk but didn't mind walking really. He'd taken some biscuits from the tin in the larder to keep him going, and it was it was a lovely morning; there were signs of spring all around. You could almost feel the burgeoning growth.

The white May blossom already lay like snow on the hedgerows and the banks of the tiny yellow buttercups his mother called Pilewort were already being joined by primroses. The lane was narrow and quiet, only used by occasional traffic. To his left was the tangled undergrowth that masked what his Aunt Gwen called Grimm's Holes.

This was an area of a couple of hundred wooded acres of deep ditches and slopes that she said was where witchcraft and human sacrifice were practised long ago. His teacher at school said that it was just heaps of spoil, left from hundreds of stone quarries that went right back to the time of the Romans, but he was still nervous to go in there.

On his right was a tall thick hedge. It defended what seemed to be a large estate though he'd never seen anyone go in or out. He passed a big gate that had been put up a few months ago. It had a big notice on it saying 'Strictly private property, No Entry!' Above it was a little camera. Beyond the gate he could just see a long gravelled track and, in the distance, a high link fence.

He heard the sound of a vehicle and he forgot about the mystery of the distant fence and walked over to the verge of the lane. It was a delivery van and, as it passed him, it almost ran over a dog that popped out of the big hedge that ringed the mysterious estate. The dog made it safely to the verge and then stood watching the disappearing van. It was about to cross the road back into the hedge but then when it saw him it stopped abruptly. He stopped too. The dog sat down on its haunches, managing to wag its tail at the same time.

He regarded the dog carefully. It was quite small with a thick black and white coat and long ears that made it look like it was wearing a long wig like those men in films about the old days. It seemed like a nice little dog but then again you had to be careful. He'd never actually been bitten by one, but you read in the newspaper about little children having their faces torn off by dogs that had acted meek and friendly right up to the last dreadful moment.

He approached slowly until he was standing over the dog. It kept its gaze on him the whole time, looking up into his eyes. It was panting slightly which gave it a kind of smile. Where had it come from? Who did it belong to?

"Hello little fella," he said. "Where do you come from then?" Its eyes lit up and it made a little squeak sound, paused, and then made it again. He had no idea why it was doing it.

The dog seemed confused too. It shook its head. It repeated the squeak several times and then stopped. Its tail stopped wagging. In so far as a dog's face could carry any expression at all, it looked distinctly unhappy.

He suddenly noticed that the dog had some sort of dark growth or scab on its head. It was quite large, about an inch across. Perhaps it had a disease, but it was hard to believe that. The dog seemed bright and healthy, with a glossy coat, and a clear light of intelligence shone out of its eyes. Even so it was probably better to stay away from it.

"Off you go," he said, "go on, go away home. Someone will be missing you." and he started to walk on. But the dog got up and not only followed him but danced around him as he walked, producing the occasional squeak and radiating the message, almost as clearly as if it were speaking, that it wanted to play.

He tried to ignore it and was relieved when the dog ran off into the hedgerow, but in a minute it was back again carrying a length of stick. It brought it up to him and dropped it in front of him. He was pretty sure he was supposed to pick it up and throw it, and he was determined not to get involved with the dog, but he couldn't help being charmed and eventually he gave in.

For the next ten minutes he dutifully threw the stick until he became bored, and in any case his mother, and Chas, would be waiting for the food he was carrying. "That's it," he said to the dog, but it continued to dance around him making little dashes away and then coming back, clearly to remind him of the procedure. Luke grew exasperated. "I ain't throwing that stick no more and that's final," he said, walking on. Immediately without ceremony the dog picked up the stick and then ambled along beside him, carrying it in its mouth. You could swear it understood what he said.

He decided that the dog probably wasn't dangerous. "You're a good boy ain't you," he said, reaching out to pat it, but the dog danced away and then briefly squatted to urinate. Luke laughed aloud. "I'm sorry gel," he said. "You're a girl of course. Ain't I daft." The dog gave another little squeak and danced around him again, tail thrashing and gazing up at him with its curiously bright eyes. They walked on together as comfortably as if they'd been friends for years...

Daisy was having a really interesting time. Although she was sometimes taken in the car by Jess to the Biomed laboratory at Canine Division Central, the place of the white coats and the strange smells, she had never been outside the big field before on her own and she had never met a real Small One, a boy, before. A whole new world was opening up for her. There were a multitude of new sounds and smells. There was an absolute barrage of susurration from the woods and undergrowth that lined the long dark car-smelling space, and a heady mix of new odours of plants and flowers from the hedgerows.

She stopped to take a good smell of the tiny yellow flowers that were scattered in the grass but then snorted at the acrid smell of diesel that the passing van had left on them. She looked up, the small human still walked on ahead of her so she decided to follow him. The way his smell and posture had changed as she first approached had warned her that he was frightened but, as he had relaxed, she had realised that she would be able to play a Game with him, just as she did with Jess.

She decided she liked him. Now he was calmer he had a nice smile and smelled fragrantly, of underwear that needed washing and biscuits. He was also carrying something she hadn't smelt before but it was intriguingly meaty. She was disappointed that she couldn't ask him about it, she'd become used to having Jess understand what she wanted to communicate, but it didn't really matter. Jess would fix that when she saw her again. Meanwhile she looked forward to a host of new experiences with her new friend.

Chapter 14

Peter Guy put down his phone. A voice from the little speaker on his desk said, "Peter? Dr Blake says he's finished now and he'll see you whenever you can get over."

"Good, tell him I'm on my way. Meantime I want to see every spare security man in the Main Meeting Room in ten minutes. Pull in the men on weekend stand down as well. No argument. Stress it's a Code One."

He left his little office and made his way through the larger room where a dozen or so people were seated at desks, each one studying their computer screens intently. There was a palpable air of tension in the room. He stopped by a young woman who, with her spiky hair, piercings, and elaborate arm tattoos looked as if she wandered into the office by mistake. She chewed steadily as she worked the keyboard.

"Marika," Guy said, "Anything? Anything at all?"

"Nah," she muttered, without looking up. "Not yet. I've stripped out the headers but these people are good. I've chased down the DNS chain but the host ID is stuck behind a load of dynamic proxies."

"OK, keep working on it," he said. "If anybody can crack it you can."

"That's it boss," she said, managing to keep chewing as she spoke, "fucking 'girl with the dragon tattoo', that's me."

He would have laughed if he weren't so worried. He opened the door to the corridor.

"I can tell you one thing," she called after him, "whoever set this up knows a heck of a lot about our systems *but* I don't think they've managed to hack into the links to the other local centres yet, and they won't if I can help it. I'm adding layers to the walls that'll take them fucking years to get through."

With a nod he left the room. One floor down he arrived at the office of Dr. Samuel Blake, Head of the Canine Division. He went straight in without knocking. Blake was working at his computer.

"I've got to bring you up to speed quickly, if you don't mind Sir," he said.

Blake sat back from the monitor. Guy stood opposite.

"It's about BC38."

"Ah, Ruby, nice dog."

"Yes. Last night her trainer Jack Sampson got a secure mail from BioMed. It said that in the dog's last check up there was evidence of neural degeneration and it would need to come back to Division Central for more tests."

Blake's face fell. "That's really worrying, but I heard nothing about this."

"No sir, neither had anyone else, but first thing this morning a two man team arrived at Jack's unit to pick Ruby up. The problem was that the dog flatly refused to go with them. Some sort of fracas ensued, during which Jack reckons he was injected with something. It knocked him out anyway. When he came to, the dog was gone."

Now Blake's expression was thunderous. "Why did local security let them in Peter?"

"I was on their backs immediately but you can't blame them. The original message had the right tags, at first glance it looks totally authentic, but it was a fake. Someone had hacked into BioMed's link to the DAC local centre."

Blake's fingers drummed on his desk as he tried to see all the implications.

"What about the other dogs? Have these people hacked into links to *all* the local centres?"

"We don't know yet. I don't think so, but it was very well done; whoever sent it knows a hell of a lot about how BSDL works, and the I.D's of the men who arrived to pick up the dog were faultless."

"Do we know anything about the men?"

"Jack said one was tall, well spoken, the other shorter, more of a working class accent, probably London. They somehow buggered up the security camera, so we've got no images of them, and the vehicle plates were fakes. I've got Jack working on identifits but that's all we have for now."

Blake said nothing. He seemed to have difficulty grasping what Peter had told him. For a moment he stared into some distant horizon. Eventually he spoke, "I'm sorry Peter, I've never experienced anything like this before. What can we do? What does it mean?"

"What I think it means is that someone has decided it's well worth grabbing the Project dogs. All I can do for now is put the other trainers in a shut-down situation."

"Good. Is Jess OK?"

"I've called her as soon as I realised what was happening and warned her to keep Daisy close by. I'll send out backup security as well."

"I'd better alert Leicemann," Blake said. "They might try something in Selections. But the real point is who wants our dogs, and why?"

"As yet," Peter said, "I have to say that we really don't know."

Leicemann's phone was muted, but its vibrations resonated on the polished steel of the laboratory table, creating their own harsh call sign. He picked it up.

"It's me." It was a man's voice with the well-rounded tones of a public school education. "How's it going your end?"

"Very well," Leicemann said. "Blake's just officially informed me that you've got a dog. Now we go to stage two. If my surmise is correct, Guy will send out teams to boost the security at the local centres. He'll have to give them the location of the training centre for each dog. The dog you're looking for now is officially nominated as DAC32. As soon as I know who's allocated to protect that dog I'll let you know."

"And we move in, check."

"And don't forget to get a collar this time. I must have those programmes."

"Check!" The caller rang off.

Chapter 15

When Luke finally got back to the cottage, his mother was in the kitchen standing at the sink. The dog followed him in. He unloaded the groceries onto the tiny kitchen table.

"Thank goodness you're back," she said, "Chas is desperate for his breakfast."

"Is that him?" came Chas's voice from the bedroom above. "Where the hell has he been to, Leicester?"

"Where did you get that from?" His mother said, looking at the dog. The dog dropped the stick and went over to sniff at the wood-burning stove in the corner.

"It's a stray," Luke said, "it followed me home. It's a nice dog Mum."

At his words the dog lost interest in the stove and came and sat beside him, looking up at his mother. Ears pricked and face relaxed and open, with its doggy smile the dog's whole attitude said, "Yes, this is me and my mate."

"It's a pretty little thing," his mother said, "somebody will be missing it, hasn't it got a collar or anything?"

"No," said Luke, "not a thing." The dog wagged its tail.

"What's that on its head?" his mother said. She wiped her wet hands and bent over the dog, which obligingly presented its head. "It looks like some kind of growth but it feels like plastic," she said. "Surely no maniac has stuck a hat on its head. Mind you, people do the queerest things these days, it's always in the papers."

She tried to get a fingernail under the edge of the little hat but the dog squeaked a warning and gently extricated its head from her hand. "Leave it Mum," Luke said.

"I'm not trying to hurt it love," she said, "but there's definitely something wrong with it."

There came the sound of Chas descending the narrow little stairs that opened straight into the kitchen, and he emerged pulling a t-shirt over his head.

"Where the hell have you been Lulu? You know I like me fry up on a Saturday morning. Christ knows it's the only break I get." He stopped when he saw the dog. The dog in turn tensed slightly and its nostrils flared and then narrowed. It snorted and shook its head as if trying to shake off a bad smell.

Chas glared at Luke. "Where the hell did you get that from?" he said. "What's up with its head?"

Luke was all set to tell Chas that it was none of his business, and it was his dog now, he was going to train it as a guard dog. It would be his true friend, and many other things, but instead he said, "I didn't get it, it followed me home."

"Where from?"

"Just from along the back lane."

"Well you'd better put it back. It looks like some kind of pedigree; it probably belongs to some well off folks. You might even get a reward."

"Well whatever you do with it, we'd better give it some water, dogs always need water," his mother said.

At the word water the dog sat up brightly made a little squeak and came over to sit at her feet and gaze into her eyes, tail swishing gently.

"Look at that," she said, "he knows the word water."

"She's very clever," said Luke, "and she's a girl not a boy."

"Dog or bitch, don't make no difference." Chas said. "Put the bloody thing in the shed until I decide what to do with it." As he spoke, the dog's whole posture changed again. It backed away from all of them towards the closed door, the tail dropped and ears laid back and it growled gently.

"She don't like you, Chas," his mother said cautiously.

"I don't give a shit if it likes me or not," said Chas, "and I want my breakfast."

He suddenly lurched across the tiny kitchen, grabbed the dog by the scruff of its neck and lifted it into the air. The dog went mad, barking and snarling, and trying to bite him. As he struggled to control it, the freshly filled milk jug on the table got knocked over and milk puddled all over the floor.

"For God's sake Chas!" Luke's mother shouted.

"Dogs need to know whose boss. I'll larn this one," and he swept out of the kitchen, walked the few feet to the old barn opposite the back door, threw the dog into it, closed the door and shut the padlock.

"Now perhaps I can get me fucking breakfast," he said. "What are you looking at?"

Luke, who had followed him, was standing uncertainly by the kitchen door. "You're not going to cry are you Lulu?"

In truth Luke was on the edge of tears, but he said nothing as Chas went back into the kitchen shouting, "Now come on Linney, where's me fucking egg and bacon?"

"You can just wait till I clear this mess up!" he heard his mother say.

Luke went over and stood silently outside the door of the barn. "Don't worry gel," he said finally, "I'll get you out of there." But from inside the barn there was only total silence.

Daisy sat in the gloom of the barn. She was very upset, her heart still beating wildly. She could smell the small human outside. She sensed he would help her if he could, but it was impossible to speak to him. She produced a little squeak. Not a word. Still at the back of her mind, she knew that Jess would fix that when she went home. Jess could do anything.

But how could she go home? Despite her innate optimism, she had a terrifying feeling that perhaps she would never get out of the barn. Perhaps the big one who frightened the others, especially the boy, would keep her in there a long time. There was something profoundly wrong about him, he smelt wrong, even the beat of his heart and the pace of his breath were somehow wrong. She hadn't been able to understand exactly what he was saying, but all her instincts told her that he was bad news. She had known he would try to hurt her. "Bad, bad man" she tried to say aloud, but nothing came out but a squeak.

She did know however that her doubts and worries were effectively freezing her from working out what to do next, so she decided to wait and let the Calm take over. A less intelligent dog would have run around the barn scratching at the door and the walls, but she already knew that was pointless. She lay perfectly still with her nose between her front paws and allowed herself to slip gently into the half awake state which she could maintain for hours.

As the soothing alpha waves began to soak through her brain, her nose automatically checked out the rich cocktail of musty smells and ancient traces in the barn. She didn't recognise most of the smell signatures and there was dust everywhere but there was a strong smell of the bad big one and she gave another little snort to clear her nostrils. At the same time she shaped the smell so that she could identify it without letting the powerful evocative associations it carried swamp her consciousness. Then she packed it away into the enormous smell dictionary in her brain and got on with checking out the opportunities for escape.

The answer was that there weren't any opportunities. The floor was hard concrete, the walls were stone and the door was tight shut. Even so, now that she was calmer she got up and carefully smelt out every inch of it. There was a work bench, boxes of various sizes, a couple of bicycles, one with a wheel missing, various tools and all the other detritus that accumulates in a rural barn. At the back there was a large pile of cut logs and next to it a plastic barrel. Above the barrel was a small window with a frosted glass pane. The window was propped open.

As soon as she saw the window, she acted. She sprinted up the log pile and took a flying leap to land on the barrel. It smelled strongly of fuel oil and she heard the liquid slosh about inside as it rocked slightly on its uneven base, but she managed to maintain her footing. Now when she stood up on her back legs, she could just reach the window sill with her front paws, but she could get no higher and even if she had been able to the opening was too small for her to get through it. She could just get her nose through the narrow gap.

The small human was waiting outside the window. He too could only just reach the lower sill. "Hello little gel," he said, "are you OK?" Daisy understood every word he said and she was bursting to tell him she wasn't ok, and she would greatly appreciate him getting her out of there, but of course she had lost her voice. He put his hand up to the narrow gap and Daisy licked it, despite her determination to be brave, but she couldn't stop herself from giving a little whine. "Don't you worry gel," he said. "I'll get you out of there". Daisy gave him another appreciative lick. She decided he was definitely Good.

As she stretched up to the window she got a clear message from the bacon and eggs frying in the kitchen. She didn't know what it was, Jess was almost entirely vegetarian, but it was a delicious warm fatty smell, seething with energy. Her stomach rumbled and she suddenly realised how thirsty she was.. As if reading her mind the small human said. "I bet you could do with a drink, little gel." Giving up on trying to speak, she just wagged her tail enthusiastically.

"Just you hang on a minute," Luke said to the dog, and then realised how daft that sounded, there wasn't anywhere else for her to go. He went back into the kitchen and started to fill a bowl from the tap.

"What do you think you're doing?" Chas said, through a mouthful of buttered toast. Even at a moment like this when he truly wanted to murder Chas and everything he stood for, Luke couldn't help being amazed at the sheer amount of butter Chas went through, half of the pack he'd bought that morning had already gone.

"I'm just taking the dog some water," he said.

"No you ain't," Chas said.

"Oh Chas," his mother murmured. "That's not right. Dogs need water. I do know that."

"Don't worry, I'll see it gets water. It might be worth money, that dog. But it can bloody wait until I've had me breakfast. And you," to Luke, "just keep your nose out of it. Get down to your little hut and have a wank or whatever you get up to in there."

"Chas..." His mother said weakly.

"I am taking the water," Luke said firmly.

"Ooh," said Chas in falsetto, "getting all ballsy today ain't we. Well you ain't taking nothin' nowhere without this." He held up the key to the padlock. "And you ain't getting it." He put it in his pocket and resumed his steady chomping, levelling a steady stare at Luke as he chewed.

Luke was so close to tears of frustration that he put the bowl of water on the draining board and ran out of the kitchen before Chas could spot his eyes brimming. He went back to the window at the back of the barn. The dog was still waiting patiently.

"It's no good, Chas said he's got the key. But he'll have to open the door to bring you water. Just wait. I'll think of something." The dog gave a little squeak, licked his hand and then hopped down to settle on the floor, nose between its front paws.

Poor little sod, he thought, she's got no idea what Chas can be like.

He went down to the end of the long narrow garden and crawled into his private den. The only thing he could do was to wait until Chas opened that door.

While he finished his breakfast, Chas considered the opportunities offered by the dog. There was no point in keeping it, they didn't need a dog and it was a waste of money. It might be possible to find out who owned it, though it was funny that it didn't have a collar. He had one contact, a dodgy character called Den, who would often pay up for a stray dog for his own purposes, but for the moment, since he was an unforgiving bastard, and Chas owed him money, it was best to keep out of his way. No, the best bet was to find out what that little plastic hat was about. It could be worth something. He wouldn't be surprised if it wasn't some new kind of computer to control dogs, like those collars that let you give them a shock when they needed it. Problem was that, although Chas knew a lot of geezers who could get you almost any kind of dope, or smuggled ciggies and beer, or even the odd iPhone, he didn't particularly have any good contacts in computers. Still that didn't stop a man of wit and determination. He could start by getting hold of the hat.

"I'll give it some water," he said to Lynn, as she started to wash up the remains of his breakfast.

"What are you going to do with it?" she said. "We could keep it as a pet for Luke, he's so isolated out here."

"Don't be daft Linney," he said. "He wouldn't know what to do with it. He ain't got the sense he was born with and you know it. Anyway, dogs cost a fortune, they need all them injections and things, and I'd rather spend the money on you." Although Luke's mother couldn't remember when exactly when he'd ever spent money on her, she smiled at the kind thought.

He quietly slipped out of the kitchen. There was no sign of Luke, which was fine, and with luck the dog wouldn't hear him coming. He stood next to the woodpile next to the backdoor and listened. Silence. Then he stealthily unlocked the padlock of the barn door. He kept it well oiled and maintained since, unbeknownst to Lynn, it had been necessary to keep one or two dodgy items stored in the barn at various times.

He slipped through the door. There was no sign of the dog but it couldn't be gone. There was no other way out. Just as he realised it must be hiding behind the door, the dog shot round behind him, and would have slipped out if he hadn't quickly slammed the door against it, trapping it half in and half out of the door. He dropped the water bowl, grabbed a piece of wood and began beating the rear end of the dog as it struggled to escape.

"You crafty little bastard," he shouted. "I'll larn you, I'll larn you." Suddenly the dog stopped struggling and howling and went completely still. He reached through the gap, grabbed it by the neck with one hand, threw it back into the shed, slamming the door shut behind him and slipping the inner bolt across.

"Just leave it, just leave it," Luke begged outside the door, audibly crying. Chas heard Linney taking Luke inside, telling him everything would be fine, Chas knew what he was doing, he knew all about animals.

Chas regarded the dog. The dog regarded him. "Yes, you little sod," he said quietly. "No water for you. You know whose boss now, don't you?" The dog stood perfectly still, its tail wagging low and slow, and watched him with its deep bright eyes. "Well I tell you what," Chas said. "If you're a good dog, I'll put you on a lead and we'll go outside for a drink of water and a nice walkies. Or would you rather have this?" He held up the piece of wood he had used to beat the dog.

Daisy was in a state of acute shock. Every time this bad big one came near her, he hurt her. He smelled strongly of the delicious breakfast but she had lost her appetite. In her experience big ones said what they would do, and then they did it, but this bad big one was doing bad things and saying good words. Her innate wisdom told her that it was better to trust her reaction to the stick and disregard the words. As Jess had taught her, she tried to arrange the possible futures into options, but it was hard to organise her thoughts and there were no clear decisions to be made. She was perfectly prepared to attack him, but she knew that at this point attacking him was a waste of time. He still held the big stick. She decided the only option she had was to do as he said, and wait and see what happened.

A few minutes later Chas had her securely trussed up and stretched across the workbench. She had cooperated at first when he put the rope around her neck, but by the time she realised what he intended it was too late and she couldn't stop him. Jaws bound and legs stretched she couldn't move. She was so frightened that she tried to beg for mercy, whining and attempting to lick his hand but it had no effect.

Chas took down a chisel from the rack above the workbench wiped it with a rag, and then bent over her. Close to, the little cap was clearly made of some kind of hard plastic. It fitted tightly to the dog's skull. He pressed hard on it and the dog whined, its eyes rolling and showing the whites. It began to drool. He inserted the edge of the chisel at the junction between the cap and the dog's skull and pushed. The dog strained against the ropes and let about a thin high scream. Chas pushed the chisel edge in a little further...

Suddenly there was a crash and the screws that held the bolt on the door flew clear of the old wood, as the door was abruptly forced open. Luke and his mother almost fell through the door as both had thrown their weight against it, and Luke rushed past her. He was holding a length of log and, without stopping, or making a sound, he brought it down with all his force on the side of Chas's head. Chas fell down, then started to struggle up again, but Luke was already at the workbench, scrabbling to loosen the ropes holding the dog down. A thin line of blood ran from the point on its skull where Chas had inserted the chisel. It paid no attention to Luke, lying perfectly still until, before he had finished untying it, it gave a sudden convulsive wriggle, leapt off the bench, squeezed past Luke's mother, and was gone.

Luke looked down at Chas as he slowly tried to get to his feet.

"Oh you little fucker, you little fucker," Chas moaned through gritted teeth, "I'll fucking kill you, I'll kill you."

He got to his feet, one hand pressed to the side of his head and started to stagger towards Luke.

"Luke, run, run," His mother called from behind him. "Just get out of it." Luke ran down the garden path and pushed through the gap in the rickety fence at the bottom. He glanced behind him to see Chas, driven apparently by pure determination weaving his way towards him. He put his head down and ran for his life.

He did not see that behind him, as Chas reached the fence, he abruptly stopped and fell flat on his face.

Two men were driving down a lane in a newly acquired and nondescript grey van when the phone buzzed abruptly. It was Leicemann. "What's happening?" he said without any preliminaries.

"Glad you called back Alex," the well-spoken man replied. "I was just about to call you. That went very well. We're on our way to somewhere called the Stone House. You are now talking to the Canine Division security team of Jackson and Jones. I'm Jackson now. I like the sound of it. Suits me."

"Where are the originals?"

"They're fine. We picked them up as they left the car pool. My boy here gave them a little shot. They're asleep and secure. By the time they're found we'll be well away."

"What's the I.D of the target dog?"

"DAC 32. Trainer Jess Stewart."

"That's good, very good. Things are going well. Keep in touch."

Leicemann disconnected and the man he had spoken to turned to the driver as he manoeuvred the van along the narrow lane. They were just about to pass a small cottage, the first habitation they'd seen for a couple of miles. "Now Mr Jones," he said, "I think Jackson would call his number two by a nickname. The officer class do things like that. I think I'm going to call you Jolly. What do you think?"

"Never mind that," the other grunted, "what's that woman doing standing in the middle of the road?"

Chapter 16

Jess had returned to the kitchen of the Stone House. Where was Daisy? She was trying to keep calm. Her mind raced round various possibilities. The most hopeful option was that the dog had simply gone exploring in the wooded buffer area outside of the fence and would wander back soon. The worst possibility was that it's disappearance was somehow connected with the call from Peter pressing her to take special care. The latent fear of messing up when faced with a challenge began to struggle its way to her consciousness but she resolutely thrust it away.

She felt a strong urge to ring Peter immediately, but she hesitated. There was no need, she told herself, to call out the whole security procedure on what might just be a false alarm. She might well be able to handle the situation herself. The best option seemed to be to make absolutely sure that the dog was not somewhere nearby and then, if the worst came to the worst, try to contact Peter.

She made a decision. She had a window of opportunity. She had perhaps a couple of hours to search before Canine Division Central would automatically start querying the lack of activity from her mainframe.

She put on a fully charged Bluetooth mike and headphone set, went to her little potting shed and took out some wire cutters, then went down through the vegetable garden and out through the door. How had the door been open anyway? She was certain that she had shut it the night before. When she reached the point in the meadow where Daisy had escaped she only had to cut a few more links and she could squeeze through the gap in the fence herself. She was surprised how easy it was.

Dusting herself off, she walked carefully through the untended scrub of bushes and small trees that populated the buffer area between the inner fence and the outer thick hedge. She called softly, "Daisy, Daisy. It's Jess. Come. Come. Let's play." The headset mike had a pickup range of about a hundred feet, so with luck the dog would pick up her voice even if it couldn't see her. Eventually she had walked almost the entire perimeter without success. It was nearly two hours since she had last seen the dog, and she had decided she would have to give in and call in an official search when there was a rustle in the bushes and ball of black and white fur exploded into her arms.

The dog licked her face furiously, tail thrashing. "Bad man! Bad man! Bad man!" boomed in her headset. "Bad man HURT me! Hurt me!" The headset was buzzing and booming, with frequent dropout. Despite the grim message she felt a huge surge of relief, hugging the warm furry body to herself, and taking a deep breath of the familiar reassuring smell. As the dog struggled to continue licking her face she resisted the urge to let it continue and pushed it away from her slightly. It was then that she noticed the thin line of blood drying across its skull. She felt an immediate rush of both anger and guilt. "Oh shit," she said. "Let's go home honey." Holding the dog tight in her arms she went back towards the gap in the fence, the dog still babbling.

Chapter 17

Luke was frightened and depressed. He had hidden in the woods behind the cottage for a while after he ran away but no one had come after him, and now he was wandering along the lane with no real sense of where he was going or what he would so next. There was no sign of the dog. He was amazed at his own temerity at hitting Chas but his feelings of fear for the inevitable retribution due to him were mixed with a deep satisfaction with the recollection of the solid sound the log had made when it hit Chas's head. It was almost worth all the punishment he was going to get. But what would the punishment be? How bad could it get? Chas would certainly give him a good hiding, but what if he took him to the police? What if he was sent to one of those detention centres where they bullied you so much you hung yourself. He simply didn't know what to do. He could only cling to the hope that his Mother would protect him.

He eventually found himself walking back to the cottage. The road back seemed all too short but eventually he was standing at the gate to the tiny neglected garden. He braced himself, took a deep breath and walked past the front door and down the side passage to the back door. It stood open. The barn door stood open too. It was very quiet. He looked into the barn, nothing. He stood at the entrance to the kitchen and called tentatively, "Mum, it's me. I'm back." Still silence.

He walked into the empty kitchen and through into the tiny sitting room then back and up the stairs. Both bedrooms were empty. The tiny bathroom was empty, but he wasn't desperately worried, Chas must be alright now, he was so big and strong, perhaps he'd got a lift to Tamborough to get his head looked at, and his Mother had gone with him. They'd return eventually. He waited patiently, and, after a long hour, even went out into the lane to catch the first glimpse of them coming back, but of Chas and his mother there was no sign at all.

Jess stood in her kitchen of the Stone House breathing heavily. She had managed to carry the dog through the gap in the fence and then across the meadow and up through the garden. Once in the house she took Daisy into the kitchen and gave the dog a substantial drink of water. As it finished, water dripping messily from its chops, it sat back on its haunches and wagged its tail. "Me happy," it announced.

 The dog's emotional resilience was amazing, Jess thought. After going through God knows what experiences, it was rapidly regaining its equilibrium.

 She went into the office, the dog close behind her. She left the feed from the Bluetooth unit to the computer disconnected. It was better that any information about this incident was organised and censored by her before it went back to Canine Division Central. She sat the dog down on her desk and then went and fetched gauze and disinfectant. "What a big smell!" the dog said cheerfully, as Jess uncapped the bottle. She carefully wiped the area around the cap. It was very strongly fixed in to the dog's skull and could not have been shifted without the proper equipment and expertise, but although the skin around the junction had been disturbed, it had already stopped bleeding.

 The device itself seemed unharmed, the hairline crack around the top, which was the only sign of the tiny lithium-ion battery, was intact. She gave an audible sigh of relief. The dog quietly gazed into her eyes. She checked it carefully all over. As she touched its sides the dog gave a little whine and laid its head on her shoulder. Looking carefully she could see scratches and swelling. Someone had given the dog a heck of a beating.

 "What did they do to you honey? I don't want to take you through this but we have to do it." She paused, "DAC32 make report."

 This was the verbal signal by which the dog went into its trained mode. She knew she was placing a huge demand on the dog, not only because she was asking it to recall traumatic events but to do so in their order of occurrence. Its primary mental experience consisted of a series of 'now' moments of various emotional hues. Many of these were not actually conscious, and those that were much more likely to be arranged in their order of impact rather than their temporal sequence. However her acquisition of language had changed, and was still changing, the nature of the dog's consciousness. Like all dogs, she could make a clear distinction between past, present, and future, and she seemed to have some grasp of the idea of a sequence. She had been taught to call it 'making report.'

The dog stiffened and sat back on its haunches. "DAC32 present," it said. Then it stopped to consider.

"Long time ago," said Jess encouragingly, "Daisy eats dinner."

"Me eat Rustlers!"

"Yes, Rustlers," Jess agreed. The dog considered the happy memory. "Me hungry."

"Long time ago," Jess persisted, "Daisy is in the garden."

"Me in garden," the dog agreed, remembering. "In garden is fox. Fox!" She corrected herself. "No, Fox gone. Where is fox? Fox in work place, me in work place. No Jess."

Jess was fairly easily able to work out that Daisy had trailed the fox out into the meadows where they worked together on her training.

"No fox," Daisy went on. She struggled for a while and then triumphantly, "No fox. But!" She stopped for a moment savouring her use of the preposition. "But fox make door!"

Jess could have kissed her. "No fox," she agreed. "Gone, but fox makes little door."

"But yes, but yes!" The dog exulted, enjoying its use of the difficult concept.

"Long time ago," said Jess, "where was Daisy?"

"Where was Daisy?" The dog agreed it was a good question. "Me was in car place." Jess had not yet assigned the word 'road' to the dog's analysis of the location since the dog hadn't walked there before. It was clearly the lane outside, based on the residual smells of passing cars.

The dog paused for a long time. It seemed to lose interest but the background signals showed it was thinking hard. It settled back on its haunches to scratch its ear and then stopped as it encountered the injury to the skin of its skull.

Then all of a rush; "Me play with good boy, me go with good boy. But! Me go in bad garage, here is bad man, bad man!" The dog stopped again and snarled quietly and then looked up at her, looked deep into her eyes. It didn't speak but just whined.

"It was bad, eh girl?"

"Bad. Me alert for go. Me standby for attack."

They were both shocked. The dog had been trained to take part in military manoeuvres and to work under close control, even to attack under extreme circumstances, but its primary intended function was simply detecting and reporting on the activity of designated targets. This was what the 'games' in work time were all about. Daisy was not naturally aggressive. She must have been under a lot of threat.

"But, but, me can not attack," she said. "Can not." She shivered. She started to scratch her ear again but abruptly stopped.

"That was pretty bad, eh?"

The dog cast its eyes down and the speaker whispered, "Bad-bad, very, very bad-bad."

Then abruptly it shook itself and cheered up.

"But. But! Good boy comes, good boy stops bad man, me go! Yes, yes, me go!"

"And here you are home again," said Jess, "safe if not quite sound."

"Me home!" the dog agreed, dancing about. "Me home with Jess! Me hungry!"

Once again, Jess marvelled at the dog's emotional resilience.

"Ok," she said, "it's hours yet until suppertime, but you've had a hard morning. Let's get you a little bit of dinner, then you can have a little nap."

Afterwards, while the dog dozed beside her, using the calming influence of the rise in its blood sugar to help it take a break from its recent experiences, Jess sat at her desk and tried to consider her options. Even though it had come back safely, the dog had been injured, and its foray into the outside world might constitute a major threat to the security of the Project. The proper procedure was for her to report the whole incident.

She wasn't exactly sure what the fallout would be from that, but it seemed likely that at best she'd get a severe reprimand and the dog might even be taken away from her. Her heart sank at the thought. Still, she consoled herself, without a Bluetooth-sensitive receiver there was no way that Daisy could have vocalised in front of the witnesses. There was still the real possibility she could cool the whole thing down.

But it wasn't clear exactly what had happened. The dog had somehow finished up confined in a garage or shed with someone it considered very bad. The dog had no moral sense of good or bad. 'Bad' was a pragmatic description of anything or anyone who hurt or threatened her, 'good' was what gave her pleasure. Then the 'good boy' had somehow stopped the bad individual. Like all dogs, Daisy, could distinguish between men and women and between children and adults, but just who was the 'good boy'? And who was the 'bad man'?

She pondered and then finally decided. Rather than just dump the problem on Guy, who was already well occupied, her best plan was to go and find out what had happened without revealing her own identity. She went over to her computer and called up the secure satellite scan of the whole area provided by Peter's department. Daisy had been gone for less than two hours. She already knew that the only near and permanent dwelling was a small cottage about a mile and a half away. That was a likely suspect. She clicked on the image and a small window appeared beside it. She read: 'Hay Cottage: CE11 4AH. 78.4 square metres. Two bedrooms, no telephone. Owner: GoodFarms Industries. Occupants: Lynne Ellen Davies 40, Luke Davies 11, Charles, 'Chas', Garvey 28, Farm Labourer.' That could well be it.

She called Daisy. The dog woke up and stretched. "Daisy and Jess work time?" the speaker said.

"No, we're going in the car," Jess replied.

"The car, the car!" The speaker said happily. Daisy enjoyed going out in the car when they made their regular visits to the Canine Research Division headquarters. Jess would often allow her, securely fixed in a safety belt harness, to sit on the back seat and look out of the darkened rear windows. When they were using quiet back roads she would even give in to her entreaties to open the window so that the dog could stick her head out and allow the airflow to stream over her head.

"Jess and Daisy will go Central. 'Hello Mike. Hello Dave.'" The dog reminisced happily about its regular meetings with the staff of the Biomedical unit who checked its health.

"No," said Jess. "Daisy, look at me." The dog looked carefully at her. "Do you know Lynne?" No response. "Do you know Luke?" The dog sat up ears pricked. "Charles? Chas?" The dog stood up and began alternately growling and barking.

"OK," she said, "we've got that sorted, but…" there was no point in lying to the dog. "We'll have to go and check it out."

The dog looked distinctly unhappy and its ears drooped. "No, no," it said. "Me stay home."

"DAC32! " Jess said sharply. The dog's official designation was Digitally Articulated Canine number 32 and use of the acronym put it into its service mode. It was also evoked when she was put into a working harness. The dog stiffened. "DAC32 present!" it said.

"DAC32 and Handler will go and check Chas," Jess said. "We will assess location. And this time you'll wear your collar."

There was a pause, and then the speaker said. "Yes," and the dog went back to sit by the door.

Jess rang the day shift man, Joe, at the checkpoint. He answered immediately. He was a local man in his fifties, made redundant last year from his job delivering milk. "Morning Jess," he said cheerfully. It was hard to find a job in this mostly agricultural area and he was very happy to sit in the little hut at the inner gate and watch TV all day.

"I'm going out for a bit Joe," she said. "I'll be through in a minute."

"Righty'o, missy," he said. "I don't like to ask, but is that alright, with this security alert on?" He was competent at his job but always deferred to what he saw as her superior judgement.

"I think it'll be alright," she said. "The dog will be with me."

"If you think that's OK then," he said. "I suppose its just some kind of exercise or something, but I'll keep me eye open."

A few moments later Jess drove with the dog down to the checkpoint where Joe was waiting with the gate open, and they set off for Hay Cottage.

Chapter 18

Following the satnav, Jess turned the car right at the Stone House gate, then drove about a mile before she was directed to turn left up an even narrower lane. Another mile or so and by the side of the lane stood a small stone-built cottage fronted by a tiny untended garden. There was a rickety looking barn by the side but no sign of a garage.

Standing by the gate was a small boy. He looked about nine years old rather than eleven but she guessed it was Luke. She pulled up next to him. To be on the safe side she'd left the dog's speaker collar switched off and was wearing a single mini-earphone that allowed only her to hear the dog.

In her ear Daisy said, "Are we there? Where are we?" Fighting her instinct to compliment Daisy on her excellent grammar, she got out of the vehicle. The boy looked at her uncertainly.

"Hello," Jess said. "My name's Mrs..." She snatched a name out of her subconscious, "Duncan. Can I speak to your Mum?"

"Not here," said the boy reluctantly

"When is she coming back?"

"Dunno."

"Is there anyone else I can speak to?"

"Just me."

"Ok, fine. You wouldn't be Luke would you?"

"Yes." It never occurred to the boy to ask how she knew. Grown ups just knew things about you.

"Hello Luke. I'm Jess. I wonder if you can help me with a couple of questions?"

"What's that in your ear?" The question was used to satisfy curiosity rather than out of rudeness.

"Oh, I'm a little bit deaf. It helps me. Now what I wonder is, did you happen to see a stray dog recently, a little black and white cocker spaniel?"

The boy's attitude became even more defensive. "Why?"

At that moment Daisy barked from the back of the jeep and at the same time shouted in her ear, "It's good little boy! Good little boy!"

"What's that dog?" the boy asked hopefully. "Is it her? Is it the dog with the little hat?"

"It's me, me, me," shouted the dog in her ear. "Me come Jess."

"Can I see her?" he said. "Is she there? Is she OK?"

"Yes, she is," Jess said, "but the thing is that she's been a bit ill and there's this new treatment she's getting, with a special plaster."

"I know I know," said the boy. "Is she alright?"

"Yes," she said, "do you know what happened to her little hat, her plaster?"

"It wasn't my fault," he said. "It was Chas."

She waited. "Ok, where's Chas now?"

"I dunno, I don't know where he is. I don't know where Mum is." His lip trembled.

In her earpiece Daisy bawled, "Me come. Me come." Jess decided she might as well let the dog out. At least it would reassure the boy it had come to no harm.

Daisy tumbled out of the boot. The dog rushed over to him and as he knelt, put her paws on his chest and gave him a good face licking.

"She certainly knows you," Jess said.

"She does," he said proudly, "we're good mates we are, ain't we?"

Daisy's thrashing tail, and continuing attempts to lick his face, confirmed his claim.

"I tell you what," said Jess, "let's go in the house and wait for your Mum, and you can tell me what happened. I'd be really grateful. I was so worried while the dog was away."

"What's her name?" said the boy suddenly.

"Her name? It's Daisy."

The dog looked up at her

"Daisy. Daisy," he said, carefully stroking the dog. "I'm Luke." It was clear he was besotted with her, and the dog's response to him made it clear it was pretty much a match made in heaven.

They went into the house. She recognised the odour of souring milk. For once the dog trailed behind her. It stood outside the barn opposite the kitchen door, refusing to go in. "Bad garage," her earpiece said, Daisy's only previous experience of a small outside building was the one Jess used as a garage.

"Let's go in the kitchen," Jess said.

"Wait!" The earpiece said.

"What?" she said to the dog. The boy regarded her curiously.

"I know her so well," Jess explained. "I can almost read her mind."

Suddenly the dog ran down the path into the garden, head down. They started to follow but within moments it had returned. The dog looked back to Jess.

"Bad big man dead." Her earpiece announced.

"Dead!" Jess couldn't stop herself.

"Who's dead?" said the boy. He was clearly frightened.

"It's all right," Jess said, "I just come out with things."

Luke was terrified. "I didn't kill him," he said, "I didn't kill him. I just hit him a bit on the head. He was hurting Daisy. He had to stop." he started crying.

The dog had returned to its careful examination of the pathway. The two humans waited. Abruptly the dog looked up. "Revised assessment," it said in Jess's ear. "Man not dead." Jess could have sworn it sounded disappointed.

"It's alright," Jess said, "don't worry. I'm absolutely sure he's not dead. Just passed out or something I'm sure he's all right. Do you think your Mum took him to the hospital?"

The thought had never occurred to him. There was no phone to ring an ambulance and his mother would have had to walk to the main road to flag down a car. There was no bus to Tamborough on a Saturday.

"I dunno," he said. "Chas ain't got no car, just a bike. I went away for a bit. When I came back they were gone."

"I'm sure they're alright," Jess said. "But, you know, Daisy's really good at tracking. Perhaps she can help us."

"Daisy," she said. "Where did they go? Where did Chas go, where did Luke's Mum go?"

The dog started looking.

Daisy trotted past the open door of the barn. It had far too many bad memories and she carefully stayed on the path outside. There was lots of information here. The minute difference in the odour from the more recent tracks told her the direction of the person who'd made them. Chas had come out of the barn, walked down the garden path, then he had fallen down, and then his scent had changed. At first she had thought he was dead. Dead things had a very clear signature. Then she had realised he was not dead. But he had become very ill.

She sprinted further on down the path, head down and tail wagging furiously; tracking scent was the most exciting thing in the world to do. At the very bottom of the garden was a little hut. She paused to register the nice friendly smell of Luke emanating from it and then moved on. Then she stopped and snuffed more carefully, using the information mainlined to her brain from the additional receptors concentrated inside the roof of her mouth to wrestle coherence from the wealth of odours.

Behind the bad smell of Chas there were other signs. The signs were stronger now, fractionally more recent than those by the barn. Here 'Mum' had come, but the intermittent tracks showed she had walked and...there was another Big One! And another! Each was clearly identifiable. Both were men but each carried a pungent distinctive smell. She packed the identifications away in her memory and hurried on.

There was a considerable gap in the rusting metal fence at the end of the garden. Beyond this the trail stopped, to be replaced by the sharp smells of petrol and rubber. She was standing on a rough track that angled back to the lane. Chas was gone. 'Mum' was gone. Both the other humans were gone.

Jess and Luke were still following her down the path. Daisy started to make a report to Jess but she was excited, and without the feedback from a collar speaker it was hard for her to organise her vocalisations. She squeaked and whined.

"I tell you what," Jess said to Luke. "I think she's getting a bit excited. I think I'll just put her back in the car."

"No, no," said Daisy in her ear, "make report, make report."

"Yes, yes, Daisy," she said in front of the boy. "In the car. We'll make report in the car."

"It's just a phrase I use with her," she explained. She pointed to the car and the dog dashed off. She turned back to the boy. "Don't worry," she said, "I'll be back in a minute when I've settled her down."

"She knows what you say," he said, "don't she?"

"Oh yes," Jess said. "She's a little marvel really."

"She's lovely," said the boy, "wish she was mine."

The dog was standing by the car barking furiously.

"I'll be back in a minute," she said again, "do you think could you make us all a cup of tea?" Luke went into the cottage.

In the back of the car she quietly switched on the dogs collar speaker unit. "DAC32 make report," she said briskly.

"Modification of information. Bad big man not dead," Daisy announced. "But," she struggled a bit with the concept, "bad inside."

"Do you know, where is the man?"

"Big man is gone. Big woman is gone. In car. Not long time."

"In a car?" Jess said.

"In car," the dog agreed. "Come to car-gone place."

"No, I won't come yet." How did Chas get to a car? Luke's Mum couldn't have carried him. "Did you see anything else?"

The dog looked at her quizzically.

"I'm sorry," she said. "Continue report."

"Man gone. Woman gone. New big ones gone."

"New big ones! How many big ones? Count."

Without hesitation the dog replied "Two. Two men." It patted her hand twice with its paw to confirm the number.

"Identify."

The dog struggled with the thought then said, "Number one is..."

The collar speaker emitted a little warble. The powerful interpretation software in Jess's laptop had not yet been used to correlate this spike in neural activity with a word. She set up the laptop for a new addition to the dictionary. In the early days of differentiating the dog's neural activity this would have taken a lot of computer firepower, but with every successful addition to the dictionary, the process got simpler.

But she needed some kind of identifying word, and quickly. In the last few weeks she had begun to get clues that as its abilities developed the dog could generate its own words if given sufficient support.

"Show me the name," she said.

The dog stopped and thought, and then moved closer to her to nudge under her arm with its nose.

"Smell like me? No. Smell like under my arm. Sweat." She logged the new signal on the laptop then assigned the associated word into the memory of the cap on the dog's head. There was a tiny click and then the dog bounced around, tail wagging. "Sweat!" she agreed. "Big sweat."

Jess was inordinately proud of the dog's growing ability to devise a mime to communicate with her.

"And number two, report."

"Number two is in 'my-bag'." She pointed to Jess's handbag with her nose.

She immediately grasped what the dog was trying to do. She opened her handbag. The dog delicately nosed into the bag and withdrew a battered empty cigarette packet, the only remnant of Jess's determined effort to stop smoking.

"Smells like cigarettes, no, smells like tobacco, tobacco." Jess said. Again she identified the new signal on the laptop, assigned the word and logged in 'tobacco' to the cap output. "Yes, number two is ... Tobacco, tobacco." The dog confirmed, enjoying the new word.

Strange that it had never been necessary before to assign a word to such common and powerful identifier.

"I'm afraid sweat and tobacco are bad mans, I mean bad men," she said. The dog regarded her levelly, but said nothing.

Chapter 19

As Jess sat in the car trying to decide what to do, the dog suddenly pricked up its ears and turned to look back down the road. "What is it?" Jess said, but before the dog could answer she heard the sound of a vehicle. After a moment an unremarkable grey mid-size van came round the bend and stopped behind them.

"Voice off," Jess said quickly. The dog obediently stretched its neck to help her to press the tiny button that switched the collar speaker off. She checked that her mini earpiece was switched on instead, packed away the laptop, told Daisy to stay quiet, and got out of the car.

Two young men were getting out of the other car. They were both casually but smartly dressed. They walked towards her, smiling easily. The taller one had the well-groomed confident look that often went with private education and a well-paid job, but there was a weary hardness to him as if he were some sort of ex-soldier or policeman. Jess looked for Luke but there was no sign of him.

"Good afternoon." The taller man held out his hand. "It's Jess isn't it? Jess Stewart?"

"And you are?"

"Of course, let's get the old ID out. We're from Division Security. I'm Jackson." She glanced at it abstractedly. The other man held a card out too. "And this is Jones." The shorter man smiled but didn't speak. He stood back a little.

"And how can I help you?"

"It's more like how we can help you actually. I don't know if you're aware but there's a bit of security flap on. We've been sent over just to check that you and the dog are OK. We were a bit worried when you weren't at your place, so we set off for a little look round. Just to be on the safe side. Everything OK?"

In her ear Daisy said, "Tobacco."

"Yes fine," she said. "I'm so sorry to put you to all this trouble."

"No harm done." He smiled reassuringly. She smiled back.

"By the way, just for the report, how come you're down here Miss Stewart?" His voice had a little more edge to it. He smiled again. He was all smiles this one.

She thought quickly. "I was on my way to Central, I thought it would be safer than just sitting around. It's a bit of a back route. Anyway, as I came past this cottage, I saw a little boy just sitting crying by the road. Although I had Dai...the dog, aboard I felt I ought to stop and help. But he took one look at me and hared off." Out of the corner of her eye she saw the lace curtain of the kitchen window stir.

"Sounds reasonable," agreed Jackson. "What do you think, Jolly? Given recent events, perhaps we should drop a word to the local cop shop to pick him up. The lad's probably all right, look after himself, but you never know. It's pretty remote out here."

Jones nodded to Jackson, and then smiled at her, but still didn't say anything. Every so often he looked around casually.

In her earphone Daisy said, "Sweat, sweat and tobacco. And bad flowers."

"Anyway, if it's alright with you Jess," Jackson continued, "I'd like you to come back with us to BSDL. Just to reassure them that everything's OK."

"Shouldn't we look for the boy?"

"Well, I'd like to sort things out with you first. He's not really our business, your security is. The cops'll sort him out I'm sure."

"Yes of course," she said. "I'm so sorry for putting you to all this trouble. We psychologists aren't very good at this security stuff."

"No, no, not at all, truth is we probably fuss over it all too much, but at least it gives us work."

The other man laughed.

"So," said Jackson, suddenly all efficiency, "we'll go back in convoy. We'll lead. The dog's OK is he?"

"He's fine."

"Good. Right let's go." He paused. "I tell you what, Jolly, you go with Jess." He smiled to her. "We're supposed to follow these security protocols. Better do things properly. No comeback then, you know."

He went back to the grey van, got in, and, using a field gate entrance, began to perform a three-point turn. She returned to her jeep. Jones got in the other side and they waited to carry out the same manoeuvre. Jones smiled at her, then turned to look back at the dog, which sat quietly as instructed on the back seat.

"Hello little chap," he said. The dog looked at him calmly. "Sweat," it said in her ear.

"He's not saying much." He smiled at Jess.

"Not today." She smiled back at his little joke. "He ought to have his belt on but it's not far." She was aware of a tiny trace of body odour. She pushed the ignition button and the automatic door locks clicked into place.

They drove in silence for a minute or two, and then Jones picked up her iPhone, lying in the pocket between the front seats. "I'd love one of these," he said, turning it over, "but they won't agree the expense."

She looked in the rear view mirror. Behind her the dog was alternately looking out of the window and studying the back of Jones's head. "Sweat and tobacco," it said thoughtfully in her ear, "and bad flowers."

She tried to organise her thoughts. Could she trust them? If Daisy was right, and she must be right, the two men were the same ones that had previously carted off both Chas and Luke's mother. Had they come back to find the boy? Why didn't they know the dog was a bitch? If they were looking for her why hadn't they just rung her cell? Were they even from Canine Research Division at all? If they weren't from Division Security, they weren't after her, or Chas, or Luke's mum, or even Luke. They were after the dog. There was only one thing she could do.

As the van ahead came to the junction with the wider road, and began to turn right, she said to Jones, "Hang on a minute, sorry." She pulled over to the side of the road and drew the car to a halt. The tangled undergrowth of Grimm's Holes pressed close to the car. "What?" Jones started to say, as she said quickly and clearly, "DAC32 come to me, now!"

As the dog hopped through the gap between the front seats and into her lap, with her right hand she pulled the door handle twice to unlock it. With her left hand she tore off the little tracker unit clipped to the dog's collar, opened the door, and threw the dog out. Beside her, Jones was reaching over to pull her back but she had no intention of trying to escape. The dog got back on its feet and started to come towards her. The only safe place she could think of was back with Luke, hopefully still somewhere near the cottage. Had she mentioned his name in front of the men? She prayed not. "Go!" she shouted. "Go! Go! Find Luke. Go find Luke. Go now!"

She heard Jackson's van reversing back towards them, and Jones had freed himself from his seat belt but it was too late. The dog stood on the verge for a moment and looked up at her.

"DAC 32, go! Good girl. Go find Luke. Stay with Luke. Go! Go!" She repeated. The dog paused for a moment longer, looking up, then in her earpiece she heard softly,

"DAC32 is go." Then, "Bye, bye, Jess," and it was gone.

Chapter 20

Daisy was in shock. One minute she was in the car the next minute she was operational. She dived into the depths of Grimm's Holes, thick with untended growth. In a panic she dashed through the dense scrub and bushes, up and down the precipitous slopes made by ancient piles of quarry spoil, as behind her she heard shouts and the sounds of car engines revving, then she stopped as she realised she had no idea where she was going.

She looked back but there was only silence. She considered returning to Jess. Then she picked up the sounds of someone moving through the bushes behind her. She could even hear them muttering, "Shit, shit and bugger," whatever that meant. Then louder, "DAC32, come on, come to me, good boy." The clear signal of his odour confirmed it was Sweat.

For a moment this put her in a bit of a quandary, any instruction prefaced by 'DAC32' was a direct order, but she'd never heard anyone but Jess issue it before. She swiftly decided it didn't count, anyway Jess had said Sweat was bad. She wasn't going to him. She ran on deeper and deeper into the undergrowth. Then she dimly heard the voice of Tobacco. "Give up. You'll never find it. It'll be heading to Luke, whatever that means. For now it's more important to find Stewart. Let's go!"

Sweat shouted, "She's broken my fucking hip!" She heard Sweat moving away, then the sound of the car engine and then silence. She waited a long time and then crawled out from under the bush and listened again, nothing. She felt a bit worn out by all the excitements of the past few minutes so she sat back on her haunches and had a good scratch of her ear. When she was finished she felt a bit calmer she got up and started moving again.

Now it was time to find Luke, as instructed. The last time she had seen him was at the cottage so that was the place to look for. She didn't spend any more time thinking about it. Her brain had evolved not for rational thought but to make instant decisions based on a constant stream of sensory input to her olfactory system, which was almost incomprehensibly more powerful and complex than a mere human nose.

She set about orienting herself, running in long loops and curves, head down, to take up the wealth of information under her nose. Dogs are not naturally very good at finding their way and many lost dogs just stay lost, but she was a highly skilled tracker and the trails were new and obvious to her. After only a minute or two, dutifully ignoring a host of fascinating trails and old scents, she had located Sweat's track and by a kind of triangulation had found her way back to the edge of the copse. She stepped out onto the lane that led to the cottage.

She lifted her head and swung it round, taking deep breaths. She recognised the lane she had walked along with Luke earlier that morning and there was a strong clear note of wood smoke from the burner in the kitchen of the cottage a mile away. Without even noticing the additional information she was getting from the direction of the breeze and the angle of the sun, she confidently followed the smell back up the lane and away from the major road. Loping along with increasing speed she soon arrived back at the cottage, sides heaving. She went through the little open gate, down the passage past the barn, made a quick check and then headed confidently down towards the little hut at the end of the garden.

Chapter 21

After the two vehicles left the cottage, Luke tried to come up with a plan but his mind was a blank. There was still no sign of his mother or Chas. The nice woman and the dog were gone. When he'd heard the van approaching he'd decided to wait quietly in the kitchen until he could understand what was going on. At first he'd thought the two men were the police, but he could see through the lace curtain that they'd arrived in a van, and anyway they didn't look anything like policemen. Now, while he waited for his mother, he decided to go to his den. It was a little hut constructed using cut logs as bricks, with a plywood roof and a small narrow door. He had put it together soon after Chas arrived. It was the only place that was his alone, a welcome escape from Chas's taunts and the noises he made with Luke's mother when he took her upstairs on Sunday afternoons. After a time he stretched out on the little old mattress that was its only furniture and went to sleep.

He was woken by a small dog standing on his chest and licking his nose. He reached up and cuddled the dog to him. "Daisy!" he said. "Where you bin gel? Where is Mrs Duncan?" The dog ignored him and continued to give him a good licking, tail wagging. "Daisy," he said, struggling to get up, "where is Jess? Is she in the car?" The dog gave a squeak and stopped wagging its tail. He got up and the dog trotted along beside him up the garden path. No sign of Jess, no sign of anything or anybody.

"Where you bin? Where is she?" He repeated. The dog sat a on its haunches and looked into his eyes, its tail made nervous little wagging movements. Then it barked and stretched its neck. His eye was drawn to its collar. It was surprisingly substantial collar for such a small dog. It seemed to be made of very hard black plastic. He looked more closely. Part of it was what looked like a tiny speaker, and there were lots of other little bumps and lumps on the surface, even some tiny letters and numbers, and a little button. Without thinking he pressed the button and the collar said, "Hello. Testing. Testing, one two three."

Chapter 22

When the dog vanished into the undergrowth, Jess had slammed her door shut and pushed hard down on the accelerator, swinging to her left to avoid Jones, who'd sprinted round to her side of the car. Even so she hit his hip a glancing blow as she took off, the engine howling.

    She looked in the rear view mirror but for the moment they weren't pursuing her. They were probably looking for Daisy. She was trying to think what to do next. Jones still had her phone but at least it didn't have her contact numbers for CRD Central on it. They were all securely logged on the direct line back at the cottage. She had no option but to go back to her base, warn Joe to full alert and contact them from there. She was becoming quite optimistic that she could pull it off.

    Then she looked in the mirror again. The van had appeared behind her and was catching up fast. She dropped the semi-automatic a gear and put her foot down hard. She took another look in the rear view mirror. They were only a couple of car lengths behind her and the skill with which the vehicle behind was being driven was terrifying. How could she hope to beat people who were professionally trained for stuff like this?

    The car rocked from side as she tried to navigate a series of tight bends at speed. Unconsciously she was muttering, " Shit, oh shit, oh shit!" but her suicidal speed seemed to be getting results. She looked in the mirror and they were actually a little further back. Then she realised they were simply matching her speed. As long as they had her in sight they could simply wait until she ran out of resolution, or fuel.

    As this sickening realisation hit her, the car clipped the high near side verge, bounced, crossed the road and was suddenly sliding gracefully into Grimm's Holes. She sat paralysed for a moment and then pushed the automatic to neutral. As she tried to brake, the car rocked and bounced down a steep incline, miraculously missing some substantial trees, finally to roll gently to a stop with the front wheels in a cheerful little stream. Above her, Jackson was hidden by the vegetation, but she could hear him shouting. "Over here, over here!" He sounded panicked.

She felt a small spark of triumph. He didn't sound so professional now. She slipped the seat belt and half fell out of the door. She wasn't injured in any way, or even shaken up, but she was shivering with shock at the suddenness of the accident. More by reflex than conscious thought she threw herself under the car. She didn't believe in God but she thanked someone for the fact that she was wearing dark unremarkable clothing. "Please, please," she muttered as she heard the men scrambling down the steep slope towards her.

An hour later she was standing at the outer gate to The Stone House. She felt sticky and tired but triumphant. The men had come down to the car, and searched it quickly without it apparently occurring to them that she might simply be under it.

They had moved further and further away from her in their search until, when she judged they were far enough away, she had carefully scrambled back up the slope to their van. She would have taken it if they had left the keys in but that had been too much to hope for. Without her cell phone she realised the only way she could communicate with Peter was to get back inside The Stone House. There had been no option but to walk the rest of the way back.

The gate was closed to, but now it swung open with a push. There was no sign of Joe, the security man in the little gatehouse. She ran down the drive to the house, serenely observed by the horse, through the back garden and up the path to the back door. She went in to her office and buzzed Joe.

"Come back Joe," she said, "it's me, come back please," but there was no reply. She was now very frightened. She hit the fast dial for Canine Division Security. The landline answered immediately and she identified herself. "Hello Jess," a voice replied, "Duty Office here, its Sean. Glad you've called back. We were a bit worried about you. Peter's tied up at the moment can I help you?"

"Listen Sean," she said. "This is urgent. I've lost my gate man. Two men have approached me. They claim to be from security but I've good reason to believe they're fake. I've managed to get away from them but I need immediate support. I need protection."

"Is the dog OK?"

"She's not with me at the moment, but I'm pretty sure she's safe. Can you send someone out to me right away, and we can pick her up?"

"Bloody hell, this is bad." The duty officer's voice had lost its reassuring tone. "Really bad. But don't worry, the thing is, try to stay calm. We'll go straight into emergency procedure now. Meantime can you describe them, did they give any names?"

"They called themselves Jackson and Jones," she said, "sweat and tobacco."

"Sorry," said the duty officer, "I didn't get that last bit."

"Doesn't matter, the main thing is I need help now. There's no sign of my gate security man and I'm pretty sure they're going to be here any minute."

"Well," said the officer after a long pause. "The thing is, according to what I have here, two men were already assigned to come to you this morning to boost security while this flap is on. And the thing is they're listed as Jackson and Jones. They are your protection. They're our people."

At that moment there was a crash as the kitchen door slammed open.

Chapter 23

Back at Hay Cottage, Daisy and Luke sat and looked at each other. He had been completely thrown by the sudden statement from the collar. He held his mouth close to it. The dog waited patiently.

"Hello," he said. "Hello. Is that you Jess? It's me. It's Luke. Where are you?"

"Me here," said the collar. The dog wagged its tail.

"Where are you?" he said, looking round. "Are you close?"

"Me here!" the speaker shouted. "Me, me, me!" Meanwhile the dog danced about, even dropping its chest and extending its front legs in an invitation to play.

"Jess, where are you?"

The dog abruptly stopped inviting him to play and sat down soberly.

"Jess gone." The speaker said sadly. He realised the voice was not that of an adult woman but of girl of about eight or nine.

An extraordinary and incredible thought came to Luke. He felt quite dizzy.

"Daisy," he said, "is that you?"

The dog looked at him and seemed to find the question difficult to comprehend. Well of course it would, he thought. It knows its name's Daisy.

The tiny speaker in the collar hissed and warbled for a moment or two as the dog seemed to pull itself together and then it said, "DAC32 make report?"

"Make report?" Luke repeated.

The dog seemed reassured. It stood up almost to attention. "Yes! DAC32 make report. Little time ago, Jess is in car, Sweat is in car, Daisy is in car. No detected armament."

"Daisy," he said. "Is that you speaking?"

The dog paused as if to concentrate and the collar continued, "Jess stop car. Jess give order; 'DAC32 Go!' DAC32 find...'" The collar gave a few chirrups. "Me go. Me find..." More chirrups. "Jess gone," it concluded sadly.

The dog dropped onto all fours and put its head in its paws. "Me hungry," the collar said as an aside.

Luke's heart thumped. It was true! The collar was the dog speaking. Wait until his Mum saw this. The thought of Chas discovering it too cast a brief shadow over his thoughts but he quickly dismissed that worry. The main thing was that Jess had sent the dog to give him a message. But was it in code? The message was incomprehensible.

"Shall I get you something to eat then?" The dog sat up and wagged its tail enthusiastically, it's depression apparently forgotten and followed him into the kitchen.

"Yes, yes, Chunky Chunks," the collar said, but by now it felt as if the dog was speaking.

"Chunky chum?"

The dog looked exasperated. "Chunky Chunks, please."

"I'm sorry gel," he said, "we ain't got none of that."

"Me not girl," said the dog, "me Daisy."

"Well Daisy, we ain't got none of that."

"Got no that?"

"No. Got no Chunky Chunks, or whatever it is."

"Rustlers?"

The dog might be able to speak, but a lot of what it said didn't make any sense at all. "You can have some of Chas's bacon and eggs," he said at last. Bugger what Chas might say, if he made any trouble, Luke would just hit him on the head with a log, and punch him in his fat gut. He could do anything now. He had a friend.

The dog waited patiently while he fried up the remaining eggs and bacon. He made some toast too. When it popped out of the toaster with a ping, the dog sat up brightly and said, "Toast!"
He buttered the toast, heaped a couple of eggs and a couple of rashers of bacon on each slice, and split the food between them. He put the dog's portion on the floor but the dog was diffident, watching the food carefully. "What's the matter?" he said. "You said you were hungry. Don't worry about Chas, he's gone." Though,

he thought nervously, he might well be back any minute. Best to eat the bacon and eggs while they could.

After a moment the dog apparently conquered its diffidence and started wolfing the meal down. Luke stuffed his portion down, he was ravenous, but down on the floor the dog had finished long before him, and licked the plate clean too.

"Toast!" It announced. "Good!"

"And bacon and egg. Can you say bacon and egg?"

"Book, black, leg," the dog said uncertainly.

"No. Bacon." He enunciated carefully.

The dog said nothing. "Bacon," Luke said even more carefully. Nothing.

Surely the dog wasn't stupid? More likely it was his fault. He just didn't know how to teach it. He should start like they did in films when you met a native on a desert island or somewhere.

"You Daisy," he said, pointing to the dog. The dog wagged its tail.

"Daisy," it agreed.

He pointed to himself. "Me, Luke."

The dog wagged its tail again. It came closer to him and looked up at him with those intense knowing eyes.

"You…" And then it just produced a warbling sound.

"Me, Luke." But the only response was same warbling sound.

"You can't say it can you. You can't say Luke."

"No," the dog agreed, clearly disappointed with itself.

It struggled to articulate a thought. Eventually it said sadly, "If cannot speak… Cannot…say." They both fell silent.

Luke felt a bit down. He'd found this wonderful dog that could speak, but he couldn't understand most of what it said, and he didn't know how to teach it any different. The dog watched him carefully. It seemed to sense that his mood had darkened. It came closer and tugged at his trouser leg to catch his attention. He looked down.

"Me Daisy," it said. Then it leapt up onto his lap and licked his nose.

"And you…You…" it was perceptibly struggling to produce a word, then suddenly its tail began to wag furiously. "Chunky!" it said loudly, and leapt off his lap. " You Chunky!"

It presented itself, chest down, tail high and wagging. "Come, Chunky!" it said. "Come play with Daisy!"

The dog ran through to the little front room and leapt on to an armchair. "Here is me house! No Chunky in me house!" It growled amiably. Luke couldn't believe it. After all that it had gone through this morning, the dog was up for some rough and tumble.

He suddenly wanted to forget all his worries and join the world of the dog. No worries, no looking back, no agonising about the future. He fell onto all fours and advanced towards the chair, growling. "Oh no, little dog," he shouted. "Here comes Chunky to take your house!"

With a delighted bark the dog leapt down and rolled over onto its back beside him. They wrestled back and forth and after a while he lost himself in delicious mindless contact with the warm furry animal. For a few blessed moments he forgot all about Chas, or his Mum, or indeed anything else.

Chapter 24

As the door slammed Jess put the phone down, stood up, and went into the kitchen of the Stone House. Jackson was standing in the outer doorway. Behind him Jones was leaning slightly to one side to take the weight off his hip.

"Sorry to barge in Miss Stewart. Needs must. Are you alright?" The question was solicitous but not the tone.

"I'm alright," she said, as firmly as she could. She went and stood by the kitchen table. She surreptitiously gripped the edge to steady herself.

"Good. You took quite a tumble back there. Are you sure you're all right?"

"Nothing a shower and change won't fix."

"Good again. But before you take your ablutions, would you mind sitting down a moment?"

She sat down on one of the old kitchen chairs at the table and a moment later he sat down opposite. Limping slightly Jones moved to stand behind her. She was dimly aware of a whiff of body odour as he leaned closer. They're all set to interrogate me, she thought. She suddenly realised how horribly quiet it was in the kitchen. The familiar background hum of Daisy's scanner had gone.

"Now..." Jackson said carefully. "Can you give me a legitimate and logical explanation for what happened back there?"

"Never mind that. Who are you?" she said.

"Who are *you*?" he said.

"What do you mean?"

He leaned back on the ancient kitchen chair then sat forward again as it gave a warning creak.

"Well, at this moment, your behaviour suggests that either you're not Jess Stewart, or else you *are* Jess Stewart but you are no longer one of Her Majesty's loyal citizens. Or perhaps, although it seems unlikely, you're having a nervous breakdown."

"Don't be ridiculous," Jess retorted.

"Whatever it is, you have attacked personnel and much more important you have endangered the safety of yourself, your client, and the security of an important and very expensive project. Are you working for someone?"

"That's even dafter! And I didn't attack anyone."

Jackson looked past her to Jones. "I should ask Jolly about that."

She resisted the urge to turn round.

"Who or what is Luke? Where's the dog now?" Jackson said gently.

There was another silence. Behind Jackson the stone sink was still full of this morning's washing up. It seemed an age ago. She had a sudden overwhelming urge for a cup of coffee.

"How do I know you're really from Security?"

"Check! Or haven't you done that already?"

"The names are real," she conceded reluctantly.

"That's because we're real!" Behind her Jones gave a snort.

"Well then, give me my phone back."

With a blast of B.O. over her shoulder, Jones's hand appeared and put her cell phone on the table. "I must get one of those," he said. Mercifully he stepped back. She picked the phone up and looked at it, as if it could somehow tell her the right thing to do.

"Do you mind?" Jackson said suddenly, taking out a pack of cigarettes. "Everyone says it's a terrible habit and they're right, but I've had a terrible day."

He lit his cigarette and snapped the lighter shut. She fought the urge to take a breath of the smoke around him.

"I tell you what," he said, "let's take it gently. Let's assume you're not mad and you are Jess Stewart, and you're not working for someone. Why did you chuck the dog out of the car?"

Before she could stop herself she burst out. "What did you do with Chas, and Luke's mum?"

"Ah, so Luke was the 'little boy crying in the road'," Jackson said. "Only he didn't run away did he? And you thought we'd done some dark deed with his parents." He looked above her again to

Jones. "Do you know, Jolly, there might almost be a credible explanation for all this? I'm getting more optimistic by the minute."

He turned to her, sending over another plume of tobacco smoke. "Now listen; when we originally came over to check your security, we came by the back lane. It's less obtrusive than the main road. Good for us. When we passed the cottage where your little chum Luke lives, a woman was standing in the middle of the road weeping."

"I had to stop." Jones said glumly. "Once she'd seen us."

"Hush Jolly," Jackson said. "He means we had to stop once we'd seen her. She was almost hysterical, desperate. She didn't mention a boy, but she led us to bottom of her garden where we found a man collapsed. He didn't look good. It looked like he'd had a heart attack or something. She asked if we could get him to the local hospital."

"She begged us," Jones grunted again.

"Yes," Jackson agreed piously. "We all have our public duty."

"We had no choice anyway," Jones muttered.

"Precisely," Jackson said, "and on the way to the hospital the woman rambled on that the whole thing was the fault of some stray dog, still no mention of a boy though. The dog was a cocker spaniel," she said, "with a little plastic hat on its head. That's when we got really interested in the cottage. And when we get back there, we bump into guess who."

"Why didn't you tell me all this?"

"Not our business, not your business. Besides we weren't too sure about you, we still aren't."

"Shouldn't you ring the hospital and see what's happening?"

"I'm sure he'll be alright. Let's pick up little DAC first, and maybe we can get the boy back to his Mum as well. Where are Luke and the dog now?" He watched her carefully, the cigarette smoke gently drifting up in the still air of the kitchen.

The possibility was steadily growing in her mind that perhaps she'd got it all wrong. She never had been good at judging people. Maybe they really were from Security. She wavered. "Probably somewhere near the cottage."

"Well done. Let's get back there," Jackson said abruptly.

"But shouldn't you contact Security at Central?"

"I'll handle that. Let's get moving. I want that dog secured, and the boy. It's getting dark. We haven't got a lot of time, but we won't panic. We never panic."

He stood up and drew her to her feet. "You'd better come with us."

They hurried her out the front door to where their van was parked. The evening light had almost all gone. They scrunched over the gravel of the drive and got in, Jones wincing as he took the driving seat. Jess squeezed into the back. The van's deodoriser had an unlikely and unlovable floral scent. Daisy's 'bad flowers', she thought. The van swept down to the gatehouse. The gate now stood open, but there was still no sign of Joe.

"Where's Joe?" she said.

"I wish I knew," said Jackson. "That's something else to sort out." Jones gunned the engine and they shot off down the narrow road.

When they reached the cottage. Jess got out quickly and was first down the path to the back door. "Luke," she called, "it's me, Jess. Are you there?" She tried the door but it was locked.

"I don't think there's anyone in there," she said.

"Needs must," Jones said behind her. "Move over miss." He prepared to throw his weight against the door.

"Hang on Jolly," Jackson said. "It's usually somewhere close." He bent down flipped over a small chopping block next to the door and picked up the key. Jones just grunted.

Jackson unlocked the door and the two men went straight through the empty kitchen to check all the rooms. Jess stood in the kitchen and looked round. A piece of paper was sticking out of the only object on the draining board, a small teapot. She took the paper out and read it. It said, 'Dear Mum. Me and Daisy have gone to Aunty Gwen, till you come back. Luke.' As Jackson came back into the room she thrust the note into her pocket. Her phone rang. It was the duty officer from Canine Division.

"Jess, is that you?"

"Yes," she said.

"This is Sean again, Have you got the dog?"

"No."

"Are the two men with you?"

"Yes."

"Really? Christ! Wherever you are get the hell out. There's been a terrible mistake. Those two aren't ours. They're hit men. Get out, get out now!"

The knowledge that her intuition about the two men had been correct was even more devastating than when she first mistrusted them. They stood quietly watching her. She took a deep breath. "OK. Fine, thanks," she said finally. "We're sorting it out. Full report soon." She turned the phone off.

"Security?" said Jackson.

"Yep, I don't know why they're calling me instead of you." Her voice trembled very slightly, and she took another careful deep breath. "I'm right in it now. I can't see me making Senior Scientific Officer."

"Don't be too hard on yourself. We'll have to do some explaining too, spooking you. We can work together on this. If we can just trace that dog."

Her phone rang again. Jackson took it from her smoothly, "It's Security again by the look of it. Let me spread some oil on the waters. Hello?"

At that moment there was a brisk rap on the door. They all froze. There was another knock and a voice shouted, "Oi! Chas boy. It's the bad lads! Time for your fruit juice!" The speaker chuckled at his own wit, and another voice shouted, "Come on Linney, kick the bugger out. We'll look after him!" From the lane there was the sound of a car revving and the thumping of music that seemed to be all bass notes. Both men tensed.

Jess took the phone back from Jackson. He didn't seem to notice. Her heart was thumping like the car radio.

"Let me sort it out," she said. "They're local boys, I know them. Just wait here."

Before the two men could answer, she opened the door, slipped out, and closed it behind her. In front of her stood two young men, both wearing identical regulation Saturday Night Out outfits of narrow jeans, running shoes, and open neck shirt, left to hang out. She couldn't see much difference between their faces either. They stared at her in amazement.

She put her finger to her lips. "Follow me." Obediently they trailed after her as she walked over to their car. It was a beautifully polished bright red Ford Fiesta, at least ten years old. Various things had been done to it. The side windows were blacked out, the chassis nearly touched the road, and it emitted a throaty rumble as it ticked over.

"Hello guys," she said, putting her hand on the shoulder of one of them and leaning in the window. The man driving the car reeked of aftershave. Daisy could have trailed him from half a mile away. Mercifully, he turned the music down. "Listen to me," she said urgently. She tried to roughen her accent. "There's bin bad business here. There's a couple of fellas after Chas. I think they're cops."

"What?" said the driver vaguely. "Who are you?"

"Fucking Chas," said the young man behind her. "He's such a fucking geezer. Is it drugs?" The other young man laughed.

Inspired, she picked up the thread. "My fault, bad deal. The thing is they're in the house now!"

"What?" said the driver.

"Lynne and Chas are well away, but they want to talk to anybody that can help them."

"Won't get no help from us, don't worry," the young man behind her said.

"No way," said the other. He sounded excited.

"We'll take 'em on," said the man behind her.

"Don't talk daft Spaz," said the other man. "Let's just get the fuck out. If they are cops, I'm carrying a little smoke here."

"Me too," said the driver. "Fuck it."

Over her shoulder Jess could see front window curtains twitch.

She turned toward the man behind her, smiling broadly for the benefit of the watchers, and leaned into him. "They haven't ID'd me yet, or you. Just help me to get the fuck out of here, please." She looked into his eyes. "I'll make it worth your while. Chas'll tell you. But be quick."

"Who are you? How do we know there's even anybody in there?" said the driver.

The whole discussion had taken just 45 seconds. Without a word she opened the rear door of the car and got in. The two young men stood for a moment undecided and then the back door opened and Jackson and Jones ran up the path.

"Stop, I'm an officer!" Jackson shouted.

"Oh fuck, they *are* cops," said the driver. "Let's go!"

The other two tumbled into the car, "Go, go, go," they screamed.

And the car roared off into the gathering night.

Chapter 25

By the time that Luke and Daisy got to Tamborough, it was dark and well into the evening. He was feeling pleased with himself. He'd packed his little rucksack with a clean shirt and underwear, left a note for his Mother, and neatly locked up the house, leaving the key in the special place.

He had managed to push the saddle of Chas's bike right down to the frame, and taken the old basket they used to store logs by the fire and wired it to the front. It had been a bit perilous to lift Daisy into it and keep the bike upright, and even more perilous to keep it balanced in the first awkward seconds before he got up to speed, but they had made it.

Most nights of the week, as is the way with small towns all over Britain, the centre of the little town would be almost completely deserted, but now it was Saturday night and the streets were busy. The normally empty restaurants were doing good business as people rewarded themselves for their efforts during the week. The pubs were busy too, and in the relative warmth of the spring evening, groups of young drinkers were already standing in the pools of light from the street lamps to enjoy a cigarette and check out the talent. Daisy watched it all in fascination as they cycled by.

Eventually they arrived in the little street of two-up two-down terraced brick cottages in which his aunt lived. Luke miraculously managed to get off the bike without crashing, and held it steady for Daisy to jump out of the basket. She immediately began checking out the interesting mix of dog urine signals and tracks of passers-by. The light was on in Auntie Gwen's front room.

He wheeled the bike down the narrow tunnel between his aunt's house and the one next door, and Daisy trotted after him. He leant the bike against the wall by the back door and bent down to her. She wagged her tail. "Listen," he said, "I don't think you should speak in front of Auntie Gwen. She won't understand. I'd better take your collar off."

The dog backed away. "Where is Jess?" it said, slightly nervously. "Me go now, go to Jess now."

"Listen," he said, squatting down beside her and giving her a rather awkward cuddle. "It's alright. We'll find Jess tomorrow. But tonight we'll stay here. You'll like Auntie Gwen. She'll give us some dinner."

At the mention of dinner, the dog seemed to relax. He was about to take the collar off when a voice came through the door.

"What is it?" It was his aunt. "What do you want?" There was a pause. "I can call the police you know."

"It's alright Auntie Gwen," he said, "it's me. I've come to visit."

A woman in her late sixties, comfortably dressed in slacks and a sweater, opened the door.

"Hello," said Daisy conversationally.

The woman ignored her. "What's the matter? Where's your Mum? Are you alright? Come on in. Is that dog with you? I can't have it in here with Polly."

At that moment the cat solved the problem as a ball of black fur shot from between her feet and past them down the garden.

Daisy turned to watch the cat sprint. "Black," she said with interest.

"You don't often see Poll move like that," his aunt said. "You come in now, and we'll sort you out."

"I just wanted to visit. Everything's fine," Luke said.

"Well that's a relief. Though you pick some strange times. If that Chas would let Linney have a mobile, she could have let me know. You go and sit down and I'll make you a nice cup of tea. Did you get your bike fixed then?"

He followed her into her little kitchen and through to the cosy front room lined with glass fronted cupboards stuffed with souvenirs. Daisy trotting on ahead, tail wagging high and all curiosity for this new source of sights and smells. He sat on the leather settee. On his Aunt's big old television a small group of people were attempting to pass soft toys to one another, despite wearing large comic masks which impeded their vision. "I always watch 'Top Family' on a Saturday," his aunt called from the kitchen, "load of rubbish."

Daisy took a brief look at the screen and turned away. The noise was meaningless and the strange movements and colours on the screen were disturbing. To a creature whose flicker fusion point was over 80 frames a second, the 26 frames of the elderly TV screen were a meaningless succession of flickering still images. She went and sat on the floor next to Luke, carefully facing away from it.

His aunt came in with his tea and turned the sound down on the television set. Now he was able to hear the sound of his aunt's old-fashioned clock ticking on the mantelpiece. Daisy looked up at it.

"Now, you just drink this, and tell me what's going on. It's not like you to turn up in the middle of the night. It's three sugars, how you like it. You shouldn't be out on your own this time of night. Have you run away? Is your Mum all right? Is it that Chas?" Daisy growled.

"Does that little dog need water?" she said. "Is it yours? What's up with its head? What's its name?"

"Daisy," the dog said.

"Oh, now that is clever," his aunt said, not missing a beat, "it's just like it was talking. How does it work, is it a nap, like on Eric's tablet?" Eric was the teen-age boy who lived with the family next door. "It's amazing what they can do these days. Where's the control? Make it do it again. I should get one for Polly."

"Me thirsty," said Daisy.

"Oh Luke, you are clever," his aunt marvelled. "You should go into computers or something like that. I'll get it a drink of water." She went into the kitchen.

Luke quickly bent down to the dog. "Sorry," he said, "but we must turn this off. Just for a little while."

"We will proceed with caution," the dog said crisply and offered its head for him to press the button on the collar.

"What did it say?" His aunt called from the kitchen. "Come in here and have a drink sweetheart."

The dog obediently trotted into the kitchen and slurped down the water, leaving puddles over the floor.

"He's a lovely little dog but they do make a mess don't they?"

Daisy looked up at her, and then came back into the little lounge to give Luke a meaningful look.

"It's a she actually," he said. "You can't tell with all that hair."

"Is it yours? I'm surprised Chas let you have it. Where's Linney? Where's your Mum?"

He was tempted to tell her the whole story there and then, but surely it would be better to leave the details, whatever they were, for his Mum to explain when she came to fetch him. He had an inspiration.

"That's why I came to you," he said. "I'm looking after it for someone It's not well. Mum says it's OK, but Chas said no."

"Trust him," his aunt observed dryly.

"Mum said it would be best to come to you with it until she persuades him. She'll be here soon."

"I wish he'd let her have a bloody phone, not that there's ever a signal out there in the middle of nowhere," his aunt grumbled. "Anyway, it's good that you're looking after it. You're a good lad. It likes you an' all. It listens to every word you say. Make it say something again."

"No," he said, "I won't just now, if you don't mind."

"Just as you like, now why don't I make you some nice egg and chips?"

The dog squeaked. "Do you think Daisy could have some too?" Luke said.

Chapter 26

As the car carrying Jess and the three young men roared away from Hay Cottage, the men with her were shouting, "Oh, fuck!" and giggling hysterically.

"Go! Go! You crazy fucker!" the man next to her kept shouting.

The driver turned the radio up again; "She think she so ratchet when she take that lean," it chanted, and they all joined in, "But she just thot. You *knows* what ah mean!" They all laughed again.

"We has the feds beat!" one shouted.

"I think they'll follow us," Jess shouted over the din.

"Don't worry," said the man squeezed in beside her, "Neck knows the back ways. He was born and bred round 'ere. We all was."

"Neck?"

"Yeah, Neck. That's Neck," indicating the driver.

"Why?"

"I dunno. He's just Neck. Always has been." He guffawed and joined in again. "You *knows* what ah mean!"

To the raucous vocal accompaniment, the little car careened down the lanes, exhaust growling, sometimes abruptly turning up dirt tracks, and then popping out again onto hard-core roads. Jess was completely disoriented, she tried to use her phone but there was no signal.

After a while, the driver eased the car to a halt and turned the radio off, and then the lights. The sun had finally slid over the horizon to be replaced by masses of thick cloud and the darkness and the silence were complete. They all sat and listened. Nothing. The man sitting next to Jess lit a cigarette and offered her one. She was tempted but managed to hold off.

"What a gas, Neck," said the man sitting next to him. "You is the man."

It occurred to Jess that for three rural labourers from the depths of South Lincolnshire, they all seemed determined to talk like the exiled inhabitants of a Los Angeles ghetto.

"Hang on," said Neck. He turned from the driving seat to face her. "I want to know what's going on here." Jess realised he was a bit older than the others. "I know all the dealers, and I ain't never seen you before. How come you ain't got no car? How come you was out there, middle of nowhere. Where's Chas?"

"He loves Chas," mocked the man next to her.

"Fuck off Chip, you pencil prick," Neck said amiably.

"Look," Jess said, "I really want to thank you for this."

"She just wants an excuse to be out with three big lads in the dark," said the man next to the driver.

Jess didn't like the little pause that followed.

"Spaz is right. You could show a bit of gratitude, I suppose," said the man next to her, almost shyly. All three laughed, but there was an edge to it.

"Get it out, has your fun, but don't forget to pull the zipper *up!*" chanted the man next to Neck. The man next to her giggled and tentatively put his hand on her thigh.

"Watch his hands, love. Chip is a registered perv," Neck said.

Jess decided it was time to get the situation under control. She firmly removed Chip's hand from her thigh. "OK," she said in her best middle class voice, "I'll come clean. But you have to understand. This is absolutely confidential. I'm going to make just one call, and I want you to listen to what I say." She took her iPhone out of her pocket. Her handbag was long gone.

"Cool phone," said the man next to her.

She had been prepared to fake a conversation but mercifully the phone was at last showing a weak signal. She hit reply on the number the duty officer had used to call her. He picked up immediately. "Hello," she said. "This is Special Agent Stewart speaking." The men around her stiffened perceptibly.

"Is that you Jess?" he said. "Special what? Are you all right? Thank goodness. Where are you? We've been trying to trace you."

"I'm OK," she said. "I don't know exactly where I am but I'm in a country lane four or five miles from Stone House. I managed to get clear of Jackson and Jones, entirely due to the efforts of three young men. They're with me now, I want them rewarded." The three young heroes exchanged glances.

"Thank God. This is a bad one. We've found the real Jones and Jackson tied up in a shed. Whoever you've been dealing with, they're not ours. Keep out of their way and keep away from the Stone House. Just tell us where you are now and we'll get people to you to pick you up. Did you find the dog?"

"I had to get her away," she said. "I'm pretty sure she's in a safe house, but I don't know the exact location. I need a search." She remembered them saying things like 'safe house' in spy thrillers. "I only have a first name, Gwen, living somewhere within say ten, no, check out within fifteen miles of local base."

"Gwen. Isn't that Linney's aunt, lives in Tamborough?" said Spaz.

The others hushed him, they were fascinated by every word she said.

"What was that?" the duty officer said, "didn't catch that." She was about to repeat the name when she had a sudden pin sharp image of Jones giving her phone back. Could they have put a tracer of some kind in it? Could they even hear what she was saying? She had no idea.

She muffled the phone to her chest and spoke to the one called Spaz. "Do you know where she lives?"

"Yeah, no problem," he said. "We can take you there if you want."

"I tell you what," she said to the duty officer. "I think I've solved that problem. I'll call in when I get there."

"OK, but are you sure you're well clear of those two? Do they know where you are? Is 32 OK?"

"She's safe," she said, "me too, thanks to the guys I'm with." The men exchanged the wry smiles of heroes.

"Look. We..." She was careful to stress the 'we'. "We're heading for the safe location now. I don't think Jackson and Jones, whoever they really are, have got as much info as I have, but I'm really worried that they'll find her."

"Oh they'll find her alright," said the duty officer, "the only thing is can you get there first?"

She rang off. "You might have said you was Jane Bond," Spaz said.

Chapter 27

At Canine Division headquarters, Peter Guy came into Blake's office. "OK," Blake said, "where are we up to now?"

"Five of the six local units are now secure," Peter said. "No problems so far. Thank God things are moving on with Jess too. She's managed to get a call through and apparently she's set up a safe house for herself. She's on her way there now. She seems confident that the dog is already there."

"She's pretty good for someone who knows nothing about security," Blake said, allowing himself the ghost of a smile. "What's next? We don't know how much of our comms is compromised. They could be following every conversation we have."

"I know. That's why I'm going to suggest she sits tight when she gets there."

Blake thought for a while. "You know Peter, there is another option. I don't like to call in the police but we've got a unique chance here. With their help we could set some sort of trap and pin these people down. It would need Jess to sit tight if we don't get there before they do, but if she can do it we might be able to turn this around."

Peter was doubtful. "What if there's civilians nearby?"

"I honestly don't think they'll be in any danger. These people seem to have been briefed not to cause any serious harm and it's in their interest to keep as low profile as they can. I know she means a lot to you. She does to me, but she's a pretty tough cookie. If we take the right precautions I think she could handle it. It's chance for us to get ahead of the curve."

Peter didn't answer. "If we can catch these buggers it would go a long way to making up for what's likely to look to the Board like a serious security lapse." Blake said. He looked at Peter. "Make us all look a bit better."

Peter understood exactly the point he was making. He took a deep breath. "OK, I'll talk to Big Ed and get his assessment. If he can come up with a plan that puts her to no risk I'll agree to it, but I don't like it."

Blake's look was sympathetic, but his tone was firm. "I'm afraid I'm ordering it Peter. If we want to come out of this without egg over all our faces, there's no other choice."

Chapter 28

Twenty minutes after Jess's call from the back lanes, Neck's little red car was drawing up about 50 yards from the house in Eltham Road where Luke's Aunt Gwen lived.

"Right," said Jess. "I want to thank you all very much again. You did the right thing." There was an appreciative murmur from the car.

"It was nothing, Miss," said Neck, "and, you know, the lads was just messing about with that dirty talk back in the car." He was suddenly formal. "I really do apologise. There's no harm in them really. I would never have let anything happen, honest."

"Of course," she said, "I knew that."

"They're just animals. Animals!" He gave a mock growl.

The others laughed; "Animals that's us!"

"Terrible," she laughed, "but you go now." And may I never ever see you in my life again, she thought.

Neck turned to get back in the car then swung back. "But about Luke's aunt, are you two goin' to be all right? Don't you think we should come in? As like, back up?" She could sense his reluctance to leave this dramatic adventure.

"No, I'm fine now. If we go in mob-handed it could ruin the whole operation." 'The whole operation', she was, not for the first time that day, amazed at her own inventiveness. She suddenly felt very weary.

"You go and have your evening. One day soon we'll get together and I'll explain what it's all about. For now, sufficient to say you've done a great service to your country." She'd heard that line as well, somewhere. "But please you must not tell anyone what's happened tonight,"

"Like terrorists is it? Muslims and that?

"You know I can't say. But again, thank you."

"Terrorists eh? Terrorists in Tamborough. Would you believe it?"

She put her finger to her lips; he put his finger beside his nose. They exchanged conspiratorial glances. "Remember," Spaz called out from the car. "Any trouble, just call. We're the boys!" There was a chorus of agreement.

She checked again. There were three or four parked cars in the street, but there had been no movement in any of them while they'd been talking.

"OK," she said, trying to do her best secret agent voice, "I'm going to get out now, and I want you guys to just take off, fast. OK?"

"OK, Commander," said Neck, "Take care. Let's go team."

He did an ostentatious wheel spin that would certainly have attracted the attention of any one within a hundred yards, and shot off down the street and round the corner. She just caught the sound of someone one singing, "Dah de deddah, de da. Da deh de dah, dada!" She realised it was an attempt at the theme music from the James Bond films…

She waited until the resonant exhaust note of the car had completely faded and walked briskly towards Number 46. Her phone rang. It was the duty officer. "Are you OK?" he said.

"I'm just going in. I'll call you back," she said. She noticed the battery of the phone was getting flat. "Good," he said, "hold on a moment." There was a pause and then Peter was on the line.

"Ah, the wandering trainer, found you at last." His voice, always so calm and modulated, sounded strained.

"Yes," she said, "lucky I could reach you. I lost my phone for a while. Anyway before you ask, I'm fine. I just got into a bit of a mess with a couple of fake security men, but I'm clear now. I'll wait until your chaps pick me and the girl up."

"That's fine Ms Stewart," he said. "Just tell us exactly where you will be, Ms Stewart…"

There was a long pause. What did he mean? Why so formal? It suddenly clicked. He must know that her phone might be tapped. "You're sure, Mr Guy?"

"Absolutely sure."

"OK," she said suddenly. "I'll be right there at number 46 Eltham Road."

"OK, we might be a little while, but just sit tight."

" Will do." She disconnected.

Back at Canine Division Peter put the phone down and turned to Blake. "She's worked it out. I love that girl. Please God she'll be OK. I'll get our team moving."

Inside number 46, Luke's aunt jumped, as a car with what sounded like a broken exhaust roared down the street outside. She got up from where all three of them were sitting on the settee, Daisy with her head in Luke's lap, and went to the front window, but the car had gone. Daisy leapt off the settee and began barking furiously at the front door, which opened straight into the street. "Don't she like cars?" his aunt said.

There came a knock at the door and Daisy became even more excited, rushing back and forth between the door and Luke. The door was knocked again. "Who the hell's that at this hour?" his aunt said. "It's no good knocking at that door," she shouted. "You'll have to go round the back. That door's been nailed up for twenty years as I know."

Luke heard the tread of feet echoing down the shared little alley, as Daisy rushed back into the kitchen ahead of his aunt. His pulse rate went up abruptly. Who could it be? His Mum, even Chas, knew that you never used the front door. Was it the nice Mrs Duncan woman, or was it the two men she'd gone off with? Or even the police? Was he in trouble for taking Daisy away? Were they after him for hitting Chas?

He stood uncertainly in the doorway to the kitchen.

The back door was knocked. "What is it?" said his aunt. She had picked up a rather ineffective looking wooden spoon. "What do you want?"

"Miss Gwen Davies? Is that you?"

"It's Miss Gwendolyn Davies. Who's asking?" At her feet Daisy scrabbled furiously at the base of the door, she was not just barking but whining now.

"My name's Jess." There was a pause. "Jess Duncan. I'm looking for Luke."

"How do you know…?" said his aunt, but Luke was already pushing past her to unbolt the door. There before them, looking tired and dishevelled stood Jess, who just had time to say, "There you are Luke!" before she caught Daisy as she leapt clean into her arms.

It took a little time for Daisy to allow Jess to speak, and for his aunt to understand who she was, (the owner of Daisy, he had explained), but quite soon he was watching Jess sitting on the settee, trying to drink a large gin and tonic with Daisy sitting on her lap, licking her hand. Meanwhile his aunt rustled up beans on toast in the kitchen. It was by no means the only food she had in the house, she said, but it was quick.

Jess was in a bit of a daze. She was amazed at the depth of her feeling for the dog on her lap. She had had almost wept when she had first seen the dog again. After its initial leap into her arms it had slipped away to return a few moments later with one of the cat's soft toys in its mouth to present to her. Now as it primly sat on her lap with the toy between its front legs and reached up to snuggle its nose under her chin she felt her eyes moisten. She looked down at the dog and realised that when it came to their feelings for each other, neither needed words. A thought came to her.

"Luke," she said, "come and sit next to me." He came over. "Did you hear anything from Daisy's collar?" she said quietly.

"Yes," he said.

"So... You know?"

"Yes. But I switched it off here."

"Good. Well done." He felt a warm glow.

"It's a secret." He nodded.

"Did she speak in front of your aunt?"

"Yes, but she didn't believe it. She thought it was a trick."

"Really?" It had never really occurred to her before, but it was obvious really. When people encountered something outside their previous experience, it was often easier to assume it hadn't really happened at all. They smiled at each other.

"That's all right then." Daisy spared a moment from looking after Jess to give his hand a lick.

"She likes you," she said.

"I like her."

"Mind you," she said, "it's going to take a bit of doing to sort this out."

She realised he didn't know what she was talking about. How could he? "The main thing is to keep all the doors locked until my people come to pick me up."

"What about me?" he said. "Shall I stay here until Mum comes? Do you know where they went? Did Chas have to go to hospital? How did they get there? Have they been home yet? Did she get my message? I didn't say nothin' to Auntie Gwen."

Jess tried to stem the tide of questions. "I believe your Mum was at the hospital. I'm sure she's alright. I'm sure Chas is alright. I need to let her know *you're* alright. In fact I wish I could get you and your Auntie to somewhere…else."

"Do they know what happened to Chas?" he said tentatively.

"Don't worry," she said. "I'll help you sort that out." The relief of finding Daisy, plus the gin and tonic, was spreading a warm flush though her. She was so tired. "Sorry. I should have had a call from Peter by now. Where the hell is he?"

"Peter?" said Gwen, coming in with the beans on toast.

"From the people I work for. He'll give us both a lift home."

"That's good. Perhaps he can't find the house. All these streets look the same if you don't live here."

Jess looked at her phone. The battery was almost completely discharged.

She had started to dial when Daisy abruptly snapped awake and growled.

"Hang on," Jess said, "just hang on a sec." She got up, went into the kitchen and listened by the door. Beside her Daisy was standing absolutely still. She growled very quietly.

Outside Jess thought she could just hear some faint noises.

Gwen went through to the kitchen and listened "You don't think it's burglars, do you?" she whispered.

Behind her Jess bent down to Daisy and switched on her collar.

"Who is it Daisy?" she said quietly.

"Big ones. Men." She growled again. Jess's heart lurched. Too soon, she thought. Where are you Peter?

Quietly she called Gwen back from the kitchen.

"I don't have time to explain it," she said, "but I think those people out there may be after me, or rather Daisy." She racked her brain for an explanation. "You see she's a very rare breed, very expensive, worth a fortune to dog smugglers. She's become the target of an international gang."

"Oh my God," said Gwen, "the things they do these days. Poor little thing." She went to stroke Daisy.

"Me fine," said the dog reassuringly.

"Don't you think you should turn that off just now dear?" Gwen said to Luke. "This is no time to play games. Let's call the police."

Jess looked at Daisy. "Daisy won't speak now." She said clearly. The dog collapsed onto all fours, head on its paws, and watched her carefully.

"That's a good idea Gwen. But these people are crafty. If it is them, they'll disappear as soon as they even hear the police coming, and just come back another time. Is there any way out of here, apart from that back door?"

"Not unless you jump out of a window."

A couple of minutes later, Luke and Daisy were crouching next to Jess while she peered out of the side of the lace curtains in the darkened front bedroom. Gwen was waiting in the kitchen below, having an imaginary conversation. It had been her own idea and she was carrying it out with enthusiasm. "Anyway," she was saying loudly, "if we have any trouble at all round here the police are very good, round here in a trice."

As Jess studied the street she realised there was a car parked across the road. It hadn't been there when she'd arrived. She couldn't see whether there was anyone in or not. The confidence with which she had offered to act as bait was rapidly draining away. My God, she thought, how many of them are there? What if they get in before Peter arrives? She had to make sure the dog was safe, and Luke, come to that. She couldn't place him at risk.

She checked the room, nowhere to hide a mouse, never mind a dog. But, in the low ceiling, above the bed, was the outline of a hatch leading up into the loft. "I tell you what we'll do," she said to Luke. Daisy stopped snuffling under the bed and came back to listen. "I'll help you get up there with Daisy and with luck they'll believe me if I say you two never even got here."

She'd have to act quickly before the men outside gave up waiting and just broke into the house, and it all depended of course on how thorough a search they would then make, but, just at that moment, she didn't have another idea in her head.

"That's a great idea," said Luke enthusiastically, "they'll never look there!"

Perhaps they won't, she thought, though she had a terrible feeling they were dealing with professionals who wouldn't miss a trick. "Is there a ladder?"

"I dunno." He disappeared into the other little bedroom.

Jess looked out of the window again. Two men were getting out of the car.

Luke returned with a small set of aluminium steps. They were too short to reach the hatch but he put them on the bed and then while she held him steady he climbed up until he could push at the hatch. It swung back easily and he managed to get elbows into the opening. Working between the two of them, they managed to get him up and into the loft. A moment later a light went on. He came back to the hatch and looked down, there was a smear of dust on his forehead. "Great," he said, "it's all insulated and everything. We'll be fine."

"OK, Daisy," she said. Daisy jumped up onto the bed and she passed the dog up into his outstretched arms. "You go with Luke. Stay quiet."

"Me go with Chunky," said the dog, looking down at her from the hatch. "Jess comes."

"No. I'll be here. I will see you soon. Go on. Good girl." She'd completely forgotten to use the official instruction language.

"Me not Girl," said the dog. "Me Daisy." and disappeared into the loft.

From downstairs she heard the sound of louder and more urgent knocking on the back door. She put the steps under the bed and ran down the stairs.

Gwen was standing by the door. "I've phoned for the police," she shouted bravely, "so you'd better get out of it."

"We must speak to you urgently Madam, and to Ms Stewart," a voice said. "Please open the door."

"There ain't no Miss Stewart here," Gwen shouted bravely, "go away or I'll call the police." She looked very pale, but determined.

Jess realised there was nothing else they could do now. "You better let them in," she said. "They'll probably knock the door down otherwise."

"If you think so dear." Gwen whispered, and reluctantly opened the door.

Chapter 29

Two young men came in. Like Jackson and Jones, each of them was dressed in a smart suit, but she had the distinct impression that it was not their usual garb. She took an immediate dislike to them. Like Jackson and Jones there was hardness about their faces, and deadness about the eyes. The first one in advanced smiling, the other stood by the door.

"I'm sorry to bother you at this hour," he said to Gwen, "but it's a bit urgent. Can we sit down a minute?" He had a distinct local accent.

"Never mind that. What was all that creeping about?" Gwen said angrily. Jess decided that she had a lot of guts for a lady in her late sixties.

"I'm really sorry if we worried you. We had to make sure we got here first." He sat down at the kitchen table.

"Do I know you?" Jess said.

"Not directly. We're from Central Security. We're just helping Mr Guy out."

"Really?" Jess's voice was hard.

Gwen was watching the conversation dubiously. The man first turned to her. "I must be quick," he said. "Can I rely on your discretion?"

"Why?"

"The thing is, Jess helps look after certain very special dogs for us. One of them is Daisy. I don't want to alarm you, but we're pretty sure that some fairly nasty people are trying to get hold of her, and we think they might be close. Where is she by the way?"

Gwen looked at him carefully, then at Jess.

"We don't know," she said.

Abruptly the young man's face hardened, as did his voice. "OK, let's have it the hard way." He turned to his companion. "Check the whole place," he said. "I'll stay here with these two."

Up in the loft Luke couldn't really hear what was going on below. He looked round in the dim light from the dusty bulb. He suddenly realised that he could look all along the lofts of all the other houses in the street. To save bricks, the builders had simply stopped constructing the walls when they reached an adequate height. In both directions long corridors stretched away into the dark before them, interrupted only by the central internal chimneystack of each separate house. Daisy started to wander off to have a good sniff around but he called her back.

"Birds," she said triumphantly. "Me go catch." Her tail wagged. "Come."

"No, Daisy," he whispered. "Jess said we stay quiet."

The dog immediately sat down beside him and waited.

He dimly heard the sounds of people coming up the stairs. Daisy's ears pricked up. "Quiet!" he whispered. "Me quiet!" She whispered back.

He suddenly realised he had the light on. Perhaps they'd see it through the hatch edges. He reached forward and turned it off. They sat in the darkness together companionably. Quite quickly his eyes began to adjust to the darkness. Then he heard a voice call.

"There's a hatch."

By the time the man looking for them had got up into the loft, Luke and Daisy had gone. They quietly worked their way over the ceilings of the houses, through the gloom of the long corridor, occasionally hearing music or voices from the rooms beneath. Luke hadn't been too sure of his footing, but the lofts were all floored with insulation, and although it had become darker and darker, he had forced himself to follow Daisy as she forged ahead. Then, beneath his feet, he suddenly felt the hard surface of a ceiling that hadn't been insulated and, though Daisy trotted ahead confidently, he stopped, reluctant to risk the precarious feeling plaster and lath. In addition there was a powerful and repulsive smell of guano. There must be some kind of opening that lets birds in, he thought, perhaps they're still in here, waiting in the dark to fly up and peck our eyes, like in that film on the telly, and he stopped. Daisy had disappeared into the darkness, but returned with her tail wagging. "Come," she said, but Luke was frozen, suddenly terrified by the strangeness of it all. He crouched down unable to move.

Abruptly the man behind them turned the loft light on. He'd managed to make his way into the loft, but by then they were something like thirty yards away, too far for the dim light bulb to pick them out.

They heard him call out to the darkness. "It's alright Luke. You can come down now!" He was peering in both directions, trying to decide which way they had gone.

Luke was in conflict. Was everything really all right? How could he be sure to trust this man? He'd never seen him before.

Beside him Daisy growled quietly.

Luke's heart thumped as the man studied the floor beneath him, made his decision, and began to work his way steadily towards them, silhouetted by the light behind him. "I think we've had it Daisy," he breathed, but the dog looked at him carefully and then put her paws in his lap and licked his face. "Chunky is fine," she said quietly. "Daisy is fine." Even in the darkness he could see the brown eyes gleam. "Come," she said again. Reluctantly he got to his feet and followed her.

He slowly inched his way over the uninsulated ceiling, straining to see in the darkness and trying to keep his feet on the narrow timbers. Suddenly she stopped and he realised that in front of them there was a very faint square of light. It was the access to the bedroom below and the hatch was missing. He looked down, brushing cobwebs away from his face. The light was filtering up from a cracked and dusty blind over a bedroom window. The source of the illumination was a street lamp a little distance away, and there was enough light to reveal that the bedroom was completely empty, apart from a few boxes. It was absolutely silent. "All gone," said Daisy. Behind them the man was calling. "It's OK Luke, everything's fine now."

He carefully let himself down until he was hanging from the ledge of the hatch and let go. He landed with a crash but no damage, and clambered to his feet. He looked up and Daisy gazed down at him for a moment and then confidently launched herself into his arms. Miraculously he caught her with no difficulty and she hopped neatly out of his arms and onto the floor. A voice behind them shouted. "Are you alright?"

The bedroom door stood open. The street light through the landing window confirmed that the house was empty, and looked as if it had been for some time. With increasing confidence he ran down the uncarpeted stairs, Daisy behind him, and into a derelict kitchen. He tried the back door but it was securely locked from the outside.

Daisy put her paws up on the windowsill and tried to peer out of the grimy window. Instinctively he joined her, all he could see was a bleak little yard with a high wall at the back. But he also noticed that the window was built exactly like the windows in his Mum's cottage, just two large panes, the kind they called sash windows. The lower pane was held secure by a simple inner catch and to his surprise, with a good push, it opened perfectly easily.

Back in Gwen's kitchen, the young man, she still didn't know what his name was, sat up sharply as a dim shout came from upstairs. He stood up as the man he'd sent upstairs ran into the room. His suit was covered in dust and his face was grimy.

"They've bolted," he said. "From what I can make out, they've gone down through another house, the other end of street. It's not safe to follow on those joists."

"Shit," said the other. " Let's go. There's still a chance we'll get them in the street."

He started to leave and then, as if on an impulse, grabbed Jess's arm and pulled her to her feet. "You're coming with me."

"Don't you dare!" Gwen shouted, but the venom of his glance at her reduced her to silence.

"Now!" he said, "if you ever want to see that dog again..." He was strong and his grip on her wrist was firm and painful. Despite her attempts to pull back, he swept her out of the back door, up the little passageway. His companion jumped into the driver's door of the car parked outside and her captor opened the passenger door and tried to push her in. At that moment there was the sound of a car approaching very fast. His grip on her relaxed momentarily and she was suddenly free as the passenger door slammed shut and the car lurched away with the two men inside.

Then a number of things happened very quickly. As the car swept down the street its lights suddenly picked out a small boy running out of a passageway. As the headlights hit him he froze, as did the dog that ran out behind him. Then both the dog and the boy were galvanised into action and sprinted down the street. The driver put on speed to catch them up but then another car suddenly appeared from a side alley and started to head them off. The driver tried to accelerate but it was too late. The other car hit them squarely in the side with an enormous bang and the first car came to an abrupt stop.

Suddenly there seemed to be men everywhere. She stood rigid in shock trying to grasp what had just happened when a man's voice said, "Hi honey, I think of got a bit of a bodywork bill coming, but everything's going to be all right now. Sorry we're late." It was Peter. She literally fell into his arms.

Neither of them, nor the officers who were occupied in getting the two men out of the wrecked car, nor the occupants of the street who were beginning to look out of windows and doors, noticed the grey van parked at the end of the street. It quietly reversed a little, did a U-turn and slid away into the night.

Chapter 30

Just a minute earlier, as Luke had come out of the passageway, he had suddenly seen a big black car, headlights full on, racing down the street towards him. He was off and running without conscious thought. Daisy followed close behind and then overtook and passed him easily, stretched into full gallop, her ears flying behind her.

He sprinted after her and then stopped, as there was a great crash behind him. He looked back to see that two cars were locked together in the street, apparently surrounded by men in dark clothes. The man who had been chasing them was being wrestled to the ground by two of them. Completely confused, he just stood and watched, and then turned to look for Daisy, but there was no sign of her.

Thoroughly unnerved by the noise and confusion, Daisy hurtled down the street ahead of Luke, took a sharp turn to her left and ran down a narrow alley to a crossroads, then left again. After a moment she stopped to look back for Luke but he wasn't there. She ran back to the junction and turned down an alleyway to retrace her steps but when she emerged from it she was in a new street but there was no trace of his scent and it looked completely unfamiliar. She had another attempt at getting back but in the maze of narrow streets she was very quickly completely lost.

Like all dogs her sense of direction derived intuitively from sources like the movement of the air, the angle of sunlight and particularly the traces of familiar smells. Like a young human child she was egocentric with respect to her left and right and, without the correct cues, totally incapable of comprehending the simplest principles of direction finding. It was not the way her brain worked. She could carry out quite complicated tasks, once she'd watched a human being accomplishing them, that was one of the secrets of her species' success, but, left to her own devices, and without an odour trail to guide her, she couldn't grasp how to move efficiently through the simplest maze.

As she ran on, the streets around her became busier with both traffic and people but she ignored them all in her panic. She finally emerged onto a harshly lit pedestrianised street where crowds of young people stood about outside pubs and bars at the latter stages of negotiating possible liaisons with members of the opposite sex. As she trotted past them there were cries of, "Look at that lovely little dog. Are you lost sweetheart?" as young women in impossibly short skirts and towering heels blearily tottered forward to reach out to her.

She ran directly past three young men sitting at a table crammed with empty glasses, but they were too busy discussing their recent adventures with a secret agent to notice her. She ran on and on, leaving the crowded areas behind her, eventually descending into smaller and darker lanes, lined with tiny terraced houses, still trying to find a scent. Finally she slowed to a complete halt, her chest heaving.

She realised that she was lost, completely lost, and a long way from Luke and Jess. And now it came on to rain. She was very tired and a bit frightened. Her immediate instinct was to find a good place to lie up for the night. It didn't take her long to find shelter under an old piece of corrugated iron piled up with other rubbish in one of the alleys that ran behind the rows of terraced houses. It was lying across an old mattress that spoke to her of all kinds of fragrant human activities but after turning three times, in an ancient ritual that she was completely unaware of, she settled fairly comfortably down beneath it.

Above her head the rain beat a stentorious rhythm on the corrugated iron but the little dog, tail wrapped around her body and her head nestled comfortably into the warm fold of her hip, had sunk into deep and dreamless sleep.

Chapter 31

Back at Eltham Road it was just after midnight, on Sunday morning. Up and down the street, lights were still coming on, and there was the rattle and squeak of sash windows being lifted. Leaning out of the open windows, people watched attentively, but largely silently, as the car with a ruined bonnet was carefully eased back from the immobile black car, and the dazed driver and his passenger were equally carefully taken out by men in dark suits.

Gwen came running out of the passageway to her house. "Oh my God, Mrs Duncan are you alright?" she cried. "Where's Luke?"

Peter took her arm. "Please don't worry Miss Davies. Luke is just down the street. One of our chaps is bringing him along now," he said gently. "Look." Sure enough, coming up the street was a small boy covered in dust being guided at arms length by one of the men in the neat dark suits. Gwen ran forward to meet him.

Then there were the familiar sounds of sirens in the distance and then first an ambulance, and then two police cars, appeared at the end of the street. The grey little road was transformed. Blue and white lights were flashing, sirens ululated extraordinarily loudly. The vehicles drew up, the sirens wailed into silence, and uniformed people spilled out confidently. As policemen examined the crashed cars and spoke confidently into their handsets, paramedical workers, with the solicitous help of a couple of the men in dark suits, placed the car passengers on lightweight wheeled stretchers, and hoisted them up into the ambulance. The two helpful men climbed in with them, the doors shut, and in a moment the ambulance was away down the street, lights flashing but siren silent, followed by a patrol car.

A big middle-aged policeman, in an outfit that looked more like full battle gear than a mere uniform, approached them. "Good evening Peter," he said calmly. He nodded to both of them. He smiled carefully at Jess, "I'm pleased to see you're unharmed Ms Stewart."

Behind them Gwen was leading Luke back towards her house. Peter said, "Can you hang on just a sec Miss Davies? Luke, can you say where Daisy is?"

Luke looked at Jess doubtfully. "It's alright Luke," she said.

"She ran too quick," he said miserably. "I lost her. You must help me find her."

"Never mind that," Gwen said, "you come inside and have a bath and get to bed. We've had enough of this."

"Just one moment, Miss Davies," Peter said. "Please."

A big white four by four came briskly down the street, dramatically screeched to a halt and two men got out to bring two tracker dogs from the rear hatch. "Don't worry," Peter said to Luke. "We'll find Daisy."

But Luke wasn't really listening. He was running forward to the woman who was getting out of the passenger door of the big car, her arms outstretched.

"Linney!" said Gwen with relief. "Well, about time!"

Chapter 32

At one thirty on Sunday morning Jess was sitting in what she supposed was usually an interrogation room in Tamborough police station. She was sitting in a small hard chair at a small hard table. Abruptly the silence outside the room was broken by the sound of two men's voices approaching. They were keeping their voices down but they were plainly arguing.

She could hear Peter's voice clearly. "It took far too long. She might have been in real danger."

The other voice replied. "You should have called us in earlier. Anyway, it's worked out. Leave it." Then the door opened and both men entered the barren little room.

Peter Guy was accompanied by the tall police officer she'd spoken to in the street into. Although he'd discarded his flak jacket he was still a huge man.

"Hello again Ms Stewart. Thank you so much for your patience." He smiled. "I'm Superintendent Larkin."

"Superintendent…" she said.

"Please Ms Stewart, call me Ed, or as I believe some call me, Big Ed."

Both of the men smiled at his little joke, she realised that, despite their mutual animosity they were trying to put her at her ease.

"Ed is our contact point with the police if we get a problem we can't handle on our own," Peter said. "His people grabbed the bad guys tonight." The policeman nodded.

"I know you've had a hell of a day," he said to Jess. "I'm so sorry."

"That's OK. I'm fine now, but can you explain exactly what's happening?" Jess said.

"Just hang on a minute."

The door opened behind her and a young policeman came in with a tray carrying three very big mugs and a bowl of sugar. He smiled at Jess, and left immediately.

Shaking her head at the offer of sugar, Jess carefully picked up a stingingly hot mug of tea. "All right, Ed," she said. "Have you any idea where Daisy is?"

"I won't lie to you Ms Stewart, we don't know yet. It's late now but in an hour or two I'll have a full team looking for her in every back street, rescue centre and kennels for twenty miles around. The moment we get a result you'll know. Try not to worry. We'll find her."

"What about the two men who came to the house?"

"The bad guys, as Peter calls them. I've been sweating them out downstairs but it doesn't look very hopeful. They're just a couple of local ner-do-wells. Unfortunately we've got enough drug business going on, even in these sleepy parts, to keep people like that employed. They got a phone call offering them good money, paid in advance, if they'd go in and pick up the dog, more instructions to follow. Once they got the cash transfer they weren't interested in identifying the source, it would have been blocked anyway. We'll work on them some more but I'm pretty sure that's all they know."

"They're not the same people I got away from."

"No. The chaps you met must have smelt the rat. They sent those two in first in case it was a trap. I fear these they're pretty crafty boys. All we really have so far are the identifits we got from Jack Sampson, Ruby's trainer."

"Jack's met them too?"

"Yes, I'm sorry to tell you that they've already succeeded in getting hold of Ruby, but if they know anything about the Project they'll know Daisy is the real prize. Its even possible Ruby was taken just to give them a lead on her."

"Oh, poor Ruby. Jack must be distraught. But who are they? They're not really called Jackson and Jones are they?"

"No they lifted the names and I.D.'s of a couple of our own people," Peter said. "We're still building up a picture at Canine Division. I'll know more soon. Bad boys anyway."

179

"I didn't realise I was in any real danger. Is Joe OK?" Jess said.

"I'll be honest we don't know where he is."

Larkin's eyebrows raised. "Our gateman at the Stone House," Peter explained. "Please God he's OK."

"He may well be," Larkin said. "Our hope is that this crowd will try to avoid actually killing anyone. On paper their actual law breaking in this operation is pretty low key so far. Let's hope it stays that way." Peter was noncommittal.

"What do you think they'll be doing now?" Jess said.

"My guess is they'll be putting all their energy into finding your dog, but so will we. We can only hope we find her first." He turned to Peter. "Look," he said, "there's not much more you can do to help here tonight. I suggest you both get back to the Stone House and catch a few hours then we can make a fresh start in the morning."

Peter looked dubious, and Jess shook her head. "No," she said. "I'm going to stay here. As soon as your people find her I want to be near."

"Are you sure?" Larkin asked.

"Look, I lost her, and I want to do all I can to help find her. Can you put me up somewhere near?"

"We do have temporary stay-over room here. It's not five star, but there is a little shower unit, and we do a good breakfast if I do say so myself."

Jess allowed herself a small smile. "I'm so exhausted I could sleep in a cell if I had to."

"We can do you better than that. I'll get it organised," Larkin said. He left the room. Peter drew a little nearer to her.

"Listen," he said quietly. "I don't have lot of confidence in this guy. We depend on the police for muscle, my department is more about surveillance expertise, but he was slow in responding to our request for manpower and he doesn't seem in much of a rush now. If you're sure you want to stay here, OK. I'll go back to Division now and see if I can move things on my end... I'll stay in touch."

Larkin came back into the room. Peter nodded to him, kissed Jess lightly on the lips and left without a backward glance. Jess smiled at the big policeman's raised eyebrows. "We go back a way, as the Americans say," she said quietly.

His craggy face broke into an unlikely smile. "I'm sure you do, and good for you," he said. "Don't worry. First thing tomorrow I'll pull in a team to start looking for the dog. It's a Sunday, but people will be glad of some overtime. You can stay right with it as long as you wish. Now, you get some rest."

Chapter 33

The men Jess had called Jackson and Jones sat in the van, parked in a narrow unpaved track in a small area of rather scruffy woodland near Tamborough. It was two thirty in the morning and it was very dark and very quiet. Both men sat silent. It was raining in a steady drizzle. Serban's mobile rang. It was Leicemann.

Serban spoke first. "Hello. You're up late."

"Where are you?"

"We're parked in a side lane in the woods. It's secure," Serban said.

"Probably a dogging heaven," Penders grunted to himself.

"Dog? You got the dog?"

"No."

"Then what the hell is going on?" Leicemann was enraged. "You guaranteed it!"

"Wait. We've had some problems. Listen. When we found the woman she was off base. While we were taking her back to our contact point she sent the dog off and bolted for it."

"I told you should have given her a shot," Penders said beside him.

"Anyway we followed her back to her base," Serban continued. "She had nowhere else to go. Then I fed her, if I say so myself, a very convincing line."

"Fucking Benedict Cumberbatch ain't you," Penders grunted.

Ignoring him Serban went on. "I persuaded her we were kosher. She took us to some cottage where she said she'd sent the dog. When we got there, no dog, but then she got a call and bolted again. Luckily we'd had hold of her phone for a little while and Penders had put a tap on it. Signal strength is all over the place round here but eventually we found out where she was heading for. I sent in a couple of people I had on standby. You said no violence, and I just hoped she'd mistake them for Division Security but she twigged them. She'd already sent the dog off."

"And you didn't get it?"

"No, I fucking didn't."

"What a fuckup. This is terrible. Why didn't you just do what I told you?" Leicemann was in despair.

"I tell *you* what Alex," Serban said, suddenly threatening. "This whole fucking operation is turning out a lot more heavy than you said. We had to pull in help. That's expensive. The agreed fee won't stretch to it. We'll just keep the deposit, call it quits, be on our way."

"No, No," Leicemann said urgently. His voice became conciliatory. "I'll raise the fee to cover the extra muscle. We can't stop now."

"You sure? It will cost."

"Yes, don't worry about that. Just do what it takes. Take what action you think necessary."

"*Any* action? You said no hard stuff."

"Look, just do what it takes to get that dog. But be careful. Understand?"

"Alright then Alex," Serban said. "In that case, and since we're family. I'll stick with it. Don't worry. We've got good leads. We'll have the dog in a matter of hours. OK?"

He disconnected the phone before Leicemann could answer and looked at Penders.

"Just a few hours, eh?" Penders said.

"He's really keen to get his hands on that dog. I'm beginning to think that it might be worth some serious money," Serban said thoughtfully. "I wish I'd hung onto that first one. It must be at Anglo by now. Get some sleep. We'll regroup in the morning."

Chapter 34

Daisy woke up just before the light started to bring Sunday to life. She got up and had a good stretch and a quick smell around, and then sat on her haunches and scratched her ears to settle herself.

The rain had stopped and, as the palest white light began to reveal the silhouettes of the houses around her, there were rustles of movement from the scrubby trees in some of the backyards and a few birds began to sing in a determinedly optimistic celebration of yet another day of living from claw to beak. She went to look for a drink and quickly found an excellent muddy puddle to slake her thirst.

Water dripping from her jowls she immediately set off to make new searches for Luke and Jess, but the quiet and empty streets were packed with information and it was difficult to keep her attention on the main task when there were so many fascinating tracks of dogs and humans and a wealth of urine signatures at nearly every corner. She bumped into the remains of a large cardboard mug of milkshake with quite a lot of liquid left, and licked clean not only the cup but the place in the gutter where it had been dropped.

As the light strengthened the sun came out and her spirits lifted for no other reason than she was alive. She was a dog, she'd had breakfast, and it was turning into an interesting and stimulating day. She was absolutely confident that she would find Jess. She always had. That's what you did if Jess wasn't around. You went and found her. In any case Jess had the most awesome and incomprehensible powers and chances were she'd just drop out of the sky any minute and take her home for some Chunky Chunks.

As she wandered on purposefully, head down for any important scent message, she encountered the familiar scents of big trees, bushes, and flowers, nicely spiced with urine signatures. The cocktail of odours emanated from a big field, rather like the one where she played with Jess, so perhaps she was in there. The problem was there was a railings fence in the way. She paced up and down and even pushed her nose between the rails but the fence was unyielding.

She noticed, out of the corner of her eye, a Big One, a man, coming towards her with a young dog on a leash. She immediately ran up to them both; tail wagging slightly and ears pricked. The man stopped politely to allow both dogs to check each other's identity, using the unique odour that each produced from the tiny vents hidden each side of the anus, but then tugged on the lead and the other dog obediently began to follow him. Daisy would have liked to chat on a bit more so she followed the two of them and, lo and behold, just a bit further along, was a large gap. She followed them into the park. It was huge and empty, it was delightful to get away from the unrelenting surfaces of the streets, and for a while she just ran about, for the joy of it.

The man eventually released the other dog and it ran over to join her and crouched, chest down and rear high, inviting her to work out. To dogs, what looks like play to us, is actually much more like a really good conversation using styles of mock attack and retreat first developed when they were puppies, and Daisy was happy to take up the invitation to get acquainted, with much jaw to jaw pushing and paw boxing. Eventually, a bit puffed, she decided she knew just about as much as she wanted to about the other dog and, despite its repeated requests to re-engage, she wandered off.

Despite her resolution to seek out Jess, she stayed for most of the morning in the park. She worked out with a couple more dogs, got chased away for taking the ball away from a game of soft ball cricket, and even adopted a young couple walking round the perimeter of the park for a while, but she mostly just sat on all fours, under a shady bush, tongue lolling out of her mouth in her doggie grin, watching all the fascinating comings and goings of the people and dogs who used the park.

Many of the park visitors had nice smelling snacks and drinks with them but they kept them to themselves and, although she was able to pull a couple of ice cream wrappers protruding from the bottom of a waste basket, she was getting really hungry, when she heard a voice call. "Hey good boy, come over here. Come on. Look what I've got for you."

Sitting on a park bench was a man holding out some nice smelling meat wrapped in a bun. She'd noticed him before, but, when he had remained unmoving, she had ignored him. "Come on, come," he said. "This is just for you."

Daisy had had some very mixed experiences in the last couple of days but her primary experience of human beings was that they were on your side. In Daisy's straightforward mind, handsome was as handsome does, so she advanced carefully but confidently towards the man. He smelled of dog, even several dogs, but she couldn't identify any of them. Stretching her neck, she politely lifted the food from his hand. "Ain't you a nice little dog?" he said. "Has yer gone and got lost?" She had no idea what 'got lost' meant, but if it had something to do with these nice pieces of meat, that was fine by her. She looked up at him and wagged her tail and he obligingly gave her another piece.

Chapter 35

Penders sat back and wiped his lips. In front of him lay the sparse remnants of what the Roadrunner American Bar called the Big Bucket Breakfast. Behind him, through the wide café window, Serban could see the never-ending Sunday traffic silently streaming up and down the A1.

"My God," Penders said, "I needed that. I don't care what we have to do next, I am never spending another night in that van with you."

"Forget it, just keep your voice down," Serban said quietly, "stay with the protocol."

Penders nodded. "OK. What are we going to do now then?" he said equally quietly. "I say the whole project's fucked. Let's fuck off out of it and get out of the country before they set up checks at the airports."

"They won't set up checks at the airports. The Canine Project doesn't even exist outside of BSDL. They won't start mounting big operations all around the country. It's not like we've killed anybody."

"What about that old security man, Joe?"

"That was just bad luck, daft bugger. They don't know about that yet. Won't for a long time, maybe never."

Penders aimlessly turned a page of the newspaper in front of him. "I still say let's get out of it. The dog could be anywhere."

"And what about the fee? And who'll ever employ us again?"

Penders was silent.

Serban went to light a cigarette and then remembered it wasn't allowed.

"Believe me," he said, "I can't wait to fuck off back to Bucharest either, but there must be a way we can still pull this off."

"You're the brains, tell me how."

Serban tapped his useless cigarette on the table.

"My argument is this," he said. "We haven't got the resources to mount a search for the dog ourselves, and the police must have a pretty good idea what we look like by now. It's better if we stay out of the way. But that bastard Guy and the police unit will be chucking all they've got at it. We've somehow got to latch on to that. Assuming the dog is found, where would they take it first?"

"The police station?"

"It's a long shot but quite possible. I'll call in O'Connell and that lad Nick and put them onto it. They only have to park across the street and keep their eyes open. Where else?"

"BSDL? Canine Division Centre?"

"Well if they take the dog there we're buggered. Even with Leicemann on the inside we'll never get it out of there now. There's just a chance they'd take it to the Stone House first. That's where it's supposed to be based. It's worth a go anyway, what's to lose? Let's give it another twenty four hours."

Despite himself Penders was impressed. "Alright," he said, "what shall we do first?"

"Let's get over there. If there's nobody there yet you can put in some ears and eyes. As soon as anything happens we'll know it."

Chapter 36

Daisy sat back on her haunches by the park bench neatly taking each fragment of food the man offered her. As she chewed on the food and waited politely for the next piece, she began to notice how the sounds of barking and laughter around her had a distant and rather strange echoing quality. It became increasingly difficult to concentrate, even on the food, and she abruptly felt the need to sit down on all fours and be quiet for a while. She tried to get up but her legs somehow wouldn't work properly

"There you go," said the man taking a lead from his pocket and looping it round her neck, "broad daylight. And a lot easier than getting fucking cats." He looked casually around one more time and then got up and pulled on the lead. Reluctantly Daisy struggled to her feet and just managed to keep up with him as he strolled towards the park gate.

Once outside the park he quickened his pace and Daisy attempted to slow him down by pulling back. He responded with a ferocious tug that snapped her head up and dragged her along the ground for a foot or two. Eventually, he stopped at one of a row of parked cars, unlocked the boot and by a combination of holding her collar and her tail, threw her in and shut the top down.

In the dark, Daisy lay awkwardly on a hard metal rim of the spare wheel. The lid pressed down on her head and the rim pressed into her ribs and she struggled to get herself into a position that wasn't quite so painful. The boot smelled of dog, and diesel fuel, and bad meat, and several other things she couldn't identify but none of them were good. She felt nauseous and frightened and suddenly vomited up an acid mush of bun and meat. She felt better but very thirsty. Then she could hear and feel the car start and there was the sharp nasty smell of exhaust fumes. The boot rattled and shook and she knew from her trips with Jess that they were going somewhere in a vehicle.

In the gloom she sensed something lying jammed between the tire she lay on and the side of the boot. It moved slightly and then whimpered. She felt the warmth coming from it and realised it was a small dog. It had soiled itself but the smell was almost lost among all the other old smells. She could just reach it enough to realise that its front legs were wired together at the wrists.

With the innate compassion that many humans would never believe existed in dogs, she tried to comfort the little dog. Its trembling diminished a little and it even gave a tiny nervous wag of its tail as she licked.

The car drove on. Without conscious thought she arranged herself as comfortably as she could, rested her head on her forepaws and tried to let herself slip into the Calm but it was very difficult, she was very frightened. Every so often she couldn't resist the urge to try and somehow get out of the dark box but no matter how she squirmed or pushed or gnawed at the inner lock of the boot she was trapped. The little dog lay perfectly still.

After a time, impossible to gauge because every moment crammed into the boot felt like an eternity, the car stopped and she heard a new voice speak. "Any luck Dad? Or have you just been pissing away in the boozer?"

"I might have had a pint," said the man who had put her in the box, "but it was a good haul today. I got two. I picked up a pup from an old bag in Lunthorpe, from the good home ad. I think it barked too much for her or something." Daisy heard the sounds of boots on concrete. She could smell both men now.

"I got another one, a stray, down Ashleigh Park. It's got something wrong with its head an' all, but it don't matter. It'll make a nice bit of bait for Buster once it's come round."

The boot lid opened with a blast of strong yeasty smell and in the harsh glare of light a loop of wire came down and suddenly tightened round her neck. The loop was connected to a stout pole and the pole was used to drag her by the neck until she managed to jump out. The pressure around her throat slackened and she coughed.

She was so grateful to be released that she wagged her tail gently at the two men who looked down at her. The man holding the other end of the pole was the one who had put her in the boot and standing next to him was a new man, holding a sack. His voice was higher and he was younger.

In the way of dogs she had no resentment for having been put in there, even though she had hated it. Humans did things. You couldn't always make out why. To her the important thing was that they had let her out and she was optimistic that things were now looking up. She would have asked for a drink but her instinct told her that this was not yet the right time to try to speak. She waited politely to see what they would do next. What happened was that she was suddenly kicked hard in the side. She yelped sharply.

"Shit, the fucking things puked all over the boot," the older man said. The younger man laughed.

He took the pole from the older man and passed him the sack. The older man reached down into the boot and plucked out the small dog by its forelegs and dropped it into the sack. It disappeared without a sound.

Despite the pole, Daisy backed away from them as far as she could and looked around. She was standing in a big yard. The concrete beneath her feet smelt dimly of cattle and even horses, but that had been long ago. The traces of manure they had left behind were hard and ancient. There were much stronger odours of dogs, many dogs, and blood.

The yard space was surrounded by various structures, all of them closed up. One of them was much larger than the others. Catching the wind, she could recognise coming from it the scent messages of mouldy straw, urine, meat, and dogs and…puppies too. She focused her hearing and could just pick up faint sounds of the puppies mewling, and another sound, a muted continuous whimpering. Somewhere inside a dog was very unhappy and in the ancient tradition of her species she immediately wanted to find it and console it.

The younger man pulled hard on her choke wire and led her towards the big building. The older man unlocked and dragged open a rickety door. There was a sudden chorus of enraged barking from the darkness. A thick stench overwhelmed her and she tried to pull back but she was pulled so hard that she almost lost her footing.

An electric light was switched on and she could see she was in a long corridor between stout cages. In the first two cages there were litters of puppies with exhausted looking mothers. The puppies gave off the sweet milky smell of babies but it was almost drowned by the odour of excrement and urine in the shredded newspaper used for their bedding. Some of the puppies blundered towards the bars of their cage to have a look at her but the gaunt mothers ignored her, gazing mindlessly into the private wells of their misery.

In the next cage there were a couple of bulldog puppies, half grown. They sat on all fours and silently watched her being dragged along. One sat up with difficulty. Like his brother he had heavy chains wound round his neck. He sank back down again. In the cage next to them a solitary dog whirled round and round endlessly chasing the raw stub of its tail.

The furious barking was coming from the row of cages further down the corridor. Each cage contained a dog that emanated such hatred, of the man, of her, and indeed everything else in the world that she froze completely, and had to be bodily dragged past them. She caught glimpses of dogs with the ruins of faces, *eyes missing, ears missing, faces that had been cut and slashed and bruised, dogs that weren't dogs anymore.*

"Goo on, goo on!" the big one shouted, almost as excited as the ruined dogs. He rattled their cages with a stick. "I'll give you some prod, you bastards." The banging on the bars seemed to drive the dogs to frenzy. But to Daisy it seemed that all their hate, their pain, their despair, was focused on her.

The younger man pulled Daisy to the end of the corridor. It was even darker here. She passed a couple of empty cages and then came to a cage with another horrific dog in it. It was what was left of a Doberman. It didn't bark at her, in fact it made no sound at all. It simply lay with its ruined face lying between its paws. Except that they didn't look like paws. Both had been brutally crushed beyond recognition.

"Old Killer's still alive." The younger man said, looking into the darkness of the Doberman's cage. "Not for much longer." His father said. "When I think how much he lost me I could kick his fucking head in now, but let him suffer a bit longer, he's still too strong. He can bait for the others later."

He slipped the catch on a big wooden store cupboard directly across the corridor from the big dog, chucked in the sack and grabbed Daisy. He started to loosen the choke wire around her neck. "Don't touch its head, Den," the older man said, "that scab could be any kind of disease."

"Alright," the younger man said, "but this looks like an expensive collar." He held Daisy securely with the choke and though she raged and snarled, and tried her best to bite him, he eventually got the collar off.

"I'll have a look at that later," he said. "Actually, for such a little piece of shit, she's a game little fucker." He quickly kicked Daisy into the cupboard before she could move and put the collar in his pocket.

"Good," his father said, "she'll make good bait for Buster then."

The two men walked back down the corridor. The outer metal door clanged behind them, and Daisy was left in the darkness. Further along the corridor the fighting dogs subsided one by one into silence. There was no food, no water and now no sound except the low moans of the unseen dog in the cage opposite. Daisy stood waiting by the cage door for a long time, but no help came.

Den and his father, with whom he shared his name, were in the shed they used as a food store and kitchen at the Yards. They'd been stacking and sorting some of the merchandise his father stored there and their efforts had made them thirsty.

"Time for a nice cup of char," his father said amiably.

"Listen," Den said, as he filled the kettle and put it on the gas ring, "I got a fellar as wants a dog."

"What, gang master? You got to be careful with that lot. Cash up front, devious bastards. Nasty. Long memories." A scowl flitted across his features.

"Nah, nothin like that. It's that mate of Chas's, another wanker."

"Has he got money?"

"He don't want a fighter. He reckons he does a bit of dealing, wants to invest in some protection. I reckon he's just a wanker who wants make out he's got balls. We must have something that'll do, game but not a real evil bugger. How about Tug? Tug'd do him."

"Tug! He couldn't get the meat out of a sausage roll. He's no fighter. I should've chopped him months ago."

"Yeah, but he'd do for this."

"Maybe. Is this fella clear?"

"He reckons he's a mate of Chas's"

"Chas! He's a wanker an' all, and a piss artist. If he don't pay up soon he'll know about it. I'll use *him* as fucking bait."

He gave the saturnine chuckle, which the younger Den had always admired but could never quite emulate. He poured the hot water onto the tea bags in each cracked mug and they both waited in silence until the liquid was the requisite muddy brown then Den added four teaspoons of sugar to each mug. Both men sipped the resulting scalding syrup with satisfaction.

"Anyway, what d'ya think about Tug?" the younger man said eventually.

"Alright Little 'un. Why not? It's drinking money, and it saves hangin' him." He laughed. "Though I know you lads, you like's your fun. Alright, give your man a call, but don't shoot your mouth off. I know you. Just get him over. You meet him down at the place. I'll be around here."

"Don't you start no baiting 'til I get back Dad," Den said. "Like I say, I reckon that little spaniel might have quite a bit of game in her."

Chapter 37

The mud covered four by four, with huge wheels and blacked out rear windows, came bouncing down a rutted track and pulled up at the field gate where Neck was waiting in his lovingly customised ten-year-old Ford Fiesta. The man he knew as Little Den swung down and Neck got out of his car.

"You're on," Little Den said, "but he took some persuading. He loves his dogs, and they're all top meat."

"Thanks mate. I'll owe you one. What we got?"

Little Den scowled at him and then held his gaze just long enough to make it clear that he was no mate of Neck's.

"We got a Doberman," he said eventually. "They don't come any gamer than a good Doberman. This boy is strong, he's had his chains all his life, but he's not bred for fighting, he's for personal protection. You got be careful though. You tell him to kill, he'll kill."

"He got a name?"

"Course he's got a name. He's called Tug, 'cos you get any trouble from anybody, don't matter who, you tell him and he'll pull their fucking arms off."

Neck considered. A dog called Tug because he would pull somebody's arm off sounded like just what he was looking for. "OK."

"Got the cash, ain't you. And the gear?"

"No problem."

"Hand it over."

"Hang on, you ain't dealing with a piker. If I like him, I'll take him. Then you'll get it."

"Like him? You'll fucking love him. Let's go. Mind you, you sure you ain't time wasting? Me Dad hates that. Gets him all worked up."

"Look, let's just fucking get there. I'll follow you."

"No you won't. You'll never get that fucking roller skate over the ruts, and me Dad don't like strangers turning up at the Yards on their own. Leave that here, and lock it," he said, surveying the endless vista of ploughed fields, delicately dusted by the first green tips of the spring wheat. "You can't trust anybody round here."

Neck sat next to the younger Den as the big vehicle banged and jolted over the track through the vast fields.

"You'll need to be firm with him," he was saying. "This kind of dog, you've got to show him whose boss, right from the start, or he'll take your throat out." He was enjoying his role as an authority on fierce dogs; his father rarely let him forget that he was not only younger than him but also far inferior in his knowledge of dogs, or indeed anything of consequence.

"I know. Don't worry. He'll know whose boss."

"You want to take him round to the Wedge. His Staffie's an evil little fucker. Give him a few rolls with Duke, That'll game him up."

"Is Duke a fighting dog then?"

"Nah, he's just an evil little fucker. He likes a bump, but he ain't a real fighting dog. You ever seen a real gamer? Ever been to a fight?"

"Nah, it's a bit of a closed shop ain't it? Chas goes though, doesn't he? Likes to have a bet."

"Yeah, and he likes to lose his money an' all. If he don't pay up soon me Dad says he'll finish up as bait!"

"Bait?"

"Dog bait, stuff you use to get you get your gamer worked up."

Neck had an uncomfortable feeling he was in too deep. For the umpteenth time the four by four bounced over a ridge to land with a crash and he realised he was beginning to feel sick.

"He…he wouldn't would he?"

Young Den laughed, pleased at how he had this piker on the run. He warmed to his unaccustomed role as an authority.

"Nah, course not. My old man's a bad bugger but he ain't fucking mafia. For bait you use cats, rabbits, stray dogs. Dogs are best of course. They're not hard to find. There's a good little racket offering good homes to unwanted dogs. You just put an ad in. All these wankers, they get a cute little puppy, then once it shits on their precious Axminster, they want it out the door."

"What if the dog fights back?"

"He's not going to get very far with his jaw wired up. Amazing how long some of them last though."

"Oh, I get it."

Neck was silent for a while. He was suddenly sharply aware what a bleak and dreary area they were driving through. All the hedges had been stripped out long ago and under the low grey clouds the endless rows of ploughed soil seemed to stretch away to eternity.

"No," Little Den resumed, a little disappointed by Neck's silence. "A real gaming dog, he's a fucking maniac. Once he gets his teeth into another dog's throat, he won't let go. He'll bite through his own face if that's what it takes. He'll hold on 'til the other dog dies, or he dies."

Neck tried to imagine a dog of such horrific ferocity. "Do they always fight to the death or does one ever like, just give in?"

"No the dogfight business don't work like that. Fair enough, if he's well outclassed in the odd match, you can just go in and pull him off if you want, might even get you good odds next time. But he's got to stay in there 'till *you* pull him off. You don't want him to let you down. That's unforgivable."

"Oh yeah, of course. I can see that," Neck said stoutly. He was concentrating on fighting a rising urge to vomit.

"I mean all that training, all that money spent on steroids and vitamins and stuff. If he lets himself down, he's let you down, makes you look like a pillock."

"So what do you do?"

"What do you do? Well, he's no fucking use to you is he? So you gather all your other dogs round to have a good look, and then you finishes him off. But you make it last, make sure he knows he's dying. Make sure they know what they'll get if they don't show some spunk."

He did his best imitation of his father's grim chuckle. Neck was silent for the rest of the journey.

Little Den's truck finally pulled up next to a big old BMW in a large cattle yard. Neck could see no other buildings in sight. Except for a large gate, a substantial chain link fence completely surrounded it, and a big barn on one side dominated the space within. An uneven collection of smaller buildings and enclosures littered two sides of the open area in the centre. Some were derelict but others had been roughly repaired. Several were relatively recent constructions of corrugated iron.

Interspersed among them were weed-grown piles of building materials, rotting straw bales, timbers, and assorted rubbish. The rusting remains of small grey tractor were the only remaining signs that the sad place had once been a viable agricultural project. Around it the flat empty fields stretched as far Neck could see.

A door opened in one of the sheds and a tall heavily built man in his fifties came out. He stopped and looked carefully at Neck. Neck had never seen him before but he knew this must be the younger Den's father, sometimes referred to as Big Den. Chas had told him some disturbing stories about him, and Neck felt distinctly uneasy.

"Me Dad," Den said unnecessarily.

"You're a mate of Chas's." It was a statement, not a question.

"Yeah."

"Well next time you see him, tell him I'm done waiting. Got it?"

Neck nodded. "OK."

"He's in trouble that one." He paused as if to let the significance of that remark sink in.

"And you want a dog do you?"

"Yea, if it's a good 'un."

Big Den smiled. "Oh you knows a good dog, does you?" Behind him his son laughed. Neck didn't like the smile, or the laugh. They were just playing with him. He had a terrible feeling that they were just as likely to beat him up and just take his money as to sell him a dog. The noise in the sheds had subsided to the occasional bark.

"I know dogs."

"Not like mine you don't mate. Wait here."

He turned away and walked back into one of the smaller corrugated sheds. The two younger men waited. There was a bit of a silence.

"Lot of sheds you got here then," Neck said tentatively. "Is it all dogs?"

"Nah, we does all kinds of business. Storage. Handling. Specialised video entertainment. Whatever. You want it we can get it. Don't matter what it is. Long as you're kosher." He winked. "Anything."

Little Den's father reappeared leading a heavily built young Doberman on a stout lead. In his other hand he held a length of black plastic water pipe. The dog walked carefully beside him. It didn't look round, it didn't check the ground for scents. It just looked at Neck with its implacable slate grey eyes. It had the uneven dun colour typical of the breed. Its tail swished slowly from side to side.

Big Den stopped.

"Are you ready?" he said to Neck. Neck nodded without knowing what he was supposed to be ready for.

"Tug! Take him!"

Without a sound, the dog instantly lunged at Neck, mouth stretched in a silent snarl. He stepped back so quickly that he almost fell, and as he did so Den's father snapped back on the lead and plucked the dog out of the air. It landed on all four feet together; lead still stretched tight and still giving him that terrible glare. It snarled quietly.

The younger Den laughed. "Told you," he said, "take your arm off."

"Back," Den's father said. The dog still hauled at the lead. "Back!" He repeated, smacking the dog's rear hard with the pipe. The dog lost interest in Neck and calmly sat down.

"Hurts him, but don't break anything," Den explained. "He's young yet."

"Is that like what you was looking for?" Big Den said. He was sneering quite openly.

"He'll do," Neck said nonchalantly, trying to sound like he was completely used to having a dog try to take his arm off.

"He'll do, alright. Better than a knife, better than a gun, better than a fucking Kalashnikov. Let's see your money."

"Hang on. I don't want him going for me again, for Christ's sake. How do I make sure he goes for other people, not me?"

Little Den's father barely hid his impatience.

"For a start he'll soon work out that if he gives you any cheek he don't get no dinner and he do get a good hiding, and in the meantime you just keep his mouth shut." The older man looked over Neck's shoulder to Den the younger. "Go and get a muzzle," he said. "There's some in the back."

Little Den went over to one of the smaller sheds, built as a lean-to to the main barn. The door was padlocked. He patted his pockets until he found a ring of keys and unlocked it. He disappeared inside and shut the door behind him.

Neck and Big Den's regarded each other stolidly. Tug continued to gaze balefully at Neck. Neck was just beginning to wonder if this dog project was such a good idea when he quite distinctly heard a child's voice speaking in the shed. It said, "Bad man, bad man. Me go now, me go now. Please!"

He looked at Den's father who remained expressionless and said nothing. Den came out of the shed with a muzzle in one hand and a dog collar in the other.

"What the fucks that all about?" Den's father said to him.

"Fucked if I know," Den said. "It must be some kind of trick. That little bitch." He shook the collar, and stuck it back in his pocket. He held out the muzzle to his father. "Forget it," he said to Neck. "It's nothin'. Right?"

Neck didn't know what to do. Both men seemed completely unfazed by the voice from the shed. He watched as Den's father thrust the muzzle over Tug's jaws and handed the lead to Den.

"Right, get his fucking money and get him out of here," he said to Den. "I got things to do."

It was beginning to get dark when Little Den dropped Neck and the dog back at his Ford. The landscape looked even more foreboding than it had in the afternoon. The meticulously washed car stood out like a bright red beacon against the dull muddy landscape and lowering sky.

He helped Neck put Tug in the boot and slammed it shut. As Neck passed the money over, he was already dreading what would happen when it was time to get Tug out again.

"Right," Young Den said, climbing back up into the cabin of the four by four, "Mind how you go. Remember be hard on him. Show him whose boss. And I don't need to tell you, not a word about the Yards. Not worth your while, right? I'll see ya around."

He roared off into the night and Neck set off on the long journey home down the back roads. He was depressed. He should have felt elated now that he possessed a real killer dog but the encounter with Little Den and his father had unnerved him. They really were dangerous. He'd always thought that Chas was exaggerating but the sheer menace that emanated from the older man haunted him. And what the hell was a kid doing in there?

Chapter 38

It was almost completely dark by the time Neck got back to his house in the outer suburbs of Tamborough. Strictly speaking it wasn't his house. It was a council house, and his long-term partner Katrina rented it. Officially she lived there with her husband, but he was long gone and, since Neck pretty regularly paid his half of the rent, and the sex was adequate, she was content to let him stay.

They'd been together for a couple of years now and it was the nearest thing to a stable relationship he'd ever had in his life, but it was not an easy relationship. She was more intelligent than him, and better educated, and often reminded him of it. She presently worked at a hairdresser's in the centre of Tamborough, but she was deeply frustrated by the limitations of the job and pined for something more substantial. She just didn't know what it was.

He parked the car on what had once been a front garden but was now a bitumen-covered parking spot, carefully easing the low slung car up the kerb. He gave one last throaty rev of the engine, just to annoy the nosy cow next door, and switched off. He got out of the car and went back to the boot. He braced himself and opened it. Tug lay comfortably in the boot and looked up at him with his disconcerting slate grey eyes. "Come on," he said to the dog. "Out!"

Amazingly it followed him obediently up the path but he still had the feeling that the relationship had got off on the wrong foot. He led it to the shed behind the house and it ambled in and began checking out the apparently fascinating scents dispersed around the grubby floor.

He thought he should take the muzzle off but was nervous about getting close to the dog's teeth. It also occurred to him that he hadn't bought any dog food. Or then again should a dog like this live on nothing but meat? He decided that he could sort all that out in the morning before he went to work. He shut the shed door and went into the house.

From the back door he could see through the kitchen to where Katrina reclined comfortably on the leather settee in the tidy little lounge, watching the Sunday edition of her favourite wild life programme. He had no idea what it was about. He started to look under the kitchen sink for some kind of bowl so that he could give the dog some water.

"What are you doing?" Katrina called. "Don't mess about in there. There's half a pie for you in the fridge. Just microwave it."

"I'm looking for a bowl to give my dog some water."

"Oh, you didn't go and do it then?" The TV had switched to advertisements and she came through and stood in the doorway, the smoke from her cigarette lazily floating from her hand.

She was a tall slim woman in her mid-thirties. Her parents were Lithuanians who had come separately to England in the Sixties, met at a Roman Catholic service in Peterborough, and married soon after. She was their only child but she had little contact with them nowadays. She had no respect for their adherence to the old language and their reluctance to mix with non-Lithuanians, and she had given up their religion long ago.

She was dressed quite carefully for a Sunday afternoon but then she always took some care with her appearance. She was proud of her substantial bosom and thick hair and rightly considered herself attractive to men, although half a lifetime of smoking had already begun to age her features prematurely.

"Where is it? I don't want it in here, smelling the place up."

"He's in the shed. He won't bother you. Just keep out of his way. He's trained to attack."

"Oh great, so now we've got a killer dog wandering about the place. You daft bugger. I will tell you, if it gives me any trouble I'll have it put down before it can take a breath."

"He won't give you no trouble Kat. He's trained. You'll be safer now. You won't get no shit from those McNally kids."

"You won't get *any* shit," she routinely corrected his double negative. "I don't need any dogs to handle the neighbours. They don't give *me* any trouble. Just stand up to them Wayne."

Katrina was nearly ten years older than Neck, and she insisted on using the name on his birth certificate, which was Wayne. When they had first met she had been charmed by his youth and transparency, and flattered by his enthusiasm for her, but over the months, as their passion had waned, and the limitations of his rather timid personality had become more apparent, she had seriously begun to wonder if it wasn't time to move on.

He ignored her comments. "Can I use this?" he said.

She nodded. "For now."

He filled a washing-up bowl with water. "I'll give him this," he added, "then I'm going down the Voodoo."

"What about your supper?"

"I'll get a pasty down there. I feel like a drink."

"Well, there's a surprise. Are you taking your new poodle?"

"No. They don't allow dogs. And don't go in the shed. He's got a muzzle on but I wouldn't trust him. He needs a firm hand."

Chapter 39

In the total darkness of the barn Daisy woke from a dream. The sun had been shining; the air was thick with the scents of summer. She had been working with Jess in the big field and she had solved a really difficult problem. She couldn't remember what it was but Jess had been really pleased and had been stroking her and scratching her ears in the way only she knew how, and Daisy had felt sublimely happy.

Then Jess had stopped stroking her and the field had suddenly become dark and cold, and Jess had begun whining just like a dog in pain... and she had abruptly woken up to the terrible reality of the dark store cupboard. The whining came from the little dog beside her and despite herself she gave a little whine too. She was hungry and desperately thirsty, bruised all over, and with no idea where she was.

Without conscious thought she set about licking the mouth and ears of the little dog as much to reassure herself as the other dog. Presently despite its distress it became quieter only to reveal another, deeper, repetitive moan. Daisy pricked up her ears and walked to the cage door. The sound was coming from the big old dog across the corridor. Daisy stood and listened carefully and then gave a short sharp bark. Instead of responding the other dog abruptly stopped moaning, and then after a pause a whispered half bark.

There was such a dense mass of odours in the cupboard that she could hardly read them but through the door she could make out that the other dog was old and male and wounded. She knew that she had come into the cupboard through the part of the wall that had what they called a handle on it. So it was a door, so it must open, if you knew the secret.

She went up on her hind legs to try and reach the catch that held the wooden door closed. It was a simple traditional tap and lift latch like some of those on the doors in Jess's house but like them, above her reach. Still she kept jumping repeatedly to bang against the door. It was the only thing she could think to do. But the door remained firmly closed. It would have done even if she had been able to reach the catch. It was bolted from the outside by a simple but effective peg and ring catch.

After a time, she stopped and sat down. Then she got up and walked carefully round the perimeter of the cupboard. A jumble of odds and ends had been dumped, a range of boxes, some of them empty, others containing oily smelling tools, rotting old paper sacks of fertiliser and stale cement, all sort of bits and pieces.

She carefully investigated all of them and then, while sniffing at a rotting sack she detected a tiny flow of air from behind it. She pulled fiercely at the sacking, despite the horrible taste and managed to move it enough to reveal an area of soft, badly rotted, wood. She scrabbled and tore at it but only managed to make a hole big enough to get her head into.

She was looking into another cage but it stood empty She was filled with new energy and grabbed at the edge of the hole she had made and pulled and pulled. Nothing happened and then abruptly with a bang a substantial piece abruptly came away from the wall. She pushed herself into the new opening and suddenly, her ribs stinging from the friction, she stood in the open cage.

She turned back to try and fetch the little dog out as well, but the sharp frayed edges of the planks that had been willing to let her get out were now set to act like a one way passage. She had been able to push her way out but she couldn't push her way back. Across from her, behind the bars of its cage, crouched the big maimed dog, every breath a low moan.

Like all the members of her species Daisy had a strong sense of empathy, and a tendency to console the loser rather than to celebrate the victor in the range of life's challenges, but Daisy had been intensively bred to have an exceptionally intense level of empathy. It was a major factor in her ability to resonate with humans and, by observing them, derive effective tactics beyond her own rational abilities.

The pain of the big dog called out to her as strongly as it would to any decent human being and she desperately wanted to reach the other dog. By reaching up she was almost able to get at the wooden peg that was inserted, in a simple ring catch, to hold the cage door closed. But she just couldn't reach it.

The little dog sat down on its haunches and considered the problem. Then it came to her. The catch wasn't too high. The floor was too low. She had to find a new floor. She trotted off into the further gloom of the corridor, well away from the other dogs and re-emerged dragging an empty wooden box. Despite her exhaustion and tiredness her tail was wagging furiously. She set the box down by the door, got up on it and began to worry at the peg with her teeth.

Just how the peg held the door closed was beyond her analytic abilities but she knew it had something to do with holding the door closed. She had watched humans pulling at a variety of door catches and worrying at the peg with her teeth was the nearest she could come to copying them. She worked away at it and suddenly, for no reason that she could see, it popped out and lay on the floor beside her. Though her mouth was torn and she could taste blood she felt an enormous glow of success. She leapt off the box, seized a bar of the cage gate and pulled. The gate swung open until it collided with the box but there was room enough for her to slip through...

She went into the cage. The big old dog sat silent now, regarding her through eyes narrowed by old scar tissue. It was a grotesque sight; a substantial part of its scalp had gone revealing the skull beneath, and its body was marred all over by scars and abrasions. It had been a great fighter in its time, but age and injury had finally destroyed its willingness to fight, for which it had received its dreadful punishment. Daisy advanced carefully to lick its nose and ears and the old dog sat quietly while it received her attentions though its tail gave a tiny flicker of movement.

After a while Daisy stopped. There was nothing else she could do and she turned to go. But behind her the old dog hauled itself up and managed to follow her by scrabbling forward on it haunches. She waited until it managed to join her in the corridor. Together the pair slowly made their way along the corridor past the cages of the fighting dogs. Apart from the occasional bark the dogs made no sound, simply standing in silence as the pair struggled past them. The puppies too crowded to the bars of their cages to watch in silence the inch-by-inch progress.

At last they got to the main door but there they had to stop. Daisy leapt and banged and worried at the door but it was a waste of time. It was securely padlocked from the outside. She made her way back down the corridor to see if she could find another way out but there was nothing at the far end but a big solid door with a substantial crossbar. When she came back the old dog was sitting quietly on all fours, patiently waiting until someone should come to open the door. She came over and sat down beside him.

Chapter 40

Just before eight o'clock Neck was parking on a building site next to a rather tired looking pub well away from the expensive watering holes of the High Street. It was notionally called the Viking Club, but for some reason everyone called it the Voodoo.

Over the years the landlord had tried to give the interior an exotic atmosphere by randomly adding fake timbering and plastic stonework. The sad remnants of his ambition, along with exhausted armchairs, stained tables and an ancient odour of old beer and toilet cleanser, created an ambience that only really suited people with absolutely no interest in the physical environment but a keen eye for a bargain pint, access to illegal substances, and the proximity of easy going sex partners.

Neck walked over to join Chip and Spaz. They were both nursing tall glasses of 'Old Cock'; a traditional ale invented about six months before, and mostly distinguished by its seven per cent alcohol content. Spaz stood up. He was wearing his usual off duty outfit of filthy black jeans, monstrous boots and a tight black leather biker jacket. "I'll get you a pint mate," he said, and walked over to the bar. He moved with a characteristic, slightly hunchback shuffle, looking like nothing so much as a bad impression of Laurence Olivier's classic characterisation of Richard III.

The shuffle was inherited from a childhood viral infection that had left him with pronounced spasticity in one leg, and the twisted shoulder was one of several reminders of the various accidents he had had on his motorbike over the speed-packed years. He was tough. He had had a hard time at school for the first couple of years after the virus struck, until one day he had responded to yet another bout of baiting by bringing a brick into school, quietly coming up behind his main tormentor, and striking him on the back of the head.

Since then his preferred method of dealing with most problems was physical violence and his reliance on his upper body musculature, plus assiduous bodybuilding, had given him dangerous strength in his arms and shoulders. Still, he was an honest and essentially good-hearted man and he had known Neck, who he loved, and Chip who he tolerated, since they were at school. The three men worked together at GoodFarms Industries, an agricultural wholesaler a few miles outside Tamborough.

Spaz returned to the table and put down Neck's drink.

"Where's mine then?" Chip grunted.

Spaz ignored the comment. Chip always tried it on and the other two just accepted it. His answer to the travails of everyday life was based on a combination of guile, duplicity, and knowing when to run for it. Superficially confident and sociable, Chip's main value to the others was his connections in the nether world of petty drug dealing and fenced consumer goods. Unfortunately he was incapable of doing any kind of business without trying to cut corners, even though it usually got him into trouble.

Neck sipped his drink. "Well, I got the dog," he said, preparing to recount the tale of his encounter with Den and his father in all its gangster detail, but he was cut off.

"Did you hear about Chas?" Spaz said with barely suppressed excitement.

"What about him?"

"You don't know?" It wasn't often that any of them had news of great significance and it was a moment to be savoured.

"What?"

"He's only fucking had a stroke."

"What? What happened? How do you know?"

"We kept trying to get him on his mobile to warn him about them cops round his place, but no answer. Then Linney picked it up. Said he was in the hospital."

"What happened? Where is he?"

Chip cut in; keen to share in the story. "Fell down. Hit his head. Like Spaz says, he's in Tamborough Local." Like all the local people he pronounced it 'Tamber'.

"How the hell could he have a stroke? He's built like a brick shit house."

"I dunno," Spaz said. "I dunno, something happened anyway. Maybe it was one too many of them poppers. I used to tell him."

A thought occurred to Chip. "Don't seem right to me. Something funny going on. What about that weird bird who was at his place last night? Maybe she had something to do with it."

"Jane Bond? Nah, Linney reckons she was already with Chas in Tamborough by the time we turned up at the cottage last night. She hadn't seen no strange woman."

"So the woman, whoever she was, she was lying about all that Special Agent stuff?"

"Must've bin."

"Wish I'd fucked her now," Chip said.

Even within this little group the remark was bad taste, though typical of Chip, and the comment was ignored.

The others sat and considered. A conspiracy was always more interesting than the more probable course of events.

"Of course he owed some bad people money, didn't he?" said Chip.

"Oh come off it!" Spaz scoffed.

"He did an' all," Neck said. "I was talking to Big Den just today. He told me to tell Chas he'd 'done waiting'. It was about money. You know Chas."

"Big Den. I wouldn't cross that old bugger. He's a bad 'un. Him and that boy of his are into all sorts of stuff," Chip said.

"But they would just beat him up a bit," Spaz said. "Wouldn't they?"

"Yea, but there's others Chas done business with. Worse." Neck pointed out.

There was a silence as they all avoided thinking about the people in their world who would be prepared to hurt you badly over an unpaid debt. Then Neck broke the silence with the only eulogy that Chas was likely to get for the time being. "Old Chas, Eh?"

The three sipped quietly on their beers for a moment in a moment of sympathy.

"Anyway, what were you doing talking to Big Den? Bit out of your league," Chip asked.

"I went over to that old farm of his to get a dog. The Yards"

"Where is that place anyway?"

Neck tried to look cynical and informed. "That's something you don't need to know."

Chip snorted, "I know just where it is. I've done a bit of business there as it happens."

"A dog, eh? What is it?" Spaz reckoned he knew a bit about dogs. "You got to get the right breed or you're wasting your time."

"I dunno the breed, a Doberman I think. It's a tough little bugger anyway. Take your arm off."

"You won't get no more trouble with the McNally's then?" Chip said sarcastically, winking at Spaz.

They both laughed. The tough family that lived next to Neck was an endless source of harassment in his life.

"Too right," said Neck defiantly. "Too right. Them days is gone." He felt triumphant; he was entering a new era of street credibility. Then for a moment his mind flicked back to that plaintive little voice from the shed. What was going on there? He tried not to think about the possibilities. It was none of his business, probably just some argument with a girl friend. But she sounded so young... He abruptly switched off thinking about it, banged his empty glass on the table and glared at Chip

"Who's getting the next round then?" he said.

Chapter 41

By the time he got back to the house from the Voodoo Club, Neck was fairly relaxed after five pints of Old Cock, and the low-slung car went up the kerb with a considerable bump. He remembered to give the engine some socially disruptive revs before switching off and then ambled up to check on Tug, only to discover that the shed was empty.

His heart lurched. All that money wasted! How had it got out? Where was it? He scanned the empty street vaguely and then ran into the house.

"Kat!" he shouted. "That fucking dog's got out!"

In the sitting room Katrina was sitting comfortably as usual on the leather settee, smoking the inevitable cigarette. She was watching yet another of her wild life programmes. At her feet lay Tug, apparently also enjoying yet another repeat of the struggle for survival in the Serengeti. His muzzle had been removed. Neck stopped dead. The two of them looked up casually as he entered then went back to watching the TV.

"What's that dog doing in here?"

"He was whining in that shed, poor little bugger. I took him something to eat, that pie you didn't want. He looked so grateful I bought him in for a bit of company. He likes watching the tele. It's nature, probably wishes he was in Africa."

Neck scoffed.

Unknown to both of them Tug really did enjoy the programme. Katrina's prized high definition TV had a flicker rate in excess of 120 frames a second, more than enough for Tug to follow the action with interest. Of course he couldn't smell anything, but even so it was better than sitting in a dark shed, and the woman was like no-one he had ever met, nice high voice, fascinating smell, she didn't even hit you. He had decided he was going to like being with her.

"He's a guard dog for Christ's sake. He's dangerous. You can't have him in the house. Give him here."

Tug looked up at him with those dreadful slate grey eyes with the small black pupils. As Neck advanced to the settee he gave a casual little growl.

"I'm going to bed," Neck said. "I've got work in the morning."

Once in bed, despite the soothing effects of the beer, he couldn't relax. Kat came up twenty minutes later and after flossing and cleaning her teeth she climbed into bed with him. He snuggled down closer to her.

"Somebody's feeling friendly tonight. Have you forgotten it's Sunday?" she said in the darkness.

"Yea, well," he said. He felt a great urge to unburden himself of all the disturbing events of the last couple of days.

"I was thinking, you know, about how the world is strange."

"Certainly is," said Katrina comfortably, "you only have to open a paper. All these idle English trying to send decent people away."

"I mean you can think everything's going along as normal and, you know, safe and then everything turns upside down. I didn't tell you, but Chas, he's in Tamborough General."

"I know, Lynne Davies called me from the hospital. Shame. I was never that bothered about him myself, but he's no age to have stroke. He's even younger than me. It must be all that stuff he keeps popping."

He settled down in the bed a bit more. "Kat."

"What? I'm nearly asleep. I've got to be in the shop tomorrow."

"I know, but I want to tell you about something. But it has to be, you know, between you and me."

"Tell me your big secret then."

"No, really. This involves some bad people."

She was suddenly alert. She sat up.

"What the hell are you talking about? You haven't been trying to deal again have you? Because if you have you can fuck off. Here and now! I'm not having it." She was frightened and angry at the same time, and he knew she meant it.

"No, no. Honest. I said, never again, didn't I? And I meant it."

He was almost telling the truth too. You couldn't count a little bit of dealing between mates.

She lay back. "What is it then?"

Slowly and carefully he told her about how he had met Den and gone with him to The Yards to meet Den's father and buy Tug. He explained about Den going into a shed to pick up a muzzle and then...

"And then what?"

"I heard this little kid's voice, sounded like a girl, asking to go home, sounded scared."

"What?"

"A kid's voice. I swear."

"What happened? What did you do?"

"Nothin'. I didn't know what to do."

"Did they say anything?"

"Den just said 'It's that little bitch'."

"What did the old man say?"

"Nothing. He's a wicked old bugger."

"What did you say?"

"I told you, nothin'. He just said forget it. I just got the hell out of there."

There was a pause and she lay silent next to him in the dark.

Abruptly her breathing quickened and despite her well practised procedures for not ever thinking about that, for the first time for years, the old images, the feelings, flooded back to her. That old bastard, stinking of tobacco and her father's brandy, holding her so tightly, whispering in her ear that she was a good girl, just a bit more, while all the time her parents were just next door, thrilled that a priest should actually bother to come to their home to prepare her for confirmation.

"Oh no, oh no," she whispered to herself. "So dirty." He stared across at her in the dark.

"Kat?" he said, but for a long time she said nothing.

"My God," she said at last. "It must be some kid. It happens all the time. God knows what they're doing. You've got to tell the police."

"I thought about it. But what if it's not some stolen kid? It could just be a relative or something. God knows what they get up to up there. Then I'll be wrong side with Den and his Dad and then there will be trouble."

There was another silence for a while. Both of them knew that behind the banal frontages and leafy lanes of Tamborough there was a considerable and violent industry in drugs and various illegal commodities. It was the same everywhere, and, who knew, perhaps children were traded too. Finally Katrina spoke.

"You've got to do something Wayne. You'd never forgive yourself."

He was suddenly very angry with her for revealing his own weakness to himself.

"Don't you tell me what I've got to do. You know nothing, nothing at all. Just shut the fuck up. I don't want no trouble, right?"

"I know this much. If it turns out it is some kid, and it comes out that you were a witness and did nothing, then you *will* be in trouble, and think about her, locked up in there."

He knew she was right. "Oh, Kat," he moaned. He snuggled up to her in the safety of the darkness. "What the fuck am I going to do?"

Chapter 42

At just before midnight on Sunday night Jess realised that there wasn't going to be any news of Daisy that day. She had sat in the hastily set up operations room since eight o'clock that morning, following the impressive organisation of the six person search team set up by Larkin. They hadn't looked much like her idea of police personnel, they were mostly young and to her scruffy looking, but they seemed to know their job.

She had somehow imagined they would all be briefed and then just go out searching the streets, but the reality was that they immediately sat down at their computers. Every lead and link, however unlikely, was followed up and, despite the fact that it was Sunday, by late evening the team had made contact with several hundred sources, including dog rescue centres, kennels, breeders, and pet shops. All had drawn a blank.

At the same time the only reply she had been able get on Peter's phone was his standard mail message. No joy there. She knew he would have called her if anything useful came up.

She didn't know what to do next and suddenly she was convinced it was all a waste of time, Daisy would never be found. Her face must have shown it because she looked up to realise that Larkin was looking down at her. "Bear up Jess," he said. "It's early days yet. We'll find her. We haven't even hit the first wall yet."

"What's the first wall?"

"Well, when you start any kind of enquiry, after a time you seem to completely run out of steam. You just hit a wall, it seems there's nothing left to check out. But eventually, suddenly, with luck, a gap opens up; a whole new mass of material emerges. You've broken through the first wall."

He smiled at her. "Don't worry we'll get through the wall, and tomorrow I'll start sending out officers to follow up on today's work."

She smiled her thanks and he left.

She started to prepare herself for another restless night in the small bare room the police had provided, but then the thought suddenly came to her that she was in completely the wrong place. There was no sign that anyone had found the dog. If Daisy were free she would know that if any place was safe it was the Stone House. She might be able to find her way back. Dogs often did things like that, travelling vast distance to find their way home. She could be there now, hidden away until someone she trusted turned up.

She could almost see Daisy waiting disconsolately, but the idea of actually going back there terrified her. What if Jackson and Jones were also waiting for her? In any case Larkin would never authorise it. But she didn't work for the police. She worked for the Project. Her responsibilities were to Daisy, and anyway, she told herself, her best contact with Peter was through the secure landlines back to Canine Division Security.

More and more convinced that it was the only thing she could do, she forced her fears to the back of her mind, briskly gathered up her things, and walked out of the room. She passed quietly by the night desk, nodding sociably to the one sleepy constable who nodded back without comment.

A few minutes later, under the blackness of an almost cloudless sky, and the tranquil gaze of a moon that was almost full, she was driving through the Tamborough suburbs. The empty streets reflected the cosmic serenity above, but she couldn't respond to it, all her thoughts were on Daisy, and where she might be. In her preoccupied state she scarcely noticed the noisy little Ford Fiesta that passed her and then turned away east towards the empty Fens.

Chapter 43

Serban was abruptly woken from his doze by a sharp dig in the ribs from Penders.

He sat up abruptly from the fully reclined seat, "What is it? What time is it?"

He looked at his watch. "One o'clock. For Christ's sake, I'm not on for an hour yet."

Penders silently held up a tablet. It glowed eerily in the dark of the van's interior as across its surface a sine waved jumped abruptly. Each time it jumped it produced a tiny ping sound. "The gate's being opened," he said.

Serban came to attention immediately. "What can you hear?"

"Nothing. Whoever it is isn't in range yet." He pressed the earphones he was wearing to his head and waited.

"It's a car. It's parked now. The house door's being unlocked; there goes the alarm warning. Now it's stopped. It must be her."

"Who else?"

"I don't know yet! Wait."

After a moment a hazy but recognisable image of the kitchen appeared on the tablet screen. A figure moved across it.

"It's her, and she's on her own," Penders breathed. "What shall we do?"

"If she's on her own, nothing," Serban said. "We wait. Now leave me be. I told you, it's not my watch for another hour," and he grimly lay back and tried to imagine he was far, far away.

Chapter 44

At almost exactly the same moment, Neck and Katrina were driving slowly through the darkness along the narrow rutted track that led to the Yards. In a mixture of fear and concern for the chassis of his low-slung car, Neck was creeping along at no more than ten miles an hour.

As they rumbled along the narrow track, with the occasional sickening crunch as the underbody hit a particularly high ridge, both of them said little. Beside him, Katrina's cigarette glowed in the near darkness.

"How far is it now Wayne?" she said for the fourth or fifth time since they had entered the track.

"I dunno. Maybe I'm on the wrong track. Maybe we should go back. We could come back in the daylight." Both of them were whispering.

There was suddenly the melancholy sound of a dog barking far away, a single note repeated again and again.

"That must be it," Neck breathed. Now Katrina's stomach was churning and she wanted to be sick, instead she expertly flicked her cigarette stub out of the window, the red glow arching through the darkness like a tiny shooting star, and lit another.

"You'll kill yourself with them things," Neck muttered. It was the first time she could ever recall him showing any concern for her health. She reached down and squeezed his knee in the darkness.

Over the next few minutes the sound of the dog's melancholy barking got steadily louder until suddenly the Yards loomed in front of them. In the grey moonlight, beyond the chain link fence, they could make out the dim shapes of the long narrow barn and the huddle of sheds around it. Neck stopped and turned off the lights and they both sat and waited. He noticed his eyes were adjusting to the darkness. The monotonous chant of the dog continued. It seemed to come from the big barn but there was no sign of movement. They looked at each other.

"We gotta do this Wayne."

"I know."

He turned off the engine. Katrina picked up the torch, Neck reached back for the heavy bolt cutters and they both got out. The dog barking stopped abruptly.

"He can smell us," Neck whispered.

"Or hear us. They can hear much better than us, and see in the dark."

He looked at her.

"I saw that on 'It's A Dog's World'," she explained. It was her favourite programme.

They reached the big chain link gate and Neck prepared to break the padlock with the bolt cutter, but as he looked closer he saw that the padlock wasn't closed. He froze. "The fuckers are in there. Let's go."

"No they're not. You can feel it. There's nobody here. There's no lights or anything. And where's their cars?"

Reluctantly he pushed on side of the big double gates open and they walked in.

"Funny the dogs are so quiet,'" he said. "Just the one barking, and he's stopped."

"Perhaps they've taken most of them with them. Which shed is it?"

He led her to the shed he remembered from the afternoon. They waited in the silence by the door. "Are you there, Honey?" Katrina whispered. Silence.

Suddenly, far away across the Fens, there was an eerie scream. It sounded exactly like a child in terrible anguish.

"Oh my God," Katrina breathed.

"Don't worry love, it's just a vixen in heat." It was suddenly brought home to her that all the knowledge about animals on which she prided herself came from the TV. Wayne had been living close to the countryside since he was born. Maybe there were some things he knew that she didn't.

"Do it," she said

Neck set the cutter against the padlock securing the shed door and with an easy crunch it chopped through it and the door swung open. Katrina shone the torch in. The beam revealed some stacks of crates and cans but otherwise it was completely empty.

"Shit," Neck breathed. "They've moved her." He was deeply relieved. He'd done his bit and his conscience was clear. "Let's go."

Katrina was examining the contents of some of the open boxes.

"Look, it's mostly DVDs," she said. "Torture porn and stuff like that I think."

Another box was full of packs of heavy studded dog collars, chains, muzzles, and whips.

"Dog stuff," she reported. "Or maybe people stuff. Who knows?"

"Anyway, none of our business, she's not here. Let's go," he said.

"We can't go. Not now. We'll have to look in the other sheds. We've done one. We're already right in it if they find out it's us. Might as well try the rest."

He looked at her with real admiration.

Twenty minutes later they had cracked the padlocks on a dozen more of the sheds. One was equipped as a primitive kitchen, one or two stood empty, but most of the others were stacked with boxes and cartons of a whole range of goods: cigarettes, alcohol, mobile phones, TV sets, the catalogue went on and on. Finally they came to a shed that was more substantially built and even more securely barred than the others, with a heavy chain and a substantial padlock.

"Could she be here?" Katrina whispered. "Hello, is anyone there?" But there was no response from within.

"I dunno if I can get through this lot," Neck whispered.

"You can do it, Wayne," she said. "I know you can."

She squeezed his arm. Her apparent confidence in him gave him a warm glow and he set to work and finally managed to weaken the fixtures enough at least to create a gap. There was still no sound from within. "Nobody here," Neck said, "but I'll just check. Stay here." He squeezed through the gap and there was silence.

"Wayne," she whispered urgently, "are you alright?" He re-emerged almost immediately.

"Nothing," he said briskly. "Keep moving."

The last of the sheds they approached was open on one side. A Land Rover was parked under the protection of its rickety roof.

"Shit, I'm sure that's Den's truck. We've got to go Kat," Neck begged. "If Big Den finds out it's us..." He knew that he had a much clearer picture of what would happen to them than Katrina could ever imagine.

"I know," she said, "but he won't. He'll think its some rival gang. Let's try the big barn, then we can go." She was working at the limits of her anxiety but the terrible scream of the fox had filled her mind with images of torture.

She began to make her way towards the big barn but then Neck stopped her.

As they had worked their way round the sheds an uncomfortable thought had been nagging at him. "What I don't understand is, how come all this stuff is unguarded? You don't leave all this lot just lying about without some security. They breed dogs for Christ's sake. Killer dogs. Why aren't they set to guard? There's something badly wrong. It'll soon be dawn. Let's go."

"Wayne! For God's sake we've got to finish this. You'd never forgive yourself."

"Well be careful. There's killer dogs in there somewhere..."

The door to the long barn had a padlock hanging on its bolt, but the shackle was left open. The darkness within was impenetrable.

"Oh Christ," Neck breathed. "There's something in there. On the floor."

Her complete terror gave Katrina a bizarre determination. She knew that if she didn't march into the barn right now she'd desperately flee to the car, take off, and never come back. She pushed against the door but it was partially blocked on the inside.

"I can't move it," she said.

Neck came up beside her and pushed too. The door reluctantly opened enough for her to squeeze her way in.

The first thing to hit her was the stench of faeces and urine, and blood. Katrina took a step back, her hand to her face, but she made herself step forward. In the light of the torch she saw that the door had been blocked by a man's leg. Two bodies were huddled together in a puddle of blood on the floor of a long narrow corridor. One was a man; the other was a big dog. They seemed to be locked together in a gruesome embrace. At the same time there was a sudden cacophony of howling, barking, and snarling. Whatever spell had been holding the dogs in silence was abruptly broken. They were aware of the dark outlines of cage doors and inside them the dim shapes of dogs and puppies.

Neck made himself bend over the bodies. The man was lying face down on top of the dog, both soaked in blood. He made himself take hold of one arm to try and turn the man over. Despite his best efforts the body wouldn't move.

"Let's go Wayne. Let's go *now!*"

"Shut up Kat." His voice was harsh. "Give me a hand to turn him over. Come on!"

She forced herself to join him. They both pulled. More dogs now stood at the bars of their cages, watching them silently. Finally, reluctantly, the body half rolled over, bringing with it the body of the dog. The dog was attached to the man because its jaws were locked into what was left of his throat. "It's Den, Little Den," Neck said softly. "Look at his throat. That fucking thing killed him."

Katrina's attention was focused on the dog. "Oh Wayne," she breathed. "Look at his poor paws." Despite all the blood it was possible to see that the dog's front paws had been smashed almost beyond recognition.

A blood-covered iron bar lying next to the bodies was evidence that the man hadn't given up without beating the dog to death. But as Little Den himself had said, Neck thought, once these dogs get a grip of you they never let go. He was suddenly filled with nausea and rising anxiety

"Let's get out of here. Now. Right now." He was already moving to the door when out of the darkness down the corridor trotted up a small black and grey cocker spaniel. It was battered and filthy but despite the horror of the scene it radiated a bizarre aura of self-possession. It sat down in front of them and calmly looked up. Katrina moved forward but Neck stopped her. "Don't touch it. They're all trained to go for you." The dog wagged its tail.

"It's just a little spaniel, Wayne."

Neck relented. "Perhaps it's what they call a bait dog, you know, they use them for the fighting dogs to train on. Still, leave it. It'll be full of disease."

"My God Wayne. How do you know these things? What are you doing mixing with these people? I'm taking it back with us."

Keeping well clear of the corpses, she moved towards the dog, which sat and waited until she was close, and then gently moved away down the corridor, looking back over its shoulder. She moved closer. "Come here sweetie," she whispered. "I won't hurt you." But the little dog just repeated the manoeuvre.

"Leave it Kat. It won't let you catch it, poor little sod. It'll be terrified of people by now."

But Katrina was following the dog into the gloom. As she moved between more cages a new chorus of growls and barks built up around her. She looked into the darkness of the first cage. A snarling body suddenly hurled itself towards her, slamming into the bars of its cage and she caught a brief glimpse of a terrible scarred face and open slavering jaws. She was terrified and stepped back, but the little dog in the corridor simply stood waiting for her and after a pause she made herself go on, deliberately avoiding looking into the other dark cages. She realised that Neck was behind her.

"They're just dogs," he said. "They can't get out."

"Well there's a door open there," she said. "Perhaps the girl was kept here. Surely they wouldn't do that."

The spaniel went ahead to stand by the door of what looked like a big storage cupboard and looked back at them. From within they could hear a muted whining.

"I'll look." He opened the door. Something moved in the filthy straw at the back of the cupboard. He picked up a skinny little tan terrier. Its back and front paws were wired together. Without a word Katrina took it from him. "Let's go."

Neck looked into the other open cage. "Nothing there," he said. "Perhaps that was where they kept the dead dog and it got out."

"But how would it move all that way with no front feet? The pain would make it impossible. It doesn't matter, let's go."

They ran back out of the big barn. Katrina realised that the sky was subtly lighter. The clouds had rolled away and the cool light of the moon outlined them clearly. They ran back to Neck's car and Katrina got in. Neck passed the little dog to her and opened the rear door for the little spaniel. It was just about to jump in when it stopped abruptly and sprinted back into the enclosure. "Wayne!" Katrina shouted. "We've got to go back for it."

"Don't be so daft. We'll never catch it. We've got to get out of here, now." He started the engine and the car started to roll forward but, as he was carefully negotiating the huge ridges at the beginning of the track, the spaniel suddenly reappeared and sprinted towards them. Katrina opened her door and the dog leapt clean onto her lap. In its mouth it was carrying a blood-stained object. It was a dog collar.

Chapter 45

When Neck and Katrina got back to her house it was after four o'clock in the morning and the streets were completely empty. Neck had turned the engine off, skipping the traditional revving up for the first time for years and they had all gone into the house. As they passed the shed next to the back door Tug had started barking from within, but then abruptly stopped when Katrina told him to shut up.

Now Neck was collapsed onto the leather settee in numb silence while in the kitchen Katrina made a cup of tea for them both, and attended to the little tan dog. During their journey back she'd managed to unravel the wire from its wrists, and now she was settling it down in a cardboard box by the cooker, with one of her best cushions to make a bed.

As soon as they had come into the kitchen the spaniel had rushed forward and got up onto its hind legs at the sink to stare at the taps, giving an urgent little whine. "My God," Katrina said, "those bastards didn't even give them any water." She had quickly filled the washing up bowl with water and both dogs greedily sucked down an unbelievable amount, splashing it all over the kitchen floor in the process. Next they had worked their way through a tin of cold beans mixed with all the raw mince that had been due to go into that evening's pie.

Neck had been surprised at how much pleasure it gave him to see them feed. As soon as the spaniel had eaten, it shot out of the kitchen door into the little hallway and up the stairs. Neck had started after it but Katrina had put her hand on his arm.

"Leave it," she said, "I think it's just checking us out."

Sure enough a moment or two later they heard it lolloping down the stairs and into the lounge. When Neck went in the dog was head down busily snuffling round every inch of the room including the furniture. Eventually, apparently satisfied, it went back into the kitchen, then there was a pause of a minute or two and it returned and sat down in front of him looking up at him with its calm intelligent eyes. Looking into them he realised that those eyes reflected a completely different personality to the mindless menace of Tug's cold stare.

Despite the fact that it was battered and filthy, the dog seemed unthreatened by him, watchful, but at ease with itself and its surroundings, as if all the dreadful experiences it must have been through had somehow washed over it and away. It still held the collar firmly in its mouth, as it had, except when it was eating and drinking ever since they had left the Yards. Even then it had made sure the collar was close by.

"Do you want to give me that then?" He reached for the collar but the dog politely declined.

Katrina came into the lounge with his big mug of tea and sat down beside him. She took a sip of her own cup. "My God, what a night." She looked down at the dog. "That creature's amazing," she said. "That poor little bastard in the kitchen wouldn't settle then she came in and gave it a good licking. It's fast asleep now."

"Is it OK?" he said.

"The wrists seem to have recovered a bit since I managed to get the wire off. I think it'll live, but I don't know if it will ever walk normally again. How can people do such a thing?" She turned to him and leaned against his shoulder. The dog in front of them put its head down on its outstretched forepaws and appeared to doze off. The collar rested on its front paws.

"Oh Wayne, what are we going to do now?" Katrina whispered. "That man's dead and God knows what's happened to that little girl."

"We do nothing," Neck grunted. "Nothing at all. I wish to God we hadn't have gone. We didn't help the kid and it's none of our business if some gangster gets himself killed by his dog. Big Den will have to sort it out. He's probably hushed up worse."

"But we didn't take anything, apart from the dogs. Why would anyone bother to break in if they didn't take anything valuable?"

"We'll never know. Perhaps the kid was some sort of hostage for another gang. It don't matter. The only thing that links us to the Yards is these dogs."

The realisation of his vulnerability suddenly struck him very hard. He was not a brave man. "But if Big Den discovers where I live and finds them here, then we're fucked. We'll have to get rid of them somehow."

Katrina looked at him in dismay and the dog looked up abruptly.

"I don't mean kill them. I'm not some psycho like Den." He realised he was addressing his remarks as much to the dog as to Katrina. "We'll just take them somewhere far away and dump them into one of them rescue places." He wasn't clear how they could do it without leaving a trail but it must be possible.

"Anyway," he said, "it'll soon be dawn. We can't do nothin' tonight. Let's go to bed."

"I'll just finish my tea." she said, and closed her eyes, but a minute or two later he realised she was fast asleep. He took the mug from her hand, set it on the coffee table, sat down beside her and felt his eyelids droop. A few minutes later all four of them, two exhausted humans and two exhausted dogs, were dead to the world.

Neck awoke abruptly, aching all over, to discover he was alone on the big settee and it was well into the morning. He got up and stretched. Everything suddenly came back to him and a dark cloud descended on his mood as he was once again faced with deciding what to do. He looked at his watch. It was after eight o'clock. He had to be at FarmFoods by eight thirty.

He walked into the kitchen where Katrina was already digesting her first cigarette with toast and black coffee as chasers. The spaniel lay at her feet; the collar firmly in its mouth, and the little terrier peeked at him over the edge of its box. "The kettle's boiled," she said, "but there's no milk. I gave it to the dogs."

"Milk?"

"For their Weetabix. You can't expect them to eat it dry. There's nothing else to give them."

"What about Tug?"

"He wouldn't eat it. I gave him the last of the eggs. Boiled. That dog's been spoiled."

"Anyway, he's not the problem. I've got to get rid of these two right now. I'll call in and say I'm sick."

"No," she said. "Don't do that. If there's ever any questions, it's better if you've just turned up as usual. I've worked it out. It's a Monday isn't it?"

He looked at her in incomprehension.

"My half-day!" Shaking her head at his lack of interest in her work schedule at the hairdresser's, she went on. "There's never much business on a Monday morning. Violet won't mind if I take the whole day off even. I'll go and visit Linney Davies. With Chas away she'll be in shock, bless her, and glad of the company. She might need some help as well. But the point is I'll take the dogs and see if she'll take them until we can work something out."

He nodded.

It was a great idea. He immediately felt a lot better; as usual Katrina was a couple of steps ahead of him. He went over to her and kissed her. "You're a clever old stick ain't you? That's a great idea." She made no overt response but despite herself she was pleased by the praise, even if it was only Wayne.

"You get off then."

Chapter 46

Big Den stood at the open door of the big barn and looked down at the remains of his only son in the early morning light. After a time he bent down and almost tenderly touched the cold and bloody skin of his son's face. Then he stood up and walked down the corridor. The caged dogs stood and watched him in silence. One carefully wagged its tail. He ignored them and walked to the open cage that had once held the maimed creature he had called Killer. An empty box stood in front of the gate. The wooden peg that had held the gate closed lay on the floor.

Next he looked into the open door of the wooden storage cupboard opposite. The cupboard was empty. He looked into the open cage next to it. That floor was littered with the remains of part of the wooden partition. He tried to put the story together. Had the dogs somehow got through the wooden wall of the cupboard into the open cage? But the door holding Killer had been opened from the outside. The wooden bolt had been chewed at, could a dog have done that? Or had Den forgotten to push the bolt? It was possible. Anyway it seemed pretty clear that Killer had got out and he'd been able to get at Den. But how had that terrier got away? Its legs were wired up for Christ's sake. There were people mixed up in this somehow...

He left the barn, went over to the sheds and saw immediately that the padlocks had been cut. He went at once to the shed with the cocaine. All its locks were forced. A one-kilo pack was gone. Without looking into the other sheds he returned to the big barn and looked down again at his son.

"Don't you worry boy," he said quietly to the inert heap. "They're going to pay for this. Oh yes. They're going to pay, and they're going to pay very hard, very, very hard. Don't you worry my son." Then he went to find a spade.

As she washed up the crockery under the tap, the washing up bowl now consigned to its new function as a water bowl, Katrina heard the familiar throaty roar of Neck's car fade away down the street. Looking down at both dogs she decided to wash them before she took them over to Linney. They were both filthy and the spaniel in particular had mud and God knew what else matted in its long fur.

"Right girls," she said. "We're going off to buy some proper dog food and then you can start your hideaway holiday. But first you're going to get a proper wash and dry from one of Tamborough's leading hairdressers."

The two dogs looked at her blankly. "Off to the bathroom," she said. She had scarcely spoken before the spaniel was up and off into the hallway. She picked up the little terrier and followed the spaniel as it sprinted up the stairs.

In the little bathroom she spread a well-worn bath towel on the floor. It carried a faded image of the World Cup and the message, 'England will it bring it home!' It was very old, she was sure Neck would never miss it. She put the plug in the bath, ran the hot and cold taps together and switched the water flow to the spray head. She doused both dogs and, even without soap, an extraordinary amount of filth flowed off them. She squirted both dogs with a generous dollop of shampoo, courtesy of the hairdressers where she worked, and began to work up foam in their coats.

Ten minutes and two more rinses later, she was faced with two almost unrecognisable if still soaked dogs. The little tan terrier turned out to have a bright almost fox-like colour and the spaniel was not black and grey but instead a clear black and white, with a thick full coat and big fluffy ears. As Katrina dried them she had also discovered that hidden among the matted hair on top of the spaniel's head was a small hard button. It seemed to be made of plastic, and it looked more like some medical device than some perverse effort by Den and his father. The dog ducked its head away when she tried to touch it so she left it alone.

"I wonder what that's all about then sweetie," she said.

The dog gazed up at her with those intelligent soft brown eyes and then went over to where it had dropped the grubby collar by the toilet seat. It picked it up and brought it to over to her.

"Well I'm honoured," she said. Holding it at arms length she rinsed it under the sink tap, then looked more closely. She didn't know anything about dog collars but close up this one was very odd, covered in little bumps and ridges, even tiny letters and numbers. It looked more like a very expensive watch than a collar. It seemed to be made of some sort of tough plastic rather than leather and there was a simple catch.

"Do you want this on then?" she said.

The dog stretched its neck and kept still until she clicked the collar into place. Wagging its tail furiously, it gave several short sharp barks. It seemed to be waiting for something, but Kat had no idea what it was. "Okay, ladies," Kat announced. "We're off to buy you dinner."

Twenty minutes later Kat parked her Mini in the enormous and mostly empty car park at the new Tamborough out-of-town trading centre. She led the two dogs into the giant pet store. They were both on leads that she had improvised from old curtain chord, and they obediently followed her down the long corridors of shelves of food and equipment. The little terrier was walking without too much difficulty, but even so Katrina and the spaniel paced themselves a little so she could keep up. At a centre desk a young assistant was checking invoices. He looked up with a cheerful smile. He was quite good looking and from old habit she straightened her back to lift her bosom a little. He appeared not to notice.

"Very quiet today," he said. "Always the same Mondays. How can I help you?"

"I've just got these two," she explained, "I don't know a lot about dogs and I want to buy the right food for them, Oh, and something for a young guard dog. I think it's a Doberman?"

"Wet or dry?"

"Sorry?"

"Sorry, I mean canned food or dried, in a packet. The dry is easier to keep and serve up, and some people say the poo is, you know, easier to handle." He led her to a long shelf with various brands of dried food in enormous sacks.

"I don't know what to choose," she said, but the spaniel was now pulling urgently at its lead, looking from her back down the corridor and giving short sharp barks. The little terrier joined in with its squeaky yap, apparently just to add to the noise.

"Bitch ain't it? She seems to want to go somewhere," said the assistant. "Do you think she's used to eating something else?"

"I don't know," she said vaguely, "but I don't fancy wandering around until I find out what it is."

He looked at her and smiled. He *had* noticed her breasts. They always did. "I tell you what," he said, "there's no one else here. Just let her free and we'll see where she goes."

They exchanged conspiratorial grins and turning away she bent to slip the spaniel from its lead. Without looking, she knew he was appreciating the view of that too. As soon as she was free, the spaniel shot off down the corridor and the two humans followed, Katrina carrying the terrier.

"If this your first time with dogs," he said, "I can give you my phone number and you can always, you know, call if you have any problems."

"I will," she said, "I will."

She was quite disappointed at how quickly they caught up with the dog.

They found the spaniel up in its hind legs, tail wagging furiously, staring fixedly at a shelf of canned food. It turned to Katrina and gave a big doggy grin.

"Well," said the young assistant, "now we know. The lady prefers Chunky Chunks."

Chapter 47

At the Stone House Jess woke up abruptly to the clear light of Monday morning. She was horrified to see it was already ten o'clock and she immediately grabbed her mobile phone and rang through to the number Larkin had given her. "Operations room," a man's voice said carefully.

"Hello it's Jess Stewart."

"Oh, hello Miss, I thought I recognised the number," the voice said. "It's John. We missed you this morning. Everything OK?"

"I'm fine thanks. I'm at the Stone House. Can I speak to Superintendent Larkin?"

"I don't know exactly where he is at the moment Miss. I can tell you we've got nothing solid yet. I'll let him know you called. Meantime don't you worry, just sit tight and I'm sure he'll get right back to you as soon as anything comes up." She thanked him and disconnected the phone. Almost as soon as she put it down it rang again. It was Peter.

"Hello," he said. "Where are you? They told me you'd left the station last night. Are you alright?"

"I'm fine. I'm at the Stone House. I thought Daisy might come back here but there's no sign of her."

"Never mind. We'll find her. Is the new security man there?"

"Yes, I met him last night when I came back. I'm OK."

"Thank goodness for that. You really shouldn't be there on your own. Please stay right there. Don't let anyone in. I'll come over as soon as I can and fill you in on what's been happening. Is that OK?"

A few hundred yards away Penders pulled down his earphones and turned to Serban triumphantly. "Now we're getting somewhere," he said. "Golden boy is on his way, and he's got news!"

Chapter 48

Just after noon on that Monday morning Katrina was drawing up outside the tiny cottage presently occupied by Lynne and Luke Davies and previously by Charles Garvin, presently lying very still in a bed at Tamborough Local Hospital.

Almost as soon as they arrived, Lynne came out of the open kitchen door at the side of the house and down the front path to meet the car. By Katrina's side the terrier was asleep but the spaniel was rigid with excitement, tail thrashing. As she opened the car door the dog leapt out and immediately sprinted down the path and into the house.

She was just about to explain to Lynne why she had brought the dogs when she said, "Kat! Hello! My goodness. You've found her!"

"What? It's not your dog is it?" Katrina said, completely confused

"No, neither is that little one, but that one..." indicating the spaniel as it now reappeared from the house to disappear into the back garden, "that's the one they're looking for."

Katrina felt an immediate surge of panic. "Is it the dog fighters? Have they been round here?"

Lynne's face dropped. "I don't know anything about no dog fighters. It's the police that want her. Where did you find her? It's good of you to bring her back here, but they want her in Tamborough."

Katrina anxiety was now augmented by confusion. Had Big Den contacted the police already? How did Linney Davies, of all people, know anything about it? She stood looking at her, trying to grapple with it all.

"Hang on, hang on," she said eventually, "I'm not rushing off to the police. Why are they looking for the dog, Linney? What's happened? I don't want to get dropped in it for something I haven't done."

Lynne looked at her curiously. "I'll tell you as much as I know. But you look a bit peaky. Are you all right? You'd better come in and have a cup of tea."

Katrina followed her into the tiny kitchen. "Oh Linney," she said, "I'm so sorry about Chas."

"Yes. It's terrible isn't it? But the hospital say he's going to be alright. So we mustn't complain." She plugged in the kettle.

"Funny how it happened," she went on, "he just got up out of his chair, walked outside and keeled over. Hit his head really badly. The doctors don't know why it happened. They think it might have been a stroke. It just happens apparently, even to young people." She looked at Katrina almost defiantly, put teabags into two mugs, ready for when the water boiled, and started putting a sandwich together.

"Anyway, Wayne sends his best," Katrina said. "It must have been a shock for Luke too. Where is he?"

"He's at school. I thought it was best if he didn't hang about here. Get things back to normal. I hope you can stay until he gets back, he'd love to see Daisy again."

"Daisy, is that her name?"

"Far as I know. That's what they all call her."

Katrina braced herself to tackle the task of discovering why so many people knew the dog and exactly why they were looking for her, when Daisy suddenly reappeared, sat down quickly in front of Lynne, and gave her what could only be described as a searching look.

"Looking for Luke are you?" Lynne said, filling the mugs with the hot water.

The dog gave a short sharp bark and wagged its tail enthusiastically.

"Clever little thing isn't she?" Lynne said. "Luke reckons she can understand every word you say. Mind you he's got this little fantasy that she can talk to him too."

She addressed the dog slowly. "Luke's at school now." The dog gave a little whine and ran to the door. It turned and came back. "I mean he's gone away for a little while, but he'll back on the school bus at four o'clock. My God," she said, catching herself, "I'm getting as bad as Luke."

Katrina could have sworn the dog glanced at the big reproduction clock on the wall but immediately dismissed the thought. The dog stopped and seemed to think for a moment, and then it came over and lay down at her feet, apparently content to wait until Luke turned up. The little terrier whined and Katrina set it down on the floor. It neatly sat itself down next to Daisy and the two dogs seemed to relax.

Lynne brought a cup of tea and a sandwich over to Kat.

"You do take milk don't you?"

For God's sake, Katrina thought, let's cut to the chase. "Please Linney," she said. "Tell me. Why are they looking for the dog?"

Lynne was studying her hands, her cup of tea forgotten. "I tell you Kat, this business with Chas it's made me think. It's brought things to a head I'm not sure he's the right person for me or Luke." She promptly burst into tears.

Katrina waited. It was obvious Lynne had to work her way through this little speech. After a little time the woman gathered herself together and blew her nose on a tissue from up her sleeve.

"Sorry," Linney offered. "I'm upset but I've made up me mind. I thought it was important for a boy to have a father. That's what I would tell meself when he was bad to Luke. But when I saw the way he beat that dog, that one right there, something went cold in me. There's something wrong in Chas. I hope he gets better, but when he does, he ain't coming back here." From the floor Daisy gave a long low growl.

"What's up with you then Miss?" Katrina said.

"She don't like Chas, no wonder," Lynne said, and then began to tell her the story of how Daisy had come into her life.

Chapter 49

Big Den was standing in his kitchen shed at the microwave, waiting for a bowl of ready-made soup to finish warming up. He was in despair. He was closer to being crushed than he had ever been in his life. The loss of young Den was like an aching tooth. It was unbearable. He would manage to push the knowledge of his death away and then he'd notice some bit of nothing like Den's jacket on the back of the door and he'd think 'He's late as usual,' and it would all flood back.

The microwave bell sounded, and he took the soup out and started eating the scalding liquid. As he bolted it down, his mind raced around the options of what had happened. Who'd broken into the Yards? Why? Had Den shot his mouth off again? Who to? Was his death a message? What was the fucking message? He was careful to keep well clear of the East European gang masters who controlled the immigrant slaves used for crop handling.

They could be very nasty but had nothing against him, surely. Had he crossed somebody from the Leicester coke crowd, or worse, the new lot, coming up from London?

Word was that they were setting up women, often recent immigrants, in towns like Tamborough to act as brokers for business coming in, as more and more kids got the habit.

Killer had been let out deliberately and the bait dogs taken, but it seemed daft to use a nearly dead dog with its front legs ruined and a couple of lap dogs just to send a message. And why had they only nicked *some* of his cocaine?

None of it made sense. But whatever was going on there was one thing he was absolutely sure of, whoever was responsible for the death of his son was going to pay, and pay hard. His mobile rang.

"It's Billy," a voice said. "You got a minute?"

"What have you got?"

"This is a weird one. Middle of the morning, a woman comes in here with a couple of dogs. Middle aged, but nice tits. Anyway she says like she's just bought them, wants advice about food and that, and I think to meself this one knows fuck all about dogs, and chances are she'll want to dump them in a month, when she realises how much they cost to keep, and shit everywhere into the bargain. I always think of you Den old buddy, so I gets her number, bit of future investment. And, as I say, nice tits."

"Go on for fuck's sake."

"Yea, well, not ten minutes ago, in comes a girlie copper. She shows me a picture of a couple of blokes. Some villains I suppose. I tell her I've never seen them before, which is true."

"Go on!"

"Well, then she says wants me to put up a wanted notice for a missing dog. I wouldn't give a shit usually, but I look at the picture and it's only the same fucking dog that this woman's just bought in. And this is the thing. I chat the cop up a bit, and she reckons that this pooch is really valuable. I mean so fucking valuable that they're looking for it everywhere. There's got to be a deal in here somewhere. So of course I thought of you."

"What's the dog?"

"Looks like a spaniel, a bitch, what they call blue roan, you know, black and white. Sharp little bugger, it don't look like much to me but perhaps it's got special DNA or something."

"Did it have a scab on its head, nasty looking black thing?"

"Do you know what? Now I come to think of it, it might have had some sort of little lump. Is that important?"

"It might well be," said Den carefully. "What about the other dog?"

"Little brown thing. Dunno what breed, little pointy ears. Why do you ask?"

"Never mind. You did well Billy boy. Give me that number. Did she give you a name?"

Chapter 50

In the kitchen of Lynne's cottage, Daisy sat quietly listening to the conversation around her. She was very tired, her body ached in several places, and she was still trying to sort out the meaning of what had been happening to her over the last forty-eight hours, but she was alert. She was only used to being spoken to in direct short sentences but the range of nouns and verbs she could comprehend was very large, and she worked out that Katrina was making a report to Lynne about her rescue last night. It seemed to get both women agitated and she could smell their arousal levels go up.

Beside her the little terrier was licking the inside of her ears, which was very pleasant, but she could not relax. She wanted to see Luke again but it was now a long time since she had last seen Jess and a lot had happened. She was very keen to make a full report to her, as she had been trained to do. Although there was a nice strong smell of Luke all around the kitchen there was also the residual sour smell of Chas and she wanted to move away from it. She decided she wanted to go and lie in Luke's little house at the end of the garden. She got up and went over to the door and scratched at it, looking back at Lynne.

"That dog wants to go out," Lynne said. "She won't go far if she's waiting for Luke. Let her go." Katrina opened the door and the little brown dog got up quickly and limped over to follow Daisy down the garden, occasionally giving her tail a playful bite.

"Anyway," Katrina was saying in her logical way, "the thing is, if Big Den is looking for whoever broke into the yards, Daisy and this little one are the living proof that me and Wayne were involved. I thought I'd bring them round to you, because," she ended rather lamely, "there's no connection between Big Den and you."

"Oh but there is, there is," Lynne said urgently. "I've heard Chas mention his name. I don't know much about it but I'm pretty sure he had some dealings with him. I don't want them round here. Do as I say, get her back to the police and quickly. They'll sort it all out and you'll be in the clear."

Katrina started to feel better. She and Neck had gone to the Yards with the best of intentions and plainly Big Den was going to have some real problems when the police discovered what he was up to. They should have gone to the police immediately. Why hadn't she said that to him?

Abruptly she felt her phone buzz in her pocket. She took it out.

"That's lucky," Lynne said, "you usually can't get a signal round here."

Katrina looked at the phone read out. It was a local number. "Hello."

"Is that Miss Katrina Smith?" It was a heavy man's voice, with a local accent.

"Sorry you've got the wrong number. I'm Katrina Ossel."

"Sorry, hang on, I've read it wrong. That's right, Katrina Ossel."

"What's this about?"

"I'm glad we've found you. I'm a community support officer, er, Mr Reardon. I'm helping out the police. They're trying to trace a lost dog and I believe you might be able to help."

"Why? How did you get my name?"

"Bit of luck really. A lady said she was a neighbour of yours, thought you might have found it. Do you mind if we check up?"

"I was just going to bring it into the station," Katrina said defensively.

"Oh thank you, but there's no need for you to come to us. She's probably not even the one we're looking for. I'll send someone round. Are you at home now? Can you give me an address?"

"No I'm not. I'm visiting a friend."

"Well, if you're not too far away, we can pop over, just to check. Can you tell me where you are now?"

Down in the garden Daisy and the terrier were luxuriating on the old mattress in Luke's den. The smaller dog had discovered his cache of comics and was now steadily reducing them to shreds. Daisy watched calmly. To an outside observer she appeared to be dozing gently, but in reality she was reviewing her plans. Her primary imperative and duty was to get back to Jess, and she was pretty sure she could work her way back to the Stone House training centre from the cottage. But she wasn't certain. With Luke to help her however she was pretty sure she could make it and she very much wanted to see him again anyway. Her understanding of formal time was not precise but she had been trained to connect spoken clock times with all the odour clues she used to estimate the time of day and she was pretty sure he would be back soon.

She stood up and stretched, and at the same moment her nose caught the tiniest whiff of diesel fume. As she stood concentrating the smell strengthened and was then compounded by the faintest odour of human beings. There were several of them. She started sorting them out, and then, as clear as a bell note would be to a human being, she identified Luke. A moment later she heard the sound of the school bus engine and began running up the garden path barking steadily.

The moment Luke got off the bus he saw Daisy as she ran forward to meet him on the front path. As he knelt the dog dived into his arms, a mass of fur and wagging tail, furiously licking his nose, and letting out little yips and squeals as he buried his face in her neck. Beside them the little terrier danced around equally enthusiastically, delighted to be associated with the happy event. The bus roared away, a line of faces looking back through the grubby rear window.

"Look at that," Lynne said, looking out of the little front window of the cottage, "they're so pleased to see each other. It's a pity they've got to take her away."

"Mum!" Luke rushed up to his mother and hugged her. "Daisy's come back! She found her way back! Does Mrs Duncan know? Is she coming too? She says I can visit Daisy at the big house and play. It'll be great! What a relief! Oh you clever girl!" He knelt and cuddled the spaniel, which enthusiastically licked his nose again.

"The thing is, I don't think Mrs Duncan is coming here today," Lynne said, "but the police have called. They're going to pick her up. I should think they'll take her to Mrs Duncan."

"Oh Mum, can I go too? I'm sure Mrs Duncan will want to see me."

"No love, we'll have to wait and see what they say. I'm sure it will be all right though."

The boy's face fell and at that moment the spaniel gave a short sharp bark and went to the door, looking back over its shoulder.

"Well then," Luke said. "Can I just go down to the den and play for a bit before she goes. Can I take the little dog too?"

"I don't know, I should think so. She belongs to Kat."

Katrina started to speak but Lynne gave her a look and she just nodded.

"Go on then, you haven't got long. Go and have one of your little chats."

But the boy and the dogs had already vanished out of the door.

Down in the den Luke sat down on his mattress and as the dogs sat down beside him he reached over and pressed the biggest button on Daisy's collar.

"One, two, three, testing," the tiny collar speaker said. "Hello Chunky."

Luke laughed with delight. "Hello Daisy," he whispered. "I was worried about you. Its lovely to see you again."

The dog momentarily abandoned its reserve and jumped up tail thrashing to lick his face. "Chunky! Chunky! I like Chunky," the little speaker squeaked.

"Where have you been? What's happened?"

The dog paused, waiting for him to formally require it to recount what had happened, but when nothing more was said it took its own initiative.

"DAC 32 will make report."

Looking at the dog Luke realised that something had changed in her manner. If it was possible to read a dog's facial expression at all Daisy had always seemed merry and bright, but now there was a weariness behind the eyes, her coat was dull and the energy seemed to have gone out of her. Then she visibly pulled herself together.

"Long time ago, Daisy loses Chunky."

"Yes," Luke said, "and Chunky loses Daisy. I'm sorry."

"Me run and run. Me search and search. But no Chunky. No Jess, no satisfactory conclusion to project." The dog paused as if remembering.

"Were you lost?" The dog made no sign of understanding him so he waited while the dog looked into the distance for a while. Then it said, "Me sleep. Me wake up. Good morning! But! No Chunky. No Jess. No dinner... But! Me search again. Me go long way, go to big play time."

Luke couldn't make out what the dog meant.

"Grass, trees. Men, women, dogs…" the dog said helpfully.

It sounded like a playground or a park. "What happened then?"

The words tumbled over one another. "Man gives me dinner. Good. But! Dinner is bad. Man is bad. Bad Man takes me to bad place. Now two bad men! Many bad dogs in boxes. Many sad dogs in boxes. Me in box. Me sad."

The dog paused as if to take a breath. "Me dig. Me make door. Me open door for Big Dog."

"Wow! Where is he then? What happened?"

The dog ignored him.

"Bad men gone. But! Big door is shut. Cannot go. Cannot."

The dog suddenly seemed to lose interest in the conversation and slumped down on all fours with its head in its paws.

"I'm sorry, it must be horrible for you to remember all this. It sounds terrible."

The dog gave a great sigh and closed its eyes. It seemed for a moment as if it was simply going to sleep. Then it said, "Big Dog and Daisy wait at big door. Cannot get out! Must get out. Little bad man comes. Little bad man opens door."

"So then you escaped. Then you got out."

"No, little bad man says no! No!"

"So what happened? What did you do?"

The dog paused again. "Me make little bad man fall down and Big Dog… Little bad man dead."

At that moment the little brown dog beside her suddenly sat up and yelped. A moment later Daisy sat up too, all alert, ears pricked, head raised to sample the breeze.

"What is it?"

The two dogs looked at each other. The smaller dog gave a little whine.

"She says Bad Man is here," Daisy said.

Katrina heard the sound of a car coming down the narrow road to the cottage. As she looked out of the window a big black car drew up. A man in his fifties got out. He was a big man and his shoulders strained against the dark suit he was wearing. He came up the path and knocked at the side door that led direct into the kitchen. Lynne opened it. Close up he was even more dominating. He looked keenly at both women. "Miss Oswell?"

"Ossel, that's me," Katrina said.

"Good." He made an effort at a smile. "My name's Officer Reardon. Thanks for helping us. I decided to come round meself. I'd better look at the dog. It won't take long. Is she nearby?"

He had a strong local accent. She'd somehow expected someone more, well, educated sounding. All of a sudden the uncertainty that had been niggling away at the back of her mind since her conversation with him on the phone crystallised into an obvious question. Why would the police send a plain-clothes officer to check on a lost dog? She felt a little wrench of panic. She tried to calm herself, who knew how the police did things? But in her gut she still felt unsure. Was it possible that he was somehow involved with the dog fighters? How could he be? But there was so much she didn't know.

Her voice trembling slightly she said, "Of course. By the way Mr…"

"Reardon," he said briskly.

"Yes Mr Reardon. I know I'm being picky, but you know. Do you have some sort of ID? I'm used to seeing policemen in uniform."

The smile slipped and for a moment she saw a flash of real irritation.

"That's a very good point Miss Ozzel. You're right to bring it up but as standard procedure I keeps it in the car. Now, can you tell me where you found the dog? Where is she?"

Now the alarm bells were really ringing. Years of trying not to sound like her parents had left her acutely aware that middle class English people never made grammatical mistakes like that. 'I *keeps* it in the car'?

"You want me to go with you?"

"You and the dog, if you don't mind, paperwork and that. If it's the right dog of course."

Katrina suddenly made up her mind, Policeman or not, she wasn't going anywhere with him. Somehow she was going to get the dogs and make her own way to the station.

Now Lynne spoke up. "My son's taken the dogs down the end of the garden. They'll be in his little play house I bet."

"I'll fetch her," Katrina said quickly. As he started towards the door she slipped past him and ran down the path, tottering slightly on her heels. She had no idea what she was going to do next. Perhaps she could somehow persuade him to let her get into her own car with the dogs and then get away from him As the futility of the idea struck her she got to the den and looked inside. It was empty A blast of aftershave signalled that Reardon, or whatever his name was, was just behind her.

"Where is it then?"

"I don't know," she said. "I'm sorry. They can't be far. I tell you what, leave it to me and I'll make sure she gets back to the station. I'm sure you've got other places to go to. I don't want to hold you up." It didn't sound very convincing, even to her.

The man's whole manner suddenly changed. He seized her arm. "I don't give fuck about the dog," he said. "Who did it? Was it you? Who do you work for? Where's my shit? Who killed my boy? Who killed my boy?"

Holding her by the arm, he dragged her up the path. She felt a heel go on one of her shoes. As Lynne started down the garden towards them, her hand to her mouth, he brushed past her and half dragged, half carried Katrina past the house and down the front path to his car.

As he opened the door and threw her in, Daisy suddenly appeared from behind the shed. She shot up the path and dived at the man, seizing his arm and trying to drag him away from Katrina. At the same moment Luke pushed past his mother and tried to pull Katrina out of the car. Behind them the little terrier was yapping furiously. Lynne was crying and mumbling, "Kat, Kat, come back."

The man ignored the dog hanging from his sleeve and effortlessly threw Luke several feet onto the road verge. As Katrina started to get out of the car he punched her hard in the jaw and, as she fell back into the front passenger seat, he slammed the door behind her. He seized Daisy by the neck, tore her teeth from his sleeve and carried her round to the boot. He quickly opened it and threw her in. The whole time, growling furiously, the little terrier worried at his ankles, until he kicked it away.

He got into the driver's seat; Katrina sprawled next to him, still dazed by the vicious punch. Lynne stood by the car impotently. "Please Mr Reardon. Let her go. She ain't done nothin. Just take the dog."

He started the engine and leaned across Katrina to the open window.

"Tell them if I don't get my shit back, she's dead. Tell them one word to the cops and she's dead. Tell them if they don't hand over the fucker that killed my boy she's dead, and you too. Tell them they crossed Den, and *nobody* crosses Den. Got it?"

Lynne simply stood paralysed. As Luke struggled to his feet, the car sped off up the narrow road. The noise died away and then there was silence except for the sound of the birds singing in the trees, and the muted sound of Lynne's sobbing.

Daisy realised that she was in the same airless container that she had been in before. Once again it was painful to brace herself across the hard rim of the wheel underneath her and once again she was surrounded the bitter smells of distress and anger and despair, but a lot had changed in her in the twenty-four hours since she had last been in the boot.

The open welcoming part of her that had assumed that all humans were not only powerful but also essentially kindly had shrunk considerably. If it hadn't been for all her relationship with Jess, and her recent experience of the unreserved affection of Luke, the brutal impact of Chas and The Yards might have made sure it had gone all together.

She still had some faith in human beings but her key strategy for dealing with new ones had moved from trying to work out how to please them to trying to anticipate how they might try to hurt you next. And from now on she would be ready to defend herself. As the car sped on she managed to find a reasonably comfortable position by arching herself around the wheel and then, with nothing else to do, promptly put herself into the Calm, the mindless dream place to which all dogs can go when there's nothing else to do but wait.

Chapter 51

At five o'clock or so that evening, the Spring day still confidently sunny, Neck parked his car outside Katrina's house, gave the throttle its traditional rev up and got out. Even before he opened the car door he could hear the melancholy sound of Tug incessantly barking.

He went up the path to the shed and opened the door. Tug stood there, and as he saw Neck he stopped barking and started wagging his tail. The dog had been tied with a rope to a heavy bench but it had still somehow managed to get itself twisted around so that it was unable to reach the basin of water he'd left for it. It had soiled the floor beneath its feet.

"Bloody hell, you poor old fucker," Neck said. "Let's get you sorted." Forgetting his fear of the dog he advanced to free it. As he put his hand on its collar he had a sudden image of it leaping at him at the Yards but it stood quietly, its tail wagging gently while he untangled the rope, and then rushed over to noisily drink.

"Have you bin left in here all day?" Neck said. "What the hell is Kat up to?"

He let himself into the house. It had clearly been empty all day. Kat's empty coffee cup, with its trademark blot of lip-gloss on the rim, stood cold by the sink. He went over to the base phone. The red light was flashing on the voice mail indicator. He pressed the tab and listened to a succession of calls. Each time the caller had simply put the receiver down when there was no answer. All the calls were marked 'number withheld'.

He started to look for something to give the dog. He had just found two ancient tins of sardines and was unrolling the lids when the phone rang. He went over and took the receiver off of the base unit. There was silence at the other end and then Katrina suddenly shouted.

"Wayne, it's me. Don't." but then her voice stopped abruptly. There was another silence and then he heard Big Den say. "The Yards. Get over here. You've got until tonight or it's Domestos time for your bitch. And bring it back. All of it." And the line went dead.

Chapter 52

Jess sat alone in the big comfortable kitchen of the Stone House. It seemed very empty without Daisy. She'd been sitting like that for much of the day. She'd been going to tidy up her records but she somehow couldn't raise the energy. There was the sound of car wheels scrunching the gravel. It was Peter. She went out to meet him.

"The new security man's keen," he said as he kissed her lightly on the lips. "He made me show all the proper I.Ds. Bit late now though."

He followed her into the kitchen and sank down into the big old armchair by the stove. She couldn't help asking, "Any news?"

"Not yet, but we'll get there."

"Do you want a drink or anything? Tea?"

"Can we hit on your famous coffee machine? I seem to have been driving all day."

She went to the fridge to get the ground coffee and next to it was a half empty can of Rustlers. That reminds me, she thought, I must order in Chunky Chunks. Then the thought struck her that perhaps there was no point because she might never see Daisy again, and she felt sadness sinking over her shoulders like a heavy cloak.

She went to the fridge and got out the milk. It was still fresh. Why would it not be, she thought. It had only been thirty-six hours since she left the house on Saturday, though it felt like a week. She set it to simmer on the stove. "It's good to have you here," she said.

"And I'm glad to be here. But I must talk to you about the Project. It's not just Daisy, the whole set up's in bad trouble." His voice was strained. He sounded completely unlike the assured Peter she knew so well. Her pulse rate went up but she forced herself to go over to the coffee machine and calmly drain its rich aromatic contents into the warm milk in the mugs.

She brought them back to the table sat down and waited.

"Don't be alarmed," he said, "but I bought a pistol with me." He opened his briefcase and took out a pistol in a well-polished holder and put in on the table. It struck her how dark and evil it looked.

"Where did you get that?"

"Army days. Don't worry, I'm still authorised to own it."

"But why bring it here?"

"Because, security man or not, I think you could be in danger."

"Me? It's Daisy who's in danger, not me."

He spoke quietly. "Let's hope neither of you are, but I still think you should know what's been happening. If you remember on Friday, Jack Sampson..."

"The trainer for Ruby, DAC36."

"That's right. Two men managed to grab her. All I could think to do in the short term was send security people out to secure the remaining centres including Stone House. But two of them never got there."

Jess's heart sank. "Jackson and Jones?"

"That's right. I think I might have been double bluffed. Perhaps it wasn't Ruby they were really after at all."

"It was Daisy?"

"Perhaps. I blame myself for that." Jess saw the unease lurking behind his words. In all the time she had known him Peter had always seemed so confident.

"Do you know anything about these people?"

"Perhaps. The discipline with which they worked made me think they might be ex-army, SAS even. That gave us a good start. Most people don't appreciate just how much personal data we can get at now, especially if it involves military personnel. My people fed in every scrap of information we had about the two men who had visited Jack, not just their faces but estimated age, height, weight, accent, we looked at every incident we could think of in the last twenty years, anywhere there'd been a crime where ex- military had been involved."

"And?"

"A pattern emerged. There's a two-man team kicking around; an ex-SAS junior officer called Andy Serban, and an ex-NCO called Ben Penders. Serban is apparently a very bright boy and Penders is a technical wizard, Dutch. Both of them were chucked out of the SAS, we don't know why, but they then started renting themselves out to criminal groups, sex trafficking, stuff like that…they were last heard of in Romania. That part of the world's a bad boy's heaven at the moment. It's where Serban's parents originally came from."

"So what's their connection with Canine Division?"

"Good point," Peter sipped the coffee again. "I started rooting around at Canine Division files. I did a normative scan first."

"What's that?" Jess's coffee sat untouched by her side.

"We monitor everyone working in Canine Division, all the time. That's right Big, Big Brother. Then if we need to, we can look for behaviour that's outside the norm. We don't pry into content. Just noting people who are doing things outside their average. First Bezel, then Leicemann came up. A lot of coming and going, and cyphered phone calls. I won't trouble you with the details, but I'd had my eye on Leicemann anyway."

"Bezel?" Jess asked.

"Bezel has gone. Officially she's been on some 'special attachment' for the last couple of months, but no one seems to have a very clear idea where, or doing what. Leicemann hadn't put anything in the schedules. I can't find out where he is now either."

The thought flitted through Jess's mind, not for the first time, that Sam Blake was sometimes a bit too easy going in the way he administered the Division, especially dealing with someone like Leicemann.

"That creep!" she said bitterly. "I know he's resentful that Sam's kept him out of the Canine Project, but even he wouldn't connive with a theft from another department surely. What would be the point?"

"Whatever the point, it's not impossible."

"Oh, Peter, it's a heck of a theory. Why would Leicemann get involved in the thefts?"

"Have you heard of direct brain to computer interface?"

"BCI? Of course, but the last I heard about it, the most anyone could manage was getting a few thousand rat neurons to operate a mechanical arm or something."

"That was a time ago. A lot of work has gone on since then."

"And?"

"It turns out Bezel and Leicemann have both been in contact with a setup somewhere in Northumberland; Angelo Control Systems. They used cyphered VPN but my girl Marika made short work of that, and, guess what, that turned out to be the location of the server with the IP address that sent the original fake mail to Ruby's trainer. It's nothing to do with BSDL, it's a private corporation, but I'm pretty sure I know what they're doing there."

"What do they do up there?"

"Ostensibly they're developing control systems for a range of engineering technologies but we're pretty sure that's a cover for some covert work on battle field robotics. We don't know who it's for though. It's not DARPA." He drained the coffee cup. "Whoever it is, it could all fit. You know about battle field robots, don't you?"

"Everybody does, you can even pull them up on the Internet. They use them to carry loads over rough country. They've got four legs and can run like a horse. They look like a cross between a giant beetle and…"

"And a dog. The military used them initially just to carry loads but then people started thinking about weaponising them, extending their flexibility. If you could devise the right control system you could build a heck of a weapon, capable of moving at speed over any terrain, carrying enough armour to be virtually indestructible. Contracts have been offered to anyone who can make it happen."

"Have they got the computer systems to control these things?"

"They're a long way from that. No, at the moment the only answer seems to be for humans to try to run them remote, as terrestrial drones, TDs. But that's a lot more complicated than flying an aircraft. A remote operator just can't keep up unless he's closely connected into the TD's sensory and motor systems."

"Is that possible? "

"Yes, but you have to use what they call a non-invasive brain computer interface; NIBCI: contacts stuck onto the operator's skull. Even then it's hard to get clear signals from the operator's brain activity. It would all work much better if you could stick a lot of electrodes right into their heads, direct BCI. But of course that's unethical for humans..."

She began to realise where he was going.

"Oh no," she said softly. "Surely that's impossible."

"If it was possible, I'm not saying it is, a battle field robot built around the brain of a well trained dog could work pretty well. One that could communicate as well would make one heck of a weapon."

Jess sat in silence. "Robots with living brains," she said finally.

"That's right," he said. "To these people Daisy and the other Project dogs may just be an incredibly valuable source of raw material. From what's been happening in the last 36 hours there seems every possibility that there are people who will do almost anything to get that raw material. I must get you out of their way."

Jess was still in shock. " I can't believe it. It's perverse. It's... monstrous."

Peter sat ignoring his coffee, his face reflecting a profound turmoil.

"What is it? What do you want to say?" she said.

He was plainly reluctant to express the thought.

"Come on spit it out."

"OK, I'll tell you. Yes, it is monstrous, and we'll keep Daisy away from them somehow, but you know what? I'm just a regular guy, I'm no scientist, but I've been thinking. Is what they're trying to do really more monstrous than those little monkeys in Neurology that are nothing more than a head connected to a life support system? The pigs in Nutrition with half their guts hanging out, the rats in BioMed, injected with every disease under the sun? The truth is the Project has already irreversibly messed these dogs up. How far is too far? What's the real difference between injecting gunk into a dog's brain and turning it into an organic robot?"

She was exasperated. "Is this the time to have an ethics discussion? Of course there's a difference. We gained a real insight into the world of another species. We did it with care and we did it with respect. And we gave *them* a whole new world, a world of speech! These people just want to build a better killing machine."

Peter strode agitatedly up and down the kitchen. "And what are we trying to do with this new ability? Train dogs to help other killing machines. Who says this set up in Northumberland or wherever it is, shouldn't go even further?"

He stopped his restless walking and waited. There was a long pause and then when she spoke her voice was very quiet. "Alright, I know what you're saying. I've had my doubts too. Maybe you're right. Daisy's not a military device. She's just a little dog that tries her best for the humans she loves. She deserves better. I let her down." Her eyes suddenly brimmed with tears.

"Go easy on yourself," he said quietly.

"Alright, in the end it's only a dog. I know. But in the last few months I've come to believe that dogs have a value of their own. They're not just some inferior species."

He looked dubious. "I mean…" she struggled to express herself. "I mean dogs aren't stuck with dubious gifts like self-deceit, or ambition, or, God help them, religion. In a funny way they're actually closer to the angels than we are."

She got up from the chair and started to take the cups to the sink, her own coffee was untouched. "I mean it," she said over her shoulder. "We might well teach them to talk, but I doubt we'll ever teach them to lie."

Another thought came to her. "You know what? I realise that most of all, the wonderful thing about them is how they offer the mercy of faith, in us, unrelenting faith. Dogs, for whatever misguided reason, believe in the inherent goodness of human beings, even if we can't."

There was a long pause before he spoke. "Perhaps the most important thing about them is the way they seem to help some people to open up," he said gently. "Offer love they can't bring themselves to give to people."

She put down the cups and looked at him. "What do you mean by that?" she said, but he knew she knew what he meant. She suddenly realised that, perhaps for the first time in her life she really loved something, even if it was only a dog. But what kind of sentimentality was that? Was she one of those pathetic people who attach themselves to animals because dealing with human beings is too complicated? Did that matter?

"Look, I can't stop whatever they may be doing in Northumberland," she said finally, "but I can try and make sure that at least the one creature I'm responsible for gets a fair break. I'm going to find her."

"And what if you do? What then?"

"I don't know. Maybe we can both disappear somewhere. I don't know. I've got to find her first, even if I have to do it on my own."

"Not on your own," Peter said quietly." You know that."

They were interrupted by a sharp buzz from the intercom that linked Jess to the Gatehouse. She hit the switch. "Excuse me, er… Miss, Sir." A voice said diffidently from the little speaker. "There's a little lad down here on a bike. I wouldn't bother you, but Mr Guy said to report anything at all. He keeps going on about his dog and cat being stolen or something."

In the back-ground they could hear Luke shouting, "Mrs Duncan. It's me. Let me in. You must help us. A wicked man has got Daisy. And Kat…"

Moments later Luke was being dropped off at the back door, somehow managing to look scared and defiant at the same time. "Luke! Come in, come in," Jess said, as he stood, suddenly uncertain, at the entrance. "Mrs Duncan," he said weakly. "You must come, you must come. A really bad person has kidnapped Daisy. You must get the police." And then he burst into tears.

By the time she had got him into the house he had calmed down a bit and regained his composure.

"Luke," Jess said. "I'm sure we can sort this out, tell me what happened."

Luke was nearly in tears again. "This man took Kat and Daisy away. You must come. He took them away."

"Luke," Jess said. "Who is Kat?"

"She's my Mum's friend."

"And she bought Daisy to your house?" Peter said.

"Yes."

"Where did she find her? What did Kat tell you Luke?"

Luke looked dubiously at Peter.

"It's OK, Luke," Jess said. "This is my friend Peter. You can trust him."

"Yes Mrs Duncan. She didn't tell me nothing. Daisy told me that Kat took her from a bad place with dogs in cages."

"What the heck could that be?" Jess said.

"Some sort of rogue breeder perhaps," Peter said. "There's enough of them around."

"But why would they take Daisy?"

"It's even possible dog fighters might have picked her up to use as training bait," Peter said. "It's a lot more common than most people realise."

"My God," Jess said. "But how did Kate find her? How did she get her away?"

"I don't know. But she bought her to my Mum's cottage, her and another dog."

"Why?"

"I don't know. But the thing is, there's a man. Mum said he was a policeman but I think she was wrong. He took Kat away."

"Why?"

"I don't know. When Daisy told me he was coming, we hid away. He grabbed Kat's wrist. He pulled her. We tried to stop him, even my Mum, but he took Kat and Daisy away in his car."

"Is your Mum OK?"

"Yes, but she keeps crying. Let's get the police."

"Yes, of course we will. First can you tell me any more about Kat? Where does she live?"

"I don't know. I think she lives at Neck's house."

Jess suddenly realised where she had heard the name before. It all made sense. Neck was one of Chas's friends; the group that had spirited her away from Jackson and Jones. So Lynne would know him, and she would know his partner 'Kat'.

"I know Neck," she said. "Don't ask me how. If we really want to know where they are, I think we should start by finding him. But first lets get this lad home."

Chapter 53

Neck picked up his mobile and rang Chip. "It's me," he said. "Listen, about the stuff."

"Do not worry my friend," Chip interrupted, "all is cool." His voice dropped to a theatrical whisper. "Not only are the contents of that little package on their way, but the payment is in hand. I told you I could shift it. You can always depend on Mr Chip!"

"Oh no," Neck groaned. "Tell me you're just pulling it. Tell me the deal's not completed."

"Tasted, tested, grabbed so fast she almost took my hand off. That must be good stuff Neck baby. Can we get any more?"

"When did you do it?"

"I dunno, couple of hours ago maybe."

"Where was the meet?"

"Trade secret buddy, just a pub. She trusts me you know. I think she fancies the young hunk. She just hides it well."

"Give me her number."

"Oh, no way man. I am the key man. It's my experience, and negotiation skills you're paying for."

"Give me her fucking number, you little wanker, or I'll set Tug on you. I swear to God."

"Jesus Neck. I thought you was straight up. I never thought you'd try to cut me out. We're mates mate."

"Look I'm not cutting you out. I've got to get that stuff back, understand?" He groaned aloud.

"She'll never give you it back man. She might even have moved it on already. Forget it. We'll do a better deal next time."

Neck explained in more detail what he would do if Chip didn't give him the number, and a few minutes later he called it. The phone connected immediately and a woman's voice said, "Hello?" and then just waited.

"My name's Neck. I'm a friend of Chip's."

"I don't know any Chip. What do you want?"

"Well I believe he sold you some, err, stuff recently and…"

"Listen!" hissed the voice on the phone, suddenly coarsening, "I don't know no Chip and I don't know anything about no stuff. Don't call me again, ever, or you'll be sorry you were ever spat out of your mother's…"

"But you don't…" he began, but the line was dead. Neck called Chip again…

Ten minutes later Neck's doorbell rang. Tug growled menacingly and sprinted to the door and then stood staring hard at it, tail waving in the slow motion of a dog ready for trouble. Neck carefully grabbed his collar and opened the door. It was Chip. Tug's growl rate went up and he pulled against the collar. Chip entered cautiously keeping well back from the dog.

"Stay!" Neck said, and was secretly amazed and gratified when the dog promptly sat down.

"That's it, is it?" Chip said. "Certainly looks ugly enough."

Tug growled again but made no move.

Chip followed Neck as he led the dog into the kitchen. He was carrying a plastic shopping bag. He started taking out cans of lager and packets of crisps.

"What did they say?" he said. Neck's look was enough to tell him. " Never mind," he said cheerfully. "Celebration!" Neck ignored the offerings.

"Have you got it?"

"Yea man, of course, every penny. I haven't even taken my fee."

He handed over a clear plastic bank cash folder. It held a wad of brand new twenty-pound notes.

"Not bad eh? Nice notes. Brand new British lettuce, small denomination. None of that dodgy five-hundred-euro rubbish."

"How much is this?"

"Eight big ones."

"Eight thousand? What the fuck! I gave you a kilo pack, that must be fifty thousand quid's worth."

"Fuck off, that's street retail, after it's cut. It was good stuff, fifty per cent or more, she said it herself, but wholesale rate for that is more like twenty thousand a kilo, and she *really* didn't like it that I wouldn't tell her where I'd got it. I had to persuade her it was kosher. She gave me fifteen. Pretty good for a no questions deal."

"So where's the other seven?"

"Ah well, that's on a note, you know. That's how we do business. They pay after the sales receipts come in."

"Is that what you've done before?"

"Well," Chip said reluctantly, "I ain't never sold that much before."

"You really think you'll get the rest? You daft little sod. You told me you had a straight up contact. Guaranteed. I trusted you."

"Well maybe you should have done it yourself."

"I don't know anything about wholesale deals. With Chas gone you're supposed to be the fucking expert." Chip looked at him steadily. They both knew that the real reason Neck had entrusted the sale to him was because he lacked both the street know-how and the confidence to do it himself.

"Look," Neck said finally, "I'm in real trouble here. I've got to get that stuff back or I'm dead."

Chip chuckled. "Oh come on man. Nobody's going to kill you. This ain't LA."

"It's worse than that. I took the stuff off Big Den. He wants it back. He's got Kat and if he don't get it he says he'll do harm to her. And now I can't even offer him the money." He was close to tears.

"Oh holy shit," Chip breathed. "You took it off Den? What's going to happen to me?"

Half an hour later Neck, and Chip sat silent at the kitchen table. Tug sat on the floor watching them. He was hoping that they would give him another packet of crisps, which he had devoured bag and then torn the bag to tiny pieces. The men were drinking the cans of lager and, at least theoretically, deciding what to do next. Chip's immediate suggestion had been that both he and Neck should immediately go their separate ways as far and as quickly as possible.

He was bitterly regretting having accepted the job of marketing the cocaine for Neck. It had seemed such a great opportunity to make a packet. The affable but not very streetwise Neck was a long term mate but the chance to cream some extra profit off the deal had been irresistible, Now he was worried not only about the revenge of Den but also what Neck would do if he ever discovered that the buyer had actually paid him not eight but ten thousand pounds cash.

Neck knew Chip well and was pretty sure that he had heeled some of the cash for the cocaine. It would be against his nature if he hadn't. He intended to squeeze every penny out of him eventually but his immediate priority was Katrina. He was once again repeating to Chip that he wasn't going to leave her to the mercies of Den and that Chip needn't think he was going anywhere either, when they both heard the crackling roar of a motor bicycle with the exhaust left open. There was a knock at the front door and Tug immediately rushed into the tiny hall to stand bristling behind it.

"It's open," Neck shouted.

Spaz came in and Tug advanced growling steadily.

"Hey man," Spaz said admiringly. "Cool beast. This must be the one that rips your arm off." With no hesitation he bent down and started stroking the dog's head. "Nice boy ain't yer?" he cooed to Tug. "I love dogs."

Tug stopped growling and backed away cautiously. He was by no means used to humans who stroked you, especially men.

"All right my men," Spaz said. "What the fuck is going on and who do we do over?"

There had been no question in Neck's mind that Spaz could make a valuable contribution to whatever plan he finally devised to rescue Katrina and he set about explaining what had happened. Spaz listened carefully while throwing crisps one at a time into Tug's open mouth…

Chapter 54

Around five thirty in the afternoon, Peter's big four by four eased out of the security gates of Stone House and a moment later swept past the little side lane into Grimm's Holes where the grey van sat unobtrusively. Serban put down his binoculars onto the seat beside him and took off his headphones. They were almost lost amidst the welter of used packaging and empty bottles that littered both the floor and the seats of the van.

"What a fascinating conversation," he said. "So that's what Leicemann's up to. Anyway, that's all three of them in the car. Drive, but take your time. We know where they're going."

Jess arrived at the cottage with Peter and Luke just as the afternoon was descending into twilight. A thin twist of wood smoke curled from the chimney and the warm glow from a solitary front window shone out like everyone's idea of old style country life. It was hard to believe that anything unpleasant could ever happen there.

As Peter parked the four by four, Lynne emerged from the front door of the cottage and ran down the little front path. Her cheeks were wet with tears. She gathered a reluctant Luke up in her arms and kissed him warmly. "Where you been all this time you bad boy?" she chided, "I'm going to keep you at home in future." She blew her nose. "He wasn't any trouble was he Miss?"

"Of course not Mrs Davies. He's a good lad. It's nice to see you again. I'm sorry it always seems to be under unhappy circumstances."

"Yes, I dunno. I feel so bad for Kat. Is the police coming? What happens now?"

"Don't worry Mrs Davies," Jess said, "this is my colleague Peter Guy. He's a specialist. He's going to make sure everything gets sorted out."

"Nice to meet you Mr Guy," Lynne said politely.

"And you Mrs Davies."

"Call me Linney, everyone does."

"OK, Linney. Fine. Is that your car?" Peter said, indicating Katrina's Mini.

"No, it's Kat's. I can't drive." Lynne said.

"I'll have a look inside, be with you in a minute."

Lynne turned to Jess and Luke. "Come into the house it's getting cold." They followed her down the path. "You've got to do something quick though," she said over her shoulder. "The man who took Kat was horrible. He said he'd kill her if we contacted the police. I couldn't bear to have her death on my conscience as well, but Luke said we should tell you and I realise he's right. And there's that little spaniel. He took her an' all. Luke, put the kettle on love."

"I'm sure we can sort it out Mrs Davies. Did you get any idea where the man might have taken them, or why?"

"He said all kinds of things I didn't understand Miss. Something about people stealing his, well, his shit, he said, and somebody's killed his son. That was about it. Terrible."

Purely on automatic, she began to make the preparations for making tea.

"Oh yes, and he said his name was Den," she said as an afterthought

"Damn," Peter said, coming into the kitchen. "There's nothing much in the car but a big box of canned dog food. Do you think the little dog could use some of this food Luke?"

Luke took the offered can. It was Chunky Chunks. "That's me!" he said, "Chunky! That's what Daisy calls me."

Jess and Peter smiled, as Lynne obliviously carried on rinsing mugs and pouring the milk from the plastic bottle into a jug, as she always did for visitors.

Luke opened the can of dog food and gave half of it to the little terrier, which cleared it up in less than a minute. Lynne poured boiling water into the teapot and set it out next to the jug of milk and a bowl of sugar on the table.

"What can you tell us about Neck?" Jess said, gratefully accepting her mug. "I believe he's Kat's partner isn't he? Do they live together?"

"Yes," Lynne said, "been together for a couple of years, though I don't know exactly where they live. Chas keeps his number here somewhere, though we can never get a signal here."

"If you can find it, my network covers this area," Jess said. "Can you have a look?"

At Katrina's house Spaz was giving his balanced appraisal of the information given him by Neck.

"It seems to me that there's only one thing we can do," he said confidently, "and that's get over to the Yards and kick the shit out of the bad boy." He rolled his empty crisp packet into a ball and lobbed it to Tug who caught it effortlessly.

"But it's Den you're talking about!" Chip expostulated. "Do you realise what you're messing with? He's an evil bugger, you know that, him and his son."

"Well, from what Neck reckons, the son's snuffed it. That brings his manpower down."

"Yet but he's got other heavies. What about that big Polish lad with the tattoos, and the black one?"

"They've not been around for months," Spaz said. "You never see them now. I think they've cleared off. Den's running a one-man show at the moment."

"Even if that's true, it's Big Den we're talking about! He's a mad man. He'll chop all three of us."

"Look," Neck interrupted. "There's nothing to talk about. I don't care what he'll do. I'm going to get Kat back; it's my fault she's there. Why did I touch that fucking coke?"

"Seems entirely reasonable to me," Chip said, "I'd have filled me boots too."

The other two looked at him in exasperation, and then Neck's mobile started buzzing. They looked at each other and then Neck carefully hit the green button and hit it again to put it onto open speech. He waited hardly breathing.

"Is that you Neck? It's me, Special Officer Stewart."

"The bird in the car!" Spaz said.

"Miss Fucking Jane Bond," Chip marvelled. "What does she want?"

"Yeah, it's me Miss," Neck said. "What is it? You in trouble again."

"Sort of. The thing is I think you can help me with a particular mission."

"Look Miss, I don't want to be awkward but I got problems of me own just now. I ain't got time to go hunting terrorists."

"Speak for yourself," Chip said. "I bet they pay well."

Neck ignored him.

"The thing is Neck, that I have to recover someone who's in danger."

"Me too," Neck muttered.

"So you know Kat's in trouble?"

"What? How the …"

"Don't ask how. The point is, do you have any idea where she might be right now?"

"Well, probably. But it's complicated," Neck said awkwardly.

"It's always complicated Neck, but I think we can work together on this."

"Look, I got issues, legal issues and that."

"Don't worry about the stolen shit. I'm not the police."

He was deeply shocked to hear her use the word shit, and how did she know?

"Cool bitch!" Spaz exulted. "She knows the scene, does Jane. Get her on the job! Let's do it, man!" He was punching the air. Tug started barking. Neck could hardly hear the phone over the noise.

"You can help?"

"I mean it, you can help me and I can help you. And no questions asked. I think we'd better come over. Give me your address."

Jess disconnected the phone and turned to Luke and Lynne. "OK," she said, "thanks for all your help Mrs Davies. We'll go and see Neck now. I'm sure he can help us sort this out."

"Can I come?" Luke said, "Daisy knows me. I can help."

"That's a good offer Luke," Peter said. "But just to be on the safe side, I think you should stay here and look after your Mum. She'll need you to keep her safe."

Luke looked dubious but Lynne smiled and took his arm and put it round her waist. "That's right," she said, "I need my big man to look after me. We'll wait here son, as soon as Miss Stewart and the gentleman find Kat and Daisy, I'm sure they'll let us know. Then we can go and see them."

"But you will tell us when you find them, won't you?"

"Yes Luke, definitely," Jess said. "But for you we wouldn't even know where to start looking. We won't leave you out. Now, we'd better get moving, it'll be dark soon."

With a quick nod to Lynne over his head she and Peter were out the door and a moment later they heard the roar of the engine fading into the darkness.

"Now," said Lynne cheerfully, "Let's see what's on the tele."

Neither of them noticed the grey van that slid quietly past the house following Peter's four by four in the direction of Tamborough, nor, a little later, the other car that quietly came to a stop just down the lane.

Chapter 55

Half an hour later Peter's black four by four drew up outside Katrina's house to join Neck's Ford, Chip's BMW, and Spaz's enormous motorbike. A little way down the street a nondescript van pulled gently into the kerb and turned off its lights.

Following Neck, Jess walked ahead of Peter and Luke into the kitchen. Behind them she could hear the dog that had greeted their arrival whining to be let out of the small front room. The two other young men she remembered were sitting around the kitchen table, but now they were dressed in jeans and heavy boots and smelled more of farm manure than aftershave.

She was surprised at how neat and tidy the kitchen was. The one called Spaz stood up awkwardly and held out his hand. He gave her a big open smile.

"It's good to see you again Miss," he said. "You remember Chip."

The smaller man called Chip just nodded and looked down at the table.

"This is Peter," she said, indicating him, "he's part of my unit."

"What fucking unit?" Chip grunted.

"Shut up Chip," Neck interrupted, "and don't swear in front of the lady. Miss Stewart knows what she's doing. Listen and learn."

Chip lit another cigarette but said nothing.

"Right, let's sort this out," Jess said. "Linney told me that the man who took Katrina is called Den. Is that right?"

"Yeah," Neck said, " Big Den."

"Why did he take her?"

"Who knows?" Chip said. "He's a fucking maniac."

Jess looked at Neck.

"It's complicated," he said. "I went up there to buy a dog."

"Went where?" Peter interjected.

"Den's place. He's got an old farm over in the Fens, calls it The Yards, bad place. He breeds dogs there. Anyway I thought I heard somebody in one of the sheds there, sounded like a kid's voice. This Den, he's a bit of a character."

"Too fucking right," said Chip.

"I thought he might have been holding some kid there, well, not me, but Kat did. She said we should go up there and check."

"That's Kat all over," Spaz said. "She's a hell of a girl, that one."

"Daft idea," Chip said.

"Shut up Chip. Anyway later that night we went over," Neck continued. "There weren't any girl that we could find, but we did find a man's body. His throat was…it was tore out. It was Den's boy. They sometimes called him Little Den."

"Not to his face," Chip said.

"I won't tell you again Chip, shut the fuck up," Neck said. "Sorry Miss."

"Could it be Den thinks you killed his son?" Jess said

"I don't think so. He might, I suppose. It was one of his own dogs that killed him, before we even got there. Nothing to do with us. Perhaps somebody had put the dog on him, I dunno. Anyway we just legged it, and that was that."

"What did you take?" Peter said sharply.

"What? Nothing. Except that little terrier and another one, a spaniel I think."

"I'll say it again," Peter said. "What did you steal? We know somebody stole something. He told Linney."

There was a silence and then Spaz said, "Oh for Christ's sake tell them Neck, or we'll never sort this out."

"Look, Neck," Peter said. "Anything you tell us is below the radar. This operation is off the record."

"Is that a promise?" Spaz said.

They both nodded.

"Well," Neck said, "me and Kat, we had a bit of a look round. There was loads of stuff, must have been lifted, phones, players, perv stuff, porn."

Predictably Chip looked up, interested. Spaz snorted and punched his arm. "Twat," he said amiably.

"We found a load of cocaine. I mean a lot."

"And?"

"And he took some of course," Chip said exasperated, "and now Den knows it was him, I've sold it, and now we can't get it back, and whatever we do we're fucked."

"Couldn't you just give him the money?" Spaz asked.

Neck and Chip exchanged glances. "There's a problem with the money," Neck said, "and in any case he don't want money, he wants revenge, and he wants his stuff."

He put his head in his hands. "What was I thinking of? I ain't no drug dealer. What a dickhead I am."

"Bear up Neck," Jess said, "we can help you."

"But you don't realise. He won't kill her. He's too clever for that. He'll burn her, with drain cleaner. That's what he does to people."

There was a pause while they tried to absorb the horrific image.

"Don't worry, we'll get her out," Peter said eventually.

"Why should you bother?" Chip said. "It's not your business"

"For God's sake Chip, that spaniel's a valuable asset to us and Kat is in real danger. Who wouldn't want to help her?" Peter said

"I ain't showing you nothing if the police are involved," Neck said.

"Alright, I understand that. Show us where she is and we'll get our dog and you get Kat. No police. We're not sure how compromised they are anyway. Someone must have tipped off Den."

"There you are," Spaz said triumphantly. "Two birds, one stone!"

"What's so great about this dog anyway?" Chip said. "What's it got to do with MI5 or whatever you are? Are you bent an' all?"

"I won't try and deceive you," Jess said. "The dog's got a particular talent for the kind of work we do. It's virtually unique."

"A dog? What talent can a mutt have that's so important? What is 'the work you do'?" Chip was unrelenting.

"Look," Peter said, becoming irritated. "We've told you far too much already. The fact is there are more people than us looking for our dog. Jess came to you because you helped her before. We can go it alone but you three would make a real difference."

The three men looked at each other.

"Well I'm up for it," Spaz announced finally. "Neck?"

Neck nodded. "Of course."

"Chip?"

Chip was staring at the coffee table in front of him. He looked up. "No," he said.

"No?"

"Yeah, no. The whole fucking idea is mad." He looked at Neck and Spaz. "How do you know you can trust these people? They might be working for the cops for all we know, even if he is black. It smells like a con to me, and even if it ain't, I'm not mixing it with Den."

Abruptly he got up and drained the last of his lager.

"I'm gone," he said, "and if you've got any sense you'll be gone too." He left the room and a moment later they heard the sound of the front door shutting.

"Fuck him," Spaz said. "Chip was never an action man. Better he skips now rather than while we're out there. Right," he said, slapping his knee, Chip immediately forgotten, "where do we start?"

"We need to make a plan," Jess said.

From the front room Tug started barking urgently.

"I'll see to him," Spaz said, getting up. "We can take him too. Maybe he can help find her. I like that dog."

In their van parked just down the street from Kat's house Serban and Penders were reviewing their options.

"This location is very good news, Jolly," Serban said, lighting his umpteenth cigarette of the day.

"Couldn't have done it without my taps."

"Jolly, old chap," Serban affected the public school accent he had used in his role as Jackson, "despite being a smelly oik, you are undoubtedly a surveillance genius, as well as a GHQ class hacker. Did I ever deny it? Now we know what that dog's worth I'll make damn sure Leicemann never sees it. I know half a dozen people will take our arm off for a chance to get at it. But the kid was the key break."

"The kid was telling them the truth you reckon?"

"I do indeed. Hasn't got the sense to lie, and the woman Stewart has got a lot of time for him. It occurred to me that he could still be a valuable asset."

Abruptly he grabbed his phone and dialled.

"O'Connell."

"Yes."

"How did it go?"

"I was just going to call you. We found the cottage no trouble. We'll be with you in a few minutes. Everything's fine. Mum'll be no trouble as long as we hold the boy. I've got some dog too. I don't know what breed. Looks like nothing much. It's not what you're looking for is it?"

"No, that's just some mutt. Hang onto it though. It might be useful." Serban said.

"What's the plan then? Young Nick here wants to know what's going on. He wants to know why we've taken the boy. That's serious stuff."

"Just tell him to shut up and do as he's told. You're the superior officer."

"He don't jump for a Corporal these days, Andy."

"Well he better jump if he wants the money. The kid's just insurance. All being well you can drop him off back at his Mum's in a couple of hours. He hasn't seen your faces has he?"

"No course not. We ain't daft Andy. What happens next?"

"We're close now, thank Christ. We're all set to tail a car that will lead us to where the dog's being held. If you don't get here in time I'll call you, meet you there."

"Nick's not happy about the shooters."

"You said no bodies. I don't like bodies." A voice said next to the phone.

"Neither do I, Nick," Serban said, "but I'm not going to miss the fucking dog again. Just bring the guns anyway. We'll use the Tokarevs."

O'Connell affected a mock Irish accent, "Begorrah, it'll be like dem auld days," he said.

Serban was about to reply when Penders put his hand on his arm.

"Look," he said.

Both men watched a figure walk out of the front door of number nine and make its way to an old BMW parked at the kerb.

"Quick Ben. Go. He'll be worth a little chat."

Penders slipped out of the van and as the driver's door of the BMW closed. Serban watched him slide into the passenger seat. He waited patiently until his mobile rang.

"I think we may have got lucky," Penders said.

Chapter 56

Katrina was sitting on the floor of a corrugated iron shed, leaning back against the wall. It was almost completely dark and there was no sound but the occasional grumble of dogs barking in the distance. One would start a melancholy monotone, others would join in, and then after a period of cacophony the sound would subside to occasional whimpers.

Somewhere along the line she had lost her watch and she had no idea of the time, but she seemed to have been in the shed for hours. She felt depressed and frightened in equal measure.

Her wrists were bound behind her back with what felt like several layers of gaffer tape. She felt completely trapped. She was at the Yards and she had been put in one of the storage sheds that she and Neck had investigated the night before. It was dark but she could just make out the dim shapes of boxes and chests against the wall opposite.

A dim square of moonlight pushed its way through the grimy glass of a small window set high up in the wall but with her arms pinioned there was no way she could reach it and even if she could it would be impossible to get through it. Her jaw ached from the punch Den had given her, the earth floor felt very cold through the thin material of her skirt, and she was desperately thirsty. Although she couldn't see it, the floor felt sticky and her nose was full of the smell of excrement. She herself felt grubby and sticky. Her hair was a mess, but for some reason what upset her most was that she had lost the heel from one of her shoes.

Beside her in the gloom, the spaniel was sitting quietly, like a furry little sphinx, apparently waiting calmly for the next thing to happen. When Den had first thrown them both into the shed the dog had energetically checked out every corner of the space, apparently looking for some way out, but then it had seemed to just give up and returned to sit by her side.

Poor thing, she thought, it doesn't realise what a mess we're in. Still, it's right about one thing. There's no way out of here.

She closed her eyes and tried to relax but her mind was racing. Why had this man Den grabbed her? She had thought at first it was all about obtaining the dog beside her but once having got it, he seemed to have lost interest in it. She had tried to ask him what was going on but he had refused to answer or even look at her. She was actually pleased that he didn't. He radiated evil and she had a terrible feeling that he was capable of almost anything. She was terrified.

"Oh God," she said aloud. "What the hell is going to happen to me?"

There was a pause and then out of the darkness a voice said quietly, "We must wait."

Kat froze but there was no sign of anyone. Could someone be held in a room next this one? Was the girl they had been looking for still here somewhere? The voice had sounded quite near. "Is there anyone there?" she whispered.

She dimly felt the dog get up and stretch towards her in the dark. There was the warm touch of its tongue as it delicately licked her cheek then drew back.

"We must wait. Jess will come." She was even more confused, who on earth was Jess?

She noticed the voice was a little nearer and it suddenly occurred to her that the dog must have some kind of tiny mobile phone built into to its collar. But surely she would have noticed that before?

"Can you hear me?" she hissed in the general direction of the dog. "It's me, Kat Ossols. I've been kidnapped. I'm in some kind of shed in a farm yard." She suddenly lost all her self-control and burst into tears. "Please, please. Come and get me. Come now. I think he's going to kill me."

She felt the dog come closer again and felt its tongue licking her cheek again.

"Jess will come," the gentle little voice said close to her. "You will be fine." She was sure now, the sound definitely came from the dog. She felt dizzy.

She found herself actually speaking to the dog. "That's good," she said. "That's good. But when will Jess come?"

"Not long time. We wait."

She sincerely wanted to believe help was coming, even if it was only on the word of a dog. "That's good," she said. "Good girl, clever dog." The dog made no response. "Good Daisy," she said again, but there was only silence. I'm definitely losing it, she thought, talking to a bloody dog.

She lapsed into inertia again and then had a sudden thought. She turned slightly to show the dog her tied wrists. "Is there anyway you can help me get these off?" There was still silence and she seriously began to think she had imagined the previous conversation then in the darkness, the voice said, "Yes. Me will remove..." there was a pause as if the speaker was searching for the right words.

"Me will remove limiting factors." The dog moved until its head was behind her and she felt it begin to tug at the tape around her wrists.

At first it seemed that the dog was wasting its time. It chewed and tugged at her bonds, delicately avoiding her skin and for a long time made no real impression on the tough tape but eventually, once it started to tear, their combined efforts eventually managed too loosen it enough for her to pull her wrists free.

She sat up massaging her swollen wrists as feeling agonisingly flooded back and then fell down as she attempted to get to her feet. She giggled slightly hysterically and then sniffed at the warm stickiness on her wrists. She realised that it was blood but not hers. The stiff material of the tape had split the dog's lips. She reached over to stroke the spaniel, which was waving its tail furiously, to celebrate their joint achievement.

"You poor thing. Well done girl," she said. "Good girl Daisy."

As she spoke the dog's tail stopped wagging and it went very still. She had the ridiculous thought that she had said something to offend it, and then its head went up and up its ears cocked.

"Wait," the childlike voice said. "Not speak."

As they both sat there in silence she realised that while concentrating on loosening her bonds, she hadn't heard even the occasional bark from the dogs outside for some time. It was completely silent. Then the dog said, "We cannot wait. Must go now."

"What is it?" she said.

"Must go, bad men come."

Oh God, she thought, is he coming back with more people? What's he going to do now? Despite her best intentions she felt a rush of panic, her heart raced and her breathing rate went up abruptly. She staggered to her feet, went over to the door and pulled at it, but it was locked solidly from the other side.

Without knowing exactly what she was doing she started pulling vaguely at the stacked chests and boxes. She was able to open one or two of them and in one were some building tools including a couple of substantial iron bars. With a rush of exhilaration she grabbed one but when she tried to lever the stout door open it had no effect.

Without any clear idea of what she was going to do next, she managed to insert the pointed end between two sections of the corrugated iron of the wall. She tried to lever the section apart but the edges overlapped slightly and were riveted together every two feet or so. Despite the considerable leverage the bar gave her she could only create a gap of a few inches.

Eventually, exhausted, she pulled the bar out with a screech that must have been audible for a hundred yards, and stood staring impotently at the mildly distorted surface that remained. "It's hopeless," she said bitterly, "totally fucking hopeless." Despite herself tears began to run down her cheeks.

"Open for me," said the voice at her feet She looked down and the dog was sitting by her side looking up at her. "You big. Me small."

Clearly the dog didn't realise that a gap of a few inches was too narrow, even for her. But, simply because it felt better to something rather than nothing, she got on her knees and inserted the bar into the seam at a point a couple of feet from the ground. When she levered this time she realised that there was no rivet at the ground level. She almost easily opened a gap about a foot wide at the base, but it wouldn't open any wider. She realised there was no hope of her getting out. She and the dog looked at each other. "You go Daisy," she said. "Go and get help. I'll wait here."

Without a word the dog gave her nose a quick lick and then pushed its head into the hole but the gap was too narrow for its shoulders. Wriggling desperately it pushed and pushed, whining slightly, and then with a rush it was through and gone. It had escaped but she hated to think what damage it had done to itself to do so.

Barely two hundred yards away Jess and Peter were sitting in the front of his big black four by four peering into the darkness. Neck and Spaz were sitting in the back seat. Tug was in the boot space behind the back seats. In front of them the dim shape of the Yards loomed out of the darkness. There was no sign of movement and no sound from the dogs within the compound but it was still a threatening prospect. Jess felt a new respect for Katrina and Neck, coming here in the middle of the night with no idea what they would find, but still willing to try and help someone, despite their terror of Den.

She had the sudden thought that perhaps Kat wasn't even here. Perhaps Den had taken her and Daisy somewhere else. Perhaps this whole exercise was a waste of time. Somehow she doubted it. The Yards were Den's chosen territory, safely away from curious eyes and ears. Kat and Daisy would be here somewhere.

"We'd better make a move," Peter said.

Distantly there was a sound like two champagne corks being popped. They looked at each other.

"I think that may be a pistol," Peter said.

Spaz abruptly made a decision.

"No point in hanging about. You wait here a minute. I'll go in first." He smiled confidently at them then left the vehicle and moved towards the chain link gate carrying Neck's bolt cutter.

For a brief moment time seemed to slow right down and Jess was aware of even the tiniest details of the scene. She realised a wind had come up and, looking up, she saw dark clouds speed overhead, briefly revealing the gibbous moon, only to mask it again almost immediately.

"I think it's going to rain," Peter said quietly. "It's got colder."

As he drew nearer to the gates fifty yards ahead, Spaz began to run with his trademark awkward gait. They had previously discussed the fact that there was no point in hoping to make a surreptitious entrance. The plan had been that as soon as Spaz had opened the gates. Peter would drive his car straight into the main yard, hopefully while Den was still realising that they had arrived. He would have inevitably set guard dogs and their only hope had been to move quickly. Jess's phone buzzed again.

"I'm at the gates," Spaz's voice said. There was a pause. "But there's no padlock. There's not a sound up here. I'll go in and check."

"Don't go in alone. Wait for me," Peter said

"I'll come with you," Jess said.

Neck just nodded.

"We'll be with you in a minute. Keep it quiet. We'll leave the car here," Jess said into the mobile, and disconnected.

All three got out of the car. Neck went round to the back. He opened the boot and took out an iron bar, then let Tug out and put him on the makeshift lead he had made from an old belt. The dog was full of excitement, rocking from foot to foot, pulling at the lead, gazing towards the Yards.

"He's probably keen to go home," Neck said.

"I doubt it," Peter said. "He's almost certainly been treated more brutally here than we can imagine. Keep him on a tight leash." The three humans and the dog advanced into the darkness.

At the open gate of the Yards there was no sign of Spaz. "Damn, he's gone in without us," Peter said. He took out his phone and dialled Spaz again.

"Where are you?" he said into the phone.

"Come into the big shed, as quick as you can. There's something you should see. Come quick." Spaz's voice sounded tense.

"Why?" Peter said, but Spaz had disconnected.

"He wants us to go to the big shed," Peter said, "and quickly."

"No patience," Neck murmured. "Never did have."

"He sounded under stress," Peter said. "Let's go."

They started to jog across the main yard towards the long dark mass of the barn but Tug started whining and pulling Neck in the direction of the corrugated iron huts on the other side of the yard.

Neck paused. "You go on ahead," he said. "You never know he might have smelt something. I'll take a quick look."

"We shouldn't split up," Jess said. "We don't know where Den is, never mind any others. Let's go to the barn first."

"We've got to check as many places as we can, as quick as we can, don't we? I can handle one fat old man," Neck said, hefting the iron bar with a confidence he didn't remotely feel.

"No time to argue. Go if you must," Peter said. "But if anything looks wrong, ring me or Jess right away. Don't wait to be sure."

The two of them headed off towards the main building and Neck followed Tug to the sheds. He walked carefully but he could hear and see nothing. Then Tug seemed to lose his certainty and began to pull him first one way then another. After a time the dog stopped dead and just looked up at him. It even started to whine very quietly.

In the darkness of the shed where she was held, Kat heard the grating sound of the door opening and then she was seized and dragged out of the shed. "Keep quiet and keep walking," a voice said quietly. It belonged to a man dressed entirely in black. She had never seen him before. She was almost paralysed with shock but she allowed herself to be led away to the end of the row of sheds.

After a moment the man stopped her and they both waited. She started to ask what was happening but he just put his hand over her mouth. She realised he was wearing tight black cotton gloves. They smelt pleasantly of mild disinfectant but it wasn't enough to dispel the man's overpowering body odour. After a moment or two another man appeared from the direction of the shed she'd been locked in. "That's the lot. No sign," he said to the man who held her. He turned to Katrina

"Where's the dog?" he said.

Incongruously it suddenly struck her that he had a Dutch accent.

"What dog?" she said, "I don't know."

As he walked between the sheds Neck suddenly regretted his decision. He realised he was alone in the dark with a dog of dubious loyalty and untested ability and no clear idea of what to do if it did find something anyway. He was about to turn back and look for the others when Tug suddenly tensed, looked off into the dark and gave a short sharp bark. In response Neck heard the faintest sound.

He couldn't be sure if it was a fragment of someone speaking or the sound of some animal. He couldn't even be sure he'd heard anything, but Tug set off confidently and he ran after him. Then he was almost certain he had heard Kat's voice again. He was convinced now she was in one of the smaller sheds. He started whispering as loud as he dared, "Kat, Kat. It's me where are you?"

Somewhere nearby he heard Kat say, "Wayne!" And then her voice was shut off.

Oh God, he thought, it's Den, and his stomach churned. Why the hell did I bring the dog? One word from Den and it'll turn on me.

Abruptly Tug turned and began to pull him to one side, down the gap between two of the sheds. He followed, shining his torch forward, and the beam suddenly outlined two men dressed in black. The thought struck him that they looked like Ninjas. One of them was holding Kat by the arm. He noticed she was standing awkwardly with one heel lower than the other He was so pleased to see her that tears came to his eyes.

"It's OK sweetheart," he said, "I'm here now." He went to move forward.

"Hold it there," one of the men said. "Just stay calm."

He realised that the one not holding Kat was holding a gun, though he'd never seen a real one in his life before. It looked much bigger than he had imagined. He guessed from the films he'd seen that it must be fitted with a barrel silencer. It was pointed at him. He stopped dead. Tug stood stock-still but surging forward against the lead.

"Let her go," Neck heard himself say. "Just let her go. We won't make trouble. I'll get the money for the stuff, I promise to God. Just let her go."

"Where's the dog?" one of the men said.

Neck stared at him blankly.

"The dog, the spaniel. Where is it?"

Neck still said nothing. He was completely confused. What the hell were they talking about? He'd completely forgotten that anyone else but Jess and Peter might be interested in Daisy.

"Better to say," the man with the gun said, and calmly turned it until it was pointing at Kat's head. Neck stood frozen. The man lifted his free hand to a neck mike...

Abruptly Tug pulled so hard against the lead that it slipped from Neck's grasp. The dog leapt forward. It covered the gap between him and the men in a second, seized the arm of the man with Kat and began pulling ferociously. Before the other man could aim his gun, Neck had thrown himself at him. He swung the iron bar at the hand that held the gun but even at this moment he couldn't make himself hit another human being with real damaging force and his opponent ignored the blow. The two of them fell to the ground together.

He had dropped the bar and had no clear idea what to do next but it seemed like a good start to get hold of the gun. As they grappled he quickly realised his opponent was lighter than him but strong and very quick. He felt a jarring blow to his head. It really hurt but didn't affect his consciousness in any way. It just made him angry. He flew at the man with renewed vigour and managed to get a hold of the hand that held the gun. As they wrestled the gun went off twice, astonishingly loudly despite the silencer, and he heard Kat gasp.

Chapter 57

Jess and Peter came to the door at the front end of the big barn. It stood open. There was no light on but the smell from within hit them with an almost physical impact. There was a light switch just inside the doorway but when Jess clicked it on it nothing happened.

Tentatively they entered the darkness and advanced down a long corridor between various barred cages. Incongruously Jess was reminded of her visit to Leicemann's dog factory. By the light of their torches they saw that dogs lurked in several of the cages, their eyes blank points of light in the darkness, but they seemed disoriented and confused. Some produced defiant snarls but most of them were silent, some were even cowering at the back of their cages. A dreadfully thin bitch, with several puppies, looked up hopefully.

"Something bad's happened here," Jess said. Peter had moved ahead of her. He was looking down into an open storage stall.

"Depends how you define it," he said quietly.

Jess joined him. He was looking down at the body of big sturdy man sprawled across the dirty wooden floor. Peter bent down and held two fingers across the carotid artery below the ear.

"I'd guess this is Big Den. Was Big Den. So someone did get here before us. He's still warm."

Jess was suddenly very aware that somewhere close by were people who really were prepared to do whatever it took to get their hands on Daisy. She looked round anxiously. Her head swam.

"This is bad," she said weakly, "really bad."

"Yes, but where's Daisy?" Peter said

Jess suddenly remembered Spaz. She clicked the fast link on her phone. There was a pause and then she heard Spaz say, "Where are you?" His voice quavered slightly.

"We're in the barn, where are you? Are you all right? Have you seen anything?"

"I'm fine. Come down to the far end qui..." Then the phone clicked off abruptly.

"We'd better get down there," Peter said. They both started down the long gloomy passageway then from behind them they heard, "No, No, stop!"

Jess looked round and her heart almost melted for there in the light of her torch stood Daisy, foursquare and real as life, ears up and tail wagging low and fast. She couldn't bear to speak but just knelt down and let the dog fall into her arms. For a moment both of them were perfectly still, the dog's head resting on her shoulder, just as it used to when, exhausted by a long foraging walk, she would carry the puppy home.

"It's so good to see you," she said finally.

The dog said nothing but just gently licked her cheek. Then it sat back from her arms to gaze down into the gloom of the corridor.

"Does she know what's going on?" Peter said.

The dog tipped its head back and looked up at her.

Jess took a breath. "DAC32 make report," she said quietly

"DAC 32 make report," the dog said briskly. "In rear location are hostiles." It's voice seemed lower than Jess remembered.

"Hostiles?" Peter said in surprise.

"It's the translator, remember," Jess said, "the identification DAC accesses the military lexicon."

"Hostiles are preparing flanking movement."

"A trap?" Peter said.

"A trap," the dog agreed. "Must make tactical retreat now. Must go!"

Jess sensed that the dog's urgency to go was not just a response to the threat from the end of the building but also to the terrifying experiences it had here. The little dog was brave but it was about at the end of its tether. It was visibly bruised and battered and there were traces of blood around its split lip and deep scratches on its sides.

"I think they must have Spaz," Peter said. "And they're almost certainly armed. We'd better act quickly, get Daisy clear somehow and pull the police in. There's no reason to think they'll hurt the lads once we've gone. There's no gain in it for them."

"What was the gain in killing Den?"

"That man bad," the dog said quietly.

"I think we should get the hell out of here," Peter said.

Suddenly Jess's mobile buzzed abruptly. She put it to your ear. "Spaz?" she said, but it was a new but familiar voice.

"Miss Stewart, this is the man you know as Jackson. Hello again. I won't waste your time. Just bring the dog to the front now. But do hurry please."

Daisy gave a little growl, looked towards the door they had used to enter, lifted her nose and inhaled. "Hostiles at front location also," she said softly.

Jess and Peter exchanged glances. "You're taking too long Miss Stewart," the voice said on the phone. "Perhaps I can hurry you on. Listen." There was a pause and then Luke came on to the phone.

"I'm sorry Mrs Duncan," he said.

All the breath went out of Jess's body in a great whoosh. After a pause she said, "Luke are you OK?" knowing it was a stupid question even as she asked it.

"Tell her," Jackson said.

"He says you must send Daisy out or," Luke paused, "they'll take me away..." His voice was suddenly cut off.

"You can't hurt the boy, please don't hurt him," Jess begged, close to tears.

"I wouldn't even give you the option but we know that your colleague is armed, and that clever little dog may get hurt or even just disappear if we simply move in on you. Which believe me we could. We'll get her anyway, but this will simplify things. A boy for a dog. Seems a no brainer to me. You can always get another dog, can't you? Bring it to the front door, and on a lead, and you'll get the boy. Trust me. But be quick."

The phone went dead. She stood and looked at Peter in shock.

" 'Trust me'," she said bitterly.

Between them Daisy sat quietly looking into the darkness at the end of the corridor.

Then they heard in the distance behind them a quiet pop sound.

"That's a silenced pistol," Peter said. "Sounds like it came from the sheds."

"Oh God, this has all gone to pieces," Jess moaned to herself. "I can't give them Daisy." She shone her torch down the length of the corridor but the darkness outside the open door was complete.

"I'm going," she said to Peter. "You wait here with Daisy."

"Wait, stop. Think," Peter said. "They won't give him over. They'll just hold you as a hostage as well."

She stood frozen desperately trying to think what to do.

Her mobile vibrated discreetly in her hand. "Shame it's taking you so long," Jackson said. "I suspect you don't really appreciate how serious we are. I'll give you a little clue." In the dim light of their torches a figure appeared in the doorway. In its hands it was holding what looked like a small parcel. The figure took the posture of a baseball pitcher, hurled the package towards them and, even before the package hit the ground, had disappeared round the edge of the door again.

Before Jess could stop her Daisy shot forward, and stood over the package. Except it wasn't a package. It was the bound form of the little terrier. And she was dead.

"Oh no," Jess breathed.

Daisy stood quietly over the dog's body. The still little figure seemed even smaller than Jess remembered, the mouth slightly open in the rictus of a final snarl. Daisy made no sound but gently licked the little dog's ears and then simply turned round and stared at Jess. She saw that some of the light had gone out of those soft brown eyes; some part of the dog had died.

Jess made her decision. She opened her arms to Daisy who slid back into her embrace.

"What are you going to do now? " Peter said.

"Hush." She looked down at Daisy who lay in her arms, tail wagging ever so gently. "It's all fine Daisy," she said, " we're going to go away from this place."

"Bad place," Daisy murmured.

"And we'll play all day and we'll have Chunky Chunks for every meal and we'll sing a song every night before we go to sleep."

She placed the dog on the floor and it sank down on all fours. "You can have a little sleep right now. Close your eyes, little girl."

"Me not girl, me Daisy," the dog said firmly, but stretched its head to rest it on its paws.

"That's right," Jess said and she began to sing quietly, a song that she'd devised in the early days of teaching the dog. She began, "Once there was a little dog, she didn't have a name..."

The dog's eyes slowly closed. "My name Daisy." She could barely hear the dog's voice.

As she sang Jess reached out with her right hand and placed it on the pistol that Peter held. "Cock it," she whispered.

"What?"

"It's the only way. I'm not letting those bastards have her. God knows what they're planning to do to her. It would be worse than death. I won't let it happen. Show me what to do."

She took the cocked pistol and maneuvered it until it pointed at Daisy's head. Daisy opened her eyes, looked up at the gun and then closed her eyes again.

Jess could hardly see through the blur of her tears. There was a long pause. "It's no good," she whispered finally, "I can't do it." At that moment there were sudden shouts and crashes in the dark behind them

Out in the alley between the corrugated sheds, as his opponent's gun went off, Neck had felt the man suddenly go slack and then almost immediately he began to convulse and choke. As Neck stared at him in horror the man desperately struggled to breath and then with a little groan he suddenly vomited a terrifying amount of blood through the thin material that covered his face, and was still. Neck was still terrified. His nose was full of the sulphurous oily smell of the discharged gun. He seized it from the man' slack fingers and pointed it at him, though he had no idea how to fire it.

"Keep still! Just don't do nothin!" he shouted, his voice shrill. But the man's eyes were fixed, staring at a far off place; he was as still as a freeze frame in a movie. Neck realised the man was dead.

He suddenly remembered Katrina and, still on his knees, turned towards her. Like him, she was kneeling, staring at the man's body in horror. Beside her Tug stood, tautly interposing his body between her and the figure of the other man, who now stood undecided a few feet away. The rigid Tug gave a deep and profoundly ominous growl. The man stood perfectly still. In the dim moonlight that struggled through the clouds Neck was able to see that his right arm hung loose and ruined. Tug hadn't managed to tear it off, but he'd had a very good try.

There was no sign of a gun and as Neck stood up uncertainly the man abruptly turned and ran off into the darkness. "Oh you good boy," Katrina said. She reached out to pat Tug's head but he swung away, all his attention on the possible threats in the darkness.

As she struggled to her feet Neck went over to embrace her. He realised there was blood on his shirt and tried to back off from her but she clung to him. She looked over his shoulder at the corpse behind him. "Oh, that poor man," she said, "what have we done?"

A deep wave of depression and anxiety swept over Neck. What had they done? What had they got mixed up in? He'd killed a man, or at least been involved in his death, and his dog had maimed another. The implications of it all suddenly hit him. If they were Den's boys he would surely take a terrible revenge, and even if he somehow escaped Den he'd probably go to prison and then, when Kat found out he'd taken the dope she'd never speak to him again. He realised that her dumping him was even more frightening than the idea of Den or going to prison and he clung to her as tightly as she did to him.

"Let's get out of here, he said, "while we can."

"Did you come on your own?"

"No, Spaz came too, but let's just get out of it. He can look after himself."

"Where is he?"

"I dunno, in the big shed I think. He'll be fine. There's others too."

"We owe him to see that he's OK, Neck. He didn't have to come with you. And you've got a gun now."

"Look honey. We're not at the pictures. I've got no idea how to use this thing, and if Den's got any more boys around they're bound to have guns that they *do* know how to use. The guy that Tug took will be on his way to get them right now, let's go."

"But you've got Tug, and I've got you. There might not be any more of them. Let's at least have a quick look."

He looked at her for a moment and then, because she was firm of purpose and braver than him, and because he realised that in the end he'd do whatever it took to keep her, he reluctantly led the way in the direction of the dark shape of the barn. As they moved away his foot crunched on something. It was a small earphone and neck mike.

As they approached the long barn, now silhouetted in the brooding cloud-flecked moonlight, he realised they were approaching it from the other end to the main entrance.

"Is there a door at this end?" she whispered.

"I dunno, we never got this far last time. We should have looked for that other gun."

"It's too late now, and I'd have no idea how to use it," she said briskly

As if I do, he thought.

They crept as quietly as they could towards the rear of the building. Katrina had Tug on a short leash but he was trembling and giving tiny little moans of excitement.

"If he barks we're buggered," Neck hissed.

"Hush," Katrina breathed. "Look."

Ahead of them a dim oblong of light appeared as a door opened at the rear of the building and they saw the silhouetted figure of a man stagger through. It was the man Tug had attacked. His right arm hung at a bizarre angle and he almost fell through the doorway and out of sight.

"He must have lost a lot of blood," Katrina said. "He couldn't call them, he lost his neck mike. He had to come back to tell the others what happened."

Neck abruptly realised that, any moment now, whoever the wounded man was reporting to at this moment would soon be coming out to look for them. "Quick, quick," he hissed and dragged her towards the rear door. She was completely confused but followed him anyway.

They raced up to the door and then as she grasped his intention they both waited against the wall beside it. A moment later another figure, again all in black, came out of the door and began to move away into the darkness away from them, and it was all going to plan. He and Kat would slip into the open door behind the man, slam it shut and find Spaz or at least confront whoever might be holding him. He'd seen it happen in movies, only in the movies they didn't have Tug, who immediately gave a sharp bark and a growl and lunged against his lead.

The man whirled round and saw all three of them outlined against the dim light of the open door behind them. He grabbed his neck mike immediately.

"It's O'Connell. I've got both of them, with the dog. I'll bring them to you."

As he spoke he lifted his gun and moved towards them as they instinctively backed away, but then Neck was abruptly shouldered aside as Spaz hurtled out of the open door and smashed into O'Connell. He fell but immediately came back hard at Spaz, who lost his balance and abruptly fell down, Neck realised his hands were tied in front of him. The man stood back slightly and raised his pistol to point it at the figure at his feet struggling to rise. Everything seemed to go into slow motion and Neck stood in an agony of frozen indecision, until abruptly the man collapsed. Behind him Katrina threw down the brick she had used to hit him on the back of the head.

"Quickly," she shouted at Neck. "Help me get him up." Together they hauled Spaz to his feet and manhandled him through the open barn door behind them. They found themselves in a small room. It stank of rotting meat. The man Tug had wounded lay very still in a corner. Without stopping they half hauled, half pushed Spaz through a second door into the main barn. Neck paused just long enough to check that the enraged Tug were also through before slamming the door behind them and closing it with a mercifully enormous crossbar. "Oh thank you, thank you," he babbled into the darkness, though he had no idea what deity he was thanking.

Katrina pulled the gaffer tape that was gagging Spaz from his mouth helped him to unwind the tape that had been used to tie his wrists.

"You alright mate?" Neck said. Spaz winked at him.

"No problem! Let's go," he muttered. Neck saw that he was smiling and there was a light in his eyes. Even at this moment Neck realised yet again how different he was from this tough little man.

The little group sprinted up the long inner corridor to find Peter and Jess standing over a scruffy looking spaniel. "Where the hell did that turn up from?" Spaz said.

"What's happening?" Jess said, "Is that Kat?"

"Never mind, never mind," Spaz shouted, "Get out! Go, before they realise what's happened!"

"We can't," Peter said. "There's a man outside holding Luke and he's got a gun."

Spaz stared at him in shock and then they all whirled round to face the front door as there was a sudden scream. Jess felt an almost physical impact and her heart seemed to stop but then Luke appeared through the door, running fast.

Almost immediately a figure appeared in the doorway behind him. The man was half bent over, one hand grasping his genitals, but in the other hand he held a gun. He raised it uncertainly and almost reflexively pointed it at Luke, but, before he could take aim, Daisy shot forward and with a blood curdling snarl locked her teeth into his free hand. He screamed again and as he tried to shake the dog off, Jess stepped forward and shot him at close range.

Both he and the dog fell back out of sight. As the reverberations of the shot rang in their ears there was a moment of pause and then Tug began barking urgently and Spaz whooped in triumph.

Jess started to run towards the entrance but Peter tried to stop her. "Wait," he said urgently. "Let me go ahead and see what's happened. There may be more of them." But she ignored him and strode out into the darkness. Both Peter and Spaz made to follow her but even before they had reached the door, Jess reappeared with Daisy in her arms.

"Thank God," Peter said with feeling.

"There's nobody else here. Let's get the fuck out," Jess said breathlessly. "God knows how many others are around. Let's go!" And then they were all out of the door and sprinting for the cars.

They raced through the darkness in a bizarre cavalcade. Peter leading the way holding Luke's hand. Spaz was bouncing along beside Jess and Daisy with his weird lopsided shuffle, whooping like a Red Indian. Neck mindlessly clung to Katrina as she dragged him along. He was mumbling, "Did anyone recognise us? Did they? If anyone recognised us we're fucked, totally fucked," and Tug loped along beside them.

As Jess looked down at the inert form they passed in the darkness she distinctly heard Daisy say, "Tobacco." She looked down. The man she knew as Jackson, clutching a blood soaked arm, struggled to get up on one elbow, but no one stopped to help him. A moment later they had all reached the cars and they tumbled in and were finally gone, into the welcoming arms of the night. It was just ten minutes to eleven and it finally started to rain.

Approximately forty minutes later two unmarked cars rolled up to The Yards. The armoured men who got out moved quickly and efficiently to search the whole area. They found the body of a middle-aged man in the main barn, and several signs of conflict, including a pool of blood outside the front door of the barn, and another among the sheds behind it, but there was no sign of anyone else. They started setting up a detailed investigation.

Tamborough and Letford Fields Echo

Local man murdered in drug gang massacre.

Mr Dennis O' Neil 58, was pronounced dead at Tamborough Hospital yesterday. Police say that early evidence suggests that he may have been shot during a turf war between local drug dealers and a new breed of gangsters attempting to move into the East of England from strongholds in the Home Counties. His body was discovered at a farm that Mr O'Neil owned in a sparsely populated part of the West Fen.

Police say they also found evidence of another body buried at the farm but as yet this has not been identified. Mr O'Neil's son, also called Dennis is still missing.

Mr O'Neill had a criminal record and police say they found a substantial quantity of Class A drugs at the farm, as well as other illegal materials, including violent pornography. A number of dogs, some in very bad condition, were held there and have been taken to appropriate care centres. Several of the dogs appeared to have been bred for fighting, though others were thoroughbred breeds of the kind often farmed for sale to unsuspecting pet lovers.

Superintendent Edward Larkin of the National Police Operations Coordination Centre said in a statement today. "Local people need not fear. We are mounting a co-coordinated national initiative and we anticipate early and wide-ranging arrests here and in other parts of the country. The eradication of drug trafficking and gangsterism is our highest priority, but citizens may be confident that we will also bear down on every facet of these people's criminal activities, not least the disgusting practice of dog fighting which is an affront to the most basic British traditions of respect for animal welfare. We will prevail."

Chapter 58

Leicemann walked into the laboratory at Angelo Control Systems and closed the inner air lock door behind him. During the previous month, all Bezel's experiments had been cleared back to make space for the enormous dog-like robot that now stood in the centre of the room. Although it stood free, it was connected to a large console by several cables and clear tubes. Harris and Bezel were bent over the console, arguing quietly, but with such intensity that they were scarcely aware that Leicemann had entered the room. He took the opportunity to have a good look at the creature.

Although it was constructed in the same way as previous versions of the Predator, it was far bigger, and the heavy protective armour and the battery of weapons it carried on its shoulders made it even more menacing. Its dark metal lines gleamed under the glare of the arc lights that illuminated it. "My God, Sophie," Leicemann breathed, "that is beautiful. You've retained all the natural structure, even the jaws."

Harris and Bezel both looked up. "I might look beautiful to you," Harris said bitterly, "but the fact is that it just doesn't work. It's been connected up for hours now and all we've had is one little twitch."

Leicemann turned to Bezel. "What's the problem?"

"Nothing. There's clear signs of arousal across the whole system. She's in there somewhere. Just give it a bit longer," Bezel said abstractedly. She fiddled with some of the switches on the console and the creature housing all that remained of what once an obedient and affectionate sheepdog called Ruby gave a tiny shiver and then returned to absolute immobility. They waited for long minutes as Bezel fussed at the console but nothing else happened. Leicemann began to feel more and more frustrated but he said nothing.

Chen walked into the room. "Any progress?" Bezel shook her head.

"This is the second day since insertion, for Christ's sake," Chen said irritably, but Leicemann detected a tiny note of satisfaction in his voice. "What the hell's up with it?"

"I don't know yet. The GABA blockers are probably suppressing too many neural pathways."

"Blockers? What the hell are they?"

"They're blockers. We use a soup of chemicals, mostly benzodiazepines, to block neurotransmission during the implant. You can't just stick an entire nervous system into a new setup and expect it to just put it on like a new pair of gloves."

"With an intelligent creature like a dog, there's massive disorientation, anxiety, anger, whatever," Leicemann explained. "Without the blockers the whole thing would probably go into immediate convulsions, or worse, catatonia. Then you've just got a vegetable. It's an art not a science."

"You told us it would all be much easier than this," Chen said

"Well it's not. I'm telling you now."

"Well I'm telling you, you've got to give Cadogan some results right now or you're fucked." He turned to Bezel. "Maybe you've gone too far with the sedation. Can you give it some stimulants or something?"

"In due course we'll start stimulating the glutamate receptors." Bezel said. "That'll switch the brain back on, gradually."

"Well, do it."

"No it's too soon. I can't predict what'll happen yet."

"I knew this thing would never work," Chen said triumphantly. "I'm going to Cadogan and get this whole idiot project shut down."

Leicemann was suddenly enraged. All the work and worry he had put in, all the endless frustrations of the last few weeks, mounted up in him. He fought off the urge to hit Chen.

"OK. Just give it the hit, Sophie," he said. "I'll take full responsibility."

"You're sure?"

"I'm sure." Bezel looked at him for a long moment and then turned back to the console. The room was silent except for a liquid gurgling as stimulants flowed through a clear tube leading to the head. They waited. Nothing happened.

"More!" Leicemann grated. Bezel stood back shaking her head but Harris took her place at the console and increased the flow. Within seconds the whole creature began to shiver and then the head suddenly lifted and they all heard a sharp hiss as air was drawn in through the two dark apertures at the front of the muzzle. They stood transfixed as slowly the head swung from right to left and back, and there was another hiss of air

"I think it's checking our scent," Bezel whispered.

The creature's head turned towards her. Then abruptly, with a tiny whirr of gears, the two saucer-like structures on the sides of the head rotated slightly and changed their orientation. With a shock of recognition Leicemann realised that this wasn't just a cleverly constructed machine linked to organic material. It might have been made of plastic and metal but in some profound sense it was alive.

"I think it recognises you Sophie. It's pricked up its ears," Harris said quietly.

"It should do. I've spent enough time conditioning it," Bezel said.

"Well make it do something then," Chen said. "Has it got a name or something?"

"Its name was, is, Ruby." Leicemann said.

At the mention of the name the head abruptly swung towards him. He gazed into the great glazed lenses of its eyes, and for some reason that he could not explain, now, at the moment when all his hopes and dreams appeared to be coming true, he felt only a profound sadness and emptiness. "Ruby," he said again softly. He had a sudden clear memory of selecting, even playing for a few moments with the bright and cheerful puppy that had grown into the creature whose brain now lay deep behind the glistening carapace that was its head. "Ruby," he said again softly.

Slowly, and with infinite care, the creature picked up its enormous feet and moved towards him, its head dropping lower and lower until it was in line with his own. As it continued to move forward it casually ripped away from its feed tubes, and he felt a sudden surge of panic. "I don't like this," he said carefully, "switch it off Sophie." But Bezel stood as if mesmerised.

He took a step back, and then another, and collided with a bench behind him so that he could move no further and abruptly sat down. The creature simply came closer and with a sigh, laid its head in his lap. Reflexively Leicemann reached down and patted the grim skull like head. There was a collective sigh of relief.

"There, there, Ruby," Leicemann whispered weakly. "Everything will be alright."

"My God," Harris breathed, "it still thinks it's a fucking dog."

"Yea, well," Chen said. "It's going to have to learn it's just a machine now."

Almost as if it understood the creature suddenly pulled back from Leicemann, sat back on its haunches and lifted its head to the sky. It opened its enormous jaws and the room was suddenly full a horrific bone shaking sound. It was a combination of a howl, a scream and the scrape of metal on metal. The sheer volume of it made all the four humans put their hands to their ears, then, as one, they rushed for the door of the laboratory but it was too late.

With one bound the creature smashed into Chen, seized his throat and with a flick of its head broke his neck. It dropped his body like a rag doll and whirled towards Harris. It took a little longer for him to die but it still didn't give Bezel enough time to complete the code sequence on the keypad that opened the door.

His exit blocked by them both, Leicemann stood helpless as the creature seized her head shook her and shook her until it was only connected to her torso by a shred of skin and gristle.

By the time it finally turned to Leicemann, he discovered he was almost calm. Time slowed right down and all his senses sharpened. The world became crystal clear. From outside he clearly heard the urgent voices of the emergency task force as they attempted to open the outer airlock door but knew that they would never complete the sequence in time to save him.

His senses were drenched by the pungent odours of the fresh spilt blood and faeces that now puddled all over the floor between him and the beast, and as it drew nearer, his nostrils filled with the evocative tang of machine oil and ozone that always seemed to hang around it. He smelt his own fear. Time stopped. Then there was nothing.

Biological Sciences Defence Laboratories
Canine Research Division
26/04/2015
To: All Department Heads
Cc: Mr Peter Guy
From: Dr Samuel Blake

With effect from today Dr Alex Leicemann and Dr Sophie Bezel are no longer employed by this Division and have been discharged without benefit of reference or further obligation of contract.

The relevant authorities are presently looking for them so that they can help with a number of enquiries. Since there is the real possibility that there has been criminal activity, all relevant staff will shortly be interviewed by Head of Division Security to the extent to which the Official Secrets Act may have been compromised.

In addition, the activities of the Department of Selections and Breeding will be fully reviewed shortly, with a view to putting into place a more comprehensive and relevant range of activities. I will personally supervise this review and then articulate a revised policy that will guide any new managers of that Department.

This news is of course disturbing but I'm confident that all staff will rise above these difficulties and carry on with the outstanding work that distinguishes the work of the Division.

Dr S. E. Blake/Head of Canine Division

Postscript

As the sun slid gently into the sea, the white rollers of the North Atlantic slid amiably up the wide Sligo beach that stretched below the towering granite cliffs behind. It was almost impossible to believe that when the days shortened to winter, these unassuming crests would morph into ten foot high breakers that would eventually, over the infinitely slow rhythms of geological time, smash the cliffs into the humblest submission. But so it was, for everything changes, everything passes, and even the hardest rock must one day grind to dust.

A seagull wheeled above the water line of long beach far below, hoping as ever that some tiny movement would reveal a few scraps of nutrient to get him through the day, but the only movement came from two people walking along the beach. From that distance it was impossible to make out much detail, even to the gull's keen eyes, but he could see that the two were hand in hand, Trotting along beside them was a small dog.

Jess stopped, linked her arm into Peter's and looked out across the sea to the setting sun.

"It's so beautiful here," she said. "I almost wish we could just stay indefinitely."

"We could," he said, "but you promised Luke he'd be seeing Daisy soon. In any case, if you stayed here you'd soon get bored. Think of all the work there is to do yet with the love of your life. Let's take another week and then you can dive back into The Project."

She looked at him and smiled. "I think I'm going to find difficult to settle back into work. And you're wrong anyway."

"How?"

"I'm not sure that there might not be another love in my life. And he really needs working on."

"Careful," he said. "You're on the edge of being romantic."

"Me?" she scowled cheerfully. "I don't know what romantic means." She strode on, and behind her he smiled.

Daisy ran up at that moment and dropped a large crab in front of Jess.

"See!" she said. "Me find big-water thing. Eight legs! Must take home, show Luke."

"We'll see about that," Jess said, but the dog had already picked up the crab again and trotted off ahead of them.

Jess took out her tablet. "I must get this logged," she said. "Do you realise she put together a twelve word sentence including three verbs and a word she's made up. I swear something's happening to her."

"You know what? You're not going to have any trouble settling back to work," Peter said, and they walked on.

Daisy looked back up the beach to the two human beings. She was pleased to see that they were holding hands. It made both of them smell happier and meant she could pay a little less attention to looking after Jess and spend more time on her own interests. They were many. The world was expanding rapidly. When she had the first flash of insight that allowed her to create a new name for Chunky Chunks, she had realised that she could make up words! Behind the constantly fluctuating world of odours and activity there wasn't just one word for each thing and each action but a huge resource of other words and other groups of words! She felt on the edge of an enormous breakthrough. Meantime there was more to discover on the beach. Did they all these tough little things have eight legs? She set to work…

The gull watched as the group strolled on into the distance, becoming smaller and smaller. It was the most normal scene in the world. As the sun sank finally behind a cloud and the sky darkened the gull wheeled away. There was nothing more of interest for him here, or indeed for anyone else.

Acknowledgements

Many people have helped in the creation of this story. Tony Laryea in particular has been an unrelenting source of support and encouragement. Jo Sandilands generously edited the entire first draft, cheerfully murdering many of my babies and vastly improving the book as a result, Tania Casselle gave the resultant manuscript the benefit of her considerable critical and editing skills, and Sally Jenkins was enormously helpful in getting the manuscript into the Kindle format and inspiring me to have a shot at publication.

My sincere thanks also to my wife Susie, and all the friends, children, and acquaintances that bothered to read the book in manuscript and give me the enormous benefit of their comment and corrections.

In the end of course the mistakes and inaccuracies are all down to me but it was a terrific journey finally getting to the end of this my first work of fiction.

Now my inspiration has signalled that she's fed up waiting at my feet while I type this, so it's time to get out there and do something more useful, like throwing her favourite ball...

Martin Lucas
Stamford 2016

Printed in Great Britain
by Amazon